Trade Winds
Vagabond

ALSO BY MICHAEL L. MARTEL

More Tales from a Gimbaled Wrist

Trade Winds Vagabond

A Novel

Michael L. Martel

Edited by Robert Muggleston

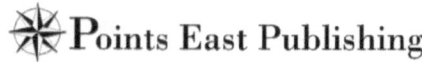Points East Publishing

ISBN 978-0-9856501-2-4

For

Christine, Kevin, and Thomas

Chapters

Chapter 1

Rugosa

"What looks right, is right."
— Old boat-builder's proverb

I went looking for a boat and although I did not have a specific make or model in mind, I knew that when I saw her, I would know, intuitively, that she was the right one. I would know by her lines, her rig, and by many different intangibles that I cannot explain. *It's much like choosing a mate*, I thought to myself, *when you see her, you'll just know*. But of course, it was not to be as simple as that. There were certain characteristics that I was looking for, including a deep-draft, sea-kindly hull well-suited to blue water sailing; a sturdy and simple rig for easy handling, and a peculiar element that I can only describe as character. I would indeed know her when I saw her.

For three weeks in the late summer, I drove along the coast of New England, peeking into old, forgotten boat yards where I might be most likely to find my boat. I made my way through the tangles of not a few wild blackberry bushes growing up and around old, sadly abandoned derelicts, all of which were clearly beyond salvage for my purposes, and I have the deep scratches and red scars to prove it. But at last I found her, indeed almost missed her, driving by an old farmhouse next to a wild, uncut field surrounded by woods, up in Camden, Maine. The field was actually on a little round hill, only a slight elevation, and propped up in the middle of it, facing me bow-on, was my sailboat. Oddly, she looked very much as I had imagined that she would. She was a gaff-rigged yawl, wooden, some 40 or so feet in length, with a peeling green-painted hull, beamy and nicely-shaped, a full keel, and bowsprit angled upward, still proud; a stout little old boat perhaps 70 or more years old, heavy-built with a pig-iron ballasted full keel and the overall appearance of a good sea-boat. There was no 'For Sale' sign in evidence, but I drove my beat-up old Volvo wagon part way up the winding gravel and crushed shell driveway and began walking through the high grass toward the boat, softly, almost in a stalking manner, much the same as one might, for example, approach a strange horse. All my senses were fully alert, taking in as much as I could of her as I approached, almost instinctively, working in concert with my intuition. To the impartial observer, my approach might have seemed to resemble a stalking, I mused afterwards, as though I were afraid of frightening a wary animal, even though it had no possibility of bolting. It might have had the appearance of gingerly approaching, as if to seek acceptance, to show harmlessness, even respect.

I reached up and touched the wood of her stem, like one might touch a horse, gently on the muzzle, on first contact. Then I ran my hand along the curvature of the hull, feeling its solidity, sensing, thinking quietly. Then I stood back, looked her over, and then approached again, repeating the process. There was no special logic or method to this procedure, but somehow it was the way that I knew that it must be done. There were still thick scales of red anti-fouling paint on the bottom planks and keel; even the shells of ancient and very large barnacles – empty conical homes now – adhered, here and there. Her planks were dry, and somewhat shrunken, yet they were still fairly tight in the seams, and the caulking had not spewed out. Her old bronze three-bladed propeller was still barnacle-encrusted, begging to be cleaned and made smooth. I walked around to the transom, where I could still make out the traces of gold leaf lettering spelling out *Rugosa*. *Rugosa*, I thought, the wild rose of the shoreline.

A rickety old wooden ladder, festooned with morning glory and purple and white trumpet vine flowers still open, leaned against the port quarter of the boat. After testing it with my weight, I began climbing cautiously. Once over the gunwale, I surveyed the deck and cabin. Peeling paint, rotting canvas, weathered wood, and green-tarnished bronze greeted me. Gray fragments of canvas tarpaulin still protected the cabin and spars in places. The cockpit was dry; the drains had seen to that. There were no leaves or debris clogging the scuppers. I slid back the hatch cover, lifted out the drop boards, and carefully climbed down the ladder into the cabin.

The air inside was warm, stale, dry, and tarry. The odor of old wood, paint, oil, and pitch met my nostrils. Still, I could see that she was a well-appointed sailboat with a roomy cabin, a little wood stove, an auxiliary engine aft under the cockpit, a head, and a forward cabin. There were two quarter berths, as they are called, under the deck aft of the main cabin. They are full-sized sleeping berths, but are called quarter berths because they are located under the port and starboard "quarters." I looked around, poked around, examining everything, lifting the floorboards and examining the deadwood and the ribs. She was solidly built; oaken frames, deck beams and carlings, and other structures; she might have even been described as over-built, solid and strong. Undoubtedly, her heavy construction had saved her from the ravages of time, from loosening up and falling apart. The now-rotted canvas tarpaulin in rags on her deck had protected her for years from the rain and snow, but now was finished. Without attention and care, she would begin to go to pieces quickly once the season changed and the wet autumn and New England winter weather set in.

The cabin had been so warm that once I climbed back up out of the cabin and into the fresh air and sunlight, it seemed of a sudden remarkably cool, the slight, salt-scented breeze flowing in off the harbor felt refreshing, since I had begun to perspire below. Now, from his high vantage point, I stood on the deck and looked out upon the sun-dappled sparkling blue of the harbor, with its merry ripples raised by the light northwest wind. The sky was a deep blue, with cottony wisps of mare's tails scattered across the great inverted bowl from horizon to treetop. Gazing at the water, I simply muttered quietly to the boat, "You'll be back out there again when I am finished with you."

It was just then that I noticed a stout elderly woman, hands on hips, standing in the field a little way from the boat, watching me. She was dressed in jeans and boots with a loose cotton work shirt, grey hair tied up in a bun under a ball cap, glasses and gardening gloves. I climbed down the ladder and walked over to her.

"You like my boat?" She inquired, boldly but not in an unfriendly manner.

"Well, I think I do," I replied.

"She is for sale, but to the right person."

"I didn't see a 'For Sale' sign on her," I said.

"The right person doesn't need one. Did you?"

"Nope, guess not."

"But you're climbing all over her anyway."

I chuckled.

"Come on inside for some iced tea and we can talk," she said, "I'm Clara." She wiped sweat from her brow. "Pullin' weeds," she said in response to the question that had not been asked.

"Thank you," I replied, "I'm Nathan."

Her old farmhouse had a rough-hewn granite slab for a front step with old wrought iron boot scrapers still embedded and potted in holes at each end. "They still work," she explained, seeing that I had noticed them. "But you don't need them. In the old days everyone rode horses and of course horse shit was everywhere. So before you went into someone's house, you scraped the horse shit off your riding boot bottoms using those."

"Being wrought iron, they never rust away," I added.

"That's right. Horse shit goes on forever, too. That's why I don't have a 'For Sale' sign on the boat. Don't want to attract horse shit."

"What do you mean?" I grinned. Her kitchen was tidy but old-fashioned, with a porcelain sink and old-style faucets. I sat down. She poured some iced tea into my glass, adding a slice of lemon; it was fresh and thirst-quenching.

"People waste my time. They come up asking questions about the boat out of curiosity, but no serious buyers. 'How old is she? Is she yours? Is that boat made of wood? Idiot talk. Wasting my time. No one wants a wooden boat anymore because no one knows how to work on one. They want to get it really cheap, then haul it off and burn it for the metal and fittings. Or they think they will look stylish in it on the water, but have no clue about the upkeep. It's not a sound stage for a big ego. It's a boat. In the old days, boat owners did some of the work, but boats were mostly maintained by the yards. Yards were staffed by skilled men who worked full-time taking care of the customer's boats. But nowadays the yards have become marinas and they are either short-handed or going out of business. They don't know how to work on anything that's not fiberglass. So it's up to the owner, and owners have no time anymore, and no skills to work on something like this."

"I'm a wooden boat builder," I said.

"You seem young for that."

"I've rebuilt a couple of boats over the last fifteen years. I learned the trade from my grandfather. It isn't my job, but it is my biggest hobby."

"My late husband was a boat builder too, you know. He didn't build this one, but he kept her well. She was built up in Maine around the turn of the century. Now, if you're a wooden boat builder, then I suppose you would know how to fix her up. That's good. I wouldn't want her to go to anyone who wouldn't take care of her or not fix her up again. She's a wonderful old boat, you know. Jake loved her. Sometimes more than me, I think. Anyhow, I don't suppose there's a lot of money in wooden boat building. There wasn't even when Jake was alive." She sipped her tea.

"I'm afraid there still isn't," I replied. "But I wouldn't be fixing her up to sell, but to sail."

She nodded; she seemed to like that response. We negotiated for a little while. She wanted four thousand dollars for the boat. I began rattling off prices, what it would cost to haul her, the extensive repairs needed, re-wiring, engine work, all the money that would be needed to bring the boat to meet Coast Guard regulations. She didn't want to budge, but finally, I persuaded her that I was the right person to take her; and she was also moved by the soft spot she had in her heart for the boat that had been her husband's pride and joy, the boat that they had sailed on together back when she could remember liking the salt water, and not minding sailing on it, packing the oak-strip picnic basket for a day trip out on a sparkling sea. Now, she thought, here was an able man who wanted the boat, who was capable enough and knowledgeable enough to fix her up, who appreciated the boat's classic lines and traditional rig. She wanted me to have it, because in his hands she knew that it would sail again. That would have pleased Jake, she knew, and she still missed him. In the end she agreed to sell me the boat for two thousand dollars. I gave her the $200 that I had in my wallet for a down payment. She wrote me a receipt, then led me out to the shed to show me the three suits of sails in like-new condition, the spars, rigging, sidelights, anchor, and innumerable other gear that Jake had maintained well. My jaw dropped; in looking over the old hull with the paint peeling off of her in the field, I would have never imagined that all of this extra gear and fittings were available in storage to go with her. They alone, aside from the boat, were easily worth twice the money she had been asking at the table. She even gave me some of Jake's old woodworking tools; Buck Brothers and Witherby chisels with their fine, highly-tempered tool steel; old lignum-vitae block planes, draw knives, spoke shaves, a fine cast rabbet plane, augers, gauges, bronze trammel points, and other antique tools that she would otherwise have never parted with, even though she had no practical use for them, but that if I could use them for fixing up the boat, why, then, I was welcome to them.

We had a deal; but before leaving, I went back out into the field to the boat, which stood still and silent, patiently resting on her poppets and blocks amidst the gently waving, straw-colored high grass that rippled and moved with the freshening breeze like the swells of a sea all around the boat. I stared at the boat, and began to grin; inside, my heart was filled with joy; she was mine now; all I had to do was to finish paying the lady. Deep within the boat's wooden soul, I mused, the boat must be happy, too. "Aren't you happy?" I asked the boat, aloud. "You'll finally say good-bye to this field; you'll be back in the water again, with the breeze in your sails, once more; not terribly soon, but when I'm done with you, God willing. And we may sail the wide oceans of the world together." It did not seem odd to me to speak to the boat; for this was not merely an inanimate object. A wooden boat has a soul, as all wooden-boat sailors know, and now in silly, giddy happiness, I put my ear to the hull, listening intently; but I did not hear a response from the wood, but rather felt the quick, excited beating of my own heart.

Once again, even though it was late afternoon, I climbed the rickety ladder, went aboard, opened the hatch, and descended into the cabin below. I will learn something new each time I go below, I knew, like reading a good book; there is something new to be discovered each time it is read, something that was missed the last time. As I poked around below, I noted a line of dark clouds approaching, a late summer thunderstorm, and heard a distant, muffled boom of thunder. The deck was dusty; a shower will do no harm, I thought. The old tarp, which I had pulled off and tossed onto the ground, had done its job; a little rain would wash the decks off. I closed the hatch and the drop boards just as the first few warm, fat droplets of rain began to fall. In the gathering darkness I sat down below on a bunk, listening to the sound of the approaching thunder outside, and the splatter of rain on the cabin roof. Inside the cabin it was silent, musty, and still. I could see the flashes of lightning through the cabin portholes, surrounded by peeling paint, and I imagined for a moment that I was in a familiar wooded cove over on Prudence Island, battened down for a squall. I could hear the whistling of the wind in the rigging, feel the gentle rocking of the boat, and sensed the motion as she swung like a pendulum on her anchor cable as the squall's wind shifted, puffed, and again subsided. I lay back in the berth, listening to the rain. At some point I fell asleep, and dreamed that I was sailing her out on the bay. In my strange dream, though, I was distressed; for despite all the work that I knew that I must have done (but could not quite, for some reason, enumerate), she was still all weathered bare wood, peeling paint and the bronze portholes were still covered with verdigris!

When I awoke, the rain had stopped and it was late in the day. I knew then how it would be. She was going to be my home, my cocoon, my refuge and fortress. She would give me a goal, a reason to work, to look to the future, to dream. We would help each other out, working together. She was a grand old lady, a lovely design of by-gone days, and she could not save herself. Yet she deserved saving, because she was so rare, and had been built so well and lovingly by true craftsmen. Built of wood, a living material, she had been crafted into a thing of beauty and purpose, an engine designed to harness the wind to move across the surface of the sea. Perhaps I would, after all, sail her around the world. We would build a relationship, a rare kind, because a good part of me would be a part of her when I had finished. Because she was a stout boat, and would be rebuilt right, I knew that she would never fail me ever of her own accord, and I would stick by her. It was a strange sort of marriage, I thought; but there are, after all, many couples like us.

I closed her up and went to the nearby marina office, at the recommendation of Clara, to arrange truck and trailer transportation, since she was not in proper condition for a sea-journey down the coast. It would take every resource that I had, but that did not concern me; for this was the pearl of great price; and I was ready to sell all that I had in order to obtain her. I stayed overnight in Boothbay at a neat little motor lodge down by the harbor, and listened to a band play Jimmy Buffett tunes on the dock next to the Lobster Claw Restaurant. There was an outdoor bar, with a big crowd of friendly locals, and I drank too much cool beer while I daydreamed and watched the many boats coming in off the placid bay. Their red and green running lights glowed in the gathering dusk as they pushed gentle bow-waves through the shimmering water that reflected the golden yellow glow of shoreside lights across the harbor. The moon was rising and the night was warm and pleasant. I saw Doug, the marina owner, at the bar with his wife and friends, and he kindly bought me a drink and paid me a compliment. I saw him speak to his wife, and I knew that he was telling her that I was the one who had come to take Clara's old boat home and fix her up.

Later, before I went back to my room to sleep, I walked down to a quiet place on the pier, and felt at peace, connected to my past, my memories of many things flowing together in a steady current down the years of my life like the brackish river flowing seaward beneath my feet. All was in motion again, headed for the open water, and I felt happy to have begun the long journey.

That night, I had a dream about *Rugosa.* I dreamt that I was on her foredeck, and that she was at sea and under way, and I was bringing her home, and she was mine. She had not been well cared for, but she was not really in bad shape at all, in my dream. A friend was towing me through the sea, rather than trailering her, and I cleated the tow-line on the bitts and exclaimed how solid the deck was, and that she would surely come through it all right; she had been well-built, and no one could ruin her, especially now that she was in the hands of someone who understood and could rebuild her. I am strong enough, I thought, and I know how to use my tools, adz and axe, chisel and saw, mallet and hammer; I will prevail. It was a strange, vivid dream, and when I awoke, it was still darkest night, in the wee hours of the morning before sunrise, and I lay on my back for a while thinking about the dream, looking for meaning, and remembering, oddly, a certain chapter in Joshua Slocum's *Sailing Alone Around the World.* It described a night where Captain Slocum was gravely ill, in a swoon from eating bad cheese and plums, while the *Spray* rode out a storm on the open sea. In his delirium, Slocum thinks that he is dockside and that careless draymen are tossing skiffs onto the *Spray's* deck, when in actuality they are seas breaking over his little vessel. But he calls out, daring the perpetrators to do their worst; "You cannot hurt the *Spray,*" Slocum cries. "She is strong!" Mine was a prophetic dream, I guessed; strong dreams often are, even if their meanings are, at the time, utterly obscure. But this one made me uneasy and I could not go back to sleep again until after the gray first light of dawn had begun to filter through the window blinds.

Chapter 2

Allowed to Pass

*"O Wedding-Guest! this soul hath been/Alone on a wide wide sea:
So lonely 'twas, that God himself/Scarce seemèd there to be."*
— Coleridge, The Rime of the Ancient Mariner

The year before I found *Rugosa* and began to rebuild her, the thought of making a voyage 'round the world' was very much on my mind, although I had not yet actually decided to do so. And yet it continued to grow, to dominate my thoughts, to the point where I was thinking about the matter as though it had already been decided upon; and why not? I had recently turned forty, and had begun to notice that things in my life and body had begun to change, changes that reminded me that I was growing older, and that the end of my life, while not imminent as far as I know, was coming and no longer out of sight or mind. The end of my life seemed like a sailing ship in pursuit of me, following from downwind, beating and tacking slowly, patiently to windward, narrowing the distance ever so gradually between us. I begin estimating the number of years left that I would be able to do this, or that; finite numbers. Nor did I wish to wait too long to pursue dreams, or adventure, or to take risks. *What are risks? Life ends just the same; there is no real safety in human life,* I told myself. I recalled a wealthy local man in his early eighties who had a custom metal sailing yacht built by a Bristol builder. He was planning a magnificent voyage. His custom yacht had every high-tech device on board to help him sail it solo wherever he wanted to go; specialized, expensive systems, labor-saving furling and electronic control devices. It was a vessel fifty feet long and more with an aluminum hull. But 80-plus is the time when death can visit suddenly even when one feels in good health. The boat was never finished; he died rather suddenly only months before its completion, and for two years and more it sat under a cover in the builder's lot without an owner, the dream that spawned it as dead as the dreamer.

I had once had a family, but lost it through no fault of my own, but rather through an accident that could probably have been prevented, had it been foreseen, but such was not the case. Suffice to say that I had lived alone since then, since recovering my bearings, so to speak, and ballasting myself to ride on an even keel once more. But I was still unfulfilled, until I dreamt one night, and then many nights running, about sailing, about taking my leave, as it were, from my current circumstances, and the idea continued to nurture and grow in my mind until it became something different and more powerful; where there had been whimsy, and then an exciting idea, there was now unshakeable conviction, and thus it went. I wanted now to live my life with greater intensity, not with desperation, but with a sharper awareness of my mortality, an awareness that I did not have in my youth, when the unseen and theoretical end of my life was hull-down on the horizon.

I knew that I needed a boat, and I also hungered for knowledge, to learn from the experiences of others who had done it already and come back. I wanted to know if the experience had changed them, and how. I had taken a part-time job as a newspaper reporter for a local sailing newsletter, and they had sent me, on assignment, to Block Island to interview a solo sailor named Jason, who had just returned from his own solo circumnavigation. It was a perfect opportunity, I thought. I did not realize it at the time, but my interview with Jason would set in concrete my decision to go.

So on a bright, brisk June morning, windy and cold, with a strong easterly wind howling across the Atlantic, I took shelter in a small breakfast café perched on the edge of a hill overlooking Block Island's Old Harbor. The wind, generated by a nor-easter low passing off to the southeast over Nantucket Shoals, had piled up great white angry surf that pounded the coast of Block Island and rattled and rumbled the round cobbles on the steep shingle beach. I could hear the cobbles grind and scurry loudly during the night right through the easterly facing window of my room in the old antique wooden harbor front hotel where I had stayed. It was an unnerving, rattly knocking sound of a million stones grinding themselves to pieces against one another with each tumbling cataract; and it made me smile in the darkness because I likened it to all the people jammed together in the city of Providence, grinding one another to flakes and fragments every day by the currents and surf of their own lives, careers, and self-imposed expectations. If you choose to live your life on the shingle beach, I thought, then that is the fate you will face. You will grind each other ever smaller until you become pebbles, then sand, then nothingness, until a gale comes along and throws up a new crop of stones and boulders to keep the cycle going.

Unlike the windy, sand-blowing abrasive chill of Water Street just outside, the inside of the café was warm, the air redolent of coffee, a hot griddle and hot oil, and bacon frying. I took a seat at a table and ordered a mug of black coffee. I was waiting for a man whom I had met the day before at the dock at the end of his solo circumnavigation in a 27-foot double-ended sloop. Jason had taken nearly five years to complete his journey, having left, initially, from the same pier here on the island. My job was to interview him for the local newspaper, but at the same time, I had many questions for him myself, for I was intensely curious about what had motivated him to attempt such a feat, and how he had managed to keep his sanity during so many months at sea, often going for weeks without any contact. I had begun to feel that solid sanity was not actually a pre-requisite for a successful solo voyage, the more of these socially un-ballasted loners I had met over time; but rather it was a touch of insanity that provided the true formula for survival; for he who seeks to save his sanity, shall lose it; whereas he who has not sanity to begin with, has nothing to lose. If you head out perfectly sane, you might lose it as some, like Donald Crowhurst did; that is assuming that he was not unbalanced in the first place. But the reverse is not true, i.e., that if you are not sane when you leave, you might possibly come back sane. The corollary simply does not work in reverse. If you cast off nutty, you will return equally nutty, if not thoroughly insane.

I was finishing my second cup when he finally arrived. He was not tall, but he was fit, from so many months at sea, of a stocky build with no fat on him. His face was ruddy from sun and wind burn and his long straw-blond hair looked damp, messy, unwashed and unkempt. He was wearing a bright yellow foul weather jacket and tan corduroy trousers. He looked a little jumpy, nervous, as though he had not quite re-adjusted to being on the land yet.

The previous day he had sailed his sloop, *Water Witch*, into the harbor and alongside the dock to much fanfare, where his family awaited him. They had arranged a happy reception for him at considerable expense, including a white convertible to serve as a limo, complete with colored balloons, to carry him the short quarter-mile from the dock to the grand National Hotel where they were all staying. But he almost didn't make it in time. The wind was blowing hard, and the sea was angry with whitecaps and spuming spindrift, as he beat back and forth in his little boat in rough seas trying to make the harbor entrance against wind and tide. But he finally made it in, in mid-afternoon, wet and tired, his boat a messy tangle, and laid her up alongside the dock as the band began to play. It was a sweet moment; his elderly parents, brothers, and sister, and his girlfriend, whom he had met in Papua New Guinea in a bar in Port Moresby, and whose plane ticket the family had paid for.

"Are you Nathan?" He asked, seeing the pencil and notebook on the table beside me.

"Yes," I replied, "I'm Nathanael Williams with the Coastal Reporter." I shook his hand. It was rough and damp and his grip firm.

He sat down opposite me; like someone who had been many days in the woods, or on safari, or in this case, at sea, he still, despite one, perhaps two showers the evening before, smelled like his boat, redolent of sweat, and oil. Perhaps it's his clothes, I thought; musty, something like the damp bilge in a fiberglass boat. But he was wide awake, energetic, jittery, perhaps, but eager to talk. Why had he decided to embark on a solo voyage around the world?

He began slowly, but then picked up the pace. His world had been closing in around him, he said. He loved to paint; he was an artist in his soul. He hated his job; his marriage was on the rocks. These were the walls that were closing in upon him, stifling him, crushing, stealing his air. He needed to breathe, to get away from everything and sort things out. Of course, a solo voyage around the world is a bit radical in terms of dealing with such problems, but I had to admit to myself that it certainly seemed like an effective way to remove oneself, not only from a bad situation or from a host of them, but also from obligations imposed by others, and even those imposed by oneself.

So he bought *Water Witch*, a used boat, but a sturdy vessel; he had done some research. She was big enough to make the trip, but small enough for him to handle by himself. Buoyant and seaworthy, she would get the job done. Family helped out with outfitting, modifying, and provisioning, and even in paying for the boat. And one cold afternoon in November he headed out from the harbor at Block Island, headed southeast, a voyage that began in a hell of cold terror, rough seas and storms, so awful that he wished that he could abandon his quest, and he would have, he said, if there had been a harbor nearby to take refuge in, but there are no places to duck into, no room for excuses, a few hundred miles at sea. You just ride it out, he said. Tripping his EPIRB would have meant abandoning his boat, and thus his voyage; he would have to go home; he owed his father and brothers; it would be a hole even deeper than the one he had escaped in the first place. No, there was no turning back; that would, he decided, be actually worse than death. So he hung on, kept breathing, and kept sailing, and in time the seas moderated, the air warmed, and he made it to the Caribbean alive. There, the sun was bright, the water warm, the rum delicious, the women pretty. He had photos of himself at parties at Tiki bars; he had a couple of dalliances. But he had made it, and at that point he knew that, even though it was less than 1,500 miles along his way, he could go on, and so he did.

He reached into the pocket of his shirt and brought forth a small bottle, with little periwinkle shells inside. It was a clear-glass bottle with a cork in the top and looked like an old medicinal bottle from the 1890s. There was a faded brown label with faint writing on it. "I carried this with me," Jason said, "All the way around the world. This was my talisman. Joshua Slocum gave this to my grandmother back in 1909. It was just before Slocum was lost at sea. My great-grandfather worked at the Herreshoff boat yard in Bristol back then and she was only a little girl and had walked over there to bring him his lunch. Slocum was tied up at the Herreshoff pier and they were fixing a few things on his boat at no charge, because old man Herreshoff liked him. So he gave her this little jar of shells from some place in the Pacific that he had visited." I marveled at this little artifact. "I kept it down belowdecks carefully stowed," he added.

Captain Joshua Slocum was the first person to circumnavigate the globe, completing his voyage of more than three years in 1898. He sailed his 37-foot rebuilt antique wooden sloop *Spray* around the world after re-building the vessel himself in a whaling captain friend's front yard in Fairhaven. I knew his story well and had read his book, *Sailing Alone Around the World*, published in 1899, numerous times.

"When I first left, it was storm after storm. I got terribly seasick and could do nothing for days. I was way off course, and every effort was a supreme effort just to do the simplest things. I couldn't sleep, so I became even more tired and weak, and then dehydrated from throwing up, and of course I couldn't eat, so that made me even weaker. Seas were, I estimated, fifteen or twenty feet at the worst, and winds were topping 45 knots, sustained. I was worried about *Water Witch's* seaworthiness. The weaker I became, the more it affected my mind. I became terribly anxious and apprehensive, with fear in the pit of my stomach all the time. I doubted my boat, myself, my goals, even my own worth. It was horrible."

Breakfast now came, and my appetite had grown sharp. "You sure you don't want anything more than a coffee?" I asked, again. I had a plate of eggs, hash, and toast in front of me.

"No, that's all right. But listen, as bad as it was, and the loneliness was terrible at first, I dealt with it, and actually got what I wanted, in a strong and strange way. I felt detached from everything, my old world, my past; everything was living in the moment and surviving. I was really in a totally new world yet still here on earth. Everything was gone; the pattern, the structure, the clearly defined role at the office, at home…gone. I was adrift and emotionally bound to nothing and no one."

"Except the boat?" I suggested.

"No, not even that, not yet. The boat was (and here he laughed) still an instrument of torture."

But he had continued onward from there, down through the Panama Canal, and out into the broad Pacific where, now attuned to being days and even weeks without human contact, he minded it less. The Pacific winds were steady and authoritative, and seemingly reliable in the latitudes where he was sailing; so he drew and painted his way across the Pacific while his boat made her own way, her self-steering vane calibrated and set, and his boom rigged with a preventer to keep it from snapping back when he descended into the deep troughs between the waves and the rig was sheltered from the driving force of the wind.

I mentioned the passage from Slocum's book where he describes hallucinating and the strange effects of the monotonous sea on his eyes and mind. "Slocum wrote that on one occasion, in a calm, a gull sitting on the surface of the water loomed as large as a ship," I said. "Did that happen to you?"

"Things can play tricks on your eyes out there. Your mind, too."

"Slocum also wrote that his mind functioned with incredible sharpness; that he could remember things that he had assumed that he had forgotten. That his mind working with great clarity."

"Yes, I know what he was talking about. It happened to me, after a few months. All of a sudden, there was no more static. What I mean is, in our every-day lives, we are so bombarded with stimuli, with interactions, with responsi-bilities, that things get buried, and problems really are never, ever resolved. We don't have time to address them, they're speaking but they can't be heard. But once you're away from the static, the effect is quite dramatic. Memories came back to me; things from my childhood, things that I never knew were buried so deeply down in there. And many unresolved things from long ago came back as well. I'm not talking about things that I can change in the physical world, for these have already been resolved in one way or another in a practical sense, willy-nilly. I'm talking about resolving them in my mind, working through them, coming out with a clean balance sheet and a sense of peace, of coming to terms with whatever the issue was and its ultimate resolution. It took a long time. And I am absolutely convinced that if I had not made this trip, those issues would still be unresolved, and perhaps I would take that unfinished business to my grave. I think many of us do, maybe even most of us."

"Do you feel a great sense of achievement?" I asked. "Like you conquered 'Old Ocean'?"

He stared directly into my eyes, searching for something, it seemed, and there was a distant, odd look in his own, somewhere between humility and awe, or maybe reverence, or perhaps a bit of both, and he was not looking at me, actually, but it seemed through me, like a pane of glass, to some visible point at a great distance away in space behind my head. He was seeing something else, somewhere else. "No, oh, no," he replied, slowly. "In the end, and even way before that, after the first terrible test, just before I arrived in Bermuda, there was no feeling of conquest, oh no. There was instead this overwhelming sense, even an understanding, if you will, that I had been allowed to pass."

I had nothing to say in response; I stirred my coffee. He continued, "I've seen some amazing things out there, things of wondrous beauty. You know that I am an artist. Well I have seen such beauty that sometimes it defies verbal description, with the earth and sea such an incredible canvas. It was like that in the Marquesas, in the Pacific, green-draped mountains and blue sea and colorful sky, awash with wild color like no artist would be skillful enough, or mad enough, to paint."

Then he said, "I heard a tale of a man single-handing who got caught in a five-week dead calm out in the middle of the doldrums and became mentally unbalanced. He had visions while becalmed, and came back predicting the end of the world. His hair had gone completely white."

"Well at least he didn't jump overboard like poor old Captain Crowhurst," I replied. "I assume that you were never tempted thus."

He ignored my question. "I understand now how that could happen out there. When there's just enough breeze to keep the sails from slatting, but not enough to move the boat, there is a great quiet like I'd never experienced before. It's a quiet so deep that I could hear the air rush past a tern's wings in the night. It's a quiet where I can hear the low hum of the radar warming up 30 feet up the mast. A sense of awe overcomes you, like being in the presence of God. It was an incredible, almost holy stillness; I dared not make a sound to break it. There was not a sound, just a silence so deep that the blood pulsing in my ears sounded like a drumbeat."

"What's ahead for you now?" I asked.

"Well, I have lots of plans, quite a few plans, actually. I want to sell reproductions of my art. I did many different sketches and watercolors out there, some that still need to be finished. I met many wonderful people out there who didn't care, really, whether or not I was an American, or whatever. They were just genuinely good. People are basically wonderful, and at times on my voyage, I felt a strange sensation when I was alone and in harmony with the world around me, the sea, the sky, and my boat, that I felt this incredible warm feeling of love wash over me, like I was being bathed in it."

"From where? Or from whom?"

"I don't know. From God, maybe. And then sometimes I would pick up radio transmissions and hear the news, with all the trouble in the world, bombings, killings, and I'd have to turn it off. It actually made me physically ill to listen to it."

"You were apart from it. But was it an escape from reality?"

"Oh no!" he exclaimed. "Let me tell you, out there it is very real, very real indeed. I didn't escape from reality, I was simply geographically removed from the everyday reality that so many other people in the populated world experience every day in their rat-races. No, I eliminated all that static, and I was liberated in a sense. It was terribly liberating, an amazing, incredible feeling. We always talk about being needed. Everyone wants to be needed. Well you know what? I was in just the opposite situation, on the flip side of the world, of life; no office, no demands, no responsibilities except to myself and my boat. I realized that for the first time in many years, maybe even in my entire life, that I was needed nowhere. And you cannot imagine how wonderfully free and liberating a feeling that is."

Chapter 3

The Boat-builder

"If a man is to be obsessed by something, I suppose a boat is as good as anything, perhaps a bit better than most."

— E. B. White

The block plane bit cleanly into the wood, shaving off paper-thin curls of pungent longleaf yellow pine. The blade was sharp and the sole well waxed, so that the tool slid along the wood smoothly all the way to the end without chattering. The curls dropped onto the saw-dusty floor where they crunched under my feet. The raspy sound of the plane was the only sound in the boat shed. Outside, the late autumn wind was blowing gusty and cold out of the northwest and occasionally slapped the outer branches of the big maple against the wall. This evening, it was cold in the shed but I did not pay any heed, as I was so absorbed in the work and working hard enough so that I kept warm.

Pine is such good wood, I reflected. This yellow pine is fairly hard, straight-grained, and strong. Also it is resistant to rot and full of pitch. It smells nice when it is sawn or cut, a fresh, aromatic scent; it makes the whole shop smell like pine incense. There is a quality of cleanness about it, and it always seems new when you cut into it, even if the piece of wood itself is quite old.

Mine was the only large wooden sailboat in the high-ceilinged boat shed. It towered over me when I walked around the hull, propped up by jack stands, occupying the better part of the center of the shed. The shed itself was built somewhat like a cathedral, with a central nave and high ceiling. On both sides of the shed were supporting posts for the roof, and then second-floor lofts, or galleries, where tool benches, work areas, painting supplies, and other stores were located. Saws, innumerable clamps, and unusually large tools hung from the walls, and multiple steel cabinets for paint, resins, solvents, and chemicals were located in one area. One wall on the first floor consisted of nothing but masts and other spars supported on frames, horses, and triangular supports, running the length of the building. Many different scents, including fresh-cut wood, old, musty wood, tarry scents, oily scents, paint, and resin, blended together to create one prevailing scent, not at all unpleasant, that embodied the defining term 'boat shed'. All wooden boat sheds have the same breath, although it may be said that in years past, it was no doubt a richer one, and never unpleasant, particularly to the nose of one whose eye holds an appreciation for the symmetry of form of a wooden hull, or the abstract beauty and intricacy of the patterns of grain in a plank of fresh-planed mahogany. In the old days, there would have been less of the odor of resin, but more of linseed oil, pine tar, turpentine, and other materials found more rarely nowadays in boat yards.

My workbench was built of sturdy maple from a tree felled in the boat yard out back by a hurricane a few years earlier. I had cut up the good parts of the tree with a chainsaw, and then cut them into planks and posts with the big 24-inch band saw in the shed. I had painted the ends to keep the wood from checking or splitting, and had stored them in a cool corner inside so that they would not dry out too quickly. After they dried for a season, I had cut them to size, planed some, and then built a sturdy workbench out of the lumber. I still had the old wooden toolbox that had been my grandfather's, painted olive green, where I kept all of my assorted planes, chisels, mallets, and other woodworking tools. They were always kept well-cleaned and sharp, and always wiped down after use. I applied a light coating of oil with a cloth before putting them away.

I stepped outside the boat shed for some air; it was cool and dry and crisp like a fresh apple that you bite into outdoors on a fall day and tastes many times better than it would if you ate it indoors. Shredded tatters of silvery clouds blew across the face of the bright full orb of the moon, scudding away before the racing blast high above. All the leaves were nearly gone from the trees, and those that had hung on until now would most certainly be gone by morning with the passing of the forecasted cold front.

Nearly all the boats were gone from Bristol harbor, now strangely empty with only winter poles marking the moorings. With the exception of the few lobster and fishing boats that would be there year 'round, the recreational sail-boats and yachts were now stacked and tightly packed in the boat yard, crowded and huddled right to the edge of the seawall as though cringing from the cold harbor waters.

Back inside, I planed some more, putting the finishing touches on the replacement plank, then stepped back to look at my work. The edge of the plank was fair. The pine was a deep shade of yellow, with no knots. I glanced at my watch; it was getting late, nearly nine o'clock in the evening, and I was tired. The series of hundred-watt incandescent bulbs high above near the roof timbers gave the boat shed a warm glow, reflecting off the naked brown aged wood walls and rafters. They provided no real warmth or comfort, although they gave the illusion of warmth when they were burning. Enough for tonight, I told myself. The bottles of beer that I had placed outside the shed door were cold now, I knew, and I welcomed the hiss of the cap unscrewing. After I had wiped down each cutting tool with a soft oily cloth and put each one away, I washed up in the cold water sink with the brown-cracked bar of soap and sat down for a moment on a stool in front of *Rugosa* and drank my beer. Actually I drank three of them in fairly quick succession and then sat for what seemed to be a very long time staring at the hull, examining each curve and comparing its symmetry until I was satisfied that all looked correct and proper, while deeply thinking through and planning the next day's work in specific order. "What looks right, is right," I recalled the old boat-builder's proverb. And she looked right.

Nearly a year had gone by now since I had rented the work space in the boat shed, and had arranged transport by trailer for *Rugosa*. When I first rented the shed, before I had even brought my boat in to work on, I had walked across the parking lot to announce my intentions to my long-time friend Neil, a wood-worker who rented a shop in the adjacent building. It was late September, a couple of months after I had climbed aboard her in the old lady's field and decided then and there that she was the right boat for me.

I climbed both steep, creaky, narrow flights of stairs that led to Neil's work-shop, on the third of four floors in what had been the old Civil War rifle factory. It was an old wooden building of massive construction and housed various wood-workers and boat building craftsmen. Some might have called it the biggest potential firetrap in Bristol, but for the furniture makers, clockmaker on the second floor, and other artisans, it was the perfect place to be creative. There was electricity, an occasionally working toilet, a dumpster outside, and now that it was late in the season the golden afternoon sun beamed in through the yellowed, wavy glass of the large-paned factory windows and warmed the place, at least in spirit, while braches outside, dropping their leaves, whipped about in the autumn wind.

Neil was originally from Wales; he was a furniture maker friend whom I had known for nearly twenty years. We had met down at the local Irish pub when I first moved to town, playing music together with a group of local amateurs like ourselves. Neil and his wife Ellen had raised a son and a daughter here. That was back in the good times, nearly two decades ago when his business was booming and he had two other men working for him.

Now it was an unusually warm fall afternoon and the building had no air conditioning and the old windows didn't open. But Neil had opened the sliding freight doors at the back of his shop, creating a big opening that let the heat out and the gentle breeze blow in. His shop was shaded by great elm trees which provided some relief during the summer but now most of their leaves were gone. The important thing was to avoid falling out the opening, I noted, as there was no rail or gate, into the parking lot fifteen feet below.

I had a six-pack of cold Guinness stout in a bag under my left arm. At the top of the second landing, there was a locked door that serviced both the east and west shops that divided that floor of the building. I knocked, and Neil came to the door, unlatched it, and let me in. I had not been over to his shop in a couple of weeks. "Brought you some beer," I said.

"All for me?" he asked jokingly, feigning surprise.

"Well, almost," I said. "Here, crack one."

Neil's house was only two blocks up the street, on High Street. His wife of thirty years lived there. Most of the time, Neil lived here, and sometimes visited there. When he showered, he showered there, simply because there were no showers in the rifle factory. Neil had been prospering at one time, when the economy had been better, but for some years now it had been a struggle. Not just for Neil, but for everyone, and every other craftsman in that building, and in many other adjacent craft businesses. It wasn't that they did not work hard, because they did; but no one had been able to put money aside, including Neil. There were no prospects for retirement, only the prospect of getting older, and wearier of the struggle, but the struggle went on, and the cost of everything continued to go up. So some took to alcohol on occasion, many on frequent occasions, and it tended to spoil things. It was a roll of the dice when, and how often, it might be, but on those occasions, even in winter, there was heat in the factory, and if you could sweep together a big enough pile of shavings and sawdust and throw a drop cloth over it, you had a bed, and not an uncomfortable one at that, even though at such times the level of comfort might have been irrelevant anyway. Those were the times of separation, of aloneness, of avoiding the home and hearth just up the street, of simply avoiding the added scolding and passion and reprimands on top of the already stacked pile of financial woes and worries carried on one's shoulders. But there was no real escape. The sun arose each day, the saws and sanders ran, the chisel bit into the clean wood and the plane sliced off fresh pine-scented curl after curl, with a false-comforting regularity, as if work would somehow make him free. But 'work makes you free' is a sinister old lie that too many already know.

The men whom he had employed were gone, well almost gone, except for George, the Irishman who had been a master cabinetmaker. Now he was a pub musician who drank far too much and often showed up at Neil's shop late in the evening to sleep, since his wife had thrown him out. Neil had made George a key. George's two children were also grown and he did not see them very often anymore. George's dirty blanket, more like an old quilted horse blanket, hung on the wall. It was for George's use only and I asked Neil one time why he himself never used it, never mind why George never laundered it, and Neil replied that George had pissed it a few times and maybe barfed on it once or twice and seemed to have no ambition for washing it, thus it was there for George alone. However, Neil reminded me, if I needed to use it on some occasion, he would not object to me doing so. I thanked him, adding that the prospect of that was highly unlikely.

"I'm your new neighbor," I said to Neil, opening a can of beer for myself, and raising it in toast. "Here's to being neighbors."

"Are you going to start making cabinets too?" he asked.

"No, you're doing a good enough job yourself of that. Moving into the barn across the alley. Renting it. I bought a boat."

His face brightened. "What kind of boat?"

"Old wooden boat," I replied, "Going to rebuild her and sail away. Don't know where. The island of St. Somewhere. That's all I know at this point."

"So you're going to put the boat in there? Will it fit?"

"I've measured," I explained, "And it will. I might even move in there with it."

"Well, you'll be paying rent to the Maritime Museum, since they own this complex," Neil said, thinking carefully. "You know, there are showers in the back, put in when the museum building used to be a spar company. You could easily use those showers when the Museum is open. You know, back behind the Hall of Boats."

"That might work," I said. Neil was always thinking like a survivor, and I liked that. "But in any case, I've got a lot of work to do, perhaps a year's worth, to get her ready for sea. I have much work to do on the hull, the engine, the rigging, the systems, you name it. My plan is to make her capable of long-distance passage-making."

"That will be expensive, no doubt," Neil said.

"I'll do almost all the work myself. At least the work that I know. But I will need to get someone who knows electrical to wire her up, and a good engine mechanic to get that diesel in there working again. I'll need to have new sails made. So yes, a lot is involved and I'm going to have to raise some money. But I will."

"Plenty of names of tradesmen with those skills over at the museum; just ask around. You're in the right place for it. So where are you going to go with her?"

"Not sure, but definitely on a long voyage, different countries, destinations, maybe around the globe. It's time for a change, I need a change."

"Who's going with you?"

"No one. Just me."

"What? Alone? Can you? That's crazy, man. You will need a crew!"

"Why? And sail with whom? A boat gets pretty small very quickly with two or more people. I don't know who would be able to stand me after a few days, or even a week, and I'm not sure that I could stand having another person aboard in my space either for very long. Besides, I would feel responsible for them. No, I think this is something that I will have to do by myself."

"Joshua Slocum had a goat," Neil mused, rubbing his beard, a faint smile beginning to form.

"Until it ate his chart, or so he said," I laughed, "It ate his lines and ropes too, so he put it ashore the first chance he had."

"He probably should have had a chicken instead."

"No animals for me," I replied. "Unless they are in cans."

When I began my work on *Rugosa,* I realized from the start that I had taken on an immense project. I began my work at the bow. There was so much to do that the only way to do it in an organized fashion was to begin at one pole and finish at the opposite. Of course, along the way there would be much digression from the strictness of such a plan, but in the end the soundness of it would be proven by measurable results. But you must always have a plan. Mine was to start at the bow and work my way back to the transom. That's ironic, because I found out at the beginning that the stem timber needed to be replaced. I was getting no breaks from this boat. Then I discovered that the transom had to be replaced, plus a whole lot that was in-between. I shook my head, and set to work.

I determined from the start to use the best materials I could find; good timber, proper fastenings, quality paint, and to take no shortcuts. Taking shortcuts in your ship can cost you your life later at sea. If something didn't come together right, then I started over. If a screw twisted off, I bored a new hole beside it and drove in a new fastening. If a screw turned in the hole and lost its bite, I would remove it and fill the hole and find a better spot to drill a new one nearby. Every mating surface of wood was treated, oiled, painted with red lead, glued, or bedded with compound, so that it would not be a place for rot to begin.

The days passed through three seasons, and although my work was hard, after a while I began to enjoy the solitude of it, and, just as Slocum had said of his work rebuilding his Spray, I could easily say that there was something to show, at the end of the day, for every day spent working on her. It might only be small, but I knew that all progress was cumulative, and thus, significant. I knew enough from boat working that it is never good to expect to accomplish too much too quickly. If one does, one will rush jobs that should not be rushed, or will become frustrated and despair, and give up. And once deeply into the boat project, I found myself lying awake at night visualizing well in advance each little job in succession that needed to be done, far down the tunnel, like a chess master plans his game moves far in advance as he plays, in order to win. At times it became almost an obsession, and kept my mind working well into the night, yet I awoke refreshed in the morning, so focused was I on the realization of my dream. I would think about my boat all the time, much the same way a young man thinks about sex every thirty minutes or so, not because he wants to (or perhaps he does), but because his chemistry drives him to. I would plan each stage and step of what had to be done next, seeing the finished product in my mind's eye. These planning and calculating exercises helped my memory and sharpened my mind, keeping it busy before I went to bed, so that I could sleep on these plans and process them in my subconscious.

I found my old leather-bound 'nothing' book that I had started many years ago, filled with notations and crude drawings and scribblings and measurements, and lists of 'needs' for each boat that I have worked on. I stopped at consignment shops, big-box DIY home stores, yard sales, any place that I felt I could find the tools and materials that I knew that I would need. I became the 'dented can guy' at the boatbuilding supply shop, buying heavily discounted paint and epoxy in dinged and rusted cans so that I could put that saved discount money toward a tool that I needed, or another can of paint. What did I care about what the can looked like, as long as the contents were intact? Let the can look ugly, and the boat pretty!

Summer time was a good time to work on Rugosa. Although it was often hot in the shed, I would open the big wooden bay doors and let the afternoon prevailing southwesterly breeze blow in, coming up off the water of Bristol Harbor.

It would cool the shed and bring with it the salt tang of the sea and fragrance of the wild rose bushes along the shore. It was the sweet aroma of the wild rose, or *Rosa Rugosa,* for which my boat had been named. The bright, cheerful sun-dappled ripples of the harbor as the breeze freshened filled me with a soothing contentment and there were times when I would pause and find myself looking out onto the bay, meditative and trance-like, while my body rested and the perspiration slowly evaporated from my saw-dusty skin. In my mind's eye I could see my boat sailing out of the harbor and into Narragansett Bay, outward bound for parts unknown, but with the watery world, as Ishmael might have said, awaiting me. I'd be up on a ladder under the shade of the hot roof hammering away at the hull and sweating, I often wondered if in some way the boat could smell the salt breeze, too. As I ground, chipped, and primed ten feet above the ground, my mind was hundreds of miles away, crossing the Gulf Stream, my boat plunging headlong into the great troughs between the sapphire-blue warm swells of the stream, happily surging toward the empty horizon and islands of spices, palm trees, coconuts, rum and white beaches that lay at the far edge of my imagination and well over the distant horizon. I was riding that dream, and it sustained me and kept my bow pointed ahead and water moving beneath the keel of my mind and energy. Other fellows working on their boats in the boat yard in the summer tend to play their radios and listen to music, I had noted, but although I like music, when I am working, I prefer to work in silence; in this way there is nothing to distract my concentration.

Now, on a late fall evening, after working on the interior of the cabin for a couple of hours painting, repairing, and re-installing hardware, I took a break and sat down at the nav station and happily surveyed my progress while the little electric heater on the deck of the saloon hummed away. I knew that I was back into my boatbuilding groove, and it felt natural, comfortable, and satisfying. *It's a good place to be,* I thought. It's a place in time that's almost meditative; time and schedule have become meaningless. There's no rush; do it right, take your time, and savor each little bit of progress. Until you arrive at this place, it's all painful, uncomfortable work, fraught with worries about weather, timing, schedules, what the neighbors are thinking, the immensity of the project, and you begin to doubt whether you will ever finish it. But once you're in the 'groove', life attains a certain balance, and it becomes a pleasure to watch the slow transformation of the vessel beneath your hands. You are no longer trudging along, strapped into the traces; you are now riding the dream. I have been to this place before, every time I got into building or re-building a boat. You don't know when you're going to get here, but when you finally do, well, you're here. The mind, as Milton correctly observed, is its own place.

I recall that evening of contemplation; the cold, blustery November wind was whistling through the bare tree branches outside, a front coming through, a gift from Canada. It blew in from the northwest under a star-lit evening sky. It rattled and shook the walls of the boat shed, but within that cocoon stood my boat, on its jack-stands, surrounded by the scaffolding I had built, ladders, and hanging beat-up shop lights shining an eerie fluorescent glow on the upper works while the hull below the waterline-level scaffolding was enfolded in darkness and shadow. There was a surreal peacefulness to the scene; I yawned. It was time to quit for the evening.

Throughout the final summer season, I had finished restoring the decks, and now the hatches were all in place and the boat could be closed up to contain the feeble output from the little space heater. It actually made a difference, because when it's very cold, water hoses become rock-like; the solid block of an engine numbs any fingers that touch it; paint won't flow and epoxies become heavy syrup and hard to mix and apply. Varnish goes on like painting molasses. But with the boat closed up, I could work inside, continuing into the winter, at least through the milder earlier parts of it. January may be another matter, I knew. But even now, later on a dark weeknight evening, the dream kept me going. While I worked, I thought of sailing the broad ocean. When I installed a new timber or deck beam, I thought of a ton of green water crashing down on it from a rogue wave, and I made sure to set it in right, and strong. I wanted my ship to be stout and seaworthy, as strong as solid wood and sound hardware could make her. She would be far stronger than my arm, and yet it is lifting small shovelful after shovelful that a mountain is raised or moved. I often considered the wooden framed colonial houses in New England that still stood solid and strong, centuries after the many arms that had raised their beams to the sky had turned to dust. *Good work gives lasting results,* I thought. By forming a strong oak framework, fastened into place with galvanized steel bolts and stout hardware, I will build with my flesh and bone arms a seaworthy framework that will stand a ton of green water on the deck. And so it went. During the off season, rarely did any-one work in the cold boat shed except on weekends, so most of the time I had the place to myself.

I worked alone, in part because I did not have the money to pay for help; and also because I do not have the patience to teach someone else how to do what I already know. I teach by doing, by showing; I am not talkative and not very good at instructing others, and when I am working and concentrating, oddly, my speech is not very articulate if I try to explain what I am doing while I am doing it. Without another helper, I learned various ways of doing things by myself that would have benefited from another pair of hands; but there being none other available, I used lines, tie-offs, block and tackle sets, and other means of moving things about or into position. It often took longer to do things this way, but what other choice did I have? And so I carried on and was exceedingly careful not to drop or damage things such as hatches that had been carefully rebuilt and refinished.

"The dream is what sustains you through the long process of refit," I said to Neil one afternoon, as we were drinking cold cans of Guinness in his workshop. "It's a daydream, and like a warm fire on a winter evening, and imagination is the kindling. Once you get it going, the intimidating, huge project becomes simply work, and who is afraid of work? When people tell me that I'm crazy, or that the task is too big or impossible, I simply respond that it's only work and you just keep plodding away. That's all it is. You buy the materials and tools that you need as you go. You make time to do the work, and the key to success is to stay in it; do something every day that you can, even if it is a small thing, for all accomplishment is cumulative. If you start making excuses to do something else when it is cold outside, or too hot, or find yourself avoiding it, or going too many days without doing anything on it, the flame will begin to fade, like a candle flame sinking to a tiny blue dot."

"It's only wood," Neil replied. "Anything made of wood can be repaired."

"And yet people will ask me "But when will it be finished?" The question is asked in an almost desperate manner. "When it's done," I reply, "Whenever that will be." Sometimes this frustrates them. And yet you cannot set a schedule for a project like this any more than a *Farmer's Almanac* can predict the weather. But you can think each separate project through and make sure that you do it right. A job done right is time saved because it does not have to be done over."

"That's true," Neil replied. He lit another cigarette, drew deeply on it, and then nodded.

The dream drives you; you ride it, I said to myself. And the dream is not about what you are doing now, or any part of the rebuilding schedule. It is simply all about what you are going to do with the boat, and where you are going to go with it, once the work is done and the oft-dreamt-of launch day has finally arrived.

I was always consciously planning ahead for a long voyage, so I had to make sure that my boat was strong and seaworthy, but also that her systems were designed and built to handle long-distance passagemaking rather than just a day sail, or an 'overnighter' on the weekend. In addition to planning for fuel and water tankage and capacity, I also had to make provisions for generating electricity, since my boat was not large enough to be equipped with a diesel generator.

I needed a constant source of power to run my small reefer unit and navigation systems, so I devised a propeller shaft and generator rig, with a drive belt that when sailing, with the propeller spinning from the flow of water, a sliding adjustment bar allowed me to tension a small drive belt that turned a 12-volt generator. It was simple; now when the engine was not running, I still had all the electricity that I wanted as long as I was moving through the water.

I remembered where my love of wooden boats had originated, and vaguely, when it had all begun, many years earlier with my grandfather. I grew up in and around boats. My grandfather Andrew, whose nickname was always 'Amp', had been a boat-builder and had worked for the Herreshoff yard in Bristol, Rhode Island; he began working there just before the Second World War. During the war years, when the famous yacht yard was given over to the war effort, he helped build Patrol Torpedo, or PT, boats.

For a number of years he had built small boats in his basement, much to my grandmother's chagrin. Boatbuilding was, and still is, a very time-consuming affair, and occasionally noisy and saw-dusty. At least he knew enough to build small-enough boats so that they could be removed from the basement without having to take the house apart. But over the years he always owned a boat of some kind, usually power boats, kept them out in the backyard and worked on them there, scraping, painting, waxing, and alternately hammering on the engines. He was a true fixer-upper, a handy guy who could repair anything in or around a boat or around the house. In the summer, we always had the means to get out onto Narragansett Bay, to go cruising, or fishing, or just knocking about, for in the end it really was all about just being out on the water. We were not wealthy people, and did not own yachts, but because Grandpa was a boat builder, we always had some type of craft to venture out on the Bay in.

I barely remember Grandpa's Popeye-ish little motor boat, *Fish Tales*. This was an open-cockpit boat some twenty-odd feet long with a hull shape more like that of a sailboat than a power boat, a sea-kindly rounded hull tapering back to a smaller transom, with an engine box in the middle of the cockpit and a simple small gasoline engine installed under it. It was an in-board engine, and Grandpa steered the boat with a bronze tiller.

For shelter, *Fish Tales* had a bent wooden folding dodger- type rig that could be raised in a rainstorm, with a canvas cover, that created a cuddy half-cabin and would provide some minimal shelter from the weather. *Fish Tales* also had a wooden mast, although I don't ever recall seeing a sail hoisted. I was barely a toddler at the time and I was told, years later, that as a baby, I had often been put on top of the engine box, since it was a flat, convenient place to put a baby, and had slept there quite comfortably when the boat was under way; thus do we make boatmen.

While I was still a young lad, Grandpa would bring me to the boat yard where he worked, occasionally, on a Saturday or a Sunday, when he was working on his own boat. He had acquired a big wooden cabin cruiser that had been built in the 1920s; these were the early '60s, now, and he was fixing it up. He'd cut a deal and acquired the old cruiser it for a very reasonable sum. It was the biggest boat that he had ever owned, perhaps forty feet long or more, and he was determined to fix it up and get it into the water to take his family out on. But when he first bought it, it had been neglected for a long time, and was up on blocks and boat stands in Mr. Pierson's boat yard, its seams yawning and the hull much in need of caulking, painting, and just plain wetness. For weeks one spring, after work, the caulking hammer pounded and the irons rang out like channel buoy bells in the early dusk, as long strands of soft tawny cotton were twisted and gradually fed into the seams, then hammered out of sight. The last whack of the hammer was always the one that rang true; it had a certain tone, I noticed, and when it achieved that tone, Grandpa advanced the iron ahead in the seam another iron-length.

I asked Grandpa what he was going to name the boat; "*Fish Tales*," he answered; it was the same name that his other boats had carried over the years. One afternoon he was busy with a putty knife, forcing some thick reddish goop into the seams where he had pounded the caulking. I asked him what the stuff was; "Compound," was his one-word answer. He was not going to try to explain to a little boy what compound was all about, or why it was used; there was no point. I was to learn all of this much later.

Boat yards were interesting places, I discovered. In the springtime, they were always worlds of strange odors. Back then, copper bottom paint had some-thing of a pleasing, oily aroma, not like the synthetic antifouling polymeric stuff they formulated later that stank horribly and made one queasy with its smell. There was also the odd, sweet, strong, strangely pleasing chemical smell of curing fiberglass resin, polyester resin. To me these were the two scents that said 'boat yard' to me. The boat yard was a dangerous place though, with splintered wood, fiberglass, gooey stuff on the ground and upward-pointing rusty nails to step in and on. Grandpa often brought my cousin Mack and I to the boat yard while he worked. Mack was Uncle Jed's son and a year or so younger than I was. Grandpa did not like us to go wandering off; but we often did, as there was not much excitement in watching Grandpa work, at least not after the first ten minutes had passed.

We were told not to bother other men working on their boats, to stay away from them lest we should become troublesome or distracting. The weeds grew amazingly tall in the boat yard; long, discarded scraps of wood became swords. Once, we 'borrowed' a wooden ladder that was resting up against a boat. We did not realize that there was a fellow working inside the boat, but Grandpa soon knew it, and knew who was responsible, when he heard the fellow hollering across the boat yard for his ladder so that he could climb down. The other great thing about the boat yard was that it was a man's, and a boy's, place. If you had to pee, well, you went behind a boat where no one could see you. Grandpa had told us that this was okay. This was an act almost sacrilegious to us lads; there was something very naughty and at the same time appealing in this freedom to make water on tall weeds in the outdoors without catching a scolding or spanking for it; so whenever we could, we peed in the boat yard. It was a symbolic act of male liberation.

During those years, Gramp had a close friend named Russ. They had been friends since boyhood and were both members of the local Yacht Club. Russ had an old-fashioned motorboat, smaller than my grandfather's big motorboat *Fish Tales,* and used to take us out in it, Gramp, Mack, and me. I remember, in particular, the wonderful coziness of the forepeak, with its old-wooden-boat smell of paint and oil, musty, but feeling solid with the old exposed bent oak frames and planks, under the foredeck, dark, hiding away, feeling the up and down motion of the bow as I nestled in there on a cool spring morning, hearing the slosh of the water around the bow and feeling the gentle vibration in the hull as the old Chrysler flathead gasoline engine busily labored away with a steady thrumming. Looking aft, I could see through the length of the cabin and out on deck, Russ standing next to the big shiny bronze tiller, steering; and I could hear Gramp and Russ talking loudly over the sound of the engine and laughing. Mack was out there with them in the bright sun, sipping an orange soda through a straw. That is something that always stays with you; the sound, the smell, the feel of a snug wooden motorboat, the kind that would do no more than six to eight knots comfortably, but that was plenty fast enough and in fact at times too fast.

One summer afternoon some years later, Gramp took me and Mack out fishing in Bristol Harbor in Gramp's eighteen-foot flat-bottomed motorboat. It was a plywood "sharpie," hard-chine, a simple boat with an outboard motor and a tiller extension. Grandpa had sold big *Fish Tales* after its size had become, with his advancing age, too much to manage and maintain.

On that particular day, we weren't catching anything, the day was warm, and thus we ventured out further, around the backside of Hog Island, near the little black and white fireplug of a lighthouse that was the only visible part of Hog Island Shoal above water. It was a fine day, sunny and bright with blue skies above, and we decided to break for lunch, going ashore in the little sheltered cove of Hog Island's southeast end.

Mack and I decided to take a little walk on the beach, to do a little beach-combing; Grandpa had taught us the value and fun of that; one never knew what one might find, from old lobster trap buoys to driftwood and fragmented lengths of multicolored rope and line to odd shells cast up from the deep.

We stumbled and ran along the rocks, and at some point, Mack cried out, "Look, there's a boat washed up." We hurried up to it; it was a sorry-looking beat up old plywood pram, the paint all peeling off of it and mostly weathered away, sitting upright and very dry and nestled in the dried band of cast-up sea-weed and salt hay that ran along the beach above the high tide mark. We looked the derelict boat over carefully; it was not tied to anything, and appeared to have been resting there for some time. We ran back to Grandpa, who was still sitting on the log, smoking and looking off into the distance at the green and sloping distant shore of Bristol.

"Gramp, there's a shipwreck on the beach!" I exclaimed, excitedly. I wanted to be the first to announce the find.

"But I discovered it!" Mack chimed up; "I saw it first!"

"So what," I said. "It was my idea to rescue it."

"I want it!" Mack whined, and I almost thought he was going to cry, for the telltale bottom lip began to protrude in a pout.

"Oh, big baby," I said.

"Hey now, you guys stop that," Gramp scolded, sharply. "What did you find? A boat? Let's go have a look. Come on, get along with one another."

Grandpa hiked over the beach to the boat with us, for it was only a hundred yards or so away. When we arrived, he stood next to it for a moment without saying anything, first puffing his pipe thoughtfully, then poking and scratching at it with his folding knife. He had an old rigging knife that he carried in his trouser pocket all the time, and now he alternately scraped parts of the boat with the blade, pried at the seams, and then poked the lethal-looking little folding marlinspike on the other end of it into holes and soft spots.

"Hmm. Ripe as a plum," he muttered.

"What's that, Grandpa?"

"Oh, nothing. Naaaah." He spat a tobacco-brown stream of spittle onto the shell-litter of the beach. Then he asked us to stand on either side of the pram and lift. It was not very heavy, actually, but to a couple of small boys, it seemed so, so we carried it a short distance at a time, dragged it some, staggered along with it some more, until we finally brought it, what seemed an interminable time later, to the shore of the little cove on the opposite side of the point, where we had come ashore.

Grandpa brought the anchor up and then tied a line from the stern of his boat onto the ringbolt on the battered pram. Mack and I could see that the pram was leaking quite a bit. Gramp got the engine going and we quickly began heading out of the cove and into the more open water of Bristol Harbor. For a while, the pram towed along behind the boat nicely, surfing along, but Mack and I, in our orange life vests, sitting on the thwarts and looking aft at the pram, could see that it was riding lower in the water all the time. Mack and I wondered if we would make it back to the boat ramp with the pram or if it would sink down and out of sight and maybe even pull us down with it. The afternoon breeze had freshened and had set up a good chop in the harbor. Even though we were riding with it, it was bumpy water, and to compound matters, the pram soon swamped, and was very difficult to control. It dived and broached, capsized and rolled, much like a live, reluctant, big fish on the end of a fishing-line, being towed in. Grandpa had to slow the boat down, and it took all his skill as a boatman to keep us moving without being 'pooped' from behind by the stiff, choppy seas, or having to cut the pram loose to keep his boat from swamping. After what seemed forever, we brought the pram in to the dinghy launching ramp at the yacht club, turned it over and dumped the water out of it, and then, for it was much heavier now for having been wetted for an hour and soaking in the sea, Gramp helped us put it up on the shell driveway upside-down where it would dry out for a couple of days before he came down again in his old Ford Country Squire station wagon where we would load the pram partly into it, partly onto the tailgate, and tie it down. Then, Gramp, Mack, and I brought it home to his house, where it was immediately put up on sawhorses out under the big maple tree in the far southeast corner of the backyard.

Grandma just shook her head disapprovingly, a sour look on her face, as she stood in the doorway of the screened-in porch facing the yard, watching us carry our beat-up old treasure out back. "Now Andrew," she addressed him. "Not another one! Not another old *piece of junk!*" she scolded, with special emphasis on the last three words. Mack and I cringed, but Grandpa puffed his pipe and ignored her remark.

As we were standing around the little derelict, staring at it admiringly, Grandma called us in for a bowl of chowder that she had just made. Grandma always made the best Rhode Island-style clam chowder, not creamy but grayish-clear in color, strongly flavored and seasoned with lots of black pepper, celery, onions, and her secret, a few pinches of poultry seasoning. Of course, there were lots of chopped fresh quahog clams and their juice in it as well. She would also serve saltine crackers with it, or nice bakery-fresh Portuguese bread rolls and butter. We all sat down and ate; she did not ask about the pram; she already knew everything there was to know about it from past experience.

"The first thing you do," Grandpa began explaining the next day, when we were gathered with him next to the pram (and had dutifully packed his pipe with Cavendish), "Is to rip away all the rot and bad stuff, and see what you've got left to work with." We were excited, and we listened attentively.

As the ensuing days passed, Grandpa ripped away the old wood, the broken pieces of gunwale and such, and made new ones. He scraped, sanded, and filled the plywood sides and bottom halves, and under his careful patient work, surrounded by the aroma of blue pipe-smoke, the pram gradually began to look new again, took proper shape, and when it was finally painted a medium blue, it was beautiful, with new bronze oarlocks and hardware. It sat on the water like a little blue duck and Mack and I took turns rowing it around the dock at the yacht club under Gramp's watchful eye. What had been old and cast-off had been made like-new again, and the whole idea of being able to do that fascinated me. The little pram skimmed along and bobbed on the afternoon waves in the harbor, light, graceful, and strong. It was wonderful. Gramp had taken something dead and brought it to life, and I wanted to learn to do that, too.

Chapter 4

No Return

"[Death is] to lose the earth you know for greater knowing; to lose the life you have, for greater life; to leave the friends you loved, for greater loving; to find a land more kind than home, more large than earth."

– Thomas Wolfe, You Can't Go Home Again

While I worked on the restoration and rebuilding of my boat, I needed an income to live and purchase supplies; I had money set aside, but did not want to slowly deplete it. So after I was done with the little coastal sailing newspaper, I took another part-time position managing a tidy little one-room nautical chart and book shop in Newport, to help pay for the materials and supplies that I would need to bring my dream to reality. As the winter season closed in and Christmas approached, I would often stay at the shop well after closing time, sitting in the silence and enjoying the quiet peace at day's end. I liked this tidy little nautical book shop in the north end of Newport. It offered all types of charts, nautical books, and cruising guides for sailors. The office girls had taste-fully decorated the shop with festive Christmas decorations including a small, trimmed artificial tree with gaily-wrapped and ribbon-tied empty boxes beneath, and had strung frosty white miniature lights around the frames of the big front windows on the street. They gave the place a soft, old-fashioned Christmassy air and I would shut off the main overhead lights at dusk and sit in my desk chair for a while after the girls had gone home and the shop was closed, watching the deep blue of winter night descend behind the ancient rooftops of the clapboard colonial homes across the street with their massive chimneys. The big windows faced westward, so after the sun set and the sky turned steel-blue, the bare branches of the trees would whip about in the strong, cold winter winds that blew across Newport Harbor from the sea beyond. Often the wind would carry the incense-like aroma of a hardwood fire burning in one of those ancient hearths and I would catch a whiff of it on the frosty air and it would make me wish that I could curl up on the warm bricks in front of it, wherever it might be, listening to the crackle of dry oak and basking in the flickering light from the flames and, perhaps, a tallow candle or a Betty Lamp.

It was a festive, sad, and quiet time all at once for me. The shop's display racks were stacked with colorful glossy guides to dreamlike destinations in the warm Caribbean, slices of paradise characterized by turquoise-blue waters, white coral sand, green coconut palms, and trade-wind breezes, but all so far away, so unreachable from this land of northern winter cold at the bottom of the year. They constantly reminded me of where I was, rather than where I would rather be, lounging on a beach on my insular Tahiti, subject of my yearning and soul-hungry longing, the fruit within sight on the display rack but in reality well beyond reach.

The quietude was a balm for my soul and my spirits; I might daydream for a time, focused on the cover photography of one of those richly-illustrated guides. I had the job of being the shop's keeper, though not its owner. I had finally found a place of comfort and security, or so it seemed, but it was not in fact secure, and in the deepest regions of my heart I knew that it would never work. I was too restless; I was eager to move on, for all security is, in the end, an illusion, and its wages are stagnation and inner rot. It was a false comfort, for although it felt neat to be a shopkeeper with a key, a purveyor of charts and books, all things that I loved very much, with a quiet dignity and distinguished saltiness to it, it could not last. But for now, for a few brief months, I was in another world, one that I had always sought to be a part of, but it was like finding oneself at long last on a beautiful, small desert island somewhere in the middle of the Caribbean, or the Pacific; you have arrived at the place where you always wanted to be, but without anything to eat, not enough to live on, too few coconuts.

Down by the waterfront, the varnished dark masts, yards and spars of traditional sailing vessels moored at the wharf shone dimly in the glow of street-level lamps, then disappeared like phantoms into the dark sky, vanishing and merging with the black winter night the higher I lifted my gaze. Like a vision into the dark nebula of the past, they stood silently over the jumble of old rooftops and brick-laid alleys, stolidly mute while beneath their loft yards, naked young trees were hung with garlands of twinkling Christmas lights that cavorted gaily in the wind like draped necklaces of jewels wrapping a ballroom floor assemblage of mad dancers as the wind whipped their branches about.

After closing the shop on such evenings, I would wrap my scarf around my neck and don my dark Navy wool pea coat and venture down to the quiet and empty waterfront to see the lights and simply breathe the fresh, salty air and contemplate the strange juxtaposition of past and present that characterizes Christmas each year in a quirky centuries-old town full of anachronisms. The waterfront was especially empty on these frequently cold and windy nights; I liked it best that way. Occasionally a bundled-up shadowy phantom scuttled from one corner to a doorway or down the street mutely into the darkness, paying no notice and no heed to anyone or anything about; heads lowered, hands in pockets, they scurried from shelter to shelter. As I walked, my footfalls on the brittle bricks clicked out sharp and keen and reverberated off brick and clapboard alley walls. It was my town, at such times; cold, but that was the price of ownership.

It was for me a time of contemplation and introspection; I could be alone with my thoughts under the moonless sky. On the wharf, I stood in the wind and stared out blankly onto the dark, unseen harbor, choppy and sloppy in the windy night; I could hear it better than I could see it, but for a few twinkling lights standing out from the far shore. At such times, I remembered people who had passed on, and I could almost hear their voices in the wind. They had passed through the lighted mead-hall full of feasting revelers like the swallow, in from the darkness, into the brilliance of the raucous Heorot, and then back out into it again. At such times, past and present merged in a wave of melancholy sweetness, the memories of good things and times keeping my heart from weighing heavy. But then I felt, all the more keenly, the wish that I could board a fine, big yacht, heading south out of these winter seas of my soul, headed for the bright, warm islands of green palm fronds rustling in the afternoon trade winds, where life and warmth were forever intertwined, where these dark hues characteristic of every day of life in these latitudes can only be found in the deepest of shadows down there. I would gladly hand, reef, and steer the ship, eager to abandon these melancholy shores of living memories and disappointments, to start a new life, make a new beginning, clear my mind of all things sad and haunting, to leave my ghosts behind me, shadows of woe unable to follow me across the cleansing, purging waters of the sparkling Gulf Stream.

But now, nothing stirred; no ship was leaving with the morning tide with a course set for the islands in the south. Small ice crystals began to fall from an overcast sky. I turned my steps homeward, desperately mindful of time's ticking clock.

I remembered that, years ago, my father became weary of his job that never changed; it was the same old desk and office in the same location every day. He used to express his dream of retiring, and purchasing a small convenience store and gas station, perhaps, a small business to run, up in New Hampshire, perhaps near Lake Winnipesaukee. He mentioned the town of Wolfeboro many times. As a young lad, the prospect of this made me feel insecure; it meant moving to a new, unknown place. And yet I wished for it, because I knew that it would make my father happy. In the end he never realized his dream; it simply never happened. The four sons grew up, and had their own ideas and dreams, and eventually wives and babies. Like ripples moving away from the pebble dropped into the still waters of a pond, so went the plans and intentions. The sons remained in close orbit around the star, but as worlds of their own. Inertia is a powerful force; it has been the smothering blanket of dreams of most people since time immemorial. But now I was determined to live mine, no matter what the cost.

Since I knew that I would be leaving, and was unsure whether or not I would ever return, I took a little time, in the months before my departure, to visit places that I had known in my childhood, and yet had not returned to in many years, to see if they resembled the hazy images in my memory, to confront my fears, and to settle with my past, to find peace with myself before pushing off from the dock for possibly the last time. I don't wish to sound morbid, but on such a small-boat voyage there is always the ever-present possibility that one will not return at all, that a storm or collision will end one's life. So of course the first place I went was home, to the home of my childhood, a place that I had not seen in decades.

Thomas Wolfe said it right when he wrote that you can't go home again. I tire of this quote; it is overused. It may be true, I often reflect, but if you can't go home, at least you can drive by it. I did that one afternoon in late August. It was the first house that I had ever lived in, situated in an aging neighborhood on a still partially-wooded hill in Woonsocket, Rhode Island, on the west bank of the Blackstone River. I had not laid eyes upon that house in nearly a half century. It made me sad to do so, and I was not sure why, at first, but it affected me so much afterwards that I concluded that although one can do such a thing, it is not necessarily always advisable. Some old river-bottoms, settled and layered with years of gently accumulated sediments, are best not stirred up, and yet I cannot explain why I was so emotional, since my childhood was not an unhappy one at all, but perhaps because disturbing years of sediment refreshes the realization that life passes and that there is the eventuality of one's own mortality. Life ends; it is linear, not cyclical. *You can never return to being that child, in that year,* I reminded myself. It lives only as a faded, distant, confused memory, and the voices of people long gone are but echoes in one's soul. Nothing more; and those echoes echo only for you. All recollections are individual and personal, ultimately.

Sometimes awakening old feelings is a good thing, I mused. After all, when something hurts, even just a little, it reminds you of the fact that you are still alive and capable of feeling; because if you lose that capability, you have died in perhaps the only way, other than physical, that truly matters.

Back in my little neighborhood, in my recollection, the end of the street, seemingly half a mile away, had now shrunk to less than a hundred yards. My world was very large back then. It is still incredibly large, but my horizon has shifted, as a few lines from Tennyson's *Ulysses* come to mind:

> *I am a part of all that I have met;*
> *Yet all experience is an arch wherethrough*
> *Gleams that untravelled world, whose margin fades*
> *For ever and for ever when I move.*

Now I drove back up the street and turned, going up another long rise to suddenly realize that a new neighborhood on the hill had once been woods, and that this nicely paved road had been a steep gravelly dirt road. We used to have a good accumulation of snow in the winter, and often plenty of snow for sledding. Once, we had a Flexible Flyer, and my father and I climbed the hill through the snow and he set the sled down, and placed me, facing forward, between his knees, with him seated behind me and his feet up front to steer the sled. We began going down the hill, faster and faster, and then all of a sudden the sled plunged into a big powdery snow drift that he hadn't seen. For me, all went wet, dark, and stinging-cold on my face, and I remember the shock and surprise, and perhaps a few tears, for I was kindergarten age, and my father laughing and doing his best to wipe the snow off my face. That unnerved me, and I never forgot the sensation of accelerating into and being momentarily buried alive in a snowdrift, or snow-bank, as my mother called it.

So now I was in a decidedly unfamiliar place much unlike my hazy, distorted dreams from a half century ago, yet I knew that this was the place where I spent my early years and from where my earliest recollections were drawn from. I looked at my old house, now somewhat run-down and looking its age, and felt a kinship with it; I, too, am showing the weathering of my years, and I thought, poor old house, poor old me.

I had come home, but to my earliest home of memory, and was no longer home, really, but one home of several in succession down through my life. I had come full circle, but the place I had returned to was not the place that I had left. You can only visit, like a visitor at a museum of your own life, politely kept behind the brass stanchions and blue velvet ropes; view, but do not touch. After all, Dad, now, is gone, gone for a few years already. The only place I can find him is in my mind of memories. He joins the fast-moving sled and the snow drift; I can hear him laugh. He is in the same place as many more recent memories too, of course, clearer and brighter and more recent. In this storehouse I keep them all, well-filed, accessible, and treasured. As we grow older, it is what we have, growing larger and larger as living reality grows smaller proportionately, less relevant, of less concern, and ultimately runs down the clock. In my end is my beginning/In my beginning is my end.

But now I had only echoes fading into the recesses of my mind and distant recollection, like orbs spinning away from me out into space, an ever-expanding universe of consciousness in which everything gradually becomes more remote from the center and from every other object and place in time. There is no road back; the rising tide has effaced my footsteps from the beach; the path behind me is overgrown and blocked. There is no possibility of stepping back into that same place.

Chapter 5

The Argument

Don't part with your illusions. When they are gone, you may still exist, but you have ceased to live.

— Mark Twain

All things having to do with my life before, and my life on land, had now come to an end with the completion of my boat, it seemed. I felt as though I were suspended on the margin between what my life had been before, all up to this moment, and a new life that lay ahead, one that I had planned, and which in itself harbored endless possibilities. And it would be entirely different, in every way, from what I was leaving behind. My long-time friend Jim was trying to dissuade me from steering my plotted course, but was becoming increasingly frustrated by my intractability.

Jim and I were down at the pub on the Bristol waterfront on a Saturday afternoon. It was a mild, early fall day and we were at the outside bar that was still open even though it was near the end of the season. The sun was warm yet, although its intensity was fading, and it felt good on my face and neck, a reminder of the summer that was now, in truth, gone.

"I'm leaving," I said, with a tone of finality.

"When?" Jim asked.

"In a day or two. As soon as I can fuel and water her up, and finish provisioning. I need to make another trip to the grocery store and the chandlery."

"Where are you going?" he asked.

"South," I replied, "And then from there, who knows."

"Maybe around the world? Like you have sometimes said?"

"I could," I said, "Although the only problem with a circumnavigation is that in the end, after all of it, you end up back in the same place you started from."

"Any idea when you'll come back?"

"No," I replied, "That's my whole point. I might never come back, in fact I probably won't. Why would I?"

"You grew up here," Jim said, "This is your home."

"But there is nothing here for me anymore," I replied. "Nothing and no one. I think sometimes it is not a good idea to stay in the same place for too long. You get stale. First stale, then you rot from the inside out. And meanwhile the clock is ticking. You don't have another life in the bank. The one you have is all that there is. So you need to refresh everything sometimes, move on, explore, learn how to learn again, to see, to discover. I think I have tarried here for too long."

"You're going to miss it," Jim replied, shaking his head.

"Maybe. Just in the beginning if at all."

Jim tossed what was left of his cigarette down on the ground and snuffed it with his shoe, grinding it hard into the dirt. "It's still hurricane season," he said.

"By the time I get out there it should be all right. Besides, it's getting on in the year and the tropics have been quiet of late."

"Why would you want to go live down there?" Jim asked me, shaking his head.

"Because it's paradise," I replied.

"I've been there. It's not paradise," he remonstrated. "There's nothing to do down there!"

"That's the whole point of paradise," I replied. "No obligations, no conse-quences, needed nowhere."

"You'll get tired of it quickly. People go down there and just drink them-selves to death on cheap rum."

"There are worse fates. Besides, you can go sailing, scuba diving or snorkeling, or explore the islands, walking the trails and paths. Stroll the beaches, swim, lie in the sun or under a palm tree in a hammock. You can paint or write if you like to do either."

"Walk the trails when it isn't too hot," Jim picked up and continued where I left off. "The woods are full of biting bugs and prickly plants that hurt your feet. You'll get a fungus. The sea is full of things that sting and bite. It's hot and humid and doesn't cool off at night."

"Then I will sleep out on the open deck," I said.

"The boredom will drive you nuts. You cannot make any money there; all you can do is spend it. Thieves are everywhere. There is only so much eating, drinking, and lying around that you can do. Soon you will find yourself broke."

" *"Tis not too late to seek a newer world...my purpose holds, to sail beyond the sunset, and the baths of all the western stars, until I die,"* I recited.

48

"*Ulysses*. Yes, of course. Romantic garbage," Jim concluded.

"I might think about you back here once in a while," I said. Then I put my empty pint glass down on the bar and walked away.

"There you go," he called after me bitterly, "Just walk away."

I stopped in my tracks, and turned around, and walked back slowly until I stood practically nose-to-nose with him.

"What you don't understand," I began, slowly and deliberately, a little bit irritated now, "is that walking away is the hardest part. It's huge, in fact. It's like stepping off a cliff. But I don't want to be one of the many who had the chance to take that step, and never did because they were afraid, and regretted it for the rest of their lives. The first step is enormous. The first few steps are very hard, I understand, but if I don't do it now, I never will. I will keep putting on a tattered winter coat every year and one day they will lower my box into the gravelly soil as the first snowflakes are flying out of a gray sky and that will be the end of my story, and all because I could not take that step."

He just looked away. "I couldn't," he said, with an odd quaver in his voice.

"Yes, you could, too."

"No," he repeated, "I could not. I could not walk away from that much all at once."

"It has to be a clean break, a total break, or you will never be able to do it. You have to think about what you are walking away from. What it means to you. Sometimes the things that you think are valuable to you are only anchors, in the end."

"I couldn't. Even though Jennie has passed on. I just couldn't. Just because I'm alone isn't enough of a reason."

"I wasn't trying to be insensitive. Listen to me. I feel like a sailor who has been left on the beach, while others sail away; or a man bound and harnessed, feet in his traces, with no option but to continue pulling endlessly like an ox for his daily bread while time and life slip away. Opportunities for exploration, adventure, and mental and physical refreshment diminish as the road to life's terminus grows ever shorter. I look around, frantically, and see only my life, proscribed by circumstances, with its attendant baggage of stagnation, frustration, and endless demands. I keep turning and turning, making a complete circle, like a broken compass, knowing no direction for progress away from the center. Jim, I yearn to go, but not on a comfortable cruise-ship; I don't want a stateroom, but rather a hammock in the fo'c'sle. Give me strong black coffee and let me handle rough lines in the middle of the night. Let me know the feeling of being there, for then I will know that I am truly alive."

"Why take that risk?" he replied.

"Jim, I used to collect silver dollars. Every once in a while I would take the box down from its high shelf and look at them, slowly run my fingers through them. Then I got very sick as you remember, and when I finally got better, I took the box down one day and realized that these were the same coins that I had bought at estate auctions, left behind when someone else had passed. They were just discs of cold metal, a heavy box full. Just another anchor. Lying in a dark box collecting dust and serving no purpose than to occupy shelf space. So I took them down to a coin shop, sold them, and with some of the money I bought a compass."

"Good luck then," Jim said, his voice quavering with emotion. "I wish you well. Maybe I envy you for doing what I know that I cannot do. You go sail; I'll opt for the box in the ground with the falling snow. Godspeed."

In the days before I left, perhaps two weeks at that, and they flew by like birds on the wing, I took some time to visit my old haunts and favorite places, knowing in my heart that I would quite probably never see them again. An old Irish folk song stuck in my mind:

So here's a health to the company and one to my lass
Let us drink and be merry all out of one glass
Let us drink and be merry, all grief to refrain
For we may or might never all meet here again.

For if my wanderings were to take me far afield, to the distant corners of the world, and the world is a big place, I noted, I might not come home again anyhow, but settle elsewhere; I often thought that I would need a lifetime of a thousand years or more to see every part of this world that interests me, and see it up close in a personal way, more than just flying by or hurrying through. Then too, if my life were to end abruptly for whatever cause, the result would be the same; my bones would bleach on some far plain, or rest in a dry hole, or at the bottom of the sea. I thought about this one afternoon as I was taking a last long walk on my favorite paths and trails down by the old colonial farm property on Mount Hope Bay. The first leaves of the sugar maples had started to turn, lighting up in flashes of brilliant reds, yellows, and orange color, fluttering in the afternoon breeze.

I took a side path down to the shoreline and stood there at the edge of the oak and maple woods, taking it in; the golden late afternoon sun, low in the sky; the sea-breeze, or *'Sea Turne,'* as our Puritan forefathers had called it, out of the southwest, its summertime direction, still warm and smelling of the sweet brine, a reminder of the season past. At that moment I thought of many things, recalled much in a flood of memory, and then thought to myself how sweet this moment really was, how sweet this place, so much a part of my whole life and of me, and how I should miss it; and tears welled up in my eyes as I thought of passing away on a foreign shore, and how much I would dearly love to somehow have my bones brought back and interred in this rocky New England soil, if that were possible. I would be in the same ground with my family and ancestors and wear a winter mantle of snow as they do every year, and rest even with the bones of the native peoples whose unmarked and unknown burials of centuries ago still dot the landscape, hidden anonymously beneath the humus.

But I knew that this would probably not be; some things simply are not achievable, or simply cannot be guaranteed, due to circumstances that we cannot control. So I shrugged, turned about with my walking-stick and once again began making my way back up the path. It is enough, I thought, to hold this place in my heart, and thus as it has become a part of me, so also have I become part of it, whether I am present here or not. And then I began once again to question my own motivations. For if I love it enough that the thought of being eternally parted from it should move me, should I even go, after all, if I do not hate it? Why leave, then? But then I realized that indeed few things in life are ever black and white, north or south; few decisions are ever clear, or without compromise. And so thus they are never easy. But I knew that I must go, even if it meant parting with this place. For there is no point in staying in a place for the sake of bones in the soil; one must not mistake the dead for living memories of them in one's own heart. Let the dead bury the dead. It is time to go, to move on while still alive.

As I mentioned earlier, my circumstances were such that I had been alone for some time; the details regarding how I had come to that point, I must confess, I am not ready yet to divulge, but they were part of the tumultuous past, events of misfortune, and all grouped together in what constitutes a man's past. You cannot sail away from your past, this I knew; for while a man may geographically remove himself from those surroundings that remind him daily of his loss, he will still carry them, along with his regrets and other cancerous baggage, in his mind; but it is true that such thoughts are more easily suppressed when in different surroundings.

So as I followed the wooded path along the shoreline, I suddenly remembered my old friend Arbuckle, whom I had not thought of in quite some years since his death. He had been a fisherman, poet, odd-jobs laborer, a heavy drinker, skinny and bearded, a friend many years ago when we had lived in old Newburyport up on the North Shore of Massachusetts. Divorced for a few years when I knew him, Arbuckle watched his daughter, whom he loved dearly, growing up, soon to become a teenager, in the same town where he lived. He could visit her at appointed times, and they would often be seen walking the brick sidewalks of downtown Newburyport on Saturdays in nice weather. But since she and her mother lived in Newburyport, and so did Arbuckle, he was too close to the scene of his sadness, the cruel reminder of his life gone wrong, whether or not it was his fault. He would not move away, for he could not bear to be away from his daughter, yet he kept his respectful distance from his ex-wife, as the law required, but like a ship without wind or power, rolling uncontrollably in a steep swell, he "wallowed" as a friend described it. Everyone felt that the best thing for Arbuckle to do was to move away and start life anew. He drank unceasingly to dull the sharpness of his pain, but found no respite in it, and when he was finally convinced to move away, to work up in Maine, he found that he could not bear the separation. His new existence was not indeed new; it was merely another re-run of a tragic-comic play, yet another mattress on a floor in a barn never meant to be a sleeping-room, another year of life out of a duffel bag, another shared communal existence devoid of privacy among a gaggle of ne'er-do-well nomadic drunkards and failures. More cigarettes, rough jokes, drinking bouts and quarrels until three in the morning, laughter amid denial, a jolly facade of perpetual inebriation, hangovers, hard work, and discomfort, in that daily order, among peers who refused to face their own lack of a future.

His life had become a ship with a broken rudder, leaking, the rising water gaining on her pumps, adrift without any progress or direction. He looked at what he was, and his will withered at his own fatalistic perception of the mountain of resistance ahead of him, and knew in his heart that his voyage was over, and he was not yet forty years of age. He had abandoned hope; and where there is no hope, there are no dreams, and where there are no dreams, lassitude and despair quickly follow, the creeping teredo-worms of the heart, eating and devouring all from the inside out, remaining just beneath the surface, leaving only a shell that is infinitely more fragile than it looks. So, on a cold late fall night in a tool shed and garage in the woods of Maine, where he had come to work and live, yet another sad chapter in a book of all similar chapters, he closed the doors to the garage, started the engine of his old pickup truck, and then sat in the driver's seat until he fell asleep, and never again awoke to the unending cycle of pain and failure that had been his life. At one point, he had published a little book, no more than a few pages, of handwritten poems and short essays that he handed out to his friends at the bar. At the very end, he wrote that *"The outcome is to see; as in the eye, and I; Seas of salt encircle the Globe, made of tears."* I stopped for a moment, and looked out on the bay; somehow, I knew, this outcome, my outcome, must be different. I had memorized lines from Tennyson's *Ulysses*:

> *"'Tis not too late to seek a newer world...*
> *Though much is taken, much abides."*

I remembered the afternoon a year or so earlier when I had stood beside my old friend Jon in the aft cockpit of his buddy Captain Bill's steel trawler. The engines were stopped and we were gently lolling in the swell a couple of miles east of Plum Island, up on the North Shore of Massachusetts, off of Newburyport. It was barely an hour before sunset, in the middle of October, and the sun peeked out golden from behind a bank of purplish blue clouds stretching across the horizon. Jon opened the plastic bag containing his father's ashes and poured them into the sea, pinkish-white sandy grains that looked for all the world like powdered plaster, making a light cloud in the deep greenish clean Atlantic water. Jon had waited for weeks for this moment, joking from time to time about how he had Dad still in the trunk of his car, and how Dad's journeys were not ended yet. He laughed; for some reason, the way Jon said it, it didn't seem creepy. After all, Dad really wasn't much more than a bag of mortar mix that wouldn't set even if wet. Now Jon's dad, who had lived well into his nineties, was a part of the place that he had always loved, and that his son loved, this very ancient part of America, old Yankee North Shore Massachusetts, a storied, farming fishing pilgrim-settled place where his family had lived for generations.

Jon had asked me to come up to Newburyport for this little ceremony. His long-time friend Captain Bill had brought his steel trawler back up to New England two years before, and lived on her now that his divorce had become final. He used to be a great guitar player before terrible arthritis had taken over and turned his knuckles and joints into oversized, painful knobs and odd shapes that made one cringe to look at. He still had a phenomenal voice but now he did not sing anymore, although you could still hear the strength and mellifluous lubricity in his fine baritone voice when he spoke. Now he lived on his boat, and worked some, but he drank a lot and had been drinking for quite a long time since his marriage had gone sour and his boat had begun to resemble Slocum's old *Spray* down below in the years before she disappeared, unkempt and in need of a good cleaning from keel to truck.

Captain Bill lived for his boat and loved the sea; his boat was his last freedom, ever since they had taken his driver's license away for good, and he had then sold his car, as he no longer had any use for it. After all, there were bars near the marina where he lived aboard his boat that were open all year long and they were well within walking distance. Bill kept his boat in the water year 'round in Hampton and sometimes the salt river froze over but it was not much of an issue because the hull was heavy steel and the ice never hurt it.

On the trip out I had noticed a faded photo of Bill's brother, a small black and white photo in a wooden frame, standing next to the compass box on the control console next to the helm. The last time I had known Bill, his younger brother had been alive, though he had a terrible drug and alcohol problem. In the intervening years that problem had claimed his life, and I never knew it until now. I remember that Bill was tough on his younger brother, but one night his brother had died while fishing at night off a Plum Island jetty. He loved to fish, but he had been drunk and unsteady, and had slipped on some slimy rocks and had fallen, struck his head, and drowned. I looked again at the photo, nicely though inexpertly framed and carefully positioned where it could always be seen by the helmsman. His name and the short span of his lifetime were penciled in at the bottom of the photo.

When Jon had phoned and asked me to come to Newburyport to go out with him and Bill to scatter his dad's ashes, I did not think twice; I got into my truck, and pointed the bow north. I never knew Jon's dad very well; the few times that I had met him, he was a gentle, quiet, balding man, puttering around his house or yard, mostly of kindly words and a very dry but ready sense of humor.

We had motored out of the mouth of the mighty Merrimack River in the late afternoon, and gone southeast to a spot that Jon had picked out on a chart; it was a place where he and his dad had gone fishing once many years ago, and had had a very lucky time of it.

It was a beautiful, pleasant evening, a slight hint of dry chill in the air, as the darkling lumpy-dune low profile of Plum Island worked its way north to south along the western horizon. The sky had the look and feel of fall, and as I gazed out to the eastward, to the emptiness of the blue horizon with the low bank of clouds stretching across it everlastingly, I felt the pull, the draw that had always tugged at me, the yearning, the longing, just to go, just to head out in that direction and forget all, forget the world, forget all mortality, trouble, and things of the land, and simply go, gliding through the air above the waves, skimming low over the water like a gull, and never looking back, no, not even for an instant. It was a pull that in my youth had drawn me to the sea, onto big steel ships and a life that was far from free, at least for a while. I had found my way out there, onto the deep, to be sure; but I had yet to find what I had been seeking as a youth, that ill-defined thing that cannot be described, but only felt; something disguised, perhaps, as something else. Maybe, I began to think as I grew older, whatever I am seeking is not out there, beyond the horizon; maybe it is within; but that is not necessarily a safer quest, either.

But no, I could not go out over the horizon now, not today, not even in Captain Bill's big, old, heavy, comfortable, cozy though unkempt, diesel-growling steel ark. It was not my ship, nor my time; instead it had been Jon's dad who went, poured out of a bag like dust and in an instant joined with and become a part of that endless wave-lapping happy blueness that stretched away forever to every last corner of the world where billow meets rocky cliff or tawny strand at its margin.

Out on deck, now, it was nearly sunset. Jon folded up the bag and put it in his pocket. He said a few rambling things in a folksy way to the water, as though addressing his dad personally in conversation. He tearfully said good-bye, thanked him for all the years of good times and raising him, hoped that he was in a better place, and told him to take care of himself. Jon was never a man for oratory or open emotion. Yet now, tears welled up in his eyes as he spoke; he sniffled a few times, and I knew that he was remembering the good years with his father.

Captain Bill brought out a good bottle of Haitian dark rum and three little shot glasses so that we could drink a toast to Jon's dad in remembrance. We drank a first, then a second, and even a third (each one of us had to offer one, of course) and then we began reminiscing about how the years had seemed to have flown by, and how none of us were very much the way we were when we used to play music together two decades ago, and yet we marveled how, in our hearts and minds, we still seemed to be the same. We compared notes about changes in our lives and then the subject drifted to Captain Bill and his decision to move aboard his boat and live aboard even during the cold North Shore winters.

Bill stood in the cockpit, glass of neat rum in hand. "I always wanted to live aboard a boat," he said. "Many people want to. Many people dream about doing it and say that they are going to do so, but never do. They keep putting it off. The truth is that most people live like they've got another life in the bank." This stopped me; for a moment, Jon and I had nothing to say, we could only nod agreement, and sip some more rum. But it rang very true, I thought, and it bothered me. His words kept coming back to me in the days and weeks and even months that followed.

Chapter 6

Departure

There is a time for departure even when there's no certain place to go.

—Tennessee Williams

Launch day arrived. Burnell Marine's truck and hydraulic trailer arrived and the trailer backed into the boat shed slowly, gradually, while a small group of us, Peter, Neil, George, and I removed the poppet-stands, all but the last two in the vary back of the boat, practically under the transom. *Rugosa* was carefully balanced, but with only two stands supporting that balance, she was now in the most precarious position that she had been in all the time that I had been working on her. The driver pushed a hydraulic control lever and the big pads and support arms lifted up into place, pressing against the hull, holding her securely. The trailer had been lowered to its lowest possible point next to the floor of the shop, and once the support arms were in place, hydraulics lifted the entire trailer chassis and boat up so that the trailer could properly negotiate the road.

Even though the launch ramp was barely a quarter mile away, the trailer moved slowly along the shore road, with people along the way at the side of the street, out walking in the cool late summer morning, staring at *Rugosa*'s classic shape and glistening painted hull admiringly, like a scene out of yesteryear, with her varnished bowsprit pointing ahead and deep keel and shiny bronze propeller casting a shadow on the tarmac. Several young women stood by the roadside briefly and they were carrying bunches of flowers from an event at a nearby church and it seemed as though they were carrying flowers for *Rugosa*'s launch. I felt immensely proud of her; she was about to 'swim' again, something that she had not done in many years, and I was happy and nervous all at the same time, my fingers crossed, my heart racing, my head light, and my feet practically dancing along.

As the trailer backed down the launch ramp and into the water, proceeding with almost unbearable slowness, I watched her rudder and then the back end of her deep full-keel hull disappear slowly into the flood tide, and then at the very end, when her transom was about to touch the water, her stern began to slowly lift and remain steady as the trailer continued to back down. There was a whine from the hydraulic pump as the support arms, deep below the surface of the water, gradually relaxed their support and allowed the hull to float free, bobbing and riding high, her round hull buoyant like a duck.

At that point she was level, and afloat, free of the trailer, and each of us held the dock lines that I had already secured to her cleats, and walked her backwards along the floating dock into deeper water while the hydraulic trailer was gradually pulled, empty, out of the water.

We tied her off to the cleats on the floating dock, and then stood back. Neil brought out his handy silver flask of brandy, and passed it around. *Rugosa* sat bobbing on her lines like a duck, easy-buoyant, perfectly aligned with her waterline; she looked like she weighed no more than a corked empty bottle. I climbed aboard, and invited the others to do so, but they declined.

"We'll wait here," Peter said. "If everything looks fine below, let's go over to the pub for a few pints to celebrate. The harbormaster said you're good here until after noon."

I went below, and saw that all was quiet; there were no leaks and there was no water in the bilge. Everything was dry, including the seacocks. I felt, for a few moments, a wave of emotion, but it was a feeling of deep satisfaction, joy, excitement, and relief, all at once. My heart felt full to bursting. I patted a varnished bulkhead, almost like one might pat the side of a horse. I could think of nothing to say, so after a few moments I went back up the ladder and into the bright sun of the cockpit. I went over to the trailer driver, gave him his check, signed off his paperwork, and he drove away, his wet trailer leaving a trail of salt water dripping a path onto the street.

"Time to celebrate," I said to my friends at the bar, "And I've got the first round. I couldn't have done this, this morning, if it hadn't been for all of you and your help along the way."

After cruising for a few weeks through the fall around Narragansett Bay, Buzzard's Bay, and the islands, it was time, in early November, for departure. *What day of the week is it,* I ask myself. I have totally lost track of time, these last few days of intense activity running into one another in a continuous stream. *Well actually it doesn't matter; doesn't matter at all, really,* I reply to myself. The calendar is now meaningless. It has taken three years to reach this point. My *Rugosa* is at the dock, provisioned and ready, the last few months having been absorbed in the effort to make her ready for the voyage; but at long last it is time to go.

I step out onto the early-morning on the dock beneath a sky of low, scudding clouds, and a strong breeze coming across the land from the distant sea to the southeast, smelling of sweet brine. It is warmer than it ought to be, quite humid, and I pause, for there is strangeness in the air, a feeling of someplace else. It sparks my senses, tickles my memory; it is a memory of a time in the past. After barely a minute, I know what it is; it is Bermuda in November, a few years ago, and a gale is building. In my mind's eye, the big orange wind-sock atop the far hill across the harbor is out straight; and the palm trees are being lashed by the wind where they stand in profile and unprotected high on the hill above the northeast end of St. George's. It has rained during the night; there is the scent of wet limestone, ancient coral, and always the sea on this low island, a spot of land in the midst of a wide blue ocean, a low archipelago that the ocean's winds blow across practically unhindered and without taking notice. I feel my pulse quicken; I know that it is time to be on my way, and that there can be no turning back. Of late, I had dawdled; perhaps flirting with uncertainty. This bothered me, because I knew that I had to depart before it became too late in the season, before the weather turned bitterly cold and the weather rougher. So now, a week after I had spoken with Jim, I stood on the floating dock at the town pier, ready to leave; and yet I felt my heart flutter, and I was filled with trepidation.

A small group of friends had gathered on the dock on this Sunday morning to see me off. All were dressed in their jeans and light sweaters or sweat-shirts, hands in pockets, caps pulled low. Jim was there, my woodworking friend Neil, Peter, and George.

"We'll handle the lines," Jim said, "You get your engine going."

Neil pulled a silver pocket flask out of his coat, "Gentlemen," he said, offering the flask to the next in line, "A toast to Captain Nate. Safe voyage, fair winds and following seas."

The others repeated it, "Here, here!" Pete added. Already standing on deck, I held onto a shroud, and reached across as George handed the flask to me. "Have the last of it," he said in his thick brogue, and I took the last long pull of the potent brandy. As I handed it back, I felt, all of a sudden, strong emotions welling up within me, and a strong desire to stay tied to the dock, to remain here with the few friends that I had in this life; but it was extinguished by the bucket of cold water that is reality, and the understanding and shared knowledge that I had already committed myself, and that there was no turning back, no matter what the future held. I recalled the words of the tragic English sailor Donald Crowhurst, who had said that he was going because he knew that he would have no peace if he stayed. But his voyage had ended in his loss, so I put that thought quickly out of my mind, suspecting that even thinking about it would bring me bad luck.

Small talk, a few laughs, a joke here and there; but what each of us was thinking, now, we all knew, but most all of it remained unsaid. New England men are like that; and what remains unsaid becomes more powerful by being so, and this we all knew.

The diesel growled to life with a cloud of smelly gray smoke, and my friends cast off the dock lines, seeming reluctantly, but with hearts full of kind wishes, hope, and goodwill, the kind of good will that men who are old friends have for one another when one is embarking on a journey from which they may never return to the same place again. There is finality, and inevitability to it, perhaps even a wish that they themselves could go along as well, even though they probably could not and would decline the opportunity if asked. We all waved as my boat and I pulled out into the gray, cold harbor; and they stood patiently on the dock for a few minutes, and then filed up the ramp. They are going to the familiar, warm Irish pub right up the street, I thought to myself, and I smiled, knowing the habits of my friends all too well, and also realizing that, even though I was heading to sea, for a short time at least, I would still be with them in spirit at those rough wooden tables, with a pint of dark porter in front of me.

Chapter 7

Chasing the Dog Star

I hate storms, but calms undermine my spirits.

— *Bernard Moitessier*

The first night at sea, after leaving the dock in Bristol, was cold, dark, and seemingly endless. The seas were high and the wind blew strong and gusty under a hard black sky. The stars were brilliant sharp points, unmoving and crisply defined, and the sea around all but invisible, even though its sound and fury was everywhere on either side and above, filling the world, indeed it was the entire world to me. I spent much of the night at the helm, steering south by Sirius, the bright Dog Star, keeping its blue-white blaze of cold fire in front of my mast, not bothering to attempt to stare long at the dim compass in my weariness. The black shadow of the mast swayed wildly against the star-studded backdrop; I could see only the black silhouette of it as it blotted out the stars behind it, the mast top like the tip of a great quill pen writing furiously with flamboyant script on the night sky overhead. Despite the cold wind, I remained warm through my exertions at the helm; and my anxieties began to grow, indeed pile upon one another, as I realized that I was sailing alone out into a watery world of emptiness. I was scared, I must admit; yet I had spent months making certain, and repeatedly so, that everything was in readiness, as far as I could determine. I had checked and double-checked my work, my stores, and my systems. In my mind, I had departed as well; I had mentally prepared for this, but at the same time, because I could not see the future, I was filled with apprehension, feeling insecure in myself, my physical strength, and my mental strength to confront the awesome challenge that a voyage alone constituted. And in the midst of this shaking fear, in the cold darkness at the nadir of my energy and fortitude yet so early in the voyage, at the perfect time for them to do so, the dolphins came, and in truth they rescued my spirits from the deep black well into which they had begun to sink.

I first saw the dolphins out of the corner of my eye, in the wild blackness of the night under a waning moon as *Rugosa* sliced through the growing seas amid the howl of the rising gale. The distant flash of the Aquinnah Lighthouse, now well beyond the horizon, had faded to a faint luminescence in the cold mist and I knew then that it was many miles away and that we must be well southeast of Nantucket and the islands. I was feeling very alone until I saw them again, in the periphery of my scope of vision; first one, then more, black and silent and moving quickly, as quickly as the wave tops and in perfect synchronization with them. It was like chamber music, I thought, first one instrument in an orchestra playing, then a duet, and then a trio; and soon there were more of them, sleek, slick black shiny torpedoes in the night, emerging in succession from the waves and as quickly looping back into them in a symphony of motion, now perfect black silhouettes against the ghostly moon-glow path on the water, near to the boat, almost near enough to touch. There was a mystic quality about their appearance, for just as suddenly they were all gone, only to appear ten minutes later. It felt good not to be alone, of a sudden, and I felt, despite my misgivings and anxieties, a strange kinship with them, now a belonging with the sea, not out of place, not so alien, or an abject stranger in an alien world. For after all, I thought, did we not all come up from the sea, many eons ago?

I could sense myself smiling in the roaring darkness, for the company of the dolphins cheered my heart, even at this very late hour. I had thought at first that they were simply illusions brought on by my condition of being cold and fatigued, but once I realized that they were not, the night took on a small amount of wonder for me. I recalled the old man, Santiago, in *The Old Man and the Sea*, realizing that no one is ever truly alone on the sea, for the birds, animals, and fish are our true brothers, he mused. Their world is very different from ours, yet it is still one that we share together.

Sometime after midnight, the wind began to moderate, and the seas to settle down some; a brightly-illuminated fishing trawler passed to starboard, steaming in the opposite direction; headed home, no doubt. In the distance, as it approached, it appeared as a phantasm, hovering in the air, floating toward me through the void, a white ghost, surrounded by a swarm of flies, or moths, pale as it grew ever larger as it emerged from the curtain of blackness. In my semi-aware state, I wondered why the bright white ghost-ship would be beset by insects, "It's the light that attracts them," I spoke aloud, then as she closed, I realized my folly; it was a cloud of gulls following the big fishing vessel, coming in with her hold full of fish. We were so far from land at that point that I knew that this boat, if going to New Bedford, would not arrive in port until the middle of the coming day.

I remembered how, when I was a boy, my grandfather used to take me for rides in his old Studebaker on Saturday late afternoons every so often in the middle of winter. We would drive down to Fort Phoenix in Fairhaven, at the end of the day, and watch the big commercial fishing boats come in. They came in from far out at sea, black dots trailing a plume of black smoke, draggers and trawlers and every different rig including the old wooden eastern rig boats that looked like schooners without their spars, seeking the safety of New Bedford's inner harbor. They came in one at a time; as soon as one loomed large and we could see it approaching the hurricane barrier, another dot would appear on the horizon, and so forth, right up until sunset. Grandpa would sit smoking his pipe, a big bowl of sweet Cavendish, and run the motor every once in a while to keep the car warm. One time, after they seemingly had all come in, and it was sunset, the day fading to bright orange in the west and dusk beginning to creep over the deep blue waters, Grandpa started the engine, but I protested,

"Wait, there is one more. We have to see him in safely," I pleaded, as if our leaving, by taking our eyes off him, it would somehow jeopardize his chances of making port safely; the sea would as suddenly swallow him up. So we waited until that last black dot came in from the horizon, an old steel boat rusty and laden with gear, and Grandpa observed, almost like an afterthought, "Perhaps it was the farthest out." And I remember replying, "Perhaps the ship that has gone the farthest out has brought in the most fish." He simply puffed his pipe and nodded in agreement.

At long last, I had to sleep, so I set the auto pilot and went below, wrapping myself in double woolen blankets and after shivering for a while, shivering myself warm, I found sleep. But it was uneasy and fitful, and I arose at the first light before dawn and climbed out into the cockpit just as a big, rusty old freighter riding high out of the water was passing swiftly astern from left to right, close enough to make me a little nervous. It was painted blue, like the sea and sky were becoming in the first of the day, with its big bulbous bow making a sloppy time of it breaking white water all around as the ship raced at what must have been nearly twenty knots through the choppy seas. I watched its dim lights vanish ghostlike into the growing orange glow of the eastern horizon, and was glad that it was gone. He must have seen me, I thought hopefully, but no matter, now that the day is come I can watch for others. I was well out at sea now with land long lost from sight and having passed far beyond the faint sweeping glow of the outermost lighthouses that I had last seen before midnight.

My destination was the island of Bermuda, first; then, the Caribbean; and after that, who knew. I had not planned that far ahead, although the Pacific was also a possibility. I felt as though I had spent too many years in one part of the world and had grown stagnant. *First you grow comfortable*, I said to myself, perhaps too comfortable; but gradually as the years pass you begin to feel uneasy and you don't know why. It is because you are stagnating while your clock is running down; because you are rotting from within and, although there is no pain associated with it, you have a vague inkling that indeed your soul is decaying from the inside out. Soon you will be dead, and will have never seen the world, or tested yourself for the final time.

A man cannot ever be satisfied with testing himself once, even if he tests himself to his limits and makes it through alive, I often thought to myself. He must test himself again and again. I had been to sea many times and sometimes under truly harrowing conditions.

"What you need," my older sailing friend Bryce told me one night in the dew damp cockpit of *Rugosa* in Cuttyhunk Island harbor, in early September, "Is to have the shit scared out of you. " It was one-o'clock in the morning under a ghostly-hazy, luminous moon and we were drinking dark rum and talking about his adventures and misadventures as a youth sailing with the famous Don Street on *Iolaire* in the Caribbean. We were anchored in a mirror-still harbor and the island was quiet but for the occasional strange voices of birds over in the shrubs and grasses of the shore nearby. I had not been out on a passage across the open sea in many years and when I had, I had been a young man serving on a Coast Guard ship. So I was apprehensive about making a small-boat passage out on what my Grandmother had often referred to as 'The Deep', and Bryce's response, of course, because he knew no fear of anything at all except being overcharged by an unscrupulous merchant, was to dismiss my confession of fear with a huff. "Remember, we are Men of the Sea," he reminded me.

"So you're going to take this boat around the world?" Bryce asked.

"Not sure," I replied. "But I'm leaving in a month or two, probably early November."

"Ah, how well I remember it, having done it many times on late-fall trips to the Caribbean. November cold, shivering on deck in the warmest of clothes, strong gales. Then November cold gives way increasingly to Caribbean warmth."

But even despite my apprehension, there was always a yearning, and I know not where it came from, unless it was, perhaps, a universal wanderlust that so many of us share. They say that desiring is much better than having; that wanting is a powerful thing, and that the fear of something is ten thousand times worse than the thing itself. And so it was for me with wanderlust and the desire to go voyaging. Imagination is a powerful thing, a driver, and the more potent a man's imagination is, the more capable it is of creating whole worlds that exist outside of reality and yet have the flavor, feel, sound, and smell – though not, but almost the touch – of real worlds.

So after having spent a weekend in Cuttyhunk with Bryce, I climbed the big hill of the island and stood on the highest point on a cool and brisk early fall summer afternoon, just before sunset, and took in the panoramic, 360-degree view if the waters surrounding Cuttyhunk and the land masses both near and distant. To the southeast were the high, streaming-colored clay cliffs of Gay Head, and the bight of Menemsha; to the west, the nearly setting sun, and the faint outline of the Romanesque towers of the Pell Newport Bridge, barely discernible in the reddening glare of the setting sun on the horizon. To the south, where lay, to my imagination, the distant warm land of Paradise, only empty ocean, at this height seeming to be only light-blue ripples on a vast flat blue expanse. Block Island, to the southwest, was beyond the horizon, but even so, perched at the end of the world before the endless ocean, I loved it more than most places.

I looked down over the harbor to the northeast and saw my own *Rugosa* riding contentedly and obediently on her rode in the outer harbor, small as a little toy, and realized as I watched her that I soon I must make my way back to Bristol with the next sunrise, returning to family and friends and familiar mooring. I felt a twinge of regret; for I thought, I could spend a season here on this quiet island; there is something almost timeless about it.

But then I spied a sailboat, a cruiser of perhaps some forty feet, plying its way across the blue to the south, heading southwest from Vineyard Sound out into the wide cerulean expanse, and I suddenly felt a wave of emotion, of yearning, envy, loneliness, sweeping over me like a rogue wave all at once. That boat could be headed to Block Island, I reasoned; but it was late in the day, and wherever it was going, it would be still well at sea by nightfall, so it was probably planning a more distant passage.

The tall golden grasses covering the hillside leaned in the sea breeze that swept over the hilltop, bent over by the breeze that flowed over the island, the same breeze that, deflected temporarily but not delayed, then coursed back down to the water on the opposite side like a williwaw and drove the sails of the anonymous vessel that had seized my heart's desire, or rather had allowed it to stow aboard with my consent, and was now carrying it, with my imagination, across the sea and away from me to the vanishing point of the horizon. And then did I pledge to myself that I would follow in that track out to the blue beyond, wherever it might carry my heart and soul, to whatever discoveries and freedoms might lie ahead, but for the moment I stood helpless on the promontory, unable to move, to pursue. And yet I knew that the boat, as it moved away totally unaware of me, had already taken a small part of me with it.

Now, I had finally made my departure, and was leaving my own wake across the trackless sea. And despite the cold, I was well on my way. I had provisioned *Rugosa* as best I could, sparing neither money nor detail and doing my best to plan meticulously as well as strategically. I realized that I had to make certain accommodations; for example, choosing foods in packaging that would resist dampness and moisture, which would ruin them, and avoiding things that required a great deal of time and cooking energy to prepare. So, as might be expected, I laid in a generous supply of canned goods, including soups, protein items such as fish and meats, hash, beans, and prepared foods such as chili. I avoided overly-prepared foods in packets that were high in sodium or contained objectionable ingredients and preservatives. Freeze-dried soups would do well, as would the newer sealed foil packages of foods such as tuna that were soft and easier to stow than cans, requiring less space. I found re-sealable plastic food containers handy for snacks and crackers that could not withstand a moist environment. I packed cans of evaporated milk, and boxes of the 'Parmalat' milk that would keep until opened. I brought jams and jellies and freeze-dried mushrooms, chocolate bars for energy and bags of dried mixed fruits such as prunes, apricots, pears and apples. I brought packages of fruit and nut trail mix for snacking, and some hard cheeses that would keep well with minimal refrigeration, perhaps, I thought, they would keep well in the hold until I reached the warmer waters of the tropics, at which time they would either be gone, or what was left would go into my chiller, assuming that it had not broken down by then.

I have been told by sailors that eggs do not require refrigeration, but will keep, yet I still did not trust them, and after three weeks, even though they had been kept fairly cool in the chiller, I chucked them over side. The same went for meats and sausages; even dry salami sausage has a shelf life in the chiller, and no matter how well preserved, if not canned, I do not trust it, and will not bring ground beef to sea at all for anything more than a weekend trip. Food poisoning at sea can mean death, if not from the illness itself, from the storm or effects of the weather while you are incapacitated and unable to work the ship.

Realizing that I would have little time to bake bread, and would not want to run the oven in the warmer tropics anyhow, I stowed aboard a good number of quart-sized cans of brown bread. It's one of my favorites; dense and nourishing, ready to slice and eat right from the can, keeps nearly forever, and is comprised in large part of the two major staples that sustained my Yankee forefathers in colonial times and generations of sailing folk, molasses and corn meal. I brought biscuit mix in tightly-sealed plastic ware so that if the mood took me, I could mix up a batch of ready to bake biscuits.

To this fine mixture I added a few durable plastic jugs of cooking oil; salt and a complete spice rack, and condiments. I also purchased a few packages of re-sealable plastic freezer bags in the gallon size, since these always came in handy for fish fillets or leftover food that one might want to preserve in the chiller for the next day's meal or so.

Coffee was, to me, an absolutely essential vice. I insisted on having fresh-brewed coffee in the morning, except in stormy weather when any kind of galley work was all but impossible. In such situations, I had no choice but to suffer. Sometimes I might chew a few roasted coffee beans, and that helped, but I always knew that in time, the wind would moderate, the seas would lie down, and I would be able once again to make a pot. I brought roasted whole beans tightly sealed in vacuum-sealed packages. Once the package was opened, I kept the loose beans in a re-usable round tin can with a screw-top.

I had brought along a French Press pot, so I simply ground my beans coarse, added boiling water, and let it steep as is proper. This made fine, smooth coffee and it was much easier to boil a kettle of water on the galley when things were swinging, than it was to tend a percolating pot. I brought quite nearly fifty books along with me, because there is much time at sea for reading when the weather is fair. I brought books that I had read before, and had planned to read again; books that I had wanted to read, and then finally books that I had no idea whether or not they were any good, books that friends gave to me or recommended. I would read them all, good or bad, and no matter how bad any book might be, I would not deep-six it. I figured that I might swap them for other books when I met up with other cruisers.

The clear sunrise the second day at sea brought faint warmth from the deceptively bright November sun. The sea roared as the fresh, blustery wind blew out of the northeast, the seas foaming along hurriedly, as blue and beautiful as in summer by appearance, but with almost winter cold as *Rugosa* rose and fell on the big rollers passing under her, rhythmically romping along. High above, the long, wispy cirrus clouds stretched across the light blue sky from north to south, up at the very ceiling of the sky, their flowing curves reflecting the form of the seas below, like an abstract painting of the rolling sea surrounding me. I was tired; I was bundled up in my warmest coat, sitting in the cockpit wrapped in a blanket that I wore partly as a hood over my knitted cap, my back to the wind, my arm over the wheel, trying to stay warm and to have some degree of comfort on this early morning that would have been exhilarating had I not been so groggy and tired.

I dozed from time to time for the first two hours. *Rugosa* remained on course nonetheless, her rig essentially balanced on a broad reach, so she did not want to round up into the wind, and my arm draped heavily over the wheel helped keep her steady, her rudder quite nearly amidships. I would doze off for five minutes, or perhaps ten, never fully asleep but always with the motion and the roaring of the sea in my consciousness, then wake up with a start, and thinking that I had been asleep for a half hour or more, see by my watch that it had been barely ten minutes. Yet each little nap refreshed me, and I was pleased to see, when I awoke each time, that the sun was quite possibly a tiny bit higher, and that the wind remained strong and steady and the weather clear. Occasionally a dolphin would break the surface, swimming alongside, grey-blue and sleek and lovely, venturing near, then away again, seeking prey. Once again, they reminded me that I was alone in their space, their world, and yet not alone, for they knew that I was there, scudding along on the surface, and each time they leaped, I could see that they were looking at me, catching a brief glimpse, curious to know who and what I was.

I began to feel chilled, and knew that I needed to warm up, and the only way to do that would be to go down into the cabin. Accordingly, I lashed the helm to keep the rudder in her current position, and then went below. Since the wind direction was off the port quarter and across the deck and out to sea, I felt that I could light the cabin stove without concern for sparks setting the sail afire.

I had saved a bin full of chunks of white oak, scraps from the kiln-dried timbers used in the replacement of frames and beams in the transom. They were dry and clean and I had cut them into bite-sized pieces. They would burn hot, I noted. I packed the lower part of the stove with them, opened the dampers, and lit the wood with some kindling. Before long the black cast-iron stove was radiating heat, as was the chimney, and up on deck, smoke blew downwind. I put some fresh water in the water deck iron at the base of the metal chimney, or Charley Noble, out on deck, and then closed the dampers until the wood was burning slowly in almost airtight fashion. I had stowed a fifty-pound tarpaulin cloth bag of anthracite nut coal in the bilge, and now added a scoop of it over the oak wood in the stove and readjusted the draft and damper. Soon the cabin was toasty-warm, and I had put a kettle of water on the stove to heat for tea. Despite the motion of the boat, the pot rail around the stove top kept the kettle from sliding off, and the little stove put out so much heat that I did not need to put the drop-boards in at the main scuttle; besides, I wanted it open just in case I had to get out into the cockpit to take care of something in a hurry. I pulled the sliding hatch closed, and now had a window out to the cockpit, as well as a source of fresh air. Looking out one of the starboard cabin ports, I could see the gray stove smoke streaming off to leeward in a line in the strong wind. Occasionally, I gazed through the other cabin portholes to see if any vessels were visible; but I saw nothing, and had turned on the radar unit and set the 3-mile alarm limit so that no matter what I was doing, such as reading or making soup, I would hear an audible warning if any ship hove into range. I made myself a simple sandwich of whole-grain sliced bread and peanut butter; I did not have the stomach for anything else. Then I bundled up and went back out onto the deck.

On the second morning, after sunrise, I noticed that the air had become slightly warmer, even a little humid, and there was a low mist everywhere on the sea, forming a bright haze that diffused the sunlight all around and put me in a world of luminosity. As I was adjusting some lines, I heard a sound much like a 'whoosh', or a powerful exhalation, and looked off to port to see, in the shifting mist, the backs of two silvery gray whales swimming together no more than fifty feet away. Their hot breath, exhaled, looked just like the plumed 'spouter' cloud of old paintings and drawings. We must be in a warm eddy of the Gulf Stream, I thought to myself, and the more southing I make, the more comfortable my circumstances, at least with regard to temperature, will become.

Encouraged by this prospect of a gradually moderating voyage, I went down into the cabin and fried some bacon and a couple of eggs; the aroma of the frying bacon, in the stove-warmed comfort of the cabin, sparked my appetite. Before I cooked the eggs, I carefully poured off the bacon fat into a tin can, to reserve aside and let solidify in the cool air. It would come in handy later, I reminded myself, should I catch some fish, because no matter what kind I caught, if I caught any, it would taste better fried in the bacon drippings.

Chapter 8

In Perpetual Motion

One must always say goodbye to all things. Ports, towns, human contacts, and pass on. I went on again and again with a little spark glowing inside of me.
— *Vito Dumas*

My world was always in motion. Even in my sleep I felt every rise and fall of my boat on the broad seas. I sensed her sliding through the water under pressure from the wind, steady and buoyant, accompanied by the constant and never-ending voice of my *Rugosa*, the creaking of the rigging and the graunching of the leather chafe-gear in the gaff jaws. I awoke on the fourth day underway shortly after the sweet brass chime of the ship's bell clock rang four times; it was six-o'clock and I could feel a warm shaft of sunlight beaming down through a porthole to touch my face. The wind had freshened slightly during the night, and from the pronounced rise and fall of the boat, I surmised that the seas had built somewhat during the night's run.

I climbed out from under the blanket, shivered a moment as I stood up and braced myself against the motion of the boat on the high seas, then looked around. The cool, fresh, salty early-morning breeze, smelling sweetly of the broad ocean, coursed down the hatchway from the cockpit. The smell of the land had been gone for several days and now there was only the salt-cleanliness of the brine, deep blue and clear. The sky overhead, glimpsed through the hatch-way, was a lovely light blue with very high wisps of mare's tails far above, in the stratospheric world of the big jets, which, whenever I saw them, seemed as tiny slivers of shiny metal, and that was when I could even see them at all. But this morning there were no signs of anything, not even a contrail, and I felt very much alone. Still, I had this lovely morning sea-breeze to enjoy, and I reminded myself that one should always be thankful even for small kindnesses and comforts at sea. These are things that the landsman takes for granted, or considers not worth noticing or mention as he hurries down the city block in his suit, with his work under his arm, racing against the current of the moving crowd to beat the clock to get to the office to begin yet another day of the rat-race, his head full of fears, plans, strategies, and the vagaries of life at work, focused intently on his impending tasks for yet another day, and oblivious to the world around him. Perhaps I will see the dolphins again today, I thought to myself, and be travelling companions for a little while, as they often have during this voyage.

My ship had sailed well during the night, and this morning she was, without any wind shift, still on course for Bermuda. She was sailing with a double-reefed gaff main, the fore club staysail, which was a small triangular sail on a boom, self-adjusting, riding on a traveler; and a reefed gaff mizzen, to balance her out, the helm lashed amidships. Once I had her balanced this way, she would sail perfectly on a steady course relative to the wind direction. Of course, if the wind shifted, her course would shift too; but it had remained steady out of the southwest.

Best time to say,
What weather's on the way,
Is at the start and end of day.

The sun was already high in the sky, and the big seas were a beautiful, cerulean blue; patches of yellow Sargasso weed drifted by and the bluish iridescent bubble-floats of the deadly Portuguese Man-o-war jellyfish bobbed like half-inflated, cast-off plastic sandwich bags. I could feel the warmth of the sea and the humidity in the air. These big, lumbering swells that we were riding over like a duck were the color of sapphire. "We must be crossing the Gulf Stream," I heard myself speak aloud. My heart was cheerful.

The long, high swells rolling down from the northwest were lifting the boat gently and setting her back down, seeming to pay no heed to her as they hurried along on their determined errand. My boat was even less than a small annoyance to them; they bore her on their backs for merely a moment, and then passed on, unimpeded. The wind was freshening, and the sea foamed and seethed under the port side as the hull pushed purposefully through the deep blue water. Far in the distance, the turquoise sky to the northwest was peppered with small, puffy fair-weather cumulus clouds, all on a single flat plane of altitude, stretching away to eternity.

My boat seemed happy; I had lashed the helm and adjusted the sails before going to bed, and had been up to check my course during the night. The cockpit had been very dark, wet, and chill. But the cool northwest wind had held unerringly and she was sailing well and comfortably on a starboard broad reach. She was not exactly on course, but I could now make corrections.

I was now, I felt, well on my way on a voyage that I had anticipated for a very long time. I had survived the initial few days of stormy, cold, rough late-autumn North Atlantic gales, passing through that maelstrom to emerge unscathed and still strong, perhaps now stronger. Having done so distilled and concentrated my resolve to continue on, and also confirmed my sense of conviction that my plan was sound, my judgment correct in doing so. I felt more confident, with less doubt and trepidation lurking in the back of my mind.

My old gaff yawl worked, flexed, and muttered, in her own way, with steady and determined motion through the seas, just the way she was expected to for a timbered vessel. Her sails were full, and she was heeling slightly to port. Sailing away alone on a long voyage this way was what I had always wanted to do. Below decks, standing in the aloneness of the cabin, I could hear the water racing past the hull, the creaking of the timbers, and especially the groaning of the leather-covered gaff jaws as they worked against the main and mizzen masts. That sound, resonant and reminiscent of a growl, though not an angry sound, was transmitted through the solid masts to the wood of the vessel, and it rang like the notes of a big bass viol. I could also distinguish the gentle rumble of the propeller shaft turning, making electricity for my boat's systems.

I climbed out into the cockpit, and scanned the horizon with my binoculars; there were no vessels of any kind in sight, and the sky was empty but for clouds. A wave splashed aboard, and some of the spray struck my face; it was warm and tasted sweet-salty, clean and good. Satisfied once again that I was completely alone, I went back below again, for it was time for morning coffee. The blue propane flame of the burner on the galley stove danced in the light breeze wafting down the hatchway, so I stood in front of the stove to shelter it from the draught, bracing myself against a bulkhead while the little metal percolator pot sputtered and filled the cabin with the aroma of coffee brewing. The galley stove swayed on its gimbals, the pot snugly locked in place by the pot rail and holders. Fair weather today, I thought, but there may be more wind tomorrow. I would sit and enjoy my mug-up, then it would be time to wash up a little and do some chart work while listening to the single sideband radio. I had balanced the rig by reefing the mainsail and adjusting the mizzen and headsails to balance and sail a steady course relative to the wind. Unless it shifted, I would be able to stay away from the helm for a while. Later on, I would steer for a few hours if the sea got up, or if I needed to correct my course. I would run the auto steering, powered by the batteries and generator, at least until afternoon.

In the evening, when the weather was fair, I would scan the horizon for contacts before turning in to get some precious sleep. I would set the auto-steering and secure the main boom with a preventer, light a lamp or two, and spend some time reading, covered with a light blanket, in the main cabin. I ran the radar and set a 6-mile alarm limit, in the event that a ship should come within range, so that I would have enough forewarning to alter course and avoid being run down. I left the VHF radio on, tuned to Channel 16. Most evenings, I would pour myself a 'neat' scotch, and then doze off, less successfully when the sea was running high. When reading, and even when dozing, I would always be listening, and even when I was asleep, on a higher plane toward consciousness than truly deep sleep (and I had become accustomed to this, and to waking refreshed even thus), I knew that I was listening. But every once in a while my body and mind would simply decide to sleep, and I would sleep much longer than I had planned, deeply and in the darkness at the bottom of the pool. It was thus also this morning, bright and blustery and lovely, and I had slept for six hours uninterrupted. I glanced around, and thanked God that nothing had gone amiss during the night, such as a squall, or a change in wind and sea conditions. I had not been run down by a freighter, nor stove by a whale or collided with a partly-submerged cargo container. I had made certain provisions for the boat to take care of itself while I slept, from the commonly-understood technique of lashing the wheel and adjusting the sails, to rigging a preventer on the big mainsail's boom so that if the wind shifted while I was taking a nap, for example, I would not experience a dangerous gybe that could damage the rig. I was now a long way out at sea, and I knew it, and also knew the simple truth that there were no chandleries out here or boat yards for repairs.

After a couple of hours, after a little bit of boredom had set in, and since there was apparently no one else around, I turned off the radio, the radar, and the auto-helm. I'll steer for the balance of the day, I said to myself, and let the generator top the batteries back up. I grabbed an apple, a snack bar, and a bottle of water, and headed out on deck. I sat in the cockpit for a while, enjoying the feel of the boat bowling along, and the rise and fall motion of the seas, like riding a smooth-running horse over small hill after hill. The sea was empty and endless from horizon to horizon, but it was full of energy and activity. It was alive, and my boat was alive too, her sails full, climbing and falling, buoyant like a gull swimming on the surface. The sun was warm, and the air, though damp, was warming too; we absolutely must be in or passing through the Gulf Stream, I was now certain.

I had equipped my boat for long-distance cruising, with adequate storage tanks installed for water and for diesel fuel. I did not have a water-maker, such accessories come at great expense, and in places such as the Caribbean, fresh water is not available everywhere, and when it is, it is available at a premium. I treated my water with a solution to keep it fresh, and had a good-quality charcoal water filter installed with a foot pump so that I could safely drink the tank water anytime. I had also stowed some bottled water to be used sparingly with meals.

I equipped the double sink with a hand pump connected through the hull to the sea, so that I could do the bulk of my dishwashing with raw seawater, which, when used with certain liquid detergents, lathers up well and cleans effectively. A very light fresh water rinsing would follow, very conservative, to save fresh water, which at sea is precious unless you have a way of replacing it or literally 'making' more on a continuous basis.

A white bird with a long, whip-like tail appeared, seemingly out of nowhere, and circled the boat some twenty feet above the masthead. I felt cheered; this snowy-white, sleek bird was a white-tailed tropic bird, and from its appearance, I knew that I must be at least halfway to Bermuda.

Sometimes, in the days, weeks, and even months before my departure, I had, in times of stress, spoken to the dead; seeking guidance and advice from my father and grandfather; but in my heart I knew that there could be no conversation. The only voice that came back was that of my own conscience, my own good sense, spoken by them in my mind's eye, saying what I knew they would say or to advise on any given subject, based upon how I had known them during my lifetime when they had still been in the world.

Now I was alone at sea, and I knew that I was alone and at times even called on Joshua Slocum, but I knew that Slocum was, like my father and grandfather, no longer around to listen or to reply. Still, it gave me comfort, like speaking and praying to God, because it gave me the false sense that someone was listening, watching over me and my boat, even approvingly, and had some interest, however small, in my welfare or the purpose of the voyage itself.

But I also knew that history is full of tales of men who called out to God for mercy while the sea was battering their ships to pieces. God does not intervene. If He is here, along for the voyage with you as an invisible friend, He is always going to maintain his distance.

The sea has no malice, unlike men; thus it is, to a certain extent, predictable; but it is no less fearsome, nor is it any less destructive for it, but its lack of deliberate cruelty makes its excesses easier to accept, at least for me.

Two nights earlier, a storm had come up after eleven in the evening; I was still awake, lying in my bunk reading, when it struck. The air changed, and I failed to take note of it; it smelled different, perhaps more moist, or cooler in temperature, but I did not become aware of its approach until I heard the wind begin to rise, and it arose quickly; it was all I could do to get out on deck and take in sail before the full intensity of the blast hit. It was a squall, of course; at night, when you can't see much of anything, every onset of sudden bad weather is a squall, and if there is a technical differentiation between one type of weather system and another, it doesn't make much difference. It could blow and rage for an hour, or for three days. Usually it will be the latter.

Storms at sea tend to intensify relatively quickly, and thus they strike hard.

There is no land, and thus there are no trees or mountains in the way to restrain the wind, or to inhibit the development. The sea is an endless plateau and if the conditions are right, a storm will develop into something quickly when the conditions are favorable, and you have no choice but to ride it out, hang on, and survive, until it expends its energy, moves on, or simply wearies of being wrathful.

It came up quickly and blew hard, and blew all night, with occasional downpours and sheets of cold rain, and I steered and kept her steady until sunrise when, at long last, utterly exhausted, I hove-to and went below to sleep for a few hours. Slowing the boat down, even though the seas had built up to fifteen feet or more, seemed to impart a relative quiet to the whole scene, and I slept through the day, after drinking a great quantity of fresh water, at ease in my mind. When I awoke it was late afternoon; my stomach felt acceptably well, even hungry, so I ate, and went back out on deck to make sail again. Thus it went, day after day. I listened to the weather reports every morning on the single sideband radio, and sometimes I was able to get updated reports from passing ships by contacting them on my VHF radio.

After initial queasiness the first night, all nausea had left me and my appetite was robust. I was eating well, but after seven days at sea my fresh foods were running low, and I was reluctant to start digging into my canned goods and dry stores. I would be approaching Bermuda in a few days, despite my relatively slow pace, and would be able to replenish there.

I had read accounts by other passagemakers of their occasional good luck fishing, by trailing a line and lure or baited hook off the stern. I did not know much about fishing, but I did know that success would depend on crossing paths with a fish well offshore, and it would have to be a surface dweller and feeder, since I had read that most fish are found in the vicinity of the continental shelf, and that the abyss is generally devoid of fish, in the main. So I rigged a lure from the tackle box and trailed it astern about twenty yards. My boat was sailing well and I did not have any great expectation of catching anything if I was moving or trolling too quickly through the water, but one never knows, I thought, depends on the fish.

I had read stories about how flying fish would come aboard in the night if one were to hang a lamp in the rigging. I had never tasted flying fish before, and Captain Slocum did not, in his accounts, complain about their taste, but I had a sneaky suspicion that he might not complain anyway, given the unappealing nature of the rest of his diet at sea as he described at times. So I sent a white kerosene lamp halfway up the mainmast and secured it with a downhaul so that it would not swing around and bang itself to pieces should the sea get up during the night.

The first night that I rigged it, it did indeed bring aboard a flying fish, but I was tired from not sleeping well the night before and I forgot to check the decks for fish until nearly nine in the morning. There was a flying fish all right but by that time the sun had been on him for a few hours and it was, in my opinion, already spoiled, being partly dried out and looking rather unattractive, with smelly fluids oozing out of it onto the deck, so I threw it overboard, immediately regretting having done so, for it occurred to me, as I watched it spin through the air and plop into a following wave, that I could have attached it to the lure that I was trailing behind the boat. The next morning, however, I turned out at sunrise, and found two flying fish, one in the cockpit, and one on deck. They were still cool and fresh from the night. I found a third one a few minutes later, but it was the smallest of the three and I decided to use it as bait rather than to eat it. The two larger ones, I judged, would be sufficient fare for the fry-pan and breakfast.

Oddly, it seemed that when flying fish came aboard, they most often slapped and flapped their way into odd places on the deck where they were not quickly or easily spotted, rather than lying about in the middle of an open area, so I had to look carefully. The two that I had in hand were a decent size for flying fish, nearly ten inches long, so I decided right then and there that these would be my breakfast-steaks. The third fish was promptly hooked onto the lure and cast back into *Rugosa*'s wake. I headed and gutted the two fish in the cockpit on a small plank that served as a cutting board, and where I could minimize the amount of mess generated which, when cleaning fish, can expand rapidly.

The sun was up now but it was behind some high, milky clouds, and so the day was not yet hot, but damp and smelling richly of the foaming brine. I scaled the fish and brought the fillets with the silvery skin on them down below to the galley, dusted them with flour and fried them in my leftover bacon fat in my black iron skillet with some leftover sliced boiled potatoes that I had in the icebox. I seasoned them with black pepper and a dash of sea salt. They were tasty fried, but I found the flavor oily and a little strong, like bluefish that I used to catch in New England waters. The taste was not unpleasant, and I was so eager to taste some fresh fish that I thoroughly enjoyed them. But I surmised that, like bluefish, these oily fish would not keep well; they were best eaten fresh, or at least on the same day that they were caught, and I knew that the strong flavor would probably only intensify with time even when stored in the icebox. My icebox not only held ice, but contained a cold plate, part of a small refrigeration unit, often referred to as a 'reefer'. IN the old days, small boats had a simple ice box, an insulated box that held block ice. But nowadays, small refrigeration units could be installed with the 'cold plate' inside the icebox, so I used a combination of block ice and the reefer unit when I could run it. And with this catch, I was elated; I had now a reliable daily supply of fish, and all for the price of a thimbleful of kerosene, which I had an abundance of stored in tins, at least three gallons of it which would be able to supply my lamp and indeed all of the lamps for months.

I soon found that I was in for even greater luck, for Old Neptune could provide even better fare. Right after I had finished cleaning up the galley, conveniently enough, I heard the fishing reel start to spin and relinquish line against the drag. I scampered into the cockpit and took up the pole; whatever was on the end of it was fighting like hell and I hoped that the line would not break as I sought to pull it in against the speed of the boat through the water. But then it leaped clear of the sea and I could see that it was a mid-size wahoo, its long metallic bluish body shaking and curling violently as it threw itself clear of the sea and water flew off of it in an explosive blast of spray. My first thought had been that it might be a barracuda, since they have a similar appearance, but once it drew closer I could see for certain that it was a wahoo. I fought it for nearly ten minutes, and the line held and eventually I brought it aboard, gaffed it, and set to work filleting it and stowing the fillets carefully in the icebox in sealable plastic bags. They would be my dinner, and what was more, I had enough to eat from that fish for at least three days, figuring on a little more than a pound a day out of nearly three pounds of fillets.

After filleting, I put the bones in a small pot with fresh water, discarding the bony head overboard, and covered and simmered them to make a stock for chowder. I put in a garlic clove, some onion flakes, a little chicken bouillon, celery powder, and a bay leaf and simmered them for a while. Later, I threw out the bones and put some small-diced potatoes in there and an onion sautéed in butter, evaporated milk and some 'Parmalat' boxed milk that keeps without refrigeration until opened, salt and pepper and chunks of wahoo, and thickened it with a little flour, to make a wahoo fish chowder. I poured just a little white wine in there and added butter and some Bermuda sherry pepper sauce, and it made a fine late dinner with enough for two more days with refrigeration.

In the weeks before my departure, during which time I put my vessel through trials and tests to see how she would behave under different conditions, I recognized that, at some point, I would probably be beset by storms and gales, and would eventually need to heave-to in the heaviest weather. Sure enough;

five days out, the first strong gale came on rather suddenly and I felt it building and thought that it might be prudent to get everything down and stowed early before the situation got out of hand. Accordingly, I dropped the headsails and secured them well, then the mainsail, securing it by wrapping it in line, and then I motored for a while with the mizzen as a steadying-sail.

But by nightfall the winds were gusting past 45 knots and the seas were building and at times breaking over the boat. So I lashed the helm and hove to with barely a scrap of reefed mizzen set as a storm trysail, and the benefits were almost immediate. I went below, nervous and afraid of what situation might unfold, but the change was profound; the action of the boat became quieter, a comfortable rise and fall, with less sound and fury. I lay down on the cabin sole for a while, and lifted the center floorboard, looking down into the bilge. It was dry, and the timbers looked solid and unmoving where they met the deadwood. My ship is solid, I thought, she will ride this out. The storm increased in intensity during the night, so much so that I could hear the wind whistling in the rigging, and heard the dull thunder of the occasional sea that boarded the boat and washed over the deck, but everything still held. I remained on the cabin sole with a blanket under my head and at last fell asleep. When I awoke shortly after dawn, the wind had abated remarkably, and although the seas were still very high, I was confident that I could soon make sail again.

After the stormy weather had passed and the seas had begun to lie down, my appetite returned and it was strong. I had been eating tinned fish and dry goods, and I yearned for some fresh food, in this case fish was the only option, and I liked fish. The coffee pot had been happily percolating away on the stove these past couple of mornings, and I felt that it was high time to drop a line overboard with a lure and trail it for a bit to try my luck. I was south of the Gulf Stream now and the waters were warmer and still clean and deep blue from the Stream. I thought of a delivery of a big catamaran from St. Martin to New York City that I had been on some years ago with my friend Steve. The catamaran had been back and forth from the Islands a few times and the propane tanks had been refilled in Marigot, on the French side of St. Martin. For some reason the French propane stank and only a little less when burning so we did not want to cook very often unless we could run with the hatches open. So we ate a lot of French canned tuna and kippers and exotic whatnot and Portuguese sardines with the scales still on the fish in the can, guts and all, that the owner had bought in Marigot. We had a lot of it and not a lot of anything else and soon we were pretty tired of it. Then a storm came up and for a day and a half we were all a little bit queasy, nothing dramatic, except for our crewmate Josh, who hadn't seemed well when we left Marigot and now was quite seasick. We were not concerned that he would die, but we were sick of pulling his watches for him and so we wanted him to recover quickly now that the storm had abated somewhat. He needed liquids and he needed food. Steve spoke up; "I have just what he needs. This always works, never know it to fail. It's a dish that you feed to people who have been seasick, it helps them recover faster."

"What is it?" I asked.

"It's called 'Tuna Shit'."

"What?"

"Tuna shit. You boil up some noodles, I think we have elbow noodles? And then you drain them and put the canned tuna in and you mix it all up. That's Tuna Shit. You feed it to the sick person and they get better."

"Prompted, no doubt, by the desperate desire to be allowed to resume eating regular food," I said.

"Fuck you," Steve replied, grinning.

So we lit the stove to boil the noodles but had neglected to open the hatches first, as we had not had them open in three days, and the propane smell was strong. I heard Josh puking into his bucket down in his cabin.

"I think he's calling out for some," I said.

Steve did not reply; he merely stirred the pot of Tuna Shit more vigorously.

But now I was trailing a fishing line and within a half hour something hit it hard and I found myself fighting to bring in a very energetic fish. It fought like hell and was leaping clear of the water, and at that point I saw its greenish yellow metallic coloring and blunt head and knew that it was a Mahi Mahi, or dolphin-fish. Just like the Wahoo that I had caught a few days before, it was a slow and careful job reeling in the Mahi, and it reminded me of the first time I had ever tasted it. Our Coast Guard ship was working in the Gulf of Mexico many years earlier taking water samples for the NOAA weather research people. It was a warm Saturday afternoon and a couple of the guys off duty went fishing over the side of the ship. One fellow caught a decent-sized Mahi and when he hauled it aboard, I saw its brilliant rainbow colors fade to silvery grey as it died. The crewman donated it to the officer's mess in the ward room, where that week I was serving as mess cook in rotation. The crewman who caught the fish had filleted it, and brought them up to the small wardroom galley. The fish was translucent white with a slight purplish tinge to it. It reminded me of the flesh of bluefish up in New England. I treated it simply; I dusted it lightly with a little black pepper and sea salt, with thin slices of lemon on top, and broiled it in the small galley range and served it with a garnish of parsley and dusting of paprika, French fries, and Cole slaw. The officers had it for dinner and loved it, or so I remember. But I had reserved a small piece in secret to taste and satisfy my own curiosity, and found my morsel to be delicious and full-fleshed.

Now I brought out my small wooden cutting board and sharp fillet knife and made quick work of it, cutting out two prime fillets of Mahi Mahi and tossing the rest over the side where a lone bird of some sort that had been following my boat dived after it with a splash as soon as I had it overside, and promptly began pecking away a nice meal from what was left of it before it sank. "Enjoy it!" I called out to the bird as it disappeared in my wake. I took the fillets below and put them in the chiller; this would be my early dinner. I felt happy, as though I had accomplished something. I knew that I was on my way, making fairly good time, in good shape, and with food and water in abundance. Water was moving beneath my keel, and my compass told me that I was pointing due south. My ship was solid and seaworthy; and the weather was fair, for the moment; I could count my blessings, and felt that they were many. In a couple of days I would be in Bermuda.

Chapter 9

Bermuda Landfall

A ship is safe in harbor but that's not what ships are for.

— *William G.T. Shedd*

The night before landfall in Bermuda, the wind piped up out of the southwest to thirty knots, so there was much work to do. I donned my harness and clipped on, then took in a double reef in the main and double reef also in the mizzen, furled the jib and just left up the staysail. I wanted to slow her down a little bit, so that I would not reach the island under cover of darkness, which, according to my calculations, I would at my current speed. The boat also behaved better when not over pressed, slower and happier and more buoyant even in the building seas.

In the cockpit, steering, I was wide awake, and excited. My boat was slicing across the seas, on a close reach, roaring ahead in a rising gale, but I felt confident now, because we were headed for landfall, and all the anxieties of the past week were dissolving as my mind focused in anticipation on only one goal; reaching Bermuda. I was truly exhausted, physically and emotionally, since a near-winter voyage like this, with its attendant sleep deprivation at times, quick and often inadequate meals, and physical demands all take a great toll on the entire human system. I would make port, surely, but I would need time to rest and recover before the next leg of my voyage.

Seated in the cockpit by the wheel, with my back to the wind on a starboard tack, I watched the half-moon rise over the eastern horizon, cheerfully illuminating the flying crests of the building seas with a soft, silken glow reminiscent of a dreamy, romantically wild 19th-Century oil painting of a seascape at night. Beethoven's Moonlight Sonata came to mind. But this was no still-life; this was very much a world in motion, as it had been since the beginning of the voyage.

Every so often, a sea would break against the bow, sending warm, dark spray flying aft to the cockpit; it tasted clean and briny. The motion was suggestive of the art of riding a horse; the boat moved in long and gentle, steady, measurable leaps through the seas. Odd, I thought, how pleasurable this particular moment is, this stretch of a few hours sailing so gloriously along out here in the middle of a trackless ocean, despite the physical discomforts and perpetual weariness, in the middle of the night when the rest of the world's citizens are comfortable in their motionless beds ashore. I myself was ready for a break;

I was weary of cold, strong gales, and rough, lumpy seas, and dearly sought a full night's sleep in still waters.

My eagerness was tempered by the recently gained knowledge that another 40-knot gale was brewing, and would be fully upon me within a few hours, in fact by morning, according to what snippets of weather forecasting I had been able to glean from the broken transmissions on the SSB radio. This created some anxiety for me. I did not want to be in another stiff gale so soon. I had begun to be able to pick up scratchy, static-punctuated weather forecasts from Bermuda Radio. The prediction was for the gale to blow out of the southwest. It was already blowing out of that direction and at nearly thirty knots at that, and was growing stronger by the hour. I looked at the chart, and figured that since I was approaching Bermuda from the northeast, I would find relief by being in the lee of the island, where I could stand off in quieter waters until dawn, and then motor into St. George's harbor. The approach to Bermuda is complicated by the fact that the island of Bermuda itself, which is not really a single island but a collection of many small islands, all in close proximity, is surrounded by a perimeter of deadly coral reefs and shallows extending some ten miles out from the actual shoreline. The only safe and reliable route into sheltered St. George's is from the northeast side of the island. No other approach from any direction is safe or feasible due to the deadly encirclement of reefs. One can go into St. George's through a man-made cut channel, or follow another channel around the island and inside the barrier of reefs to enter Hamilton Harbor from the southwest via Great Sound.

I was going into the old town of St. George's through a passage hewn through rock, known as Town Cut. My plan was perfect in theory, except that the island of Bermuda does not really provide a very effective lee, since the land overall is so low. Without mountain peaks or anything of the sort to impede the blast, the wind literally howls over the little archipelago as though it's hardly there. Couple that with the fact that one must stay well offshore, in the darkness, to stay prudently outside of the deadly reefs, and one might as well be out on the open sea, for all the shelter that its lee is worth.

Distances at sea can be deceiving, especially at night. For a few hours now, I had been able to see the very faint, unnatural glow of Bermuda against the cloud ceiling in the distance. It was colorless and barely discernible, yet still visible against the absolute murky darkness all around. So I thought I was closer, when in fact I was still many miles distant, even too many miles for VHF radio contact; and over the next few hours that glow of the island still over the horizon would grow brighter and larger, eventually punctuated by the flashes of light tower beacons against the undersides of the clouds. The lights themselves were still beyond the horizon; yet the comfort that even that faint glow, no matter how distant, imparts to the mind, is powerful. It gives new-found strength and energy, and fosters a change of mind-set and perspective. Everything is transformed by a new inner light, a paradigm shift; the mind is indeed its own place, as Milton observed. At long last, I would be arriving in my own boat under sail to this lonely outpost of land in the middle of the ocean, formed of ancient volcanoes, exposed seamounts, land that simply does not belong out here in the heart of Neptune's realm.

As I drew closer, I heard the weather broadcast from Bermuda Radio coming through with increasing clarity. It was a live broadcast, it seemed, even though it was the middle of the night, delivered by a pleasant, professional radio operator, a fellow with a British, if not decidedly Scottish, accent. Hungry for human contact, and thinking, mistakenly, that my transmission might be heard as clearly by that operator as I could hear his, I tried to call him on the VHF, because the weather forecast transmission had been spotty and broken up, but the words "forty-knot gales" had been quite discernible. I queried him about the forecast, and asked him to repeat it.

He came back to me by saying that I was still too far away for him to make out our transmission, and that we should contact the station again in a few hours when we were closer to the island; but he had heard me ask for a repeat of the marine weather forecast, and although he did not say so over the air, I believe that he detected some anxiety in my voice, and as a result, he quite remarkably, and patiently, repeated the forecast, speaking slowly and distinctly, a kindness and professionalism that I had not anticipated, and which of course would have been an impossibility with the automated broadcasts heard on weather radio here in the states. It was contact, though, and it cheered me even more, although that cheer was tempered by the validation of my concern, that I would be in the heart of another gale in only a few hours, long before I would be in the safety of the harbor. Well, I thought, I will simply have to make do, and manage. It would be a long, long night.

The rig was balanced and the wind did not seem to be strengthening. So I lashed the wheel and pulled my hood over my head to keep the spray out, and crouched back against the cabin so that the spray coming over the boat washed over me from behind. I could remain dry this way, in my foul weather gear, and the water and spray were not cold, so I did not expect to be chilled. Thus braced, I began to doze, and dozed for three or four hours, waking quickly and suddenly, not due to any alarm or incident, or change in circumstances, but through odd intuition that I needed to look around.

After what seemed an interminable night of endless tumult, I saw the welcome glow of the gray dawn in the east, and it cheered me; my pulse quickened and I felt excitement like that of a child as my heart beat in anticipation of landfall and the relief of quiet waters. At long last, I was headed in. I looked upwards at the sky. It was a high dawn, broken clouds of a mottled mackerel-scale ceiling far above and still well before the sunrise, but I thought it beautiful, and so much like the many daybreaks I had seen at sea in years past. Despite whatever conditions one has at the surface, a high dawn at sea is a time of peace, contemplation, and joy, even though it is usually a harbinger of strong wind later. But for the moment, a new day, with all its possibilities, challenges, and fears, is about to break, and the sun will rise.

Out of the dusty recesses of my mind came, inexplicably, a fragment of an old rhyme, and in the half-light, and it brought a faint smile to me:

> *"The evening red and morning gray,*
> *Are sure signs of a fine day."*

Off to starboard, in the growing light and through the haze of sea-mist, I could see a chalky, high cliff of the island, and a lighthouse, as well as the steel light towers that marked the perimeter of the reef at Kitchen Shoal, North Rock, and Northeast Breaker.

It was blowing half a gale as I motored around the channel markers and into narrow Town Cut, a channel blasted through a limestone cliff, and into a strange calmness of the inner harbor, a calm that I had not known for a week. I felt my stress melt away; my body began to relax, as I realized that I had now safely attained a quiet harbor where body and mind could rest. I was wet and weary, and the wind was high and it was freshening, as had been predicted, but under bare poles now and maneuvering with the engine, after being at sea, it seemed child's play. I had already called in my passport information and answered the appropriate questions to Bermuda Maritime Operations; I simply needed to go to the Customs dock and clear in. There would be forms to fill out and fees to pay. But as I motored in, it was sunrise, orange, groggy, damp, fatigued sunrise, and with my mind dulled by lack of sleep, sights and sounds were coming to me as through a frosted lens, fuzzy and dark around the edges. Scrubby trees like windswept evergreens hung on tenaciously to the rocky ledges around the harbor entrance and for the first time I realized that the strange sweet scent reaching my nostrils was the smell of land. Land does have an aroma, indeed, but one is not conscious of it until one has been away from it for a few days.

St. George's Harbour was lined with steep, close hillsides and pastel houses with tall palm trees between them. The strong wind sent low clouds scudding across the sky seemingly barely above the rooftops and the branches and fronds of every palm tree had been turned into a windsock. When I finally had pulled up to the dock and secured my boat, I stood on the dock at the 18th Century stucco-walled Customs House and the solidity felt strange.

There were boats in the harbor from many places, most new, some older, and I saw an old friend, a white sloop of approximately the same size and with the same traditional lines, hull shape, and color and appearance but for her rig, as my *Rugosa*. This was *Destiny*, the same boat that I had seen the first time that I had entered this harbor two years earlier when I sailed in as a crewman aboard the schooner *Christina,* on which I was crewing as part of a delivery to make some extra money. At the time, the appearance of *Destiny* in the harbor had seemed like an early-morning vision, and it reminded me of my own *Rugosa,* at that moment propped up under repair in the boat shed in Bristol, more than six hundred miles away. I had felt a twinge of guilt and homesickness; I wished at that moment that I was looking at my own boat in the harbor. "One day I will sail you here," I had said, inaudibly, more a thought than an utterance, speaking to my boat far and away across the expanse of sea. But now here she was again, and I was motoring by her in my own vessel, my promise fulfilled. "Look, *Destiny,*" I called out, "As I promised, I have brought your older sibling!"

When the sun ascended above the hillsides, now white and full of the strength of day, it shone upon impossibly bright turquoise waters, clear and reminiscent of an Olympic swimming pool, but with a misty, cloudy haziness that reminded one that it was salt water, not fresh. The gale was blowing hard but I was now secure to the commercial wharf in St. George's, so let the wind whistle and howl under a brilliant blue sky, I thought. Tomorrow I would put her on a mooring or anchor her.

Walking the streets; winding, hilly, cobblestoned, everywhere stone, brick, stucco, painted. From a hilltop, I had sweeping views of the harbors and islets and the great sea beyond, from horizon to horizon a carpet of flat and everlasting blue. *This place does not belong to the land*, I said to myself.

Before heading off walking, I had made myself a drink down below, and would have slept, but as has always been my habit when visiting a new port, or one that I have not been to in a while, I like to walk about a bit and stretch my legs until at long last sheer exhaustion drives me to my berth. The Bermuda sun was blazing brilliant and dazzling white on the terra-cotta and white-plastered rooftops, under clear blue skies, and it was time to explore. Somehow my legs found energy, driven by my relentless curiosity that even fatigue could not quell, and soon I was walking the hilly, cobbled streets of the old town, and past lush greenery and plants with broad leaves, succulents, banana plants, and many unusual and beautiful things on this archipelago of low islands, a place in-between many things, between continents, barely above the surface of the sea, an annoyance perhaps to the ocean.

I ended up at a tavern near the docks called the White Horse, and after dusk, when I finally grew tired enough, I walked back to the boat in a storm of rain and thunder with wind and lightning, and slept solidly.

I spent what seemed like a season in Bermuda, although in reality it was barely two months, at first resting up after my voyage down, and then exploring the island and thinking hard about what I was doing. I spent a lot of time contemplating my next move, the next stop along the way to my distant and unknown destination. I moved ashore, renting the upstairs floor of a dark, old stone house that had once been a blacksmith shop a century or more before. On gray winter days when the sun was hidden, and when low, wet clouds off the ocean scudded by overhead just above the chimney-tops, I watched the strong ocean winds blow through the tortured, shredded fronds of the palm trees on the hilltops, blown ragged as they leaned away from the blast. The wind made a deep roaring sound as it passed over the islands, but it brought in an almost-palpable freshness from the broad ocean that I always welcomed in the early morning as I stood on my small upstairs balcony. My balcony overlooked the rooftops of houses further down the hill and afforded me a rare view of St. George's Harbor and surrounding hilltops, and was the perfect place, I thought, to drink a cup of hot coffee and feel the wind in my hair without having to be on the deck of a ship. The sun would occasionally peek through the layers of fast-scudding clouds and I could, at such times, imagine that I was at sea but on a stable deck that never moved; such was the deck of this great coral-encrusted ship, Bermuda.

On cooler winter days, I would light a small fire of hard, brittle, hot-crackling Casuarina logs in the blackened brick fireplace and sit on a threadbare, ancient woolen prayer rug on the floor in front of the hearth. The room, with its uneven plank floors worn smooth with age, was dark but for the bright, stark gray illumination of the bare, undraped windows, and I would dwell in the shadows in the semi-darkness of the big, empty room, listening to the low crackle of the fire and the spatter of fat rain drops against the wavy antique bubble-peppered window panes. Some late afternoons I would drift off to sleep, lulled by the sound of the wind whistling around the eaves and humming about the chimney flue while the low glow of the coals kept the damp chill off.

I took most of my meals at a pastel-painted stucco café down the street where the locals ate. It was affordable Caribbean food, always different, with sauces and grilled wahoo or rock fish, cooked plantains and different ingredients and spices that always made it interesting.

St. George's winding, brick and stone walled, cobbled streets are lined with stone and stuccoed houses jammed together. They are painted gay pastel colors and their chimney flue tops are graced by slanted notched panels known in old times as "'praying hands'" and now called "'rooster combs'", designed to prevent downdrafts from the strong winds.

It was never cold in Bermuda, there was never ice nor snow such as we had back home in New England. But there were days when it was windy, raw, and damp and the air smelled always of the sea. It was a penetrating dampness and the only defense against it was a warm woolen sweater or a jacket, and a tot of rum. The faint scent of wood burning on the cool air was reassuring and pleasant, and reminded me in a small way of home, which was now something on the order of six hundred miles away across open sea.

I was surrounded, in the center of the little town, by lush greenery every-where. Fat succulent leaves, cacti, banana trees, every sort of green thing that could grow in the thin soil of Bermuda seemed to have taken root, and it made me think that I had found a little corner of Paradise here in the middle of the Atlantic. *In Paradisum*, I mused, *deducant angeli. The angels have led me to Paradise.*

I went out to *Rugosa* nearly every day, usually in the morning. I didn't take her out of the harbor, or go anywhere in her; that would have involved too much radio traffic with the authorities, but I did make sure that her fuel and water tanks were filled, her mooring lines secure, and that all things were well below. I went swimming in the clean, clear brine around her, cleaning her propeller and hull in spots, keeping her free of growth as well as I could. I provisioned her with canned and dry goods from the grocery on shore.

I found a few new friends, and went fishing with them in their small boat out to the reef, catching rockfish and wahoo. There seemed to be a lot of Bermuda when riding around her winding roads on a bus or in some other con-veyance, such as the bicycle that I had rented; but when I went out in a small boat to the reef and looked back at the island, I realized what a small place Bermuda really was, a speck out in the middle of the ocean, not much more, when viewed from a distance.

I explored the island every day, from one end to the other, ultimately, and all the small islands and connections in between. I found every pub, every beach, every interesting place, but I did my exploring alone.

After about three weeks of satisfying my curiosity, I began to think about my situation and my aloneness, and I began to realize that while being alone at sea on a long single-handed passage was unavoidable, it was a totally unnecessary burden to be borne while on an archipelago of islands surrounded by generally pleasant people. I was not seeking friendship beyond casual acquaintance, since I had neither the desire nor the energy to invest in developing strong or deep attachments. But being a curious sort, and always interested in people even though I liked them at arm's length, I thought I might meet some people while on the island if for no other reason than to have some friends to drink with, and occasionally talk to, since at sea there was plenty of opportunity to talk to myself.

I began by exploring all the well-known bars on the island frequented by the tourists, with the only result being that I spent too much money and the places were noisy and the people generally obnoxious. I visited the Hog Penny in Hamilton, taking a bus there one warm night just as a violent thunderstorm was breaking over the island and water ran down the hilly streets of St. George's in rivers with the drenching downpour. White flashes of brilliant light like giant flash-bulbs lit up the old town from the sky and the local people cowered under umbrellas and yet were soaked anyway. The beer was good but it was like being hidden in plain sight, as they say; sometimes one is more alone in a crowd than on a deserted beach, with the added disadvantage that one is unlikely to be jostled or deafened on an empty beach or to have someone's drink spilled upon you. The only advantage to the crowded place is that one is not physically alone; there are people all around, but it is not a satisfying companionship; it is nothing more than physical proximity, which is of little value really; it does not palliate loneliness, on the contrary, it amplifies one's sense of emotional isolation. So after a couple of nights there I decided that it was not worth the hike to go there alone.

But on a tip, on a rather hot day, I decided to find a local watering-hole that the bartender at the White Horse Pub and Tavern told me about, a laid-back beach bar on the other side of St. George's. I walked through the village center and up a very narrow street flanked by coral stone walls and flowering lush vines to the crest of a hill that bisected a golf course. I was on my way to find a small cabana bar on the other side of the rise on a small body of water named Tobacco Bay. On the way there, I paused at the edge of a steep hill to look at the remains of yet another old fortification. It consisted of a sheer wall of grey limestone or coral rock perhaps fifty or more feet high, with huge rust-red iron cannon from a bygone age scattered in a jumble around its base in the tall grass. Wild fennel was growing everywhere and it filled the air with a spicy-sweet aroma.

It looked as though a part of the hill had been cut away, like a boule that has had a third of it sliced away and eaten, and the raw cliff side, cut into stone, was featureless except for an old steel door at the base, shut but with a broken lock. It covered, it would seem, a passage cut into the base of the rock face, and I climbed the short talus-covered incline to the door, grabbed it and pulled it open, creaking and groaning as it did, to reveal a cleanly cut passageway leading up a slight incline into impenetrable darkness.

Cool, stagnant, musty air greeted me; I imagined myself a latter-day Howard Carter entering an ancient Egyptian pyramid. A small collection of dirty empty beer bottles lined the passageway on either side by my feet. I carried a small light on my keychain, and as my eyes became accustomed to the darkness, it seemed brighter to me, and I thought nothing of advancing further into the straight passageway. Every few moments I glanced back at the rectangle of brilliant white-hot light that marked the entrance, and the outdoors, and even though the time that I walked was a few minutes and no more, it seemed longer, the deeper I penetrated into the passageway.

At the very end, or what seemed to be the very end, the corridor expanded into a much larger space, a rectangular room, actually. The air was very cool and damp and made me shudder; it was stale, like a tomb, and my dim little pocket light did not penetrate far. Everything was covered with gray dust and at one end of the room was a cocktail bar, of all things, with old-fashioned round stools, all dust-covered. There were busted shards from old liquor bottles on the floor, and in one corner the broken remains of a heavy glass oil lamp. The place was creepy, I thought, and then as I looked around, I began to feel, growing quite suddenly, an overwhelming and powerful sensation of dread, and the prickling sensory alarm that I was not alone, and was being watched.

Now my attention immediately focused on the far end of the room, where there was a blackness that was impenetrable by my light, whether it was simply a dark wall, or a continuation of the passageway, I could not tell, and yet I dared not approach it; and as I stared at it, knowing now that it was the focal point from where my strange feelings of fear and warning were emanating, I attempted to discern features from the silken, velvet blackness. As I stared at it, to my horror it suddenly seemed to begin to move and undulate, like some huge menacing creature in the darkness that had been disturbed by my approach, or a pile of black headless snakes, and I was seized by terror, a terror that washed over me like a cold wave breaking over the boat, immobilizing me, making me a helpless, frozen observer about to be devoured and destroyed by an inescapable threat that I could neither identify nor define.

It was strange, because I have never been a believer in ghosts, or the supernatural, demons or devils, and am not generally taken to unreasoning fear, but in this case I stood transfixed, like a mouse hypnotized by the eye of a cobra about to devour it, looking for identifiable features, such as eyes, or teeth; but I saw none; merely an undulating darkness. I likened it to a troll, or great black hairy gorilla or octopus or something huge and threatening, yet undefinable, as I stood there fascinated, mesmerized and in a state of unholy terror, unable to turn and run, and yet…I could see nothing, nothing definable. I lost my sense of time; how long I stood there could have been one minute, or ten.

And although I dared not approach that writhing darkness that occupied the entire width and height of the wall, I saw that neither did it advance toward me, and although I was shaking like a leaf with my shirt now dank with a profuse cold sweat, I began to back up, one shaky step at a time, until, after what seemed like an eternity, I was out of the room and into the narrow passageway, and as the gradual intensification of light washing in from the doorway began to brighten the walls and banish the darkness to the distant end of the hallway, now a world, a reality away, I found myself once again stepping out into the blinding sunlight and heat of the day. I closed the door, nearly falling on the uneven talus as I walked down the path with weak and unsteady knees.

A brisk walk soon set me to rights, however, and as I descended the slope of the hill, I saw the cheerful light blue painted walls and white roof of the cabana bar and the turquoise clean waters of little Tobacco Bay adjacent, with its odd stands of wave-hollowed limestone boulders scattered here and there, surf rushing through their strange brown caves and perforations, spouting and spraying here and there with each wave driven in by the stiff onshore wind.

It was mid-afternoon, now, and I knew that I wanted a drink badly to settle my nerves. I still had no clue regarding what I had observed in that cave, or why I had been so terrorized by it. I sat at the bar and ordered a 'Painkiller' rum punch from the friendly bartender, a big tall fellow with dark slicked-back hair and a half-beard who wore an island shirt printed with colorful parrot images. His name tag read 'Dan,' and he had an easygoing way about him that helped me settle down. The first Painkiller went quickly. By the end of the second, I was beginning to feel more relaxed, and tried to push the phenomenon that I had observed from my mind. By the third drink, I had become all but dismissive of it, alternately as the embodiment of my fears of the voyage ahead, or of facing the sea alone, or of death; perhaps I was looking at my own death, I thought to myself. Or perhaps I had an odd onset of claustrophobia, but that makes no sense, I chided myself, after sailing alone for hundreds of miles in a little boat. Perhaps it was nothing but an unusual and rare hallucination, I reasoned. But in any case I soon decided that I was not going to come to any viable conclusion about what I had witnessed in the old cavern, or what I thought I had witnessed; that was a job for another day. And so, with that experience receding into the wake of my thoughts and considerations, I turned my eyes to the sea and the horizon, the aqua-blue white-capped waves coming in from the edge of the reef ten miles out, and a sailboat plying its way from left to right mid-way, its white wings carrying it steady and smoothly on a rhumb line down the main channel to round the headland and Fort St. Catherine and perhaps then the channel from St. George's out to sea. It was a beautiful scene, and in the afternoon wind and sun and the relaxation from the rum, I began to feel whole again, riding on my lines, and on an even keel.

My eyes turned to the water in the little bay, and the beach, where a half dozen people were swimming and splashing in the gentle surf. One bather caught my eye, a pretty island woman, standing in the water a little off by herself, perhaps in her late thirties, I thought, lithe and shapely with limbs like smooth milk chocolate and a generous head of black curly hair. I watched her for a little while, as she was pleasant to watch, and I did not notice anyone with her. And although I scanned the sea and the many different beautiful sights of the Bermuda shore and landscape, my focus kept drifting back to her, like a moth drawn to a lamp, and at one point, when she looked up from the beach and towards the cabana bar, she saw me looking at her; our eyes met for a moment, and I, embarrassed slightly, turned my head slightly away, but yet at the same time delayed doing so for a second or so more, so that she would know that I was noticing her, though not rudely staring, but pretending not to notice while at the same time pleased at being caught.

Aware that she had been noticed, she took some pleasure in her bathing, moving a little closer, and had I been a photographer, I might have observed that she was purposely giving me the best possible views for shots for the swimsuit cover of a magazine.

When she left the beach she boldly came up to the cabana bar, wrapped in her towel, and sat down next to me on the nearest empty seat of a row of empty seats. "May I?" she asked. "Please do," I replied, followed by some silly line such as "How's the water?" although perhaps it was not that trite but in any case I do not remember precisely; I was feeling few inhibitions thanks to the drinks that I'd had. She introduced herself; her name was Amélie, she said, and I offered to buy her a drink. The water droplets in her hair were like tiny prisms and they sparkled in the sun. She seemed to have a perpetual slight smile, as though she were quietly amused. She was easygoing and pleasant, and I noticed that her eyes were a mixture of brown and blue. She spoke in a very crisp British accent, but in a voice soft and melodious.

"That's very decent of you," she said. "I like rum, especially the Black Seal Bermuda rum, in a nice rum punch." She turned to the bartender, and he smiled when she said, "Danny, make me a swizzle, will you, dear? One of your very best as always. Thank you."

We talked for a little while, then moved over to the grill, where the smoke from grilling cheeseburgers was being carried on the wind and making every-one hungry who was within reach of the grill's aroma. "Let's eat something," I said. So we ate cheeseburgers while we talked and drank Danny's rum cocktails out on the deck of the cabana bar until nearly sunset.

Amélie was a Bermudian, she said, family came originally from Barbados, her great-grandfather was a white planter, her great-grandmother a servant in his house. It was all a very long time ago.

"Do you always go to the beach to watch ladies in the water?" She asked quite suddenly, putting me oddly on the defensive; there was no good or easy answer to such a plain and unexpected question.

"Actually never. I came here today because I heard that this was a nice outdoor bar, a relaxing place where I could kick back for a bit in peace for an afternoon."

"Do you swim?"

"Only when I have to these days, like times when I have to clean my propeller."

"So you came here by boat? Where is your crew?"

"Right here," I replied. "I am sailing alone."

"To where?"

"Don't know yet."

"Then you might not get there!" She replied, puzzled. "But I mean, really.

Why alone? Why here? I'm sorry to ask such probing questions, but your voyage intrigues me."

"A lot of reasons, not all clear to me yet. I had to get away, and I've wanted to make this trip for a long time. I thought I might sail around the world. But if I don't, it will be because I finally have found what I have been looking for, wherever that may be, whatever that may be."

"Don't be on a fool's errand," she said, playfully.

"I hope it isn't," I replied, "But you know, there is an old folk fable about a man who had spent too many years at sea, and left his coastal town in New England, walking due west with a pair of oars over his shoulder. And he pledged that as soon as someone asked him what those things were that he was carrying, that's where he would stop and buy a farm. As soon as he was far enough away from the sea. Maybe I'm working it backwards. I've left the farm and gone to sea."

"Sailing alone is dangerous, though. You could lose your boat and your life. Aren't you afraid?"

"I'm not afraid to die," I replied. "Death comes to everyone eventually. I'm afraid of not living while I am alive. If there is sin, perhaps that is the greatest sin of all."

She looked at me in an odd way, without a smile, critical, perhaps, or as one would look at someone entirely cuckoo, and not understanding. She said nothing, and then finally turned her gaze away and shook her head.

"But you are not fearless?"

"No," I replied. "I have known much fear at sea. Only a fool would be fearless. The key is not to let fear debilitate you. Any intelligent man knows fear when he truly understands the odds in his situation."

"When was the time that you remember being most afraid?" she asked.

I thought for a moment. "Once, when crossing the Gulf Stream. The winds were high and opposing the Stream, under clear, sunny, beautiful skies, I was in the middle of these mountainous, sometimes breaking seas. And I really do mean mountainous. And yet the color of the sea was so sapphire-blue, transparent, and beautiful. I think the great beauty of the Gulf Stream made it all the more terrifying."

"There are dangers in the shallows, too. As far as swimming in Bermuda goes, I think you should be careful when you do, especially at the beaches.

Stinging jellyfish frequently wash up on the beach, and even the dead ones tend to collect in the shallows when the wind is onshore. They are dead but they can still sting. I'm always afraid of swimming into one without seeing it. I've been stung before, and it is terribly painful."

"I will be careful," I replied.

We walked up the tree-lined road to the top where the breeze crossed over the island and then down the hill past the ruins of the old brick church and into the village. It was just after sunset, and I was growing tired. "Will you be at the beach tomorrow?" I asked.

"Oh, perhaps." She smiled, "Stop by if you are not busy. It will be Sunday. Come on by for a swim in the afternoon. There are never any jellyfish in Tobacco Bay." And then she quickly turned and walked away, turning once to wave to me, smiling.

I went back to my apartment room and for the first time since I had rented it, it seemed empty and hollow, and the darkness in the shadows reminded me of the strange horror of the tunnel in the fort. I lay on my bunk watching the sky through the window as the last light of the day faded from deep blue to black.

I thought about Amélie for a while afterwards. Perhaps, I told myself, you are more vulnerable than you realize at the moment, being alone and without a clear direction. Perhaps you have discovered a weak spot, a chink in your armor. But in any case this is not any kind of involvement that you want, I chided myself. But for some reason I could not sleep, so after a while I got up and dressed and went outside. The night was still warm and the street noisy, with cars and a motor scooters noisily clattering down the cobbled streets. I walked the short few blocks to the White Horse and took a seat at the bar. It was only nine-o'clock by my watch.

Morgan, the manager, was tending bar. I never did learn his last name, we all simply knew him as 'Morgan.' He was a tall, elderly black man who had lived in Bermuda for most of his life and was a part-owner of the tavern. He had been working here for more than forty years and had a deadpan, dry sense of humor. I liked him and chatted with him often when visiting the tavern. On this evening, the bar was crowded and there were four members of a big yacht's crew at the bar, four men who had just sailed a big Hylas yacht in from Halifax. They'd had a stormy ride of it and had cleared customs this morning and this was their first night in port and their first visit to a bar since they had left Canada. The two younger guys were eyeing all the women in the place, coming and going, rather comprehensively. But being sailors, we were all soon talking and comparing notes about our crossing, and sailing in general, as Morgan filled and re-filled our frosted mugs from what seemed an endless tap drawn from a beer aquifer somewhere beneath the island. I sat by myself for a while until I grew tired, then slowly picked my way back along the cobbled street to my apartment in the Old Forge.

Chapter 10

Amélie

Dear as remembered kisses after death,
And sweet as those by hopeless fancy feigned...
Deep as first love, and wild with all regret;
O Death in Life, the days that are no more!

— Tennyson

The next afternoon I went back to the cabana bar at Tobacco Bay in the afternoon. As I descended the hill toward the beach, from a distance, I could see that Amélie was already in the water. I watched her swim for a little while, and then went down to the little beach myself wearing my old Ron Jon bathing suit and waded in. The surf was running high again with a stiff onshore breeze from the west and the day was warm and the water wonderfully tepid. Amélie saw me, smiled and swam over to me and we talked for a while with just our heads above the water. She seemed pleased to see me, and of course I had come down to the beach for the sole purpose of seeing her again, although I did not want to seem to be too anxious. We made small talk for a little while and then she asked, "Did you hear about the storm developing?"

"No, I didn't; I must have missed that. I was cleaning down below and fixing a leaky water hose. What kind of storm?"

"A cyclone of some kind, a big one. Developed from a tropical wave off the coast of Africa. The long term outlook has it coming this way in a week or so."

"I didn't think it was hurricane season," I replied.

"I don't know. But it seems like it might come this way in a few days. But then again it might not, they aren't sure."

"If it does, I'm going to have to secure my boat," I said.

"Are you on an anchor?"

"Yes. Like most everyone else. What I mean is that I would have to reduce wind resistance by taking the sails off the spars so that they won't get torn up, things like that. I don't imagine that I would be able to be hauled out."

"St. George's is a pretty sheltered place; you would probably ride it out just fine in there. They only haul out boats for the biggest hurricanes most of the time."

"I'm sure that I would not be high on the boat yard's priority list, and that it is probably extremely costly to do so. If my anchor is set well I should be fine with extra lines on and chafing gear. It's a bunch of work but should not be too much of a problem, but it all depends on the projected intensity of the storm. I need to make sure that my anchor is buried well and won't drag."

"Would you stay aboard the boat during the storm?" Amélie asked.

"I might. Sometimes I do. Or I might ride it out at the White Horse," I grinned. "All depends."

"On what?"

"On how I feel at the time. If she breaks loose, there isn't much I can do even if I am aboard. In fact, staying on the boat is really a dangerous place to be if she does break loose. You're basically at the mercy of the wind and seas, since you can't do much to fight it. So you end up on the rocks or on the beach, and you figure that if the boat is going to end up there anyway, you're better off not being on her when she does. Thinking of that, I might dive down and look at the condition of the anchor chain as soon as I can to assess my chances. But, in any case, there's plenty to do to prepare the boat to ride out a storm."

"Can I help you?" She asked. The question took me a little by surprise.

"Well, certainly you could help stow the sails and tie things down, but would you want to? It's just a bunch of work, not very much fun."

"I don't mind," She replied, "I've spent plenty of time on boats, living here in Bermuda. Besides, I want to see your boat."

I smiled, happy to hear this. "Well of course I'd love to show her to you, but she's no grand yacht, just an old wooden sailboat that I fixed up and sailed here."

"That's fine with me, even better, I think."

She reached into the water and playfully splashed me. "You're starting to burn!" She laughed.

"Maybe I should sit under the umbrella up at the bar," I said.

"Better yet that I rub some lotion on your back," she said. "I have a bottle of it with my towel on the beach."

Up at the bar she rubbed the creamy liquid on my back, very smoothly, not hurriedly at all, taking her time and taking pains to cover every inch, especially the back of my neck and my shoulders. Her hands felt very smooth and soft, yet her touch was firm, and when she was finished, I felt aroused.

"That was very nice," I said. "But they say that you have to apply that stuff frequently."

She chuckled softly in amusement, "Yeah, well once will be good enough for you this afternoon, Captain!"

I was thinking about the weather now and as I drank a rum punch, I asked Danny the bartender what he knew. He was wiping big cocktail glasses with a white terrycloth towel and doing so in a disinterested ho-hum manner. "Always a mess when one of those things blows through here," he began, shaking his head. "Still too early to tell how bad it will be, we'll know in a couple of days."

"Don't hurricanes and tropical cyclones usually miss this island?" I asked.

"Usually, but not always. This one isn't following the rules. But we could get nearly hurricane-force winds they say, sixty or seventy miles per hour, so it could tear things up a bit. You got your boat here?"

"In the Convict Bay anchorage," I replied.

"Tie her down good is all I can say if the storm begins to head this way. You have maybe five days yet before you need to be thinking about it. But if it comes here, there will be a frenzy of haul-outs in the yards. Good luck getting a reservation if that's what you want to do. The locals get first dibs, always, so if you're a visitor, don't get your hopes up."

I turned to Amélie. "I'll keep an eye on the forecast. If I need to batten down, and if you'll come out to the boat with me to help out, I'll buy you dinner for helping me."

"I'd help you anyway, she replied, "You don't need to buy me dinner for that. Buy it tonight instead," she replied, playfully.

"You bet. Let's go for drinks at the White Horse first."

There was always a crowd late in the day at the White Horse. The tap was busy, with Morgan and two other bartenders keeping the patrons wet. We took up seats at the bar; Morgan looked at Amélie, and then looked at me; he had not seen us together before, but I was sure that he knew her, and of course he knew me; but whatever he might have been thinking, his eyes and his expression gave no clue. He smiled a little, in his characteristic warm way, and filled our pint glasses with cellar-cool ale. Amélie thanked him as he put them down, and he nodded; that was all.

Amélie talked about her job, working in the island's insurance industry as some sort of analyst, and living in an efficiency apartment at the other end of St. George's alone. She had been married once, married too early to a businessman from the U.K. who was looking less for marriage than for an occasional night of sex. She didn't know this when she married him, but quite early on she discovered that he had a wife back in Twickenham, so the whole marriage was a sham anyway, and he was back off to London and she never saw him again. It had all happened so fast that she was left dizzy for a few months by it. Only her mother was living now, and she was an invalid in a nursing home. "When David left," she said, "There was nothing I could do. I could have started drinking or doing other things. But I had to keep my job and keep Mom in the home, since I am paying such a big share of it."

Her father had been a merchant seaman who had died more than a decade earlier. "He was on a container ship and used to hide bottles of liquor away and drink when he was off watch," she said.

"One night he drank too much and fell overboard during bad weather and nobody saw him fall. The ship lost a day; they went back looking for him, retracing their course, but there was no sign of him, so they turned around and continued on to Jakarta."

"So it's just you and your Mom?"

"Just me and Mom. I have no sisters or brothers, and David and I never had children. I wanted to have a baby but he really didn't. I couldn't understand why at first, but it wasn't very long before I found out why."

"Did he and his wife in England have children?"

"Oh, yes. A son and a daughter, both in private academies in London."

We sat at the bar and as we drank, I looked around to get the 'lay of the land' so to speak, and to see if there was anyone in the place I might know. After a short while my attention was drawn to a corner table, where a tall, middle-aged seaman with long blond hair down to his shoulders, a bushy moustache, and a ruddy complexion was laughing heartily and roaring out about one thing or another. He seemed a rough and ready sea-type; his hair was drawn back in a ponytail, but he sported a blond, untrimmed moustache and bushy brows, and his manner of speaking and overall style put him somewhere between an 18th century fighting frigate captain and a 70's rock and roll musician. He was dressed in faded jeans and a worn chamois shirt with its long sleeves rolled up, a big oval scrimshaw belt buckle plate punctuating the two, and raggedy leather old-style boat moccasins and no socks. He wore an ancient Spanish coin, a silver treasure doubloon from a shipwreck, suspended from a chain around his neck like a holy medal.

"You see that fellow over there," I heard Morgan, behind me, speaking in low tones into my ear, "He's one of your Yankee captains, probably from your end of the beach. That's Captain John Carver, he's from Massachusetts. Brought a really sweet antique schooner some time back and just sailed down here a few days ago, planning on taking it down to the Virgin Islands."

"Does he own it outright?"

"Oh, yes. Quite a story there. I guess he worked on it as the hired captain for a few years, loved the boat very much. The owner, however, took ill somewhat, and what with money troubles couldn't keep her up. About the same time, Captain John come into some family money, yes he did. So he made an offer and bought her outright. Her name is *Gleam*. Now he just sails her around, down to the Caribbean in the fall, back to Massachusetts in the spring. Says he wants to sail to the Pacific. You should go over and meet him. Introduce yourself, he's rather approachable."

"Maybe," I said, "or maybe later. He seems to be pretty well occupied with his crew around him."

But soon enough Captain John came barreling over to the bar to refill his drink. Morgan had it ready for him. "Captain John's signature drink," Morgan said, as Carver came up alongside. "Mount Gay rum, orange juice, and pineapple juice to top it off, over ice."

"Sounds tasty," I spoke up, "Morgan, I'll try one of those, too."

"You want to try one?" Captain John spoke up. "Morgan, give him one too, please, on me." He extended a big hand, and squeezed mine in a firm, strong grip. "Hi, I'm John Carver. Nice to meet you."

"Nate Williams," I replied. "Morgan here says you're from Massachusetts? I'm from Bristol, Rhode Island."

"Bristol? Rogue's Island? Why, I know Bristol well. My staysail schooner *Gleam* was originally built by Herreshoff. I'm from Falmouth, down on the

Cape. I grew up paddling a punt around Quisset harbor. But that was a long time ago, ha, ha!"

Carver told us about his youth, joining the Coast Guard, and his experiences serving on a Coast Guard patrol boat, which then became a Navy patrol boat, drafted into the Navy, as were many Coast Guard vessels during the Vietnam War. He wound up on patrol in the rivers of South Vietnam, then went AWOL, was caught and spent time in the Marine Brig up in Portsmouth, New Hampshire. He told me of many other similar misadventures, as well. He took to sailing schooners and traditional square-rigged ships during the late 1970s and around the Bicentennial, and then switched to running tugboats in New York Harbor and making yacht deliveries on the side. He lived like a Bohemian; grew his hair long, lived by his own rules, had a girlfriend in every port of call. He told us about his schooner, *Gleam*, invited us aboard for a party after the storm had passed.

"We'll have a great time," Carver said, "But first we have to get past this gale coming in a day or so."

After drinks, Amélie and I quietly slipped out after dark and walked down the street to a quiet little bistro that she liked. It was right on the harbor, a cozy place where the food was known to be good. The tablecloths were starched and white and there were tapers lit and the golden light refracted through our glasses of white wine. It was a nice touch, the kind of setting that both of us liked. Afterwards, we walked up and down the quaint streets and alleyways hand in hand in the cool of the evening as we talked, a puffy breeze off the sea rustling the leaves on the trees and the palm branches, and we felt happy to be together, just alone and without anyone else around, tranquil, and feeling as though we had known each other much longer than we had.

The next day Amélie met me at the White Horse just before lunch. She was dressed in jeans and a work shirt. I had been waiting for her out on the patio, eating an order of conch fritters and fries while watching the rockfish swimming around in schools in the water below the little bridge nearby. I was watching them break the surface of the light blue, slightly cloudy seawater. It made me think of what someone's swimming pool back home might look like if it had been filled with this clean salt water rather than fresh.

"Want some?" I offered.

"No, they are no good here. Whoever cooks for this place can't cook at all. They ought to put him in that ducking stool over there that they have rigged up for the tourists."

"Ooh. I hope it's not Morgan." I threw what was left into the water; the rockfish ignored them, as much as if I had tossed a handful of pebbles into the water.

"How about a beer?"

"Draft for mine," she said.

Then we went out to *Rugosa* in my small inflatable dinghy that I had named *Skidbladner* and had brought along for the trip. It was just big enough for the two of us.

"Why do you call it skin-bladder?" she asked.

"*Skidbladner*. It is a ship in Norse mythology, a super lightweight ship built from cobwebs and bird spittle. The ship can be folded and kept in a pocket, even though it has enough space for thirty men."

"Well this one's barely big enough for the two of us," she replied, "And she doesn't keep her air very well."

"Don't be running down my boat," I replied, "It's unlucky to do that," and then I started the little outboard motor. We putt-putted out across the choppy harbor, and all the while she used the air pump clumsily to firm up the inflatable chambers. I had waited for her at the White Horse while getting weather updates at the old Cruise Ship Terminal building on Ordinance Island on the harbor. Many other boat owners and visiting yachtsmen were there for the same reason, looking for information about the approaching storm, with much discussion going on. The building had showers and other facilities and information, and it was a favorite hangout for cruisers.

"From what I'm seeing and hearing, it looks like we're going to catch it in a couple of days," I told Amélie. "So I will try to get everything secured today, with extra chafing gear. I'll dive on the anchor this morning."

There was a lot of work to do and Amélie did not seem to mind. "I've worked on a lot of boats," was all she said. At noon, with the sun directly overhead behind an increasing haze of high clouds, I wanted to dive, for the day had grown warm, but there was still much to do getting the boat secured. I had decided against removing the sails; that was a job to be done at the dock, and there was no room for a poor man's forty-foot wooden sailboat at the dock alongside of seventy-foot modern yachts preparing for an imminent cyclone. Instead of removing the sails, I wrapped them tightly on the spars with line so that the wind could not pull them free and tatter them, as I had initially favored. They were snugly lashed and as such were also tightly compressed and offered little resistance to the wind.

Everything down below was secured and all seacocks closed except the cockpit drains and the bilge pump outlet. I was not going to remain aboard during the storm. I donned a dive mask and dove over the side and in the clean, clear water, and worked my way down the anchor chain some ten feet or so. It was all good, strong chain, and the links were solid and not worn thinner at the contact points, since I had bought the chain fairly new. The shackles were all good and the pins were twist-wired well and I had no worries for that. I went down a second time, holding my breath until I thought my lungs would burst, and dimly saw that the entire anchor and most of the heavy chain at the end were well-buried in the harbor bottom. *Rugosa* might as well try to pull the foundation of St. George's out of the sea bottom, I said to myself.

I wrapped a piece of thick drainage hose around the anchor rode where it passed through the chock in the bow, to prevent chafe, and tied it off well. My anchor rode was spliced into the chain that made up most of the anchor rode, and I attached a heavy-duty snubber so that if the bow pitched, the chain would not go taut and rip my bitts out. As I worked from the uncertain dinghy, and then went back into the water to inspect the underside of the hull, Amélie jumped into the water with me to help.

"Can you put out an extra anchor?" she asked.

"I don't want them to tangle or wrap around each other," I replied. "The boat will need to swing, because the wind will change direction in a cyclone."

Now the boat was secure and the swim had taken away the overheating and perspiration from the work, so once we were back aboard, I uncorked a bottle of chilled white Italian wine and we sat in the cockpit resting and drinking the wine and chatting while the seawater slowly dried, leaving a dusting of fine salt on our skin. I had pulled a small block of hard cheddar from the icebox and put it out on the cockpit table. I sliced a fresh apple from the market, and opened a jar of cranberry chutney. In the Bermuda warmth and humidity the cheese soon had its own perspiration, and it began to soften. I had some English crackers that I had bought in the village and we snacked on the cheese and crackers and apple slices with the chutney, and washed it down with the dry white Soave while we slowly dried off.

What happened next was quite sudden and unexpected. I had gone down below looking for something or other, and she followed me down the ladder. When I turned around and faced her, she embraced me, and pulled me in to a long, eager, and sensuous kiss. There was a hunger in both of us; I surprised myself, for it had been many months, even a couple of years since I had held a woman in such a way; and everything in her caress and embrace seemed to want, to absorb, to possess. I did not resist, but returned the anxious desire. Her mouth tasted wine-sweet and warm, and she hugged me hard, squeezed me with her arms, and in a few moments, we had quickly stripped off our bathing suits and were making love on the bunk in the forepeak, paying no heed to anything else but the enthusiastic consummation of a desire that had grown quickly in the fertile ground of mutual deprivation, and which demanded full and complete satisfaction. There is no need to elaborate details; the reader's imagination and knowledge from experience can supply all that is needed. Amélie was small-boned, and only after we were lying together did I realize how delicate her frame actually was, but there was much energy in her, and in her strength there was gentleness, too. It was warmth; smoothness; firmness, squeezing, and searching, all at the same time, seeking pleasure while seeking to please. I thought that I knew all there was to know about making love to a woman since the time of my raw youth, but even now I found that I still had some to learn. Suffice to say that our lovemaking reminded me of my friend the old boat-builder's comment about steam-bending oak frames. They come out of the steam box pliable and rubbery, and before they are cool and no longer bendable, they must be quickly bent and fastened into place on the hull by the crew, working purposefully. "It was eager work," the old man said, reminiscing; and such was our lovemaking, or so I was thinking as we were doing it, eager work. It was passionate and over quickly, perhaps more quickly due to its intensity, and for a little while afterwards we lay on the bunk listening to the sounds of the wind in the rigging overhead and the slapping of the little waves of the harbor against the hull. A big powerboat went by, unseen by us, its wake rocking us slowly and slightly a few moments after it had passed. It would be dark soon.

"Come over to my flat," I said, "I have more wine, and besides, you can get a shower. I will light a fire in the fireplace; it's a very nice one." She nodded assent, happily.

We powered in on *Skidbladner* in the gathering dusk, after I had closed everything up and secured the hatches. The wind had begun to kick up in damp, restless gusts, and I could feel in the pit of my stomach that there was a significant storm coming.

Amélie followed me the short distance back to my apartment upstairs in the old Forge and with the help of some kindling of dried palm husks, I soon had an aromatic fire of Casuarina logs crackling away. We sat together on the small woven rug in front of the hearth basking in the warmth and the flickering yellow flames of the fire. I brought out a nearly-full bottle of aged Haitian rum that I'd traded an old ash shell block for, traded to a fellow from Australia who needed a traditional block for his Bermuda sloop that he had been rebuilding. The rum was old and sweet and smooth like black velvet, easy to sip and rich with molasses and it warmed my throat as it went down. The wind was buffeting the rooftops outside and I had seen the single red flag with the black square, signaling a whole gale, flying from the staff outside the Customs House as we were coming in with the dinghy.

"It will intensify during the night," I said, "God knows what it will be like in the morning."

Amélie leaned over toward me and rested against me, then put her head down in my lap, watching the fire. "Storms will come, and storms will go again," she said. "As they always have and always will." She turned and looked up at me, and beckoned for me to come closer; she pulled me down to her, and we lay together on the floor as the gale outside began to rattle the windows and roar in the chimney flue. Every once in a while the chimney would backdraft and send a cloud of blue smoke belching out of the fireplace like the exhaled snort of a disgusted dragon, forming a stratified smoky mist up near the ceiling. Amélie wanted to make love again, and this time we took our time, relaxed now from the effects of the rum.

"Do you remember the afternoon that we first met?" I asked her, as we sat on the rug afterwards in front of the fire, sipping rum.

"Of course I do. It was only a few days ago!"

"Oh, I know, but what I was going to tell you about was this awful thing I saw maybe an hour before I saw you in the water." And then I told her about the apparition in the stone passageway that I had seen on my way down to the beach.

She shuddered. "I can't go in there," she replied, shaking her head. "That place is haunted they say. It was once an old fort, and a place where they stored gunpowder."

"I won't go near it again," I replied. "It gave me the willies."

"But what do you think you saw?"

"I don't know," I replied. "Maybe I saw my death."

"Don't say that," she said. "I don't ever want to think about you dead. Thinking about death is unlucky, anyway."

"Right afterwards, I began to think that perhaps I should forget about continuing on this voyage," I said. "I have thought about that. Perhaps it was a warning. But then I realize that death comes to us all, and that there is no shame in death, only, as I said before, in not living while alive. So when death comes, it comes. *Cuando la muerte viene, viene.*" And with that mention, she hugged me in a comforting way. Then we sat for a while staring at the fire and at the little imaginary ghosts and demons whose shadows were cast upon the hearth by the flames. We spoke little, just sipped the rum and watched the fire and listened to the wind whistling about the baffles at the top of the chimney. When she finally moved to rise, I said, "Stay," and she stayed the night, both of us moving to the bed after a while so that we would not be sore in the morning from sleeping on the floor.

Of course, this was to be but the beginning; the novelty of lovemaking after such a long sabbatical for me did not grow stale. And Amélie's lovemaking was always very matter-of-fact; it was a cleanly and freely given in the same manner as a back-rub, or a massage of my shoulders, without drama, expectation, complications of guilt or things hidden or suspected of being hidden; it was out in the open. But was not shallow; it was loving, every movement, touch, and motion done sensually and with a purpose of contributing to the complete sensuality of it. When I had once been in high school, I had dated a girl who kept pet dogs, and loved horses. When we had sex, she would pat me like she patted her dogs, I had observed, which was unsettling, and even though I was a teen-ager in the prime of my sexual drive, I lost my taste for sex with her. Amélie had an enthusiasm that was whole and complete. She was energetic and gently strong, like a coiled spring, but without conveying tension. Is such a thing possible? And she literally became almost hot to the touch, which I had not experienced before with some of the cold northern girls from Massachusetts in my high school and even college years. So this was very different, and when the opportunity presented itself, why, unless the boat had sprung a plank and was sinking, I would always find time for it, I pledged to myself.

But now it was the morning of the gale, she was with me, and I got up first to put on a pot of coffee and get the weather forecast on my small VHF radio. The fireplace had long been cold and the first gray light of morning was filtering in through the wavy glass windows.

The Old Forge, being a stone building, did not shake or stir with each pummeling storm-driven gust, nor was it affected in any way other than the windows buffeted such that they rattled. Amélie took a steaming cup, and then donned her Musto foul weather jacket, rumpled khaki shorts and boat shoes.

"Are you going down to the boat?" she asked, groggily.

"To the sea wall, anyhow," I answered, pulling on my yellow oilskins.

"I will come with you," she said, "But I should go check in on Mom first."

"May I walk with you?" I asked.

"If you like, but only to the outside door, you know, I don't want her or the staff to see you, or questions and such from her this morning. We have to stop at my apartment first."

"I understand, believe me. Be sure to keep your head low," I cautioned, "Lots of stuff will be flying around."

Her flat was nothing more than an efficiency apartment in a rooming house down along the waterfront on the east end of the village, closer to the Town Cut inlet. "There's not much to the place," she apologized as we went in. "Looks nice," I offered. "Ground floor floods sometimes in big storms like this, but only when they hit at high tide," she added.

I noted that she had little clear jars of sea-glass everywhere, and a few small antique cobalt-blue and light aqua-colored bottles, even a couple of deep red ones, on shelves and window sills. "I collect sea glass," she told me, "I've been to every beach. The bottles come from old wrecks; there are many of them here in the waters around Bermuda. Diver friends have given them to me, and some I have salvaged myself."

"How?" I asked. "Are the wrecks in water that shallow?"

"Some," she said. "I used to scuba dive, you know. Not deep, just around. But no time anymore with Mom to take care of. You have to dive with a buddy, always. I certainly have friends to go with, but I just sort of lost interest in it a year or so ago."

Then she had to visit the little managed-care facility up the street where her mother lived. I waited outside in the rain and it seemed an eternity before she finally came back outside.

"Mom okay?" I asked.

"She's fine today. Has no idea that it's blowing a gale out here. She has good days and not so good days. Let's go."

She would not bring me to meet her mother, and quite frankly, I didn't want to meet her mother anyhow. I really wasn't interested in getting involved in any manner of familiarity with aging parents or family. I had my friendship with Amélie, and my sexual relationship, and was quite happy to leave it within that circumscribed boundary. Apparently her mother was not in a good way, not very well in terms of physical health, so Amélie preferred to see her alone.

Down at the cruise ship terminal the gale flag was snapping violently in the gusts that nearly blew us over as we tried to walk down the streets and alleys. A big palm frond had blown loose and wrapped itself like a mask over Sir George Somers' happy bronze face, as if God were covering it deliberately so that Somers would not have to watch the gale bust up and lay waste to the harbor. The skies were gray, with scudding low clouds dumping wind-driven sheets of streaming rain. The gale was blowing in from the southeast, racing across the low sky and through the tortured, shredding palm branches.

The main room of the terminal building was packed with wet, steamy, sweating, noisy sailors of all nationalities in oilskins, foul-weather jackets and boots, their hair wet, clumped and stringy, all looking for answers and help with their boats, or missing members of their crews.

I stepped out into a sheltered doorway and looked out onto the harbor. It was foaming white with spindrift from the driving wind, and boats on the harbor were plunging, pitching, and yawing in the angry chop that was whipping up to froth, but not bouncing about terribly. The relatively small size of the harbor and its sheltered nature prevented larger seas from forming. There was simply not enough fetch for them to grow. But Bermuda is a low island and there was little to stop the wind, and as a result it was howling and occasionally screaming through the rigging of boats on the docks and through trees and flag poles on shore. I could see *Rugosa* out on the harbor through the rain and white spray and she actually seemed to be doing nicely, sheltered in her position somewhat, simply swinging back and forth on her mooring pennant and heeling over a little once in a while from the force of the wind when she took a big gust on the beam. But she recovered quickly and I knew that without deep plunging or pitching, there would be little concern about chafing of the pennants.

"Does she look all right?" Amélie asked.

"She'll be fine as long as someone else doesn't drag down on her, or break loose and run down on top of her," I replied. "That's the biggest concern with a storm like this in a crowded harbor. It's not your boat you worry about, but other people's boats whacking into you."

Down on the wharf, where there was, I felt, more exposure to the harbor entrance, the wind was whipping up spindrift and mist as nearby boats on moorings and anchors bobbed and pitched uncomfortably on their pennants, like wild horses trying to break free of a hitching post. I could see Captain John Carver's big schooner out near the middle of the anchorage, a small yellow-clad figure was up on the bow and I assumed that it was Carver himself, tending to his chafing gear. I searched again for *Rugosa* in the wind and mist, straining to see her in the sea-fog and blowing spray, and turned to Amélie and asked,

"Do you see her?"

"Yes," she replied, "She's there all right."

But just then I heard two men shouting nearby, and a big outboard engine on a work boat roared to life and revved high. Two men in the boat were casting off their lines as fast as they could. They were Bermuda Maritime Ops boys; I knew the insignia on their jackets and their boat was marked.

"What's wrong?" I shouted.

"*Gleam*'s just broke loose," one shouted back. There were only two of them.

"I'll come with you," I barked, and impulsively jumped into the boat. One of them turned around, a look of dismay on his face, "You can't...."

"Coast Guard," I shouted. "American. Friend of Captain Carver!"

"Fine then," one of them shouted, "Put this life jacket on and let's go!" And the double-hulled skiff leaped away from the pier and out onto the wild harbor. I turned around, momentarily, to see Amélie standing on the pier, watching us, and she waved a good-luck wave, or so I assumed, as we bounded across the angry lagoon. In the turbulence I managed to get the life jacket on and secured properly. I held on; the senior man, whom I later learned was named George, motioned that I should toss a coil of heavy line to *Gleam* when we got close. Spray and spindrift were flying through the air all around us, and in only a matter of moments I was practically soaked. Now while we may not have been able to tow the big boat far in the storm, I knew, we would at least be able to get her bow into the wind and slow down her deadly downwind drift across the harbor to the inevitable rocks and shoals at the far end. I could see the figure of Carver moving toward the bow again; he had gone aft and started *Gleam*'s engine, and was now in the bow pulpit waiting for the line to be cast to him.

George maneuvered the BMO rescue boat up close to the schooner, and as he did, I threw the line, which landed squarely in the middle of Captain John's chest. In a matter of a few seconds he had slipped it through the bow chocks and secured it to the bitts on the foredeck. As George gunned the boat's engine and put a strain on the line, the BMO boat bucked and yawed, slewing to the left and to the right, while angry water slopped aboard from both sides. The bow of *Gleam* gradually came around, and then I noticed that Carver was gone from the bow and had moved to his cockpit and was now powering the big schooner ahead and steering to assist the efforts of the rescue boat. Gradually, we began to make headway together across the harbor to the deep windward side, in the lee of the land, where the chop began to subside due to the closeness of the land's shelter, but the wind was still horrible.

"We're going to put him on a BMO mooring," George shouted to me. "Can you go aboard and help him, once we get a little closer under the lee?"

"Yes, I can."

"It will have to be soon," he continued, "The mooring is coming up, and I don't want to get her into shallow water."

"Put me aboard now," I called out.

George revved the engine down and backed down quickly alongside *Gleam.* The schooner was still moving forward under power of its own engine, but was unlikely to be able to hold herself into the wind for very long. As we came alongside, I reached up, grabbed two stanchions, and, standing on the gunwale of the BMO boat, pulled myself up and slid under the lifelines and onto the deck of *Gleam.* George immediately pulled away, putting tension once again on the tether, and bringing *Gleam*'s bow back into the wind as both boats clawed their way toward the mooring ball fifty yards ahead. I scrambled back to the cockpit, and Carver shouted, "On the foredeck! I'll get her there, you make her secure!" And so forward I went to the plunging bow, salt spray blinding me, stinging my eyes. At least it was warm, I noted.

A strong line was already prepared on the bow with one end cleated off. Lying next to it where Carver had coiled it was the painter from the other mooring, and the line was still connected to part of a rusted, broken shackle. Now, with the good, new line that Carver had attached when we were watching him up on the bow, I was able to pass the other end to George's helper in the boat as George maneuvered it just under *Gleam*'s bow. He took the end of it and passed it through a steel ring on the top of the mooring float and sent it back to me; I was hanging off the bowsprit and it took three tries for me to grab it. At one point *Gleam*'s dolphin striker came down with the bow settling into a trough and I thought it would poke a hole through the BMO boat, but George kept the boat clear at the last minute and the striker just missed impaling George and the bottom of the BMO boat. It was quick work; I secured the end of the long loop of line to the bitts while at the same time releasing their tow line. I looked up; they were pulling away quickly, George pointing in the direction of another yacht across the harbor that had also, apparently, broken loose. Carver eased the throttle and the looped line took up the strain. The mooring held, and *Gleam* was secure and safe on a good government mooring, but I had concerns about the line chafing where it looped through the iron ring. Carver made his way forward, inspected everything, with the engine still running, and then frowned, shook his head, and motioned for me to follow him. We then crawled aft on hands and knees to the cockpit, where Carver shut off the engine and motioned for me to follow him belowdecks. At least it was dry down in the cabin and the motion of the boat stable now that she was secure and pointed into the wind.

"So, what did they leave you here?" he chuckled gruffly. "Well, *THAT*'s not nice! Here, hang up your oilies, dry off." He set two glasses on the dinette table in the main saloon and pulled the cork out of a large, ancient green tubby captain's decanter, and it came out with a deep-throated 'whum', and then poured dark rum into both glasses, each with a few anemic ice cubes in the bottom. "Sorry about the ice," he muttered, "I haven't been running the generator much. Well anyway," he lifted his glass for a toast, "I really appreciate you hopping aboard like that and helping me out. Don't know where the rest of my crew is, the scallywags! Couple of useless scamps! Here!"

I eagerly drank the smooth, silky old rum, and it warmed all the way down. "Happy to help," I said. "But I would keep an eye on that mooring connection, it could easily chafe."

"Oh, it will, but I expect this gale to blow by fairly quickly. Also as it clocks around we will be more in the shelter of St. David's so there should be less motion at the bow. Again it all depends on how long this continues to blow, but just the same, I would rather get a length of chain on it, or better yet if there is a mooring pennant shackled to the top chain below the ball, and I didn't see one, it would be good to get hold of it and secure it to the boat as insurance in case this line chafes through."

"I agree," I said, "but it might be tricky trying to work it from a dinghy."

He cradled his drink in his hands, staring down at it, or perhaps through it, "Hmmm, yes let's wait a while. I can't get you ashore at the moment, not unless those patrol guys come back for you. I have only one dinghy, the inflatable that's bouncing around the stern, and it would be crazy to try to go off in it right now. Hell, we've got rum here, no need to go anywhere!" And with that final comment his voice rose and he laughed heartily.

We rode out the worst part of the storm aboard *Gleam* all the while checking the mooring pennant from time to time, but we were becoming increasingly wobbly, thanks to the rum, the more the afternoon wore on. Every now and then, from the deck of *Gleam*, I caught a glimpse of my *Rugosa* riding out the gale. Carver gave me the comprehensive tour of *Gleam*, allowing me to inspect every cabin, engine space, and storage space. *Gleam* was a beautiful yacht, and her interior was exquisite, with beautiful woodwork everywhere in evidence. The main scuttle from the main cabin below to the cockpit could only be described as a hardwood staircase, complete with a bannister and turned spindles, and even a mahogany newel-post at the bottom.

Carver invited me to sail along with him some time. "It takes four hands to sail this old girl," he said. "I can get by with three, or even one very good hand plus myself, but that's cutting it close, and of course not for long-distance passagemaking. You need four to stand the 'round-the-clock watch schedule."

"Where are you sailing next?" I asked.

"I want to go to the Pacific," he answered, "The Society islands. Tahiti. The haunts of the great old captains, like Cook, Bligh, the early navigators. Imagine what it must have been like to be sailing a full-rigged ship in those days in uncharted waters and making those kinds of discoveries."

"There can be down-sides," I replied.

"What's that?"

"Well, Captain Cook was, well, cooked, and apparently eaten," I said.

"Oh, ha, ha!" he laughed, "Yes, I guess he was, wasn't he? Well too bad for him. Did you ever read Dana's classic, *Two Years Before the Mast*?"

"Many years ago, I think."

"Well remember they had a crewman aboard, and old guy, a Maori or something like that, and he had no teeth, and the young guys used to tease him terribly. They told him that he had lost his teeth eating that tough old Britisher, Captain Cook. And the old guy would get all upset, just like clockwork, you know, which is probably why they kept baiting him time and again. He would get all passionate and declare, 'Me no eat Captain Cook! Sandwich Islanders eat Captain Cook!' Something like that."

"They knew his hot button," I said.

"That they did."

Just before dusk, in late afternoon, I poked my head up under the pram-hood dodger covering the scuttle and saw the BMO boat approaching in the distance. The wind had moderated somewhat, clocked around from the southwest, and the sun looked as though it were trying to break through. "Looks like they've come back for me," I called out to Carver, below.

"You going with them?" he called out.

"What about you?" I said.

"I'll go ashore in a bit in the dinghy."

"It's still pretty rough," I said.

"Nah. Fuck it."

"I'll go in with you, then, if that's okay."

"Sure."

The BMO boat came near, and I went out on deck. They saw me; they looked exhausted. I pointed to the dinghy and then to me and waved them off. They nodded, indicating that they understood, and then motored away.

"Bring a change of dry clothes in a plastic bag, Captain John," I called down to him, "You can change at my place. I figure we'll get plenty wet going in." I was already plenty wet now but being half-soused on his rum, I didn't much care. I grabbed the dinghy's painter and pulled it in close to the schooner. The dinghy was afloat but full of water. I jumped into the dinghy with a big splash and began bailing it out. Carver appeared at the gunwale, looking over the edge; "Good man!" He then proceeded to climb into the newly bailed out dinghy with me, which was considerably more stable. The engine started for him, and we were off on a wild, inebriated, wet, bouncy, perilous ride to shore. The ride became smoother the closer we got to the pier, and we worked our way in to quiet water and tied off the dinghy to an 18th Century cannon that stood inverted and half buried at the edge; a quaint sight, it was one of the many antique cannon that served as dock bollards in St. George's.

"I need something to eat," he said. "How about you?"

"Just what I was thinking," I replied.

The bar at the White Horse was crowded with boating and sailing people, all wet, all becoming increasingly loud and drunk. But they were happy; nobody had lost a boat. The crowd was an array of wet yellow rubber jackets, damp shorts, and hairy bare legs terminating in wet deck shoes or boat sandals, all heads capped off with damp ball caps or heads of stringy, wet hair. English, Australian, New Zealand, French, and American voices were the dominant ones, with the air punctuated by a peal of laughter from some corner of the room every couple of minutes or so. The storm had passed and it was time to celebrate. I was soaked from bailing out the dinghy, but it was warm water in a warm climate and I knew that I would dry out fairly soon. Carver had already ordered a round of his favorite rum punch for us, and I could feel the flushed redness in my own face from the afternoon's time aboard *Gleam*. No matter, I thought. I looked around the crowd, searching for Amélie, but did not see her. My heart sank. *Perhaps she went over to check on her mother again,* I said to myself. But the fact that I could not locate her bothered me, and almost as though he knew what I was thinking, Carver asked, "So where's your little hottie?"

"Ah, well I don't know…don't see her…but I imagine that she'll be on by at some point."

I learned a lot about John Carver that night. He was a true free spirit, a buccaneer of sorts, loud and energetic, a forceful but engaging personality, and always a good soul. But he had no tolerance for fools, or idiots, or people of ill intent or sour disposition. He would not suffer them. But at the same time, he did not fit the classic mold of a Yankee skipper. He had come of age during the 1960s and had a certain part of him, from his long, shoulder-length blond hair to his Viking-style blond moustache that was clearly counterculture. "Hell," he said at one point, "I've made this trip south so many times when I was younger, we never really prepared. Whoever we were as a crew, bunch of friends mostly, we took boats back and forth to the Caribbean, sometimes with nothing more than a bunch of bread and peanut butter to eat for the trip. We'd fly home on a plane out of San Juan, and back in those days we would go into the toilets at the back of the plane and spark up a joint. That was before they put smoke detectors in the toilets. But ha ha, the next person in knew for sure what had been going on inside with the last occupant!" He laughed. "We were pretty care-free back then."

Carver was a flamboyant guy full of *joie de vivre*. He laughed when he told me about how, on occasion, he would be walking down a street only for some guy passing in a pickup truck to honk at him from behind, thinking that he was a big blonde woman, only to look in his side mirror and be mortified to realize that he had honked at a big long-haired blond guy with a big moustache. This amused Carver greatly whenever he recalled such incidents. "I would wave to them after they drove by," Carver laughed, continuing, "That made them feel even worse, I'm sure!"

Despite his age, at nearly sixty-five years old, his animal instincts were still healthy, active, and strong. A petite young woman named Sabine, and I say 'young' meaning under forty, crewing on a French boat sat down briefly at our little pub table. She had met Carver earlier in the week, and she seemed to be unattached. She was petite physically, but a known competitive sailor and the combination of physical attractiveness and sure-footed self-confidence drew Carver to her like a bright lamp captivates a moth in the night. Carver's focus shifted, suddenly; he was 'locked on', as I suppose the fighter jet pilots say, and would, if she would have allowed him, move in for the kill. She occupied his attention and his conversation almost completely. I had to smile. His response to the girl seemed almost uncontrollable and involuntary, even automatic on his part. Nor could he hide it. Never, I thought, have I seen a fellow who so obviously wants to get into a girl's pants as Carver, and he is probably utterly unaware of how visible it is, and on top of that, probably doesn't care a whit, either!

I would have continued having no one to speak to, but at last I was rescued by Amélie, who came in, made a beeline for our table, and I pulled back a chair for her. Now there were four of us, a balanced foursome, with Sabine, whose name might well have been 'Siren' as far as Carver was concerned. All was going well, until the food was brought over to the table. As mentioned earlier, the cuisine at the tavern could vary in quality, depending on who might be the chef that particular day, or how crowded the place might be, putting a certain amount of stress on the kitchen staff when business was brisk; but in general it was quite satisfactory, depending of course on the menu choice selected. As with most tavern food, the longer one patronizes a pub or tavern, the sooner one learns what selections are consistently good or reliable, and which ones are to be avoided, always. This was the case with the White Horse as well; there were a number of items that one could be quite certain that would never be quite up to snuff, on any day, for that matter. Amélie had warned me that the steak was one of them.

I had to stray from the table briefly, but as I was returning, I heard a loud commotion coming from our table, and saw John Carver standing up, his face red and his demeanor one of obvious unpleasant agitation. The two girls (and several other people around the table) seemed to be looking on in horror as Carver held a piece of his flank steak up over his head on his fork. He was shouting at the cook, who had come out of the kitchen to see what was the matter; the cook had been interrupted in the kitchen by the very agitated young man waiting on our table.

"I wouldn't feed this to my DOG!" Carver shouted angrily, now waving the unfortunate piece of beef in the air and jabbing it in the direction of the cook.

"Oh, my," I heard myself say, and I noticed that Sabine appeared to be utterly mortified, watching her Captain friend with undisguised horror. Rejoining the table, I was made to understand, right away, that the issue was the toughness of the steak. *Well,* I thought, *Amélie could have warned you, Captain.* I looked over at Amélie, and was nearly shocked to note that she was apparently quite amused by the whole scene and was doing her best to keep from laughing out loud, while it was all that Sabine could do to keep from pouting.

"Captain, it can't be that bad, can it?" I said, sitting down again.

"That bad?" he repeated, "That bad? It's like an old sea-boot. Like a god-damned horse's hoof!"

"Maybe a white horse?"

Now he laughed. "Yeah, maybe! That would be about right, ha, ha. Cripes! I couldn't chew the damned thing!"

The waiter was all apologies, and I felt bad for him, but of course there was nothing for me to say or do about it. He cleared it off the bill for the table, even though Carver had eaten most of it before launching into his tirade of indignation.

Two days later, Carver and I were having a beer at the tap late in the after-noon. It was a warm day, very sunny and bright outside. Carver was in the bar with his two young crewmen, Sam and Billy, who had emerged from the Bermudian wilderness in time to help their Captain get *Gleam* ready for sea. "Wasn't sure if we'd get Billy back," John said as Morgan filled our frosted mugs. "He shacked up with some chick over on the other end of the island, near the Dockyard. What's that, Ireland Island or something? When did you tell her you were leaving, this morning, ha ha!"

"No, she knew I was leaving," Billy said, sheepishly.

"Sure she did. But it's good that you came back to the boat. Otherwise you'd have to marry her," he teased.

"Don't want that."

"I have to get out of here in a week," I said to Carver. "My visa's up, so to speak. And besides, I have been here long enough now. It's time to be moving on."

"Your girlfriend going with you?" he asked.

"No, she can't go. And besides, this is not that kind of trip. I'm sailing alone."

"That's a bit dangerous," he said. "You could find a crewman to sail down to the islands with you, if you ask around a bit. Would you like me to?"

"No, Cap, no thanks."

"You could get yourself killed single-handing. You know that."

"I'm not afraid to, actually more afraid of hanging around here too long and not doing it."

"Amen to that, brother." He took a long pull on his mug of beer. "Well, we're leaving tomorrow. Heading down to the B.V.I's first, then we're Antigua bound. I'm heading to St. Martin along the way. Maybe we'll catch up with you down in the islands."

"Maybe," I said. "I hope so."

He gave me a strong slap on the back, and shook my hand. "Be careful, good luck, Captain Nate! Safe voyaging!"

"Aye, Captain John, same to you. Fair winds and following seas to *Gleam* and her crew." And with that, the three of them left the tavern.

On the morning of my day of departure, Amélie and I were walking and climbing around the earthworks of an old fort called Alexandra's Battery. The grasses were high around the perimeter of the little park and the air was redolent with the spicy scent of wild fennel. I walked through the high fennel, grabbing and crushing it with my hands, and catching the sweet, exotic scent in my palms from the crushed blossoms and stalks. *In the end, there is no safety in staying anywhere,* I observed, only stagnation and the gnawing uneasiness of not knowing. Life is a passage, a transit punctuated by waypoints and occasional landfalls. But there is no salvation in abandoning the voyage; that is an illusion, because the voyage that is life continues relentlessly. All one loses is time in delay, and self-denial of vistas and experiences lost or postponed. We become soft through inactivity, without the struggle to temper our spirits, like fire hardening a wooden spear-point. We lose our nerve and our spirit if we stay behind and hide amongst the palm fronds and succulent leaves in the cool, dark damp of the garden. Words of scripture came to mind: "For whoever would save his life, shall lose it."

Out on the harbor, the sun-dappled wavelets raised by the freshening breeze sparkled brilliantly, like bright diamonds, reflecting into my eyes; boats at anchor became silhouettes on a canvas of moving, fiery bold brush dots of light and color thickly applied by an impressionist. Despite my feelings of apprehension, it was time to move on, to set sail, and to head south to the tropics.

"Must you leave already?" Amélie asked, once again, her arms around me as we sat together in the grass at the top of the earthen fort. She knew that the answer was always going to be the same, but I believe that she hoped, with the slimmest of hopes, that I would change my mind. Of course she was anxious; she wanted me to stay. But we both knew that it was not to be.

"I have to follow my dream," I said. "I used to believe in what Melville once said, 'Stay true to the dreams of your youth."

"Do you still have those dreams?"

I paused for a moment, considering. "I still remember them," I replied.

"Then they are gone?"

"I don't think about them too often. I did not know it back then, but most were not practical. At least that's what others have said. I've been called a 'dreamer.' I was scolded by my grandparents for having my head in the clouds rather than on the ground. I said one time that I wanted to be a writer, and Grandmother told me, *pshaw*, that's a rich man's hobby, didn't I know better? Get a good secure job in a factory somewhere with benefits, ride it for the rest of your life. Know your place in the world; don't aspire to rise above your station."

"You rejected that."

"I have always believed that with my good mind, and sufficient energy, I could be whoever and whatever I wanted; the future was a book of blank pages waiting for me to fill in with glorious chapters. But now as the clock runs down, I am crossing out one more line after another of possibilities. It's a bitter job, but then I sigh and realize, as I look at some of them, that they never really were achievable. Most of them never had a practical chance. Sometimes you have to start out in a certain place, or with certain tools, to achieve a goal, like being born rich, or having a father who is a Congressman. I had none of that."

"But you need to have dreams that are above what you think you can do. You have to set the bar a little higher. You must have challenges, but not impossible ones."

"Some were lost simply because I made poor choices, or at the very least, not the best choice," I continued. "I have regrets, I suppose everyone does. But I do not think of them often, nor do I speak of them. What would be the use? I have a boat load of them. Dwelling on them would make me ill. The past is etched in stone; it cannot be erased. It will always come back; the past will always haunt the man who has even a smidgeon of conscience. So I try to keep my eyes ahead all the time; there is nothing else, in the end, but the ever-changing future. That is challenge enough. Remember that we do not begin to truly grow old until we cease to dream. So this is my dream now. All the old ones are dead."

"So you are resolved to go. But you know that I can't go with you," she said, and began to cry, softly.

"I know. We have already talked about this. But I cannot stay here, either. The Bermudian Government is kicking me out."

"There is nothing anyone can do about that. But what can I do? My mother is in the nursing home now. I cannot leave here. I have to stay by her."

"That is something that you must do. You have no real choice."

"I wish you would stay, though. I could say that I needed you."

"But I don't want to be needed anywhere," I replied. "To be so only makes it harder to continue onward."

"I just don't understand that," she replied, frustrated, wiping the tears off her cheeks. "But I guess you have to go and do what you have to do, all alone. Follow the dream wherever it takes you. Maybe it will eventually bring you back to me."

"The earth is round, after all," I said.

This made her smile; "Well then," she said, with a tone of finality, "Let's go get you off the dock." We went down to the pier and she helped me finish loading the dinghy, and saw me off. "If you don't come back to me, I will come find you," she called after me, as I rowed away from the dock. She waved.

And yet, as I motored out through Town Cut and onto the broad and open blue, I felt almost ill; and I realized that I had never before felt so reluctant to depart any port in my entire life as much as I did now. I had to fight the urge to turn around and head back in. I fell into a foul mood, angry, depressed, full of regret, questioning everything I had planned to do and was doing, filled with uncertainty, foreboding, and nervous frustration. I knew that I would feel better once I was back into my seagoing routine, and no longer within sight of the island, but that was as yet many hours ahead.

Chapter 11

Passage South

"The sea drives truth into a man like salt."

— *Hilaire Belloc*

I was now focused entirely on heading out to sea as I passed through the rock wall of Town Cut and motored out of the channel. I hoisted my sails once I was a mile out on the open sea. I had much work to do, and had to focus completely on navigating my boat, trimming the sails, setting my course, and essentially getting back into the rhythm of the sea and making my passage. The color of the sea was sapphire, and the sun was warm and bright with a gentle breeze blowing across the island as my ship and I passed out beyond the sea-buoy, where the reality of being out on the open ocean once again dominated all. A gentle swell was working down from the northwest, and the cliff faces of Great Head were beginning to fade into the shadows of the declining day and rising mist.

As I watched the safety and security of solid ground retreat into the distance, now rising and falling with the timeless and unending rhythm of the sea, I felt again the familiar pang of instinctive anxiety, of separation from the land, of a wish, after darkness fell, that the fading glow of the island on the horizon astern would not disappear, but remain with me. I could not stop facing aft, watching the land shrink and fade into my wake. The smell of the land now once again vanished, leaving me with the cloying salt tang of the deep, and my uneasiness would not go away, no matter how I tried to dispel it. That is the problem always with a landfall, I reminded myself. Stay too long, and you may never leave; and even a short stay can be too long, like the comparative experience of the reformed smoker who has quit smoking for years, but then smokes a single cigarette and the addiction is back with full force, and kicking the habit is as difficult as if there had been no long period of abstinence, but uninterrupted continuity.

Rugosa was motor-sailing in moderate airs, off the wind, and I had engaged the autopilot, whom I judged the best helmsman second to myself, and thoroughly indefatigable, unerringly accurate, and quite capable now that the high seas of the first leg of my passage were, at least for the time being, behind me. So I sat in the cockpit, checking the navigation system, and keeping a lookout for other vessels. I left the helm to run below for a cup of hot tea and a snack, a slice of multi-grain bread smeared with chunky peanut butter. It was now after dark and all I could see of Bermuda remaining was the flash of St. David's light barely above the horizon.

Back in the cockpit, my uneasiness persisted, and I was sitting by the wheel feeling tired, drowsy even, nearly nodding off, when I heard a faint, almost indiscernible sound that raised the hair on the back of my neck and sent a shiver of quiet terror creeping through me, a shiver of what I can only describe as a deep, detached blend of terror mixed with a greater proportion of fascination, like having a waking dream in which a Seraph of dreadful power and light is standing at the foot of the bed. I was listening to music that was unearthly beautiful, ethereal, and lush, like a choir of angels; the music was high, and strange, just out of my range of hearing, and the more I strained to hear it, the more elusive it became. I was fully awake now, and intensely focused, entranced; the music came from nowhere and everywhere at once, and was incredibly lush and melodic, ornate, sweet, complex, and captivating. Although seemingly more at sensing than actual hearing, I knew nonetheless that I was hearing it with my ears as well as with my soul. I thought of Mozart and Fauré together writing for the choirs of angels; no music ever heard on earth; the singing of Sirens. I remained transfixed, straining mightily to hear individual notes, or words, in the nearly still air.

Never have I concentrated with greater intensity, eyes staring straight ahead unseeing as my mind worked at great pace to comprehend and understand, but the more I struggled to bring it close, the further it drifted away, like fruit from the grasping reach of Tantalus. If all the great masters of music, having died and gone to the realms of Heaven were, after centuries, composing for the ranks of heavenly hosts, would this be the product of their collaboration? Masterworks beyond the comprehension of mortal man?

But then came a darker thought; what grave of sunken souls at the bottom of the abyssal plain has the shadow of my keel crossed this night? What sad wreck of drowned spirits trapped in the still blackness of the depths has the proximity of my passage disturbed? *Los Cantos de Los Muertos*. I whispered a prayer for them, as we passed, in my mind's eye, over the nameless wreck.

A fresh gust of wind suddenly puffed in from a different direction, threatening to jibe the mainsail; this broke the spell, now that there was work to do. I heard the music no more that night, or any subsequent night, but the memory of it haunted me for days afterward.

Prior to departure from St. George's, I had filled my water tanks, and had topped off my diesel at the fuel dock. I had even purchased six additional yellow fuel jugs and had secured them to the stanchions along either side of the boat, lashing them down so that I would not lose them in bad weather if she started shipping green water. I had also taped around the hatches and dorades to prevent water ingress. But after the first week I found these preparations to have been mostly unnecessary; the weather was warming, the winds and seas moderating, and the forecast that I heard on the single sideband was for lighter and lighter airs the closer I came to the waters of the Caribbean in the days ahead. Once I was certain that the weather prognosis was good, and in fact on some days I was motoring most of the time, I began to remove the tape so that I could open the hatches and better ventilate the boat.

More and more, my mast-top kept company with brilliant white tropic-birds, their long slender tails trailing gracefully behind as they kept up with my progress in long, slow, easy circles, and they cheered my heart. "We are sailing ever-closer to the islands of the coconut palms, and places where I will find RUM!" I called out to them, happily. "Green and lush tropical islands for me. So are you showing me the way? Stick around, I like your company!" And so it went, my spirits becoming increasingly buoyant the further south my position on the chart progressed.

Occasionally I fished, and on a couple of occasions landed a brilliant, colorful mahi, or a wahoo. It was by far preferable to any of my canned goods, and I have always liked fish, anyway. I did not tire of fresh fish, and it kept well in the icebox.

I deflated the dock fenders after leaving St. George's and stowed them nice and flat and stacked well aft in the storage space near the transom. They took up far too much room inflated, and I did not want to stow them on deck because they would become obstacles. Since I would not need them for some time, there was no issue, and besides, I had a small 12-volt inflator pump that would easily fill them all again once I arrived. Although I planned to anchor or moor most of the time, I would still need to tie up to a dock at some point for fuel and water, and I would certainly need them then. Many old docks and piers were stone or con-crete without adequate (or sometimes any) fenders or protection, and thus not very hull-friendly.

Before I left Bermuda, I obtained as current a weather forecast as I possibly could. The forecast predicted some strong winds for the first few days, all out of the northeast, then east, then southeast, getting lighter the further the days went on, and the further south I could manage. Coming out of Bermuda, my course, once offshore, was pretty basic; I would steer 180 degrees, due south, for nearly a thousand miles. With the exception of light airs a few hundred miles east of Florida, I should eventually be in the easterly trades, and having gained enough 'easting' on my passage to Bermuda, I should be able then to sail on my due south course on a beam reach, which would be ideal since my boat, being a gaff rig, did not beat well to windward. I would be able to adjust my sails, lash my helm, and run for days steadily with the wind always out of an easterly or southeasterly direction. But first I had to get through the stormy weather that I knew was coming for the first couple hundred miles heading south. I knew that once I reached the trades and warmer weather, or "when the butter melts" as famed sailor Don Street has written, I would also be able to run the auto-steering, with my propeller shaft generator feeding my batteries and the steering machine, I would catch up on needed sleep that had been lost in the stormy days following my departure from Bermuda. If the wind died, I could motor for many miles, and of course the electricity from the engine running would take care of the auto steering, of that there was no question. But even though I had plenty of diesel in reserve, it was better not to use it unless absolutely necessary. I also needed to run the radar while I slept.

Two days out from Bermuda, the weather turned foul, and the wind piped up to twenty-five knots and even to 45 at times. Seas grew large and steep and I had to triple-reef my mainsail. I did not sleep well, and I had little appetite. I mostly drank hot tea without sweetener, and my food was almost exclusively bread with peanut butter, or a piece of fruit, or a hard-boiled egg. I bought whole grain bread in Bermuda and to keep it from spoiling too early as the weather warmed, I kept it in the icebox. I ate crackers and biscuits, avoiding all spicy or greasy food. My stomach was tender and anything smelling strong or oily would make my gorge rise, and although I never retched, I felt like it quite a few times until after five days when my stomach adjusted. But there was no time to cook; there was too much work to do. Just grab a banana, an orange or an apple, some peanut butter bread, or in the morning, if the seas weren't too bad, I would have a small bowl of granola cereal with Parmalat milk with a piece of fruit and that stood me in good stead for the better part of the morning, and of course always with hot unsweetened tea. Days later when the weather began to calm down somewhat, I started making my coffee again, and expanded my meals to include other protein items and rounded out my diet even more. My appetite was slow to return while I was behind on my sleep, but once I was down into easier conditions and could reduce my cumulative sleep deficit, my appetite returned in force and I began supplementing my evening meal, whether it came from a can or from my trailing fishing line, with a glass of red wine, and this improved my overall outlook, as well as my mood. When I was able to finally open and relish a tin of sardines, mackerel, or other fish, or a can of small finger sausages to snack on, I knew that I was fully restored.

When the seas were high, I had to spend more time on the helm, because I could not run the auto steering in high seas. The mechanism simply couldn't handle it. My mainsail was triple-reefed and still we were going like hell, which for *Rugosa* was eight knots and sometimes nine. When the gale had finally moderated enough for me to shake out that third reef and run only double-reefed, I knew that I was gradually working my way into better weather as I approached the trade winds belt.

With the advent of gradually calmer weather, my daily routine regained some normalcy. I began my day with coffee and something to eat, and then checked the radar and my surroundings for any contacts, or other ships. If I noted another ship, and occasionally I would see a bulk carrier or even a cruise ship, though the latter quite rarely, I would attempt to contact them via the VHF radio to obtain an updated local forecast. The masters of these ships, regardless of their flag, were usually helpful and responsive and their English passable, meaning of course that I could understand it, which was as much as I needed. Then I would visit my usual favorite single sideband channels for even more forecast information and anything else in the way of information that might turn out to be useful.

I properly kept a daily logbook, noting such things as distance traveled during the night, current position, current condition of the boat and its systems, the weather and forecast, course steering, speed, sail configuration, wind direction, and other observations having to do with other ships, fish or animals seen, and of course water and fuel tankage estimates. I had kept this log since I left New England, and although I had not been able to keep it up on some days, I filled the pages in as best I could later on, as I wanted it to be as complete and accurate a record of the voyage as possible.

During the first few days of the voyage, I did not think much about Amélie; in fact I was so busy dealing with sailing my ship, handling her in rough seas and keeping my boat safe and under control that I did not have much time to think about her. In fact I think I spent a good deal of time trying not to think about her, which of course actually meant that I was thinking about her, or that she was present in my conscious mind but that I was not thinking about her in detail. I knew that I had to stay focused on the voyage, and also recognized that if I were to allow emotional matters to take control, I could compromise my own safety by becoming distracted, and out here there was no one to save me or correct my mistakes. The sea is unforgiving of the smallest lapse in judgment or focus, and that can be fatal on the broad ocean. Did I miss Amélie? Well of course I did, but then again I had not taken a great deal of time to get to know her, or her me, perhaps because she knew that my place in her life, at least for the moment, was destined to be transient. I was a sailor on a solo voyage, not a person to start growing a relationship with, since in any relationship, the closer two people grow, the more it hurts when eventually they must part, for whatever reason. So perhaps we each deliberately held ourselves back, to spare being wounded. Yet at the same time, I was determined to make my voyage, and she certainly knew this, and would not have been able to dissuade me. She must have known that even if she had, I could not be happy, always wondering 'what if' I had continued on my way. Besides, she had the responsibility of caring for her mother, I reasoned, and she could not walk away from that any more than I could abandon my voyage to remain with her. Since she had so recently been in an emotionally crushing relationship, she was reluctant to so quickly forge new bonds of the same nature which, if broken, could be equally painful once again. And yet she had asked me to stay…

I smiled when I thought about the sex; it had been so goodfor us both, but it was not the same thing as a deep relationship. And yet it was not a bad thing; something good could happen to soothe our souls and satisfy our physical needs without hurt, aye, without any damage, much less lasting damage. And hell, it had actually been fun. Now as I began to think back about it, and miss it, I suddenly realized that I was daydreaming again, falling under a spell in that remembrance, and laughing at myself, chided, "You old sea-goat, you!" and broke free of it; this was no time for erotic daydreams, forgetting myself and gybing the mainsail, probably break a running backstay and broach the damn boat. "Back to work!" I shouted aloud, to myself.

But one night during the voyage south, I dreamed of her, a very vivid dream. We were both aboard *Rugosa* and we were sailing south together to the Caribbean. I was making my way down the ladder from the cockpit where I had been steering, and as I did so, I saw that she was asleep in the berth up forward. I leaned over and nuzzled her body with my face and nose as she lay covered by a white sheet, my tanned skin against her smooth brown arm, smelling lightly of salt and sun-toasted with the faint floral aura of long-ago perfume. "Amélie," I whispered, my new beard now scratchy against her, but she did not awaken. I could hear the wind rising, freshening, and the boat had slowly begun to plunge ahead more determinedly, with a greater eagerness, it seemed, through the long swells. It would not be long before I would have to go back on deck to make adjustments to the sails. "Amélie."

And so I caressed her warm firm body and she began to stir, then at last opened her eyes and looked into mine, questioningly, her eyes moist and still sleepy behind clear dark crystal. She reached around me with both arms and pulled me down into the bunk with her, close and firmly up against her. She yawned. "Did we travel far during the night?" she asked.

"Yes, we did well. Some forty miles by the log."

"Oh." She pondered this seemingly trivial fact for a moment, then stowed it away in some inner closet where it might be examined later and become more than merely a number. "Whether or not it is significant is only relative to wherever we are going," she mused. "If we are going around the world, then it is not terribly far. Were you up all night?"

"No," I said. "I slept at times, I always do. But now the wind is freshening, and I will have much work to do."

"Is there a change in the wind?"

"Direction? No. But the glass is falling, we may have some developing weather soon."

She lay wrapped in the white Bermudian sheets, still fresh as clean muslin from the St. George's laundry, but now she pulled me closer. "You will have plenty of time to romance the wheel," she said. "But first you must pause and make time to romance me." Her lips met mine and they were warm; she was eager to make love, and I was taken by surprise somewhat when she unwrapped the warm bedclothes to reveal that she was completely undressed beneath. We made love and although it was unhurried, it was eager and intense.

"Now you can go on deck," she said after we had finished, drawing her finger across the beads of new sweat on my chest. "I will make coffee."

I awoke just before sunrise without my shirt and with beads of sweat on my chest, lying on my back on my bunk. It had been a sweet dream, seeming to be so real that I had actually thought that it was while I was dreaming. I could not go back to sleep then, so I got up and made coffee for myself, just as Amélie had promised to do in the dream. And I began to wonder if leaving her behind in Bermuda had really been what I wanted. But then I reminded myself that because of her mother, she could not leave anyway, so that was the finality of it.

As the weather grew distinctly warmer, it reminded me of voyages in the past, particularly my first solo passage in the tropics, where it had come as something of a radical thought that my clothing had little use for me, or I for it, in the increasingly warm and humid climate. Although the constant breezes such as the trade winds made life tolerable, I recognized that in the absence of society around me, or of human company or human eyes, I had no cause for modesty. So I shed my clothing, and after the initial strangeness of it, I chuckled, for I felt emancipated from the socially imposed constraints that were clothing and the ridiculous need to wear clothes. All is vanity! Each day I scanned the horizon many times, and never saw another vessel. I could go about my vessel with nary a stitch on, and with no one to notice, and with no flush of embarrassment or of shame. I began to remove my clothes until I wore only boat shoes, for the practicality of moving about on deck sure-footed during the day, and without the possibility of painfully stubbing a toe, and my wide floppy hat for sun protection. Belowdecks, I remained entirely naked all the time, and there was a certain naughty novelty to it. I smiled at the thought that by not wearing clothes, I was not wearing them out, either, or soiling them and as such was saving myself a great deal of time and trouble by not having to wash them. Sometimes in my dreams I was sailing my boat completely naked, so much did it seem to be a natural state that I belonged in and had, at long last and belatedly, come to appreciate and enjoy.

But after a while I began to think of the effect of my body upon the cushions in the cabin, and how they in turn might become soiled and oily rather than my clothing, and how more difficult they would be to clean, so I covered every cushion with a bed-sheet tucked in at the sides so that I would not leave sweat and body oils on the upholstery. As far as going topside in only deck shoes and a hat, that was not a long-lived policy either, because as the sun grew stronger, I began to burn, even through my tan, so at long last, nagged by the echoes of past conversations and admonitions from various sources about the dangers of skin cancer, I took to wearing old, long-sleeved white dress shirts on deck. White loose cotton shirts were cool and provided the sun protection that I needed, as I was not fond of greasy sunblock. I eventually took to once again wearing shorts, simply because I needed pockets to carry things around the deck in, such as a rigging knife or tools or twine. There is nothing to carry things around in when one is naked. And thus my experiment with 'naturism' had come 'round full circle simply out of practical concerns. I did not care a whit about modesty out at sea, but I did need to protect myself from the elements.

As I drew closer on my chart to landfall, and I had set as my initial destination the island of Tortola, in the British Virgin Islands, I felt a certain excitement beginning to grow and expand in the depths of my consciousness. It grew a little more every day and began to well up within me, filling me at last with almost nervous anticipation and irrepressible good cheer. I plotted my position every day on the charts and watched the distance between myself and the islands narrow each day, and as such, I had to work hard to suppress the temptation to be impatient; to burn more fuel during languid days by running the engine wastefully hard, but thankfully, I had enough breeze most of the time that I could sail grandly onward without the need for my engine.

The design and rig of my boat did not allow me to rig any manner of sunshade while actively sailing, so, but for the occasional trip to the cockpit to scan the horizon for ships and contacts, which was on the order of every half hour or so, I stayed below in the shade and out of the increasingly intense sun. I sailed along with the shaft generator purring and the auto-steering keeping the boat on course. I opened the butterfly wings of my hatch above the main cabin and, sailing on a broad reach, it was nevertheless dry with no water coming aboard or splashing down the hatch. When the breeze blew stronger and there was the occasional possibility of a sea slopping aboard, I closed the windward-facing wing of the hatch, leaving the other side open which, like a venturi, drew air out from down below and kept the cabin comfortably cool with the air flowing down the main scuttle, or hatchway, from the cockpit.

Of course, when the breeze was fresh and the day blue and sparkling, I would often enjoy steering for a few hours at the time, and for this I wore a wide-brimmed, floppy white hat with a chin strap to keep it from flying away; in this manner I could steer for hours with a bottle of water by my side and a couple of trail mix snack bars and a small sandwich bag of mixed dried fruit that I had brought along in larger containers. I wore the best sunglasses that I could buy, before the trip, to protect my vision, and the backs of my hands browned up like those of an islander even with the frequent application of sun block.

But I was sailing along across a brilliant blue, warm, beautiful ocean under a bright sky, and I realized then that, for the first time in my life, I was in a certain moment, perhaps the same one that Jason, the circumnavigator, had described to me a few years earlier, in that at last I was needed nowhere, and by nobody. When this epiphany of my state of absolute liberation came to me, on quite nearly a downwind romp to the Caribbean Sea, I suddenly felt light-headed; or was it a lightness of my soul? My spirit soared, above the water, above my own mast-head like the white tropic bird, I imagined. I thought of my life now, as Hemingway once wrote, as a life without consequences. Can there be such a thing? Without consequences to whom? Well to everyone else but me, of course. Whatever I was to do, or mis-do, would affect only myself, and I was perfectly comfortable with that. If I screw up, I thought, it's my fault and mine alone. I need no one else to blame for anything, and in fact would not wish to.

By my chart, I estimated that I had perhaps a day and a half before landfall, and at my current speed, that would be some time during the middle of the night. Since I would rather arrive in the early morning, I decided to slow the boat down a bit by shortening sail and thereby advancing at a more leisurely pace.

The barometer was steady and high, so I knew that I had good weather in the forecast for at least a day unless something sudden came up. I had also seen a couple of boats the day before, which indicated to me that I was getting closer to land; one had been a fishing boat, and another a big yacht heading more westward, probably off toward Puerto Rico. I had flying fish coming aboard every night now, even though I was no longer hanging my lantern in the rigging, but they came aboard anyway and since I was sick of them, I tossed them back each morning. The novelty of eating them had worn off very quickly, especially once I had learned how to catch enough wahoo and mahi to supplement my diet with much tastier fish. But for the moment, I had but one focus for my mind, and that was making landfall. My first stop would be the island of Jost Van Dyke in the British Virgins.

Moving along at a slower pace allowed me more time to prepare my boat for arrival. This meant stowing and consolidating things aboard, cleaning up, preparing lines, and inflating my dinghy that was tied down up on the foredeck, then carefully launching it over the side and setting it in tow behind *Rugosa*. All of this busy work took the better part of a day anyway, and by evening I was weary, yet just before sunset I thought I could see a thin, blue-grey, irregular line across the horizon to the south, most probably the mountaintops of the BVIs, and my pulse quickened with joy as I anticipated my arrival on the following day.

After darkness fell, I could sleep only in snatches due to my anxiousness. My fuel was running low, so I sailed, even though the airs were light, in order to conserve the fuel that I would need in the morning to work my way around the island and up into Great Harbour. In the meantime, it was a patience-trying waiting game.

I played my radio for a while, after pouring myself a glass of bourbon and toasted my impending landfall. I happily surfed the many AM and FM stations now available on the dial, most of them from the U.S. Virgin Islands and Puerto Rico, and quite a few in Spanish from other places as well, likely Cuba and the Dominican Republic. Since my command of Spanish was mediocre at best, and the radio voices were speaking what seemed to me to be incredibly fast, I could discern only snippets here and there of what they were saying, local dialects and inflections notwithstanding. The Caribbean is a busy place, I thought to myself. As my head grew woozy from the drink, I took one last look at my chart and my most recent plot, and then lay down on my bunk with the faint crackle of the radio being the only truly audible sound in the cabin. I was almost instantly asleep.

Sometime later during the night, I awoke, not startled, but neither drowsy; my senses were alert and alive. My boat was sailing along gently; still faithfully

130

holding her course due south, and the breeze was warm and light. The gaff jaws made a gentle, rhythmic creaking sound as regular as a clock pendulum as she rode from light swell to light swell, and nothing seemed amiss. It was a moonless night, but brightly starlit; I went out on deck to look around, and shook slightly from the chill of the cool, damp deck. There was nothing to see at first. And yet, something had awakened me, a sense of something different. As I lay back down in my bunk, nearly drifting off to sleep, it suddenly came to me: the air was different. I could smell the land.

I have read that the sleeping body cannot be awakened by the sense of smell, which does not function when one is asleep, which is why so many people die in house fires; they never awaken to the smell of smoke. One's hearing works just fine, hence the practicality of loud smoke alarms. But growing proximity to land had awakened me, perhaps in concert with the smell of the land or the change in the air. Back on deck, I scanned the horizon to the south, and saw nothing but darkness and starlight above. And the scent borne upon the breeze was earthy, distinctly floral, and no longer briny-sweet alone. I felt my pulse quicken; I had not too long to wait before landfall. And, as my eyes became accustomed to the darkness on deck, I began to see faint twinkling lights on the horizon that could only come from the approaching land masses of the Virgin Islands.

I lay back down, but awoke again at first light, after fitful half-sleep; I think I was only dozing, and waiting for the excuse that the breaking dawn would afford me to go back on deck, like a child awakening on Christmas morning to rush downstairs to the decorated tree and take in the euphoric rush of the first sight of all the gifts beneath its branches.

As the sun was rising into a warm, cloudless blue sky, and the breeze had fallen light as a breath, I cranked over the engine, and the old Westerbeke diesel rumbled to life with a growl, but a determined voice, and began its work pushing me toward the distant purple-grey silhouetted peaked British Virgin Islands on the horizon. Directly ahead, to port slightly, stood the island of Jost van Dyke. More directly ahead lay the passage between Jost and Great Tobago Island. I would transit that passage and then turn to port, motoring into Great Harbour to clear in to Customs. The sea was almost glassy, with only a long, low ground swell. I had my papers together, and I was anxious to get into port after so many days at sea. I unpacked and inflated *Skidbladner* and eased her over the side and took her in tow.

Now, the rugged outline of the islands was clearly visible. I was less than ten miles away according to my morning chart plot. The individual islands were not distinguishable from one another yet; there was a misty haze on the sea around the islands and they seemed brownish-grey and in shadow. But they were a magnificent sight under the clear blue sky of the new day. With the motor running and hot water available from the engine, and, having furled the sails, I set the auto-steering, looked around to make sure that there were no vessels approaching, and treated myself to the luxury of a brief hot fresh-water shower and soap and clean clothes. I would come in through the passage between the end of the island and the rocky islet named Tobago, then steer to my port, around the south end of the island and up into Great Harbour where I would grab a mooring temporarily or simply anchor. I was anxious to get off the boat and go ashore to socialize, and perhaps to have an evening of drinking and release. I knew just where I wanted to go, the famous Soggy Dollar Bar that I had glimpsed to port in White Bay as I had been approaching Great Harbour. I hoped that I would be able to keep myself in check; for I knew that there was a certain pent-up wildness in me that, like steam from a pressure release valve, wanted out of me, and was, unfortunately, not to be denied, but perhaps sensibly restrained if possible.

I took some time to explore the little village that basically ringed the harbor, taking note of the fuel dock, grocery store, and shops. I walked the short distance from Customs and Immigration's red-roofed cottage over to the famous Foxy's Bar for a couple of frozen daiquiris. It was early afternoon now, the bar was fairly empty, and the day was quite warm, so the shade of the bar and the cool iciness of the frozen rum drinks were a welcome relief. *Once again, I am back in Paradise,* I told myself.

I was back on the boat within the hour, looking down the anchor line into the deep and impenetrable powder blue of the harbor waters. A crab clung to the line a few feet below the surface. As clear as the water was, I still could not see the bottom; it was nearly thirty feet below.

After visiting the fuel dock, I motored over to White Bay and anchored again. The bay is shallow, so I had to anchor out a good distance from shore since *Rugosa* draws nearly six feet. I didn't mind; I had my dinghy. With my mainmast down and in its crutch, I rigged what I call the 'Lord Jim' canopy, basically a canvas shelter half using the main boom as a frame, to protect the cockpit from the sun. I could already feel myself beginning to slow down; my attitude was mellowing nicely. With my cockpit shelter rigged, I felt that I might as well mix a drink, especially since I had bought a big bag of ice cubes. Then I would lay my cockpit cushions out and take a nap in the shade. The sky was clouding up; it looked as though a rain shower might be coming. I fell asleep to the sound of fat, warm rain drops slapping into the Lord Jim, my anchor firmly and securely set. It was late afternoon when I finally awoke. The clouds were gone and the sun was nearly ready to set over the harbor and the distant islands to the west.

I felt rested when I awoke, but also, once again, very much alone. I thought of Amélie, and that bothered me, because it made me feel even more alone. I tried not to think about her, which of course made me think about her even more so, and therefore I decided that the best cure would be human company. I would fire up the dinghy and head in to shore to the Soggy Dollar, have a few drinks and a little food and hopefully meet with some lively company, and that would get me over my aloneness funk and let me blow off a little steam. I'd purchased a cheap straw hat at a shop in Great Harbour, lightweight and shaped like a Panama hat; I named it The Goat's Lunch, and put it on my head and donned a loose, colorful island shirt, jumped into *Skidbladner*, and motored in toward the beach to spend a couple of uneventful hours at the bar.

In the morning I felt ready for a good breakfast. I had been eating in spotty fashion since I had left Bermuda, and now, on my first actual morning in the islands, I wanted to do better. I began the day with a swim off the boat at sunrise. The water was comfortably warm and washed away the night's perspiration. After I climbed back aboard, I gave myself a fresh-water rinse with the 'sun-shower' bag hoisted part way up the mainmast. It felt cool and refreshing from hanging from the mast all night without the sun beating on it. I then went below and made some coffee in my old-fashioned percolator pot, and noted that I was getting low on beans, and would have to buy some more.

For creamer, when I use it, I simply open a small can of evaporated milk, which I like just fine, and will keep for a few days in the icebox. I noted that I had a small filet of mahi, so I fried it in a little butter with an egg and a banana. What a breakfast! My toast was a slice of brown bread, right from a can, the kind we serve in New England with baked beans. I toasted it over the blue galley flame. Brown bread is wonderful to stow because it keeps forever, you always have bread when you want it, even when far from land, and it is nutritious and satisfying, truly sturdy stuff.

I was preparing to weigh anchor, when I saw something out of the corner of my eye, a large sailing yacht, and I grabbed my binoculars to get a better look. She was sailing along slowly a few miles away from the east, along the north coast of Tortola, and through the glasses, her identity was unmistakable; it was John Carver's schooner *Gleam*. I suspected that he might be going around the west end of the island and into Soper's Hole, but I could not be sure; for all I knew, he was headed for St. Thomas. I went below and turned on the VHF radio and tried to raise him, but there was no response. "Damn," I sputtered, aloud. But at least I know that he's here, I thought to myself. I can catch up with him in a day or so.

Chapter 12

Tortola

Boats, like whiskey, are all good.

— R. D. Culler

The next morning, after a modest breakfast of hot coffee, oatmeal, and a banana, I weighed anchor, hoisted sail, and sailed across to the island of Tortola, around the West End, and up into Soper's Hole, the snug little semicircular deepwater harbor nestled between Tortola and Frenchman's Cay. Upon entering the harbor I immediately spied *Gleam* moored out in the middle. I was assigned a mooring not far away by the harbor master, and once settled in, rigged the Lord Jim once again and decided to go exploring in *Skidbladner*.

No one seemed to be aboard *Gleam*, even though I came alongside and called out Carver's name and rapped my knuckles on ther wooden hull; so I took a little motor tour of the harbor, which terminated, not terribly abruptly or unpredictably, at the Pusser's café on the south side of the harbor, on Frenchman's Cay. It was cool in the shade of the bar and from my seat I could easily keep an eye on my dinghy bobbing happily at the end of its short tether in the brilliant white sunlight nose-up to the dinghy dock. I could relax; for although dinghies are a popular target for theft, there was no need to worry during the daytime, and besides, it was relatively within sight, and being a beat-up and tired little craft as it was, it would have been the last choice for theft, I reasoned. So I dropped my own anchor at the café for a little while and sipped cool rum punches until I felt unsteady enough to begin my journey back to the boat for a nap.

When I awoke, it was just after nightfall, and the harbor was transformed. The stars shone brightly out of the velvet black sky overhead. Lights gleamed from the many homes built on the steep high hillsides surrounding the harbor. Surrounded by greenery, these homes were largely invisible by day, but were brightly and warmly revealed after dark. The harbor surface was calm and the little ripples reflecting the hillside lights sparkled as the sounds of music and voices drifted across the anchorage from the nearby shores. There was a band playing reggae music joyfully at an outdoor waterfront bar; the aroma of charcoal-grilled steaks and lobster floated across the harbor.

Although the harbor was crowded, the boats on their moorings were dark and invisible except when one of them turned in the current, exposing its topsides to a light from the shore. It seemed as though a perpetual party was going on, and I longed to be a part of it, even though I was, quite actually, out in the middle of it. My first urge was to jump into *Skidbladner* and head for the point on shore where the most sound came from, in this case, it was the rambling bar called the 'Jolly Roger' that I had seen on the north side of the harbor when I was coming in. there was no need to hurry, I reasoned. I could pause to enjoy my surroundings. I went below, put some ice in a glass and made myself a good drink, and then went back on deck and sat, invisible in the darkness, in my seat behind the wheel, an omniscient eye, taking it all in.

At the end of a long odyssey, I had arrived at the place I had sought, myself and my boat intact. And even if in the coming days, weeks, or months, this paradise should not turn out to live up to my expectations, I could always once again turn inward. As Melville wrote, *"For as this appalling ocean surrounds the verdant land, so in the soul of man there lies one insular Tahiti, full of peace and joy, but encompassed by all the horrors of the half known life. God keep thee! Push not off from that isle, thou canst never return!"*

After my drink I felt a growing hunger, stimulated by the aromas of a charcoal grill wafting across the harbor. I chanced another glance over to *Gleam*, on her mooring. She was still dark, with no signs of life or movement. Very well, I reasoned. I jumped into *Skidbladner*, pushed off, and slowly motored in to the dock, the light blue phosphorescence in the kicked-up prop wash leaving a glowing trail behind me all the way back to *Rugosa*.

The band played loudly; people also spoke loudly to be heard over the band. The chef at the big patio grill performed his art over black iron rods that spanned the bright red glow of coals in the fire box. The bartenders were busy mixing smart rum punches for a three-deep circle of patrons. I grabbed a barstool just as a sailor was leaving it; and then a big fellow with long blond hair and a colorful islands shirt bellied up to the bar. It was none other than Carver. He saw me, and his face lit up.

"Captain Nate!" he exclaimed, clamping an arm around my shoulder, "Good to see you here! You made it! Great! When did you get in?"

"Couple of days ago at Jost. Hung out for a night at the Soggy Dollar."

"Oh! Well that's a great place, isn't it?

"I got Josted," I grinned. "Starting to relax now."

"Good! All good. Got a drink too, they're good, aren't they? Come sit with us. We've got a table. Going to eat in a bit. Come join us."

At the table were Carver, his crewman Billy, and a rough-looking ex-pat named Jack. "What happened to Sam?" I asked.

"He flew back a few days ago," Carver replied. "He was needed back home. His father bought him a plane ticket. He also had some issues."

"Oh, yeah."

"Nothing worth talking about."

"Understood."

"Jack here is helping me with some engine work. Lives here, used to live on St. Thomas or something. Originally from Southie. We've got some engine work going, had to break down the engine to take care of a few things. I mean, I could do it myself, but it's a lot faster with an extra pair of experienced hands, and he knows diesel engines pretty much inside and out."

Jack was a tough, thin, wiry guy with suntanned skin, muscular tattooed arms, a moustache and long, stringy dark brown hair that had clearly retained its natural oils as well as some unnatural ones. His face was acne-scarred, and he smoked constantly. He apparently had felt no obligation to change for dinner; he was still dressed in carbon and diesel-stained work clothes that smelled of sweat, fuel, and cigarette smoke. His voice was a bit gravelly at times, and the most popular and frequently-used word in his vocabulary was the F-bomb, deployed in various forms, and sometimes deployed like a cluster-bomb, a devastating staccato of F-bomblets peppering his conversation or a humorous (or, alternately, annoyed) outburst. His creativity with that single word was also impressive; like a violinist playing an entire air on a single string, Jack used the F-bomb as a potent modifier for ordinary words, as a prefix, as a suffix, and sometimes as both; for example, the difference between "I guarantee that I will be there," versus Jack's "I guaran-fucking-tee that I'll be there," which obviously carries more emphasis, with the F-bomb used in this case as a mid-word additional syllable within an otherwise ordinary and unimpressive word. In this manner, he could use the F-bomb as creatively as the old Portuguese fishing-boat cooks prepared codfish a hundred different ways so that it never tasted the same twice in a week, at least that's what I recall from Kipling's *Captains Courageous*. And thus Jack could flesh out practically one-third of his speech with just that one word used flexibly and spiced and sauced different ways. But of course the F-bomb prepared and served a dozen different ways is still the F-bomb, after all, and that was, arguably, the down-side of his uniquely idiosyncratic manner of speech.

We had just finished dinner and were having another drink when Jack made an interesting suggestion.

"Let's go over to the Bomba Shack for some psychedelic mushroom tea," he ventured. "We can go in my jeep."

"How are we getting back?" I asked.

"Same fucking way," Jack croaked, his voice the gravelly low voice of the chain-smoker.

We had been told that the Bomba Shack in Cappoons Bay on the northwest coast of Tortola was a really 'laid back' kind of place, a crude shack constructed of cast-off corrugated metal and driftwood nailed together to make a shack with a bar, and that they served free psychedelic mushroom tea, which is legal to consume in the BVIs. It was not actually very far away, only a few miles.

"That's odd," I said, "That business about the mushroom tea."

"What's odd?" Jack asked, irritably.

"You get jailed down here for having weed, but it's legal to drink magic mushroom tea?" I replied.

"Everyone smokes weed anyway," Jack said. "No fucking problem. Everyone will be smoking it tonight on the beach. Later on when the chicks all get drunk, they start taking all their clothes off. It's a tradition at the Bomba Shack full moon party."

We climbed into Jack's beat-up and rusted old jeep, five people all told including Jack. It was crowded. The jeep had been painted in jungle camouflage with cans of spray paint and it was a very unprofessional job, but it was better than walking up the steep hillsides. Jack was driving fairly fast and some of the roads were incredibly steep, especially after we left the tarmac and were going up, down, and across winding dirt and gravel mountain roads. It was very dark and only one of Jack's headlights worked, and on high beam. "Gotta get that fixed, I know," he muttered as we bounced over the rutted road.

It was a scary ride until we were driving down along the coast. It seemed to take forever even though in actuality we were not in transit for very long. Fear makes time pass more slowly, I observed. But soon we did arrive, and all in one piece, by luck.

The Bomba Shack was really a ramshackle collection of driftwood and corrugated metal and other flotsam all nailed together with a sand floor, something akin to the forts in the woods that we kids used to build from discarded plywood and junk in our early teen years. Two bartenders were selling expensive drinks in plastic Solo cups and the crowd was touristy – some younger, some older,

137

some from boats, some not from boats at all, most everyone drunk, dancing around on the beach smoking joints and spilling drinks all over themselves.

Jack was milling around with a filter-less Camel hanging out of his mouth and suddenly he appeared holding a cup. "Try this," he said, "Magic mushroom tea." I took a sip. It was like old rotten wood steeped in water and burnt leaves. I spit it out. "Hey!" he exclaimed, "Don't waste it! I had to pay ten fucking bucks just to rent this special cup, and then tip the asshole pouring it…what a bloody fucking racket. But you don't get high unless you swallow it."

"Swamp water," I said, spitting again, "I would rather get drunk on bad whisky."

Jack shook his head, tipped the cup up and drank it all at once. "I'm goin' cruisin' with fucking Timothy Leary!" He exclaimed. Captain John had also been through four cups a half hour later, but looked disappointed. He shook his head. "Tastes like shit," he said, "And I'm no higher than when I got here. As a matter of fact I'm beginning to straighten out. This is bullshit. This is fake!" *Uh-oh*, I thought. *Here comes the steak-on-a-fork.*

Young crewman Billy Quintal joined us. He had been down on the beach where a small group of women had begun taking their clothes off, in what was generally advertised as the Bomba Shack tradition. It was the night of the full moon.

"Mushroom tea?" I asked.

"Nah. They're just wicked drunk. Came over on the ferry from Virgin Gorda."

"Not your type?"

"One of them is old enough to be my mother for cryin' out loud."

I looked over their way; in the light of the full moon, they looked a bit surreal. One fell down face-first in the sand and two girls helped her back up.

"Sand-bank face plant," Billy remarked.

"I went to a nude bathing beach on St. Martin once, over on the French side," I said. "I didn't know that it was a nude beach, I think all the beaches on the French side are nude. But it had a bar with cold beer and a grill where they served good burgers. My friend Zeno and I had been driving around in a rented jeep and we were hungry and thirsty. Zeno knew about this place so we drove down a sand path."

"What was it like?" he asked.

"I learned something," I replied. "First of all, a lot of people who take their clothes off really ought to leave them on. It's not like the movies. And most people with clothes on really look a lot better with them on and may not realize it."

"Second?"

"That nude beaches are not for sightseeing. Not if they serve food and you want to hang on to your appetite. Most people's nude bodies are a lot like a shoddy boat-building job. It's like the old boatbuilder's expression, "Good from far, but far from good.""

Billy laughed. "You are crazy," he said.

But it was a white tourist crowd almost exclusively, getting fleeced in this tourist trap, no Robinson Crusoe-ish adventure here, so finally, Carver said that he'd had enough. "The rum punch is horrible," he said, starting to slur his words. The so-called magic mushrooms had been steeped in it, so now it had a bitter, decayed-leaves taste. "The drinks are six bucks, no matter if you drink liquor or beer, and the mixed drinks are watery. I drank a lot of that tea and all it did was make me piss a lot. Got no higher than a gopher in his hole."

Jack had bought some of the dried mushrooms offered for sale, and after he had eaten a few, pronounced them a "Fucking rip-off" and walked off in a huff toward his jeep. "I bought better than that two days ago from that spoonbill bitch over in the Customs office," he added.

Later, as we sat out in the cockpit of *Gleam* having a night-cap, Jack said, "You have to be careful with that fucking place. Can't fucking trust anyone these days. Make sure when you go there that you don't eat or drink any fucking thing that you don't see opened in front of you. This native islander taxi driver I know named Steve, over in Cane Garden Bay, he told me that he tried the mushroom tea once and it poisoned him; he didn't walk for almost a week, his feet didn't fucking work. So ya gotta be very, very fucking careful."

In addition to helping Carver with *Gleam*, Jack was working with a local crew that were making extensive repairs on the antique sloop *Amaryllis* in the boat yard at the east end of Soper's Hole. They were in general a rough bunch, but hard workers and heavy drinkers, and would sometimes end up in the after-noon on payday at Pusser's.

Jack and I spent some time together on a couple of occasions drinking Red Stripe beer in pounder cans over at the boat yard. Jack liked rum too, and he liked eyeballing the pretty young women in bathing suits that came off the yachts moored out front of the café. The café was a good spot for 'recon', he explained. I had told him about my plans to finish restoring *Rugosa* and take her on a long voyage, perhaps around the world. He had only nodded his head, not in agreement, but simply acknowledgment that he understood what I was talking about.

Late in the afternoon a few days after I had arrived, I was feeling a little hungry, and definitely thirsty, so I took the dinghy over to the floating dock at Pusser's. There were only a few people there, nobody that I knew, so I ordered a painkiller and a plate of conch fritters. In a little while, just after 5 p.m., as though right on cue, Jack came sauntering down the sidewalk from the fuel dock, looking as unshaven and bedraggled as ever, his long brown hair oily and tied up in a ponytail. He threw a cigarette butt down on the pavement and snuffed it out with his shoe, then came over and perched himself on a barstool next to me. He was rank with sweat and heated, redolent with the noxious odor of diesel and sweat. I slid just slightly away, to the opposite semicircle of my barstool, hoping he would not notice my perspiration. He ordered a Carib beer, putting the bottle to his mouth and tilting his head back, chugging it down easily. Then, without so much as a word of greeting, he snatched my last conch fritter off my plate and ate it in two bites. I'd eaten all I wanted to by then anyway.

"You're welcome," I said.

He grunted. "That all?"

"Should've gotten here earlier," I replied.

"Well," he began, slowly, "I had things to do. Had to replace a fuel dock pump, took longer than I expected."

"I'm going to have another drink," I said, "Can I get you another Carib?"

He smiled and chuckled slightly. "I'm never gonna say 'no'"

"I'll order another plate of fritters, too."

We ate and drank for a little while, until the rum punch cocktails had settled me into a pleasant frame of mind.

"Tourist comes up to me today while I was grinding the hull on *Amaryllis*. Sure it was hot. He asks me, 'How do you guys work like that in this heat?' I told him, you just get a good sweat going in the mornin' and ride it all day!" He laughed roughly, coughing and wheezing as he did.

"Still smoking those British fags, what are they called, 'Dung-hills?'"

"Yeah, fuck you," he replied, laughing some more. "So what is this voyage anyway, solo around the world?"

"Looking that way."

"For what? Fame? No fortune in it. Not much fame in it either, maybe you get, you know, the 15 minutes that whatshisname said you would get, and that's about it. I mean, I've seen a lot of folks that have come through here, all with the same intention. You'd be surprised at how many, and how many never return, that you don't hear about. I don't recall a one of 'em that wasn't friggin' nuts."

"You're not calling me nuts, Jack, are you?"

"Oh don't get a hair across your ass, I don't mean you, but some of these folks I met really were batty. But you know what? After all that danger and pain and privation, they end up right where they started, less a few years, just as poor as when they left, and honest to Christ, no one back home really gives a rat's ass. I mean, Joshua Slocum, okay, the first guy to do it, after him, a few too. You write a book, peddle it around. Back then it was like going to the moon when he did it. Nowadays, like I said, nobody gives a shit."

"I know. But I am not doing it for anyone else, only for myself."

"Yeah, yeah. Hey Jasmine, can we have another round? Thank you….so what you really want to do is find a real nice place along the way, and stay there. Forget going back to where you sailed away from. Nobody will have missed you anyway, and what will it be, cold winters again and the same struggle and rat race. Who needs that? Find a good new place and drop anchor."

"I may do that. By the way, is that her name? The bartender. 'Jasmine?'"

"I don't fucking know. But she looks like a 'Jasmine' to me. So anyway, you're doing this voyage, and I guess you're doing it for yourself. Okay. Find an island chick. Build a little thatched cabin on an atoll like that crazy Frenchman did."

"Moitessier?"

"And live happily ever after. Who knows, you might even find Amelia Earhart."

I had to laugh this time. But then my mind drifted back to a few years earlier, to a crowded afternoon gathering at the Maritime Museum downtown in Bristol. A crowd had gathered, brought together by a publicist, the press, the Museum people, and the Joshua Slocum Society, to honor the return of Dana Parma, a 40-year-old woman who had just come home after sailing her 24-foot sloop *Parmacetty* around the world alone. It had taken her three years, but she had come through it just fine, thinner, wirier, stronger, and as brown as toast when she had returned. She was an amazingly resourceful woman, and now the Slocum Society was going to honor her with a burgee and elevation to the 'Golden Circle' of circumnavigators recognized by the Society. The local paper, and even the Providence daily, had written up her achievement and the elderly publicist who had donated his time to help her drum up support and public awareness had worked mightily.

But two weeks after she had sailed into the harbor, it seemed as though nobody cared. She had a flag now, a boat that needed cleaning, and she needed a job. Nobody really cared in part because the entire concept of sailing alone around the world was beyond the comprehension of most people who live their lives in front of a television set, who can pick up the telephone and call a friend or a relative the moment they get lonely, day or night, and whose daily danger involves no more than the remote possibility of a fender bender on the way to work. The idea of being alone for weeks at a time on the broad and changeable ocean, with only oneself to rely on, frightened people. They did not want to think about it, much less imagine themselves doing it, setting it as a goal, or emulating the feat.

"Self-reliance is not a popular ideal anymore," I said to Jack, suddenly, thinking aloud. "That's very 19th Century."

"No, and that's too bad. Everyone today has to have someone else carry them, it seems. Too many dependent sissies and whiners. Everybody is a fucking gimme."

"I mean, I knew why this lady left. It was a guilt thing. I guess she'd had a family, and then had been in some kind of car accident, or caused a car accident and a couple of people died in it. That's what she said. So she threw herself into the purifying fire, risked her life, went through the whole voyage and when she got back, she was going to use the fame and all that sort of thing to raise money for good causes, she really had plans. And she did her best to launch them, but she had no money, and again, nobody gave a damn."

"So what good did it do her?"

"Well, I think it did her a lot of good, though not right away. She was nutty when she came back, she so much wanted the spotlight, attention, not for herself I don't think. She was playing music out in bars, writing her own songs, always about her voyage. She was trying to tell her story, how she had come through the fire, how it had saved her sanity, or at least her soul. Don't laugh. I think it really did. And it frustrated her that no one seemed to care. Eventually she calmed down, was reconciled with her family, met a good man who ran oil-well boats out of Baton Rouge. When they had the big earthquake in Haiti, she helped organize a flotilla of volunteer boats to bring water, medicine, and food and supplies to the poor people who were suffering there. She worked very hard at it for months and I think it helped bring her peace."

"Well you know, what goes around, comes around, you know?" Jack said. "I mean good stuff as well as bad. Sometimes when you do stuff for others, it comes around back to you when you least expect it, and does you good, too."

I nodded; he was right. So in the end, the fame and publicity didn't matter. Dana Parma had saved herself, her mind, and her soul, and had saved it for just such an opportunity as had come with the earthquake and suffering in Haiti. Saving herself gave her the chance to help save others.

"I have no such lofty plans," I said. "I don't have her reasons for leaving, and am not sure what I want to accomplish," I said.

"One thing I learned," Jack responded gruffly, and thumped my back, "Is don't fuckin' worry about it. Don't think too hard tryin' to figure it out in advance. Things become clear in time, usually all by themselves. Sometimes people actually fuckin' *think* too much, you know? And it gets 'em in trouble. What the fuck, you're here in Tortola, in fuckin' Soper's Hole drinking rum punch while your buddies back in New England are freezing their asses off and shoveling snow and slippin' on fucking ice. So there's something right there. Take it one day at a time, brother."

In a little while it was nearly dark, and I'd had enough Painkillers, and my bar tab was getting a little higher than I liked. Jack sensed what I was thinking; "Let's settle up and go over to the Jolly Roger for a few cold Caribs, a nice fucking nightcap."

We took the dinghy across the darkening harbor in the quickly settling tropical night, and tied up. "Have you ever seen the Green Flash?" he asked me.

"Nope. There really is no such thing," I replied.

"The fuck there ain't. People talk about it all the time."

"Look, Jack, if you stare at something bright red for a minute, then move your eyes quickly over to a sheet of white paper, you're going to see a ghostly green dot on the paper."

"Yeah…so?"

"You're staring at the sunset, it's brilliant orange. You're staring at the edge of the disk and it makes an impression on your retina. Now all of a sudden that disk disappears below the horizon. What do you suddenly see, for an instant?"

"A green flash, I guess?"

"That's all it is. There is no green light. It's all in your eye."

"Oh bullshit. It's real, it has something to do with the horizon, the light bending, you know, like your elbow when you've got a beer in your hand. Don't be like that."

"Like what?"

"Ruining shit for people, you know? Let people hang on to their mysteries if they like them, true or not. Doesn't matter. They give people comfort. Not knowing everything makes some things special."

"Like faith?"

"Oh don't even fucking go there. Here, let's have another beer."

Chapter 13

The Lull

"Not until we are lost do we begin to understand ourselves."

— Thoreau

I remained in the BVIs for a few weeks, hunkered down securely while the stronger-than-usual Christmas Winds blew hard through the islands during December and January. They howled out of the east, twenty-five to thirty-five knots at times, turning the sea to frothy spindrift, and sending whitecaps scurrying across even normally sheltered harbors. They blew a little harder and a little longer than many people said were usual for them, which tended to keep many smaller boats in port, and me on a bar stool, or at times alone on the beach under gray skies as the wind-whipped sand stung my bare ankles, blowing along the beach like a low, scudding cloud with the strongest blasts. When the Christmas Winds blew under gray skies, much of the sailing tourist activity around the islands came to a standstill. Sailing in heavy air is hard work, and people do not come chartering in the Caribbean to do hard work. They want light, warm breezes and sun-dappled sparkling seas, white sandy beaches, and cold cocktails. Terribly windy days are not for the novice. So the constant winds had a depressing effect on everyone in general, and people retreated from the beaches and the bays and lagoons to the secure comfort of the bars. There was the constant ripping sound of the wind in the palms and the surf on the shore, day and night.

The strong winds did not deter John Carver and *Gleam*, however. He and his big wooden schooner liked heavy airs. He was soon to be off to Antigua with crewman Billy and a spry young French girl nicknamed Cécile from St. Martin. Cécile, or Ceci, was very much a typical boat-vagabond, finding her way around the Caribbean and the rest of the world on other people's boats, making a life of it, never staying too long on any one vessel or in any one place, earning her passage almost always by sleeping with the captain or boat owner. Her only hobby other than seamanship was gymnastics, and she was a good sailor and a capable cook as well. These are the talents that people spoke about in polite company; as for her other talents, when I asked Billy how she managed to enjoy a life of such freedom and adventuring, he merely sputtered in reply, "She's a whore!"

She and Billy were crewmates aboard *Gleam*, and I wondered how much he liked that, if at all. Carver kept *Gleam*'s complement to just the three of them in the Caribbean; for an ocean passage, due to the size of his schooner, he would need a fourth hand, and that would probably be Jack, except that Jack would have to join them later, since he was still involved with refurbishing *Amaryllis*. But I had no doubt that he would soon join Carver permanently as part of *Gleam*'s crew.

Now they were gone and I thought that soon I too should be heading somewhere else, although it certainly wasn't my intention to follow them; that would have an element of the 'stray cat' to it and I was no stray cat, after all. We are individual free-spirited men of the sea, vagabonds, I thought. There will be plenty of times when we will meet up out on the broad ocean, and they will always be 'Hail-fellow-well-met' times indeed when we do.

Before they left, we met up for one last time at the Jolly Roger. "Will we see you down in Antigua?" Carver asked.

"Maybe. But there are a couple of places I want to visit on the way, one of them being Saint Martin. I've been there a couple of times, a few years ago, and might stop in there for a while."

"Well fair winds, Captain Williams, I'm sure we'll be meeting up somewhere along the way!"

The Christmas winds brought occasional showers and rustled the coconut palm and banana tree branches angrily, and tore off dead, brown husks from the palms and scattered them along the beach and the paths leading through the undergrowth. During this time, I liked being alone with my thoughts, in contrast to the many opportunities to stay out late with groups of sailors and drink the night away while dreaming of distant ports waiting to be visited, or lamenting that Christmas didn't seem to be much of anything down here in the islands.

At one small tiki bar on Tortola, the perimeter of the thatched roof was strung with colorful lights, small plastic parrots glowing red, green, and yellow from within at night, and the wind made them dance about on their cords as though they were putting on some manner of spirited performance. Other people at the bar seemed not to notice them, but, I thought, each one of them is putting on a little dance of their own, to one another, while parroting some sort of line or pitch to each other, and they don't even see the similarity of the parrots dancing over their heads in coincidental and unintentional mimicry.

It was during such times of voluntary solitude that I could most distinctly hear the voice, which comes from within. Not that I was physically alone all the time; in fact I have found myself most alone, actually, when in a crowd, or walking down a street in Manhattan. It's like hiding in plain sight, the concept of being most alone when surrounded by people. But for the voice, which is my own, and speaks to me quietly like my conscience, a quiet spot on a cool windy beach on a cloudy day is best for hearing it.

Some of us listen to advice from others, some of it from within, and some listen to neither. It is good to listen to others, I thought to myself, for often they will provide a perspective on ourselves that we have not heretofore seen, and often they will speak the truth, but not always. Sometimes they have our best interests at heart, but more often, being people, they put their own self-interests foremost, and the two do not always agree, and harm can come to you from it when they lie, and they will lie deliberately and without any qualms if they feel that it serves their interests.

Thus, it is perhaps even more important to listen to the voice, but be careful. It is a powerful voice, and often speaks the truth, but always from the lonely and occasionally unenlightened perspective of oneself; though it is prone to mischief.

The voice will lie to you if it knows that you want to hear a lie. It will tell you the truth only if you ask it hard questions. But it does seek mischief and will work it very subtly, mostly to tell you what you want to hear. If you lose the ability to distinguish truth from fiction, then you are in trouble, because you will lose control of the voice. It will mix truth with fiction as it chooses, and in addition to losing control of it, you will begin to lose your grip on reality. Then, the bottom will then fall out of your world. You must always stay on top of things, in complete control, when you are listening to your voices within, and you must also maintain a very healthy skepticism, aye, even cynicism, when listening to advice from other sources, I say.

But the voice can be liberating, too, as can a voyage at sea, particularly when we have unintentionally locked ourselves into a box in life. I often wonder if many of us, having achieved, over time, a modicum of success in any one field, tend to subconsciously pigeon-hole ourselves or create for ourselves a well-defined box of sorts, a comfortable, circumscribed place where we feel good and secure within it, a querencia; yet in the end it is still a box, with four walls and worse, a top as well as a bottom, and it is not only the sides but especially the lid that is most troublesome, because the box prevents us from expanding ourselves in the horizontal plane as well as vertically. Once you can no longer see the outside world, it ceases to exist. You begin to believe that what is in the box is all that there is, and yet...it was the sense of the world closing in around him that sent Jason, the skipper of *Water Witch*, on a quest to find himself and to also find the rest of the world that he thought he had lost. He then found a very big world indeed. He ran from a life that he felt was constricting.

But if you are not fleeing your rapidly constricting world, if you are comfortable and content, beware that extreme swing of life's pendulum. Avoid with horror the comfortable chair, the snug hollow, the appearance of order and predictability, because that is when you are in the greatest danger of losing your soul. Break out! True life is not lived in comfort, but on the edge of experience, where new experience after new experience constantly refreshes the soul like blasts from a cool and unexpected rain squall. Stagnation is when everything seems to follow the same path and result, all the time. Stagnation is life wasted, as surely as if one were dead, but no, just wandering cluelessly, rather, among the walking dead.

From experience, too, I have learned that dreams and desire, combined with art, can indeed bring about reality. If you have a dream that you wish for badly enough, and then make it as real as you can with your art and skill, living it as though it is real in every way, then in time it will become truly real. It will happen as you have planned it, and will transition from dream to actual reality. That is the magic of the force of will, and the strength of desire. You will become it, and it will become the reality that you have created in your mind and heart. But you must follow through every step of the dream completely, and live in it every moment, if you wish to bring it to life. And it will come accompanied by an abundance of luck, because you created it out of the whole cloth of your fertile imagination and the purity of desire for a good thing. So pick up the chisel and the plane, and fair the plank; you build your reality out of the strength of your dreams, one timber, screw, strake, and rope at a time.

I had little desire for solo rambling in *Rugosa* during the time of the Christmas Winds. Could I have put to sea? Why of course. Would it be hard work? Yes. But what need was there? I was beginning to adopt an 'island attitude', doing nothing that was not in itself truly necessary. But early in February during a brief spell of moderate winds, I weighed anchor and ventured out exploring.

By luck or by chance, I sailed a little too close to a small uninhabited and probably privately owned island off of Drake's Channel, up near the Dog Islands that was surrounded by a thick forest of mangroves growing well out into the surrounding shallows. Fearful of running aground, I came about and turned my bow seaward, to seek deeper water, but just as I did, I noticed the unmistakable deep-blue color indicating a channel of sorts through the coral to my port. It appeared to be a straight, man-made cut channel leading directly into the mangroves and the island. *"There must have been a dock in there at one time,"* I said to myself, aloud. It looked to be eight feet deep or so, I guessed. It led directly into the overgrown mangrove forest. I dropped my sails, and motored cautiously around and into the narrow channel from the safety of deeper water. The cut, overgrown by and encroached upon by the growth, went further into the mangroves than the mangroves themselves would allow my boat to pass; but with one little burst of engine power, I eased in without difficulty as far as I could go and found my boat entirely surrounded by dense mangroves, while at the same time still being safely afloat in the crystal-blue waters. The mangroves were older, too; they were dense, with thick limbs, and high enough that they covered, even concealed, the hull of my boat. Only my two wooden masts stood higher. If I stood on the cabin top, my chest and shoulders stood above them, and I could see everything around me in all directions, seemingly above a green canopy of leaves, including the solid land of this rocky islet, perhaps a hundred feet away, my bow pointing toward it, through the impenetrable mangrove growth.

I had no worries about backing out; that could be done the same way I had gone in, or with the aid of ropes to tie off to the mangroves and pull the boat back out, as my stern had penetrated the mangrove forest by about two boat lengths. Ten feet to either side of my boat, the depth of the water was only a couple of feet deep, such was the sharpness of the perfectly straight channel cut. I was afloat in a snug berth, sheltered from wind and all but the gentlest seas, and the deep green mangrove leaves shaded my boat from the sun and heat of day. In a moment of inspiration, I rigged my tent-fly over the main boom to shade the cockpit from the sun directly above, and then tied off my boat with ten lines in a spider-web fashion to the thickest mangrove trunks, with my boat at the center of the radiating spokes. I could be comfortable and secure here unless discovered; so in the cool green and purple shade of the mangroves, it being the middle of the afternoon, I lay down in the cockpit for a pleasant nap. When I had approached the island, I noticed that there were many different types of birds that perched in the mangroves; wading birds that fished, large white birds that looked like egrets, small birds blue and white, all flew away as I brought my boat in. But later they returned and as I lay in the shade in the cockpit, I heard them fly in and perch, and listened to their odd speech, as different from one another as could be, and I went to sleep to the sounds of their cackles and croaks and oddly musical sounds, knowing that I was by no means alone in this strange forest.

At night it was very quiet in the mangroves; there was only the sound of of small waves lapping against the trunks and stems of the growth and against the hull. The wind rustled the leaves and through the openings between them I could watch the sky deepen from blue to purple to black, and occasionally glimpse stars. If I stood on the cabin roof I could hold a drink in my hand, my binoculars in the other, and watch the comings and goings of boats in the distance, and then their navigation lights after dark. Every once in a while a small fish would splash in the channel, or a bird would take flight, and after a while I would retire to the comfort of the cabin below and with the hatches open for fresh air, I would light the oil lamps, which filled the cabin with a soft, golden glow, bright enough to read by if I kept one near. Sometimes I would turn the single-sideband radio on and would surf the airwaves of the globe, listening to boat traffic, weather, and whatever I could find that was far away. It made me comfortable sometimes to listen to other voices, and yet at the same time I could be content just to listen to the rustling leaves, the lapping waves, and the splash of a fish. At such tranquil times it was enough.

I spent several days in my mangrove hideaway, and noted its location carefully in case I were ever going to be back here, and needed a secure place to ride out a gale. But I could not stay in any one place for very long, and one afternoon late in the day I retrieved my lines and backed her out and sailed up to North Sound and the bars of Virgin Gorda.

Before very long, however, I felt a restlessness beginning to grow within me, an itchy, irritable, nagging sense from deep within that it was rapidly becoming time to be moving again. I knew this urge, had known it well for so much of my life. It manifested itself by a general sense of dissatisfaction with everything around me, the people, the bars, the usual haunts. It was time to be moving on, and I knew it. I took no pleasure from an afternoon at the Crawl Pub, and became reclusive and unsociable, not wanting to speak to anyone very much while there, brooding in my own thoughts. But I knew that I would be happy once again as soon as my anchor was up and my mainsail was bellying with wind.

Part of it, perhaps, had to do with the departure of friends I knew; with Captain Carver and *Gleam* off to Antigua, even though I had my own boat and could venture where I wished, I still felt as though I had been left behind while my friends were going onward ahead of me. I have never felt comfortable being a follower, I reminded myself, and yet this is not really that, is it? Perhaps it is a natural thing to feel as though I am being slow, or reluctant, or somehow inadequate, when others move on and leave me behind? But there is no real reason to feel that way, I reminded myself; you are not being a rational being, but an inexplicably emotional one full of conflicting thoughts and feelings. Perhaps that is the nature of wanderlust. I stood on my boat's foredeck and looked at the shoreline of Virgin Gorda Island through the mist of a falling drizzle. Why does it seem stagnant, I asked myself. Of course it isn't stagnant; it is a beautiful, wonderful place. But you see it the way you want to see it at any given time and are powerless to change that optical and mental illusion while you are in front of it. It is much like staring at a clever work of *trompe l'oeil*; no matter how long you stare at it, even knowing that it is trickery, you still cannot see it for what it really is. And the only cure, the way to put your perspective back on track, is to get away from it for a while, to change the scenery. So I knew that I had to leave.

I decided that I would sail southeast to the island of St. Martin, a place I had visited many years before on a delivery of a big cruising catamaran from New York City to Oyster Pond, a popular cruising and chartering harbor, on the French side of St. Martin. St. Martin is an island that is territorially split in half between the Dutch and the French; the Dutch own essentially the southern half, including the harbor at Phillipsburg and Princess Juliana International Airport, and the French own the northern half, including the charming town of Marigot and a smaller regional airport at Grand Case. The distance was approximately 120 nautical miles; I would take my time and take two days to get there.

I sailed easy with the trade winds, the breeze off my port quarter as I headed south and southeast. I left in the early morning, right after sunrise, and the wind was fresh and I welcomed it, for it would drive me well on my way. I actually awoke before dawn; my energy was high, and I knew that it was the excitement of getting going. I was going to make a passage, down through these storied islands, and I knew that my ship was sturdy and that I was sound and well and ready to go also.

I made my pot of coffee, ground my beans and made a small French press pot of it, enough for myself, then breakfasted on pan-fried fresh fish and banana, and a piece of toasted brown bread. That, plus my coffee, and I was ready to weigh anchor and hoist my sails. I listened to the radio while I ate; I heard the weather forecast, and then listened to some Caribbean music and a show about the *Moko Jumbies* and how they danced on high stilts in colorful costumes at so many island parties and festivals.

The breeze was warm and dry, and filled my mainsail until it bellied. I let it out, and then bore off and away on a broad reach southward, the near islands slowly receding behind me. I sailed down past Spanish Town, then around the southern end of the island and hardened up on the wind to sail more easterly, now on a close reach, while the heights of the distant islands showed hazy purple above the horizon in the distance, slowly shrinking and eventually dropping below the horizon.

By late afternoon the soft, warm breeze had moderated, and by evening it had dropped to nearly calm. I was out in the middle of nowhere, under a deep, starry sky so full of stars and the Milky Way that the starlight was almost enough to see my way by, as there was no land near. I could barely discern some faint lights on the horizon in the direction of St. Martin and Anguilla, and perhaps some of the others were traveling yachts or inter-island shipping and commerce, but that was all. So I started the engine, and set a course for St. Martin with the auto steering, going easy at half throttle, around six knots through the quiet waters. I did not want to reach the island under cover of darkness, and I also wanted to save fuel, and I knew the most efficient throttle speed for my little diesel. As long as I was not in a hurry, my engine would burn very little fuel compared to running her throttle wide open. I turned on the radar and the proximity alarm, so that I would not risk collision with another vessel unseen should one appear and cross my path. I then made a simple dinner and brought pillows, cushions, and a blanket out into the cockpit, where I made myself comfortable, listening to the crackly distant radio stations with their Caribbean music with steel drums. I passed the night this way, dozing, nodding off occasionally only to reawaken a short time later each time with a start, but I passed no other vessels. At one point I heard something splash in the water alongside the boat, and stood up to see, but it was gone, and I assumed that I had been visited by a fish, or a dolphin. Dolphins are good companions, I thought to myself. They bring luck. And one can never have too much luck when on the sea.

At some point I dozed off and began to dream. In my dream I was a young seaman again on the Coast Guard ship cruising in the Gulf of Mexico in summer, going from point to point out on the open sea, stopping for the marine scientists to collect water samples, or whatever they were doing. In my dream I was on the flying bridge on watch during the late afternoon, watching individual squalls move across the surface of the ocean in the distance. It was during hurricane season, and even the calmest days were charged with energy and the sun and warm waters ready to fuel the seeds of storms. I watched these small squalls, dense compacts of purple clouds moving across the Gulf here and there as though they were going about personal business. They were trailing shadows and rain showers like great purple jellyfish floating through the sky with their tentacles dragging behind. Occasionally one of them would move over the ship and briefly douse us with a rain shower and blast of cool air. There was never any thunder, I remembered, but at night the beautiful heat lightning would flash in the clouds, illuminating them like Chinese lanterns. There is always much going on at sea with the weather.

I awoke completely a few times during the night and stayed awake long enough to scan the horizon and make slight course adjustments. When I awoke for the last time, it was just before sunrise and I could see the islands of Anguilla and St. Martin in the distance, with St. Martin dead ahead. An hour after sunrise, the wind began to freshen and I sailed into the harbor at Marigot to clear customs, then went into Simpson Bay Lagoon through the Sandy Ground Bridge. I set my anchor in good water, set up my inflatable dinghy, made myself a good drink and went to sleep for most of the afternoon.

Chapter 14

The True Vagabond

Like all great travelers, I have seen more than I remember, and remember more than I have seen.

— Benjamin Disraeli

I was asleep in the cockpit, my boat swinging gently on her anchor in Simpson Bay. I was catching up on the sleep that I had lost while sailing through the night, sailing southeast nonstop from the BVIs. It was already late in the afternoon, and as I lay in the shade in deep slumber, I found myself becoming gradually awakened by the sound of an approaching outboard motor. In my sleep I dreamed that a giant mosquito was slowly zeroing in on me, the buzz of its wings growing louder each moment. But then there came a voice, a strong, but kindly and amused voice, a man speaking English but with an odd slight German accent. "Ahoy there, Captain, are you awake? Or are you planning to sleep all day, sir?" There followed a hearty laugh.

I slowly sat up, and rubbed my eyes; an inflatable dinghy had come along-side, with a tall, big-boned, balding white stubble-bearded man in a ragged straw hat and Euro-style sandals sitting in it. He had long, lanky arms and big hands, and one outstretched arm grasped one of my port side stanchions, while the other hand held what looked like a tall rum cocktail. I had to laugh.

"What a welcoming committee!" I exclaimed, thoroughly amused. "I see that you travel prepared! I'm sorry I didn't have the bar set up yet, but I had no idea that you would be coming over for a gam. I hope I didn't drag over your anchor line."

"No! But you anchored close enough that I assumed that you wanted me to visit!" He was a friendly and jocular sort, I thought, as I came to being fully awake. I looked aft and rubbed my eyes, and sure enough there was a big light-blue catamaran anchored less than a hundred yards away.

"Now wait," I said, "I came in here this morning and I swear there were no other boats around. In fact I made it a point to anchor away from the crowd, I always do."

"Maybe after sailing all night, your eyes were not as sharp as they might have been," he teased.

"How did you know that I was sailing all night?"

"That's the only reason that you would be sleeping in the middle of the afternoon, unless you are a native islander on island time, ha, ha. But you do not have a native boat. You have a Yankee boat."

"That it is," I replied. "Got me," I added, and as I rigged the boarding ladder, continued, "Captain Nathanael Williams from Rhode Island at your service. Now dammit, come aboard will you? And let's be properly introduced. And pardon me while I make one of those for myself. And oh, should you need a refill, I am well supplied!"

His name was Dieter Bauer, he explained. "Just remember that my first name rhymes with 'Peter, and you will never forget me," he chuckled. I had rigged the Lord Jim over the main boom nice and taut, and although it pulsed like a drum-head occasionally in the afternoon breeze, it kept the cockpit shady. I made myself a good rum punch, and began to feel myself relaxing as we talked. Dieter's trade was as a locksmith and a mechanical engineer, and he had built a solid locksmithing business in Massachusetts before moving it to Raleigh, in North Carolina, and then retiring about five years ago, he said. He had two sons by his first wife, none by his second, and now that they were grown and off on their own, he had decided to take what was left after he had sold his business, sold his house, and paid off his wives, and bought a used catamaran that needed a little bit of work so that he could 'live like a vagabond' in the Caribbean. His boat was, appropriately enough, named *Two Blue*', as there were two hulls, and the color was blue. What else could it have been named?

"Not to live like a king?" I asked.

"No. A boat bum, a true vagabond. That is as much as I want to be."

Dieter explained that he was a 'war baby', or actually a very young boy when the end of World War II came, and his country and his town were devastated around him. As a result, he became very much a Euro-hippie growing up during the 1950s; anti-war, anti-military, with an anti-establishment, somewhat Euro-leftist view of life. He was a wanderer, spent a few years as a teenager hitchhiking around Europe as it was rebuilding. He was personable and liked hanging around with and meeting people, drinking with them, learning about them and their lives. He hated ties, formality, and anything that smacked of falseness or affectation. But at the same time, he was passionate about his opinions, and could be very *Deutsch* about expressing them.

"When my friends and I were in our early twenties," he began, "We would get together in the beer hall or the gymnasium or wherever to have a political debate, we would start out by telling each other right at the start what we didn't like about each other, even though we were barely acquainted. You see? That's how we got it going, that was how we trained. So yes I am very much outspoken," he added.

But now we were having sundowners. I looked over the side into the clear water of Simpson Bay and could easily see the coral and green growth-covered bottom eight or nine feet down. It did not look that deep even though I knew that it was. The bottom looked like a big green shag carpet. Then all of a sudden I saw an island man swimming under the boat and along the bottom. He had some sort of spear or tool in his hand, wore a mask, fins, and snorkel, and seemed to go a long way before he needed to surface for air.

"See his net bag?" Dieter pointed out. "He is crabbing. There are crabs in here and he can see them on the bottom. He is out here every day, fishing for them. He doesn't bother the boats or anyone."

"Are the crabs any good? They look small and ugly."

"Don't know," he answered, "I've never eaten one. Only the locals do."

Dieter pointed to an odd cone of gray rock sticking out of the side of the big hill on the nearest shore, up beyond a dense shoreline growth of mangroves. It looked like a miniature version of a mesa out in the west, a lava chimney from a small volcano or vent from which the cone around it has long since eroded. "We call that the Witch's Tit," Dieter said.

"Delicate," I replied. "But apropos."

He asked me if I had ever been here before, because he said that I sounded like I had, and I answered yes, indeed, I had sailed here on a delivery of a big catamaran, invited along by a friend of mine. It was a hellish trip down in mid-November, I recalled.

"I came here years ago as a crewman on a big catamaran that the owner wanted to sail down here to Oyster Pond on the other side of the island; he was planning to put it to work in the charter business," I began. "He was going to lease it to the charter company to make some money on it, but the boat actually needed quite a lot of work first. Many systems needed upgrading, and the rig needed some refurbishing."

"We sailed out of New York, the owner, plus a hired skipper, actually a friend of mine named Russ, with whom I had sailed a number of times. Russ had invited me along for the delivery. I had not been on a long-distance yacht delivery before, and indeed I had not been on a long-distance blue water passage in quite a few years, since my days in Uncle Sam's Coast Guard. One of the reasons I went was because a good friend of mine had recently been diagnosed with a terminal disease and was dying. So why did I go? Perhaps it was to avoid thinking about my friend, or perhaps because his impending closure reminded me of my own mortal clock ticking down. In any event, the voyage was like anything else, imbued with its own level of risk; but I thought, what the hell, I can walk out my front door and be mowed down by a nut-job behind the wheel of a car any day. So I decided that I might as well go. And besides, I would be sailing with my friend Russ, whom I knew to be the most competent and prudent sailor that I had ever known."

"In any case, it was a hellish trip; they call that kind of delivery a D.O.A., not 'Dead On Arrival', but 'Delivery, Owner Aboard.' It means essentially the same thing, i.e., an unpleasant trip. The owner's name was Dick Thornton, and he was an incredible asshole. In addition to that, all sorts of things went wrong with the boat, from clogged fuel filters to leaks to things."

"On the second night out at sea, a great squall overtook us from behind, from the north, probably the advancing line of a strong cold front, at two o'clock in the morning. It grew out of the peaceful and star-studded panoply of stars overhead, coming up fast from behind like an angry, dark, knitted brow, the coal-black angry brow of a giant, with scattered bolts of lightning shooting from his eyes, barreling out of the northeast. I felt the first cool wafts of the cold front on my cheek, saw the vivid lightning sparking with incredible frequency, and saw that we were in its path. Why I didn't feel terror I've never understood, but I felt a deep sense of foreboding in the pit of my stomach, an emotion that was as old and unfamiliar to me as to be almost forgotten. During the trip, I would discover many more emotions that would rise to the surface of my awareness, like bubbles in a pond, long ago forgotten. Some of these included despair, loneliness, exuberance, homesickness, longing, frustration, helpless-ness, all in full strength, and I was as unprepared for them as I was unprepared for the onset of this terrible squall that, rather than passing over, continued to blow and blow harder for hours on end, a most furious storm, and the worst weather of the entire voyage to St. Martin. In a matter of minutes, this storm whipped the seas up to a livid froth, and the wind topped 50 knots at times. Russ and Dick both took the helm while I took in sail; then after a while, exhausted and soaked, Russ sent me below, since I had already been on the helm for my four hours of watch, and it was 2:30 a.m. But sleep never came; through the next few terrible hours I lay in my berth as the catamaran rose on giant swells and surfed down them, at one time exceeding 20 knots in speed. It was all Russ could do to keep her pointed downwind, so that she would not skew sideways and broach-to, to be rolled and capsized by the seas while surfing down a big wave. With the catamaran there was another hazard, pitch-poling, something that I am sure that you know well enough about, being a catamaran owner yourself."

"That's correct," Dieter responded. "It's when a multihull boat will surf down the front of a wave too quickly, and bury its bows in the trough of the next wave. The boat comes to a sudden stop, and the wave rising behind it pushes it over, capsizing the vessel end over end. The boat will stay flipped over and you will die."

"But anyhow, we survived that of course. It was a terribly long night, an eternity, and I did not feel hopeful until I saw the orange light of dawn in the east through my cabin port. The wind had moderated quite a bit by first light, and over the tops of the waves I could see a red horizon in the east. Despite this ominous sign, red sky at morning, I was able to lie down and get a couple of hours' worth of sleep. When I finally awoke, I made my way up to the main saloon, and saw Dick outside in the cockpit, steering his boat, with a mountainous blue wave rearing up impossibly high behind him, sporting a great curling white lip."

I went out into the cockpit; Russ was out there too, but he was pale and clearly exhausted.

"Good, God, what big seas!" was the only comment I could manage.

"Well, we had big wind," Russ spoke up, and then he continued "I'm going below to get some sleep. I'm tired," and with that, he went into the saloon, peeled off his wet foul weather gear and spread it over the dinette, stripped even down to his damp briefs and then disappeared below. He would not reappear until late in the afternoon."

"Thornton was exhausted too, and told me that he'd had enough, that it was my turn to stand helm watch. The wind was still high, thirty to thirty five knots at times and never below 25, but the sky was mostly clearing and blue with white, puffy clouds. It was brisk and very cool, and I put on my coat and hat, bundled up well. He told me I should eat something, for I would be a long time on the wheel.

I stuffed a couple of bananas in my pocket, ate a bowl of cereal, and grabbed a bread roll. Once on the helm, I could not leave it, even for a moment, not in these steep seas. I would have to become fully awake and capable, and quickly, and would have to be on top of my game, with my best steering skills, all day, because in these seas, the auto pilot was useless. These seas required a helmsman with eyes, and with knowledge, and the ability to anticipate trouble.

If I failed once, and allowed the boat to broach broadside to the seas, the ocean would have no mercy."

"The seas were like great blue hills of water, rising up threateningly behind the boat, and then passing harmlessly under her. We rode down the back of each one as it passed under from behind, then tilted forward at a very steep angle to run quickly down its face, never going fast enough to outstrip them. I did not even want to look behind me at these great seas, for every seven or eight, it seemed, there came a group of three with one very high and steep one in the middle."

"At first, I felt fear, lack of confidence, and great anxiety; how could I manage this boat in such seas? I could not recall in my life being out on such a wild and empty, moving seascape, nothing but the mighty sea and the sky above, and a great roaring in my ears, the world in total motion everywhere around me."

"Gradually, though, after an hour or two, I became used to the situation. I put aside my fear and looked around me for the moment. The boat was (and had been) riding nicely, a little difficult to steer, but surfing down the face of the great seas with occasional bursts to 15 knots. We did not want her to go faster and bury her nose. Fear gave way to wonder. The wind roared; the clouds in the sky scudded by; the seascape was a fantastic scene of great moving blue and white rolling hills, as far as the eye could see, all hurrying along, massive and powerful and unstoppable, great curling crests that contributed to the great overall din of wind and sea and sky in motion."

"I began to feel exhilaration; this was fun! Fun if you did not think too hard and too long about where you actually were and what could happen to you. Do not dwell overly, at sea, on too many "what ifs.""

"My helm watch, which I stood alone was during the night. I thought about many things as I occasionally glanced up at the horizon that I knew was there but could not see. The shadows constructed within my eyes by the constant staring at the same pattern of light created a sort of afterglow effect on my retina, and as I looked up at the black horizon on an overcast night, I could see patterns of light and shadow, and I imagined it to be a near shore, maybe in Georgia or Florida, low sandy beaches and low marshlands with copses of trees, all lit by a softly rising moon peeking from behind a sky of broken clouds. This was only an illusion, though. Was my whole trip an illusion, I wondered."

"Well, was it?" Dieter asked, amused.

"Still not sure," I answered. "During the entire voyage, we were remarkably isolated, owing, perhaps, to the great distance that we were sailing offshore, and not in the regular shipping lanes. We saw but two ships the entire time, one the second day out or so, and then not another until a day or so before landfall. We saw no other yachts while far at sea, nor planes, except on one clear night, when we were south of Bermuda. We saw a couple of planes very high up, on what must have been a flyway, perhaps between Europe and Miami, but there were only two or three and they were way up at their cruising altitudes.

"Gradually warming days and gradually abating wind marked our final few days prior to our arrival in St. Martin. The last day or two were actually pleasant; bright sun, deep crystal blue seas, laughing waves, yellow Sargasso-weed, mild, steady trade winds, and beautiful sunsets. I was tired of choppy cobble-seas, poor food, damp clothes, and the dirty, sticky feeling that comes from high humidity and the long overdue need for a good shower. On the very last day, when motoring in the lee of St. Martin, the seas were calm enough for me to open the portholes in my cabin to let fresh air into the stuffy, dank cabin. For days, everything had been damp, humid, steamy, and warm, with no relief below. I decided that I would never go offshore in a catamaran again."

"Such a boat as this catamaran may be a pure delight on the relatively flat waters of Drake's Passage in the Virgin Islands, but on the open sea, they are no pleasure. Seas constantly hammer and slam from beneath the bridge that connects the hulls, so much sometimes that you wonder that the thing isn't hammered to pieces. "Remember," Russ had said at one point, in a moment of black humor, "This boat was built by guys making minimum wage."

"The last four or five days of our trip were practically windless. We made progress by racing ahead with both diesel engines, one in each hull, operating all the time. Russ and I were desperately anxious to get off the boat and away from Thornton; he was a miserable crank. But the dirty fuel problem kept shutting down the engines and gen-set. Thornton had brought only two spare cylindrical paper fuel filters; so when they clogged, they had to be removed, but the only option was to clean them. I developed a technique for cleaning them in sudsy soapy water with dish detergent, then drying them out before swapping them out, in order to keep the engines running. Soon all of them were furry and fuzzy from constant cleaning in water, but the procedure, performed day and night, kept us roaring along toward St. Martin. In the end, this saved our lives."

"The filters, when washed, had yielded a chocolaty slime which was a sure indicator of bacterial growth in contaminated diesel fuel. Thornton had not taken care of his fuel tanks, had not added biocide at regular intervals, as he should have. We would be stuck out here at sea, far longer than we wanted, if we could not keep the engines running."

"We learned that Thornton had no Weatherfax, no single-sideband radio, and even his satellite phone lay useless on his chart table. His boat had been poorly kept up. He had lied to Russ, and had thus placed our lives in jeopardy. We had only a VHF radio of dubious quality, good for 25 miles from shore at best. Russ had brought a single-sideband portable radio receiver, but we could obtain no meaningful broadcasts or information from it, mostly static. So we were essentially out of touch with the rest of the world for hundreds of miles of open sea."

"I remember the joy I felt when, in the middle of one night, I first saw the light of Sombrero Island coming up, just beyond the horizon. It was a sublime moment of inner peace, and satisfaction. The night was humid and warm, the air dense and misty, and it was almost three o'clock in the morning when I first thought I saw a faint pulse of light on the horizon ahead. I thought at first that my eyes were playing tricks on me because I was weary and had not slept well the night before; but no, there it was again, a misty, ghostly pulse at regular intervals, so I knew that it was a navigational beacon. The humid air reflected the flash, carrying its glow over the horizon to me. The chart told me that Sombrero Island was a hat-shaped pile of lifeless rubble still ten miles away or more; it actually looks like a sombrero viewed from the side; but after a thousand miles of ocean, it seemed close enough to reach out and touch. I was glad for it; I was sick of the boat and sick of being at sea and was desperate to jump off the boat at the first landfall."

"At this point, no problem was insurmountable; everything could be suffered; this was the home stretch. We were into the Anegada Passage. I was anxious for the light of morning, and my first glimpse of the green, mountainous island of St. Martin. I could see it in my mind's eye. Anguilla was nearby, in the night; I could almost feel it, taking one last look at the chart as I went off watch, pouring my glass full of the strong amber spirits. I would try to sleep; dawn would be in only a few hours, and I wanted to greet the day refreshed."

"In the morning, I awoke to the sound of the boat motoring, with almost no wind, and for the first time in days, the boat was traveling across virtually flat water. There was no slamming, pounding, or lurching, and out the port-hole, I could see the steep, rounded, vegetation-covered hills of the island, green and inviting. Such joy! In the distance were the hazy gray outlines of other Caribbean islands, gray mountain peaks rising out of the blue; they seemed to be dreamy phantasms, and yet they were real and such as I had never seen before. Here were images out of the *Bounty,* or *Treasure Island*; I had arrived in a magical place."

"That was your first time here?" he asked.

"First time to St. Martin, first time sailing to the Caribbean, yes."

By evening, right after sunset; I was beginning to feel a little bit drunk. But Dieter seemed 'right as rain', and he had been drinking two to my every one. "Let's go get something to eat," he suggested.

"Any particular place in mind?" I asked.

"How do you like Indian food? Curry?"

"That sounds great to me. I like spicy."

"Good. I know a good place and we can go there in my dinghy, actually. Ride with me, I know the way."

The wind had freshened, and under a full moon we raced across Simpson Bay, which is actually quite large and with small islands in the middle of it. The little open-air Indian eatery was perched on the edge of the bay on the Dutch side near the airport. There was a wooden stairway leading from the bar down to a small but well-maintained dinghy dock and float for customers. We reached the little dinghy dock and perched above us, on land a flight of stairs or two above, was a neat Tiki bar, and a small metal trailer that served as a kitchen for this Indian restaurant that was a favorite of Dieter's. The roar of jet engines overhead and taxiing on the runway less than a mile away punctuated our conversation, occasionally requiring us to pause.

"What's good here?" I asked Dieter, as we pulled up bar stools.

"George's cocktails," he replied. George, the big Indian man behind the bar, grinned.

"I assume that the food is excellent, too," I said.

"Oh, it's all good," Dieter said. "The goat vindaloo is very good. Have you ever eaten goat?"

"Almost, once, when I got the worst end of a deal trying to fly back to the Caribbean on a budget-priced never-heard-of-the-name airline. Predictably, the plane had mechanical problems and we had to land in Cienfuegos, Cuba, instead. This time I had to get on a Cuban plane to get back to Tortola. When we landed, this time unfortunately in a field on Grenada, you see, the compass wasn't working, my new hired crewman, Oliver, a man from Dominica, pointed to a goat tied to a stake near the plane. It was a scrawny, hungry-looking creature. Oliver handed me the leash; I looked at him, puzzled.

"For me?" I asked.

"Yes. Get used to him; he will be with you everywhere you go," he answered. I wasn't sure I liked that; Joshua Slocum had brought a goat aboard his sloop *Spray* and had to get rid of it because it ate everything it could get its teeth on, including his chart of the Atlantic.

"Everywhere?" I asked, querulously.

"Mostly on your plate," he replied.

"So what happened to the goat?" Dieter asked.

"He stayed in Grenada."

But I took Dieter's advice and ordered the house specialty, the spicy goat vindaloo. The island was full of goats, I had noted, so there were plenty to supply the island's need for spicy vindaloo. The goat was strong-tasting, even though it had been cooked long enough to be tender, and I ate all of it, with the afterthought occurring that, now that I had eaten it, and done the meal justice (the restaurant's owner, George, who was also the chef, was pleased that I had cleaned my plate), there was no need for me to ever eat it again. I had done it, I would always remember the experience of eating goat meat, and thus it would not need repetition.

After dinner, we had zoomed back across Simpson Bay for three or four miles in the bright moonlight, across the choppy, warm, shallow waters, spray on our faces, soaking us but giving no discomfort as we sped under the shadow of Witch's Tit. It was a wonderful run back to Marigot's inner harbor in the warmth and splashy darkness of the night-enshrouded bay, with colorful and mystical shore lights of Dutch Phillipsburg glaring, winking, and blinking in all colors of blue and purple and white from the shore-side casinos in the distance. The ghostly wrecks of grounded, rusty freighters, destroyed and cast up by various hurricanes over the years, now stood sentinel high and dry in the darkness, looming in the night monstrous and decrepit near the scrub-encrusted lowland no-mans-land of little bug and snake-infested islands in the middle of the bay. I prayed that the air would stay in the pontoons and that they would not spring a leak as the little craft lumped and flexed and undulated across the chop like overinflated balloon art in a breeze.

We got back to our boats late, but for some reason, Dieter wanted to bring his boat in to the boat yard dock in Marigot, on the French side of Simpson Bay, actually the seawall, because there was some work that needed to be done on the next day.

"This late?" I asked; I was already feeling rather drunk, in fact we were both drunk.

"You can stay on board, I will run you back out to your boat in the morning. Besides, there is a decent bar I want to show you."

"Another bar?"

"Never mind, I can bring her in by myself," he answered, seeming slightly irritated.

"Oh Christ, hell no, let's go, let's get the anchor up."

It was only a fifteen-minute motor across the enclosed bay to the boat yard dock, and after we tied her up, we walked across the boat yard to the street and to a row of shops and bars that were still open. I remember laughing, drinking, the company of people speaking French and English, then stumbling in the darkness back to *Two Blue* before managing to get below to a cabin without cracking my skull open.

Chapter 15

Morning in Marigot

I may not have gone where I intended to go, but I think I have ended up where I needed to be.

– Douglas Adams

The wind came up during the night. It raised little wavelets in the harbor and in the hour just before dawn, in the limpid semi-consciousness that precedes waking, I heard them lap-lapping against the hull of *Two Blue*, tied up against the bulkhead of the boat yard's pier. Each time a gust blew, the little ripples arose and came hurrying onward mindlessly across the stretch of dark water from the opposite side of the lagoon, only to slap themselves into nothingness against the hull. The restlessness of the wind and the many sounds accompanying it, including the occasional snoring snort from Dieter in his cabin, kept me from rolling back into deep sleep. The moaning of the wind came in through the open main hatch; it was joined in aggravating symphony by the sound of rustling, dry palm fronds and the clang-clanging of loose rigging against aluminum masts in the boat yard.

Gusts of wind rose and fell in a great restless sighing and I remembered from the conversations at the bar the evening before that a storm was gathering somewhere offshore. As my head cleared and I gradually reached full con-sciousness, I found myself awake in the blue-grey light of overcast dawn and felt the stiff mass of the boat press up against the fat fenders that were tied up between the boat's hull and the pier, the hull held firmly against them by the strong wind. There was wetness in the air; it carried a humid, salty and earth-fragrant scent with barely the hint of tropical flowers; but it smelled mostly like the rain that would soon come. Dark clouds were scudding across the high, green rounded tops of the mountains of the island's interior.

I had not slept well due to the heat, humidity, and closeness of the cabin. I was also uneasy, and on top of that, had imbibed too much liquor and the spicy curry had not digested well or easily.

Once we were finally back at the boat, I knew that drinking the rum, plus sweating in the damp heat, was bound to dehydrate me; I knew this when I lay down in my berth. Sure enough, after only a couple of hours of sleep I awoke thirsty for a drink of water. The sheet that I had lain upon was moist from perspiration and the cabin was stifling and close, without a breath. Even at night, I noted, there was no relief, no significant cooling. What faint air exchange came in through the cabin's open porthole was a moist, humid breath with no freshness or relief in it. What I would have given for an hour's worth of air-conditioned sleep!

Seeking water for my thirst, I groped my way through the darkness to the galley, and to the faucet and pump. I could see better with the light coming in through the cabin ports and hatchway; the inner harbor around Marigot was beautiful even at two o'clock in the morning.

I found a clear plastic cup and filled it with water from the tap, directly from the tanks. It was warm and tasted terrible, full of minerals, stale, tinny; but it sufficed to quench the dry fire of my thirst. The next morning, I filled the same cup and noted that the water was cloudy, and after sitting for awhile, whitish, chalky sediment settled to the bottom. Disconcerted some, and a little disgusted, I learned later that the water in St. Martin is desalinated seawater, and on the French side, of very poor, or nearly undrinkable, quality. "It's better on the Dutch side," a man told me, "They have an American company managing their water-making."

Later that morning, when the boat yard workers came to work, I noted that one of the helpers was not much more than a lad in his late teens, poor and black and dressed in clothes that were little more than rags; but as he came in the gate, I saw that he carried a fresh new bottle of purified water from the market up the street. No one, I learned, drinks tap water in St. Martin; even the poorest drink bottled water, sold in huge flats and pallets in the supermarkets; and when I went to the market, I saw that everyone who passed through the checkout line carried a six or eight-pack of bottled water. It was not 'spring water', for there are few natural sources of fresh water in the islands, most of which are old extinct volcanoes capped with limestone that have risen from beneath the sea over the vast expanse of geologic time. No, this is extra-purified water, and for the wealthier folk there are imported waters from Italy and France.

It made me a little bit queasy, days later, whenever I recalled drinking that tank water in the cabin, filled from a dirty hose on the pier; but that was my last draught of the muddy stuff; I resolved only to drink beer, wine, or bottled water thereafter.

I was fully awake now, still tired from lack of sleep, or unrefreshing sleep, and not a little hung over. I burped; it tasted of spiced goat and acid. I slowly and carefully felt my way up the steps and passageway to the main saloon and sat at the dinette in the semi-darkness for a few moments, then stepped outside, momentarily, into the cockpit. The cool, clammy, dewy wetness of the deck felt good on the soles of my bare feet. I looked over toward the mountains, but it

166

was still too dark for me to see if there were any goats on the hillsides above, or even to see the Witch's Tit.

Now I wanted a cup of coffee, and the eerie quality of the early morning made me think of similar mornings sitting in airports very early and watching the flashing red lights of taxiing jetliners. There is a strange, ethereal feeling to the time of day that is just before sunrise, an unreal quality, a pause before the insanity of the day actually begins. Hemingway said it right; everything was 'true at first light', even here in the Caribbean, a long way from Africa.

My body felt strange; a fleeting sense of vertigo, the kind that comes, sometimes, when you are in a strange place and forget about your position in time and space for a minute, relaxing your guard, only to have the awareness flood back in an instant; coming back with a quick shudder. It was a morning reminiscent of other pre-dawn mornings, like one many years ago when our Coast Guard ship had been cruising in the calm, warm Gulf waters off the low coast of Texas. I was an inexperienced young sailor on lookout watch on the flying bridge and there was a light gray mist and I did not know how many miles off the coast we were; for certain it was many, and we were well out of sight of land, but in my homesickness and yearning for the sight of land (it was my first trip to sea and we had been gone for many days), I imagined that I could make out a long, low coast, a thin line, perhaps, maybe that dark spot I saw was even a small building. For a moment, I forgot myself, and the simple fact that we were in fact many miles from land, too many for it to even be in sight. My imaginings were given shape by the mist, the grayness of dawn that would soon be dispelled by the rising sun, turning the gray sea once again to deep Gulf blue. Then we would see the porpoises, five or six at a time, under the bow of the ship, moving along effortlessly, keeping pace with us all day long, hour after hour, and the schools of flying-fish leaping from wave to wave always ahead of us, glinting in the sun. But that was a long time ago. Now, resting in the close cabin of the sailboat, I was beginning to awaken, and I yearned ever more ardently for a cup of strong coffee.

Looking out the cabin window, I could see the lights along the nearby inner harbor shore of Simpson Bay. These were the lights of cafés and odd decorative strings of lights that were left on all the time, even after the places had closed down for the night; so I knew that the town was still asleep. The awful, loud, raucous native rock and roll band that had played outdoors in a rubble-ringed lot on the opposite side of the harbor, playing terribly even until the wee hours of the morning, had finally quit, returning the waterfront to the eternal and far more soothing sounds of the sighing wind and the hoarse rustle of the breeze in the coconut palms.

The wind tugged at my clothes as I crossed the dusty, dry, dirt-patch boat yard. My baggy khaki pants needed a laundering; even in the dim early light I could see the dust and stains on them, and feel the clinging salt-clammy unpleasantness of my unlaundered work shirt. Today, I resolved; Today.

The boat yard was full of abandoned yachts and smaller sailboats set down into roughly dug craters in the earth, the deeper trenches for their keels and rudders dug with a backhoe. They had been there since the last hurricane several months before. They were, I noted, a bit like the pack of stray dogs, some of them sick, that inhabited the boat yard. Homeless, abandoned mongrels, they claimed the boat yard as their own and served as the yard's unofficial watch-keepers. Mangy and starving, they dug bowl-shaped depressions in the hard, limestone-gravelly, grassless earth and nested in them for most of the day and all of the night. Unrelated to one another, they were nevertheless a loose confederation, a family of sorts, and the trash-strewn yard with its monumental derelicts was their only home. About half a dozen in number, they followed me, hungry yet friendly, eager for a handout but not hopeful, some distant and ranging, not trusting, others coming right up to me, seeking a scrap of food at best or, at the very least, affection. I had no food for any of them. One of them was a light brown, short-haired bitch that seemed to have some pit bull in her. She had a wide head, black teats, and I felt bad for her, for a small part of her bowel seemed to perpetually protrude from her behind, not a good sign. I wished that I could help her and the others, but I was in no position to do so, and to bring food to them would make traversing the boat yard at any time increasingly difficult.

Banana plant leaves shook and slapped in the gusts, under the dry white glare of the yard's security lights mounted on the tops of tall, swaying poles. As I approached the gate, I heard the cars out on the main street; through the tall cane, broad-leaved green plants and shrubs I caught the occasional glimpse of headlights. Marigot was beginning to awaken; the *patisserie* would be open, with black coffee or café au lait, and I was thankful, in anticipation, for that.

It was a short walk past the open garbage bins and scattered trash and bobbing pigeons to the waterfront shops and the patisserie where I knew that I could get freshly-baked croissants, still hot, with butter and a pot of mango jam, plus other crusty breads, for short money. I sat down at one of the small tables with my large hot coffee and took my rum flask from my pocket and poured in a dollop; no, two, for this was a two-dollop morning, into the cup, and slowly drank it down. It warmed me as it went down, and even the small amount of liquor began to take subtle effect; it readjusted my perspective and pushed my consciousness back into a daydream, quenching my unease, a welcome place to be in the half light of the early morning.

As I sipped my coffee slowly, I reflected on how there are times when I cannot sleep, and must stay up all night, being able to go to bed, finally, when the first gray light of dawn begins to color the eastern sky, like white paint gradually stirred into a can of black. When I see gray through the open blinds of my window at home, my open eye on the night, then I know that it is, at last, time to go to bed, with some assurance of being able to sleep; prior to that, though, it is much like standing watch, or as I remember standing watch many years ago. Wakefulness, I note, has become easier with age.

In *The Old Man and the Sea*, Manolo, the young boy, is forced to awaken early, well before dawn to help his old fisherman friend Santiago prepare the boat. He has difficulty arising, and comments, by way of apology for his grogginess, that young men sleep long and hard. Santiago, the old man, replies, "I can remember it." Santiago wonders why old men sleep lightly and can easily awaken early; perhaps it is to have one more day on earth, he reflects.

There are many other things, in addition to the ability to sleep deeply, that I too remember from those days in my life. It is easier to remember them at night, when the world about is dark and quiet, with no interruptions, no distractions to the mind like annoying static on an old radio when the tuner can't find a strong signal or even a station still on the air. At such times I remember the groggy, half-wakefulness of being a young man of eighteen years, tormented by weariness, eager and desirous of sleep but denied it by the requisites of duty. I remember, and still relish the effects of being awake very late at night, when the usual straight sapling switch of reality becomes slightly bent, no longer straight but delicately curved, changing the perception of passing time. This is when the dream world begins to overlap, ever so slightly, the real world of wakeful consciousness, causing mistrust of all things seen, heard, or sensed. It is in a strange way slightly euphoric, a state of altered consciousness. The past intersects the present; both streams meet and mingle their waters, their confluence now great and turbulent. This river was once fresh and sparkling near the source, but different now, downriver, less pure, and like the poor old *Pequod,* tinged with sadness. For experience gives us the ability, on rare occasion, to glimpse the future, not to forecast the unknown, but to simply recognize the inevitable transitions of our own lives, and those of others. And anyone who knows true melancholy knows that it is never sweet, no, there is nothing ever sweet about it. These are the things that we had inklings of, perhaps even knew, yet never respected and thus ignored in our youth.

Yet there is sweetness in remembrance, if only because remembrance, by its nature, chooses only the good for its tableau; very well. But that of course only enhances melancholy; one must take the bad with the good, always in balance.

Sometimes, I reflect, late at night, my mind drifts back to a time where I see a young man, in blue Coast Guard work uniform trousers and jumper with a blue ball cap, standing watch in the middle of the night in a military boathouse on the shores of a muddy creek in Cape May, New Jersey. The young man, really just a boy, is eighteen years old and has rarely strayed from his home town in New England; in fact he had never even been to New Jersey before. But he had read many of the great books of the adventures of Captain Cook, and of Bligh; he had read works by Defoe, Hemingway, Nordhoff and Hall. And as might happen with any boy, these had filled his mind with dreams of adventure, yearnings for travel, and a fascination with exotic and tropical places, filled with dreams of rustling palms, great fleshy leaves of strange plants in cricket-noisy warm nights under the full moon, and ships at anchor, their dull yellow lamps gleaming down onto moon-dappled harbors surrounded by tropical shorelines.

Such are the powerful dreams of boys, when the entire world holds the promise of adventure, when Death is '…beyond the sunset, and the baths /Of all the western stars," as Tennyson wrote, no peak unconquerable, and one has all of forever to achieve, to explore, without limitations.

At the southern end of the Garden State Parkway, at very nearly its terminus in Cape May, there was a wild grove of fast-growing trees, perhaps poplars, at the side of the highway, just before the land becomes an extensive salt marsh stretching away toward Wildwood. I have seen it many times, a green landmark covering perhaps the better part of an acre, leaves rustling and quaking in the brisk summer afternoon breezes. I have always wanted to walk into that grove, and stand at the base of those trees, to look upward at the canopy of leaves, and watch them flutter, light and dark sides alternating, in the wind. Standing in the Coast Guard small boat house on watch at night, a skinny seaman recruit so many years ago, I could see the dark outline of the grove in the distance, barely distinguishable in the damp night mists against the backlit haze illuminated by the highway lights. I would rather have been even there, rather than standing watch in the boathouse, forever on my feet, for to sit was to fall asleep, an unforgivable offense. That grove represented a place, a metaphor of freedom and deliverance to me, but unattainable; it might as easily have been the island of Tahiti, for all my ability to reach it.

Of course, there was no good reason to be in the brightly-lit boathouse; there was no need to guard it or defend it, since it was on the Coast Guard base, isolated from the civilian world; but standing watch taught discipline and, as a raw recruit, I needed to learn discipline, and how to stand watch, to stay awake and attentive, something that would stand me in good stead many years later in the world of sailing and cruising. I noted, at the time, how different the shore of the mid Atlantic is from New England. In southern New Jersey, there are more marshes; the water is warmer, and there is more mud everywhere. The warm salt marshes, on a summer's night, exude a tangy, salty sweetness that seemed strange at first, but which, over many years, and many return visits to that part of the coast, I have come to love. The boathouse dock and pilings were, like all wooden pilings, coated with creosote, and if there is, to me, one scent, smell, or aroma that defines the inland waterways of southern New Jersey, it is the warm, heavy, salt-sweet scent of exposed salt-marsh mud and brine, mingled with the odor of creosote-coated timbers. But then, this was a new sensory experience to me, and I noted it, and paced impatiently, occasionally glancing at the clock; I was eager for my bunk, eager for what the next day would bring.

Cape May was a delay, a whistle-stop, in the itinerary of my life; it was not a tropical paradise, and there were neither love nor riches there for me, although I desired both. But it was, I thought, a means to an end; and was not the whole world as yet before me?

I was sitting at the table by myself, watching the blue andwhite morning sky behind the fast-moving gray clouds to seaward, when I heard someone approach from behind. It was Dieter; he sat down at the table next to me; there were only two chairs, anyway.

"Good morning, sir!" he greeted me, cheerfully, but with an odd, almost formal tension in his voice.

"Something wrong?" I asked. The girl who owned the shop came over to the table and brought him a cup of coffee and one of those wonderful croissants. He sniffed. "What is that you put in your coffee?" I handed the flask over to him. "Thank you," he said, but rather than pour it into his coffee, he raised it to his lips and took a long pull at it."

"That ought to fix whatever hurts," I said.

"I am thinking that we need to move," Dieter said.

"Move to where?"

"Oyster Pond, on the other side of the island. There is a big storm coming. Two or three days."

"Oh, bloody Deja-vu," I said.

"What do you mean?"

"Well, that first trip I made down here, there was also a gale, but it was a late-season storm. We flew home before it hit. My friend Russ and I brought the big cat over to Oyster Pond with the owner and tied her off, secured the boat and flew home. I know that drill. Can't we simply hunker down here in Simpson Bay?"

"This is a big body of water," Dieter replied. "It's shallow, there are no moorings. I don't trust the anchors in here; we'll pull loose and end up high and dry in the mangroves, or up on a pier or dashed to pieces against a bulkhead."

"Everyone will want to be in there," I said.

"But I have a friend over there, Captain Nigel. He owns a resort, and will let us moor. It is much more protected in there."

"When should we go?"

"Soon," he replied. But first we should travel around the island a little bit, just for today. And you must meet my friend, Poppa Jon."

"Who is he?"

"He is just a friend, a local guy. You will understand why when you meet him. He is a good guy. Everyone calls him Poppa."

"Does he have a lot of illegitimate children running around the island?" I asked.

"Well he might. But I don't think so, and besides, it would be rude of you to ask him that."

"Oh don't worry, I won't," I replied. "Let's go meet Poppa."

Dieter had rented a jeep and we went off riding around the island. He wanted to show me an out-of-the-way beach at the end of a long dirt road where there was a bar and cabana. It was owned by a big African fellow who was truly African, not brown at all but extremely black so that his skin bore a sheen like blued gun-metal. I was thirsty for a beer, and there were only two brands available, Carib and big cold green bottles of a cold Mexican beer called 'Presidente'. The big African's face broke into a broad grin when I asked for it; he handed me a bottle beaded with condensation. I gripped it in my hand, and he pointed to my hand and laughed, a big deep, jolly laugh, and said "Ha, ha, you see, that is what we call shaking hands with the President! Hey, you want to shake hands with the President?" I had to laugh too, but nevertheless, the beer was cold and it tasted good, even this early in the morning.

A hired cook was grilling burgers outside at the beach and Dieter and I bought a couple and sat at a table right down next to the beach where we could view the panorama of the water and eat our burger and beer lunch.

Dieter said, "Let's go find Poppa Jon now, before it gets too late in the day." So we drove back into Marigot and parked by the beach near the open-air market.

"He will be along shortly," Dieter said. "He is a famous island folklorist. He tells wonderful stories and his soul is like the soul of the island itself. It's as old, too, I suspect."

"That old?"

"No, you know what I mean, timeless. His soul is old and young at the same time, like the spirit of the island people. You will see what I mean."

"All right," I said.

"He is as regular as clockwork this time of day," Dieter added, and as he said this, I noticed a tall, older black man approaching from the other direction. He was stoop shouldered with long, gangly arms and legs like the trunks of palm trees. "See? Here he comes, right on time. He comes here to the market every day at just this time to read the newspapers and argue with the other old men."

Poppa Jon's course intersected ours, and he rafted up alongside as though we had been friends all of our lives. Poppa Jon was tall, with very black skin and very deep blue eyes. The whites were spider-webbed with red veins and a moist bleariness; but the blue was like the blue of the Caribbean water when seen from a height of land or from the sky, where, looking farther out from the shore, the increasing depth finally obscures the reflection of the white coral sand so that one can't tell comfortably where the bottom is anymore.

"Dieter! Good morning to you. Who is your friend here?" Poppa Jon began, his speech bearing the musical inflections of the odd island *Patois* that he was used to speaking to his local friends.

"His name is Nathanael Williams. He is here on his boat over in the bay."

"Is he friendly?" Poppa Jon asked, grinning broadly.

"Most of the time," Dieter laughed, "He has some hang-ups, but I am teaching him."

"Oh! That's good. You will make him mellow?"

"I will try! If an old Socialist cannot make him mellow, nothing will."

"Good! Learn to live on island time, Mister Captain Williams. First thing, then, come on," he said, "We must go have a coconut."

Then he laid his big hand on my shoulder. It was like a great floppy spotted brown flounder made of fingers but dry like leather rather than like a fish. He spoke in slow melodious Caribbean tones, "What you lookin' for, Mister Captain? Maybe we find you a nice island girl." That brought a chuckle and a smile to my face, which amused him.

"I'll leave it in your capable hands, Poppa," I said.

Poppa Jon collected green coconuts every morning in a rickety metal discarded shopping cart. He always worked the area down by the waterfront in the shadow of the big hill and Fort de France, working the beach and around the natural crescent of Marigot Harbor. He would start just after first light and by ten in the morning he had close to a full cart. He would collect the green coconuts that fell during the night and when there had been a particularly windy night, he would have an especially prosperous morning. The cart had lost a wheel and now had only three wheels on it and although all three worked, they were a bit sloppy so that directing the cart was a challenge to him unless he pushed it along slowly, in which case it always reached its destination anyway and after all there was no particular hurry.

He sold his coconuts to tourists but especially to the open-air bar nearby whose specialty was, I soon discovered, green coconuts spiked with gin. The manager of the bar often refused Poppa Jon's beach-flotsam coconuts because they were too small, or rotten, or had brown spots on them, but most of the time they bought a few, generally the larger ones, because they knew that he also had to eat and needed the money.

Dieter and I bought three green coconuts at the open-air bar and where a man with a machete deftly chopped the bottom of the husk off of each one, without cutting through the shell of the coconut itself, to make a flat spot so that the coconut could stand up by itself on a table. Then he lopped off the top, or opposite end, just far enough down to expose some of the copra and allow access to the coconut milk. Each coconut was full of milk. You drank a little of the milk so that there would be room to put the liquor in. At the small bar open to the street that was adjacent to the coconut stand, you bought the double shot of gin and they poured it right into the coconut and gave you a straw. There were tables where you could then sit down and enjoy your draught. When you were finished, the man with the machete would quickly split the coconut and scoop out the copra, the white coconut meat, hand it to you, and throw away the husk.

The copra was tender and delicious, and made a complete, if somewhat unconventional, luncheon. Only the useless, inedible outer husk and shell were discarded.

Poppa Jon took a long time with his coconut and spoke quite animatedly in his odd patois with the other old black men loitering about the bar. One of them had a newspaper and Poppa Jon asked for and was given a piece of it. He read it briefly, handed it back, and the discussion became an animated argument, presumably over some news item, with Poppa Jon jabbing at the paper with a very long, brown, knobbed index finger as he made his point. He won the argument; the other fellow with whom he had been most vehemently engaged turned away, apparently nonplussed, and would not speak further to Poppa Jon or even look at him.

We spoke on into the afternoon; one coconut followed another, but by the third coconut, I'd had enough, but it had taken us a couple of hours to get there. I began telling Poppa Jon and Dieter about my time fixing up *Rugosa*, and my passage to Bermuda, without divulging any information about how I spent my time there, or whom I spent it with. But then I recalled the incident in the hewn rock tunnel on the hillside going down to Tobacco Bay, and at the description of this, Poppa Jon became very grave.

"You were in much danger, young captain. It is a wonder that you are here now. That was a very bad island spirit, very evil. The kind that come out of the earth. Very strong."

"Was it a Jumbie?" I asked.

"No, no Jumbie, much worse than that. You had there a shape-changing spirit. I grew up on the island of Trinidad, and we always had the legend of the Ligahoo, or Loup Garou. Many old Creole families believe in the Ligahoo. He is the shape changer. He was once a wizard that became cursed. He had good magic, but when he began to turn it to evil purpose, the people drive him out of the village with spears and spikes and cursed him. At first he had been feared but respected, but now he became feared and hated. A curse was put on him. Or maybe he was burned; I forget; but he learned to change his form to that of a vicious animal, and has power over nature. There is no good in him. Now maybe worse, you saw the Soucouyant. She is the old woman who has made a pact with the devil to be able to change herself into all kinds of different forms like a ball of fire or animals."

"Whatever it was," I said, "It was almost surreal. And it was terrifying."

"You stay out of caves, then. Caves anyhow are only for wild animals and bad spirits."

Later on in the day, Poppa Jon, Dieter, and I were sitting in the tall, wavy grass, high up on the side of a steep hill, looking down at the road that led to Phillipsburg, watching the cars coming and going on the narrow, winding, pothole-pocked two-lane road at the base of the hill, the only way to get into town. The road was crowded with traffic, all bumper to bumper, as it always was at this time of early evening, and the many different flowers along the roadside that closed at dusk were already folding their blossoms. It was nearly the time of sunset, and the sea breeze was coming in light and cool now off the distant ocean. The hill was very steep and I could hear the goats that were grazing on the hillside well above us, where the slope was even sharper. I heard one goat crashing around in some brush, another bleating. Always they were chewing and grazing basically quite contentedly and not doing much else.

Poppa Jon sat beside me and put his big hand on my shoulder again. "You sail all the way down here to the islands, solo captain. But you bring too much ballast with you, unhappy ballast. You can't keep all that bad stuff inside, you know." He waved a finger at me; it was a long, brown, wrinkled finger, knobby where the joints were swollen and deformed by arthritis. "You got to get rid of all that, you know, it's not good for you. That's why from now on, I call you 'Hotpeppa.'" Dieter nodded in agreement. "You have a name now, sir."

"I never think of myself as particularly unhappy," I replied. "I guess I would say that I am not satisfied. I am restless to see what I have not yet seen while I still have the time and energy to see it."

Poppa Jon stared at me, his face serious and studying. "Always I find with you Yankees from up north, the feeling that you need to accomplish something. If you are not doing so, you feel that you are wasting your time. But you see, living is an accomplishment. Being at peace with the world. You are not wasting time, because all time comes from God, and if you do not do evil with it, then it is time well spent."

"So I should think like I am on island time?"

"It's a paradigm shift in your thinking," Dieter interjected. "Admittedly it's a big one, pretty much a one-eighty for someone like you."

"You mean I need to 'mellow out'? I think I'm pretty mellow already, basically. But you're right; I don't have the island mind-set. At least not yet."

Poppa Jon reached into the pocket of his frayed, baggy, well-worn cotton flannel shirt and carefully pulled out a big fat loose ganja cigarette. It was like a big white grub with fat teak chopsticks bringing it slowly up and out of his pocket. He rolled it lovingly between his very long, flat, oily hands, hands that looked themselves like big cured tobacco-leaves or brown leather, thin and wide, long yet still supple, rolling the cigarette to make it tighter and more compact. Then he lit it with a flaring wooden match and inhaled deeply while the seeds popped and snapped and the sparks fell onto his old motor oil-stained trousers. "This should help, Hotpeppa," he said.

I took out my pocket flask and took a big swallow of the dark rum, passing it to Dieter and then to Poppa Jon. We swapped. I drew on the big weed-roll and the choking smoke made my head light momentarily, then it settled into a quiet pool, like a rocking skiff anchored on a choppy lake when all of a sudden the wind drops to nothing and the chop lies down.

"Let's go back down to the main street," Dieter suggested. "Let's get something to eat."

"I am *sooo* hungry," Poppa Jon added. "I want a beer and half a chicken; hows 'bout you?" He was referring to the simple combination sold in several of the cooked food shops in the town below, half of a roasted chicken and a bottle of cold Carib beer for four dollars.

"That's good for me," I agreed. "Let's go."

Slowly, cautiously, we descended the hill toward the roadside. It would be easy to cross in the slow traffic.

"First we eat, hey, and drink a beer," Poppa Jon said. "Then we can sit outside for a while down by the harbor and watch the pretty girls, hey? You going to be all right, solo captain Hotpeppa."

"Glad to hear you think so, Poppa Jon," I answered.

"Just be careful, don't be like this man here," he said, laughing, slapping Dieter on the shoulder. "Don't eat the fruit on the tree if the monkeys won't eat it."

Dieter laughed, embarrassed, then piped up, "Do you have to tell him that story?" he replied loudly, feigning indignation. "That was one of my more stupid moments! But Poppa Jon here always likes to tease me about it."

"What did you do?" I asked.

"He almost die," Poppa Jon interjected.

"I can tell the story myself!" Dieter continued, "Okay, yes, me and another fellow, we took the boat over to some small island, we'd had a few drinks aboard, you know, and sailed in to the beach to go swimming. We got hungry.

We saw a tree near the beach with soft green fruit on it, they looked like little apples. We decided to taste them. It was a little sweet at first. The other guy liked it, he ate two or three. There were monkeys in the other trees around but oddly they would not eat the fruit. But within a few minutes after we ate them, something happened. It started to burn, wherever it had touched our mouths. Then came the pain and everything coming up, and everything going out the other end, and got worse. We had to radio the rescue. We both ended up in the hospital, the other guy, he almost died. His throat swelled up so bad he couldn't breathe, almost. The fruit was poison. So the moral of the story is, don't eat anything growing if you don't know what it is, and moreover, if the monkeys won't touch it, you don't eat it, either!"

"He eat the Manchineel fruit," Poppa Jon said. "We sometimes call it the 'Death Apple."

I took another pull on my rum flask. "You guys are going to spoil my appetite," I said. "Let's go for that chicken, please. And thanks for the advice about the death apple."

Chapter 16

Hurricane

Gonna be a real frog-strangling turd-floater.

– Charles Martin

The forecast was on everyone's mind; the cyclone had a name now, Alfred; and it was continuing to intensify. Thus, the third morning after my arrival found both boats, *Rugosa* and *Two Blue*, lined up in the channel with many other boats all waiting for the drawbridge to open. Some boats were coming into Simpson Bay; some, like us, were heading out to head around the island to Oyster Pond, the best hurricane hole available on St. Martin. The morning was overcast now and the bay was calm and mirror-flat. Dieter and I kept in touch on the radio and I agreed that I would simply follow him and *Two Blue* over to Oyster Pond. The entrance to the pond was tricky, I recalled, and the privately owned channel markers not always to be trusted. Although I had been there before, it had been a few years since, and my memory was a little hazy as a result. In the Caribbean everything changes constantly, and Aids to Navigation especially so. Therefore, I opted to follow rather than to attempt to lead.

Once we were into the pond, I was surprised that we weren't part of a caravan of boats coming in, but I suspected that the crowd would begin to converge on the place fairly soon, the current trickle of boats eventually swelling to a river. After some haggling on the radio, both *Two Blue* and *Rugosa* were assigned moorings. They didn't want us tying up to the floating docks, they said, because if the storm hit with predicted ferocity, lines would stretch and the boats and docks would damage each other. Instead, we were told to put out anchors, in addition to the mooring, to keep the boats from going anywhere. But of course, as most seasoned boaters understand, and as I had explained to Amélie in Bermuda, it isn't the prospect of your boat breaking loose that is the greatest threat, but rather that of other boats upwind of you breaking loose and then coming crashing down upon your vessel, doing damage and breaking you loose in a domino effect.

"It sounds like we've got two days before the storm hits," Dieter said, his voice crackling over the radio.

"We could go over to St. Bart's," I replied into the mike.

"And do what?" he shot back, "You have a safe place right here. There is no place else to go. Come on up the dock with me in a little while and I will introduce you to Captain Nigel. Well, maybe later. He is very busy right now, and I suspect that he is going to be very busy for quite some time the next few days."

After an hour and a half of hard work tying up and securing my boat, I shouted over to him, "Are you secure yet over there?" I had been buzzing around my boat in *Skidbladner*, setting out my spare anchors and extra-heavy lines.

"Almost ready. Why don't you come over in your dinghy and have a drink? I think your rotten rubber dinghy has more air in it than my rotten rubber dinghy, ha, ha."

"If it does, it's not much more. It's getting pretty soft. I'll be over in fifteen. I'm running chain from the bitts to the mooring shackle."

"Make sure you put a shock absorber on it," he said.

I tied up alongside *Two Blue* and climbed aboard. Dieter mixed me a rather large rum punch with ice. I could smell the alcohol in it; Dieter always made strong drinks. He liked them that way, and so did I.

We sat at the big dinette table in the main saloon and he showed me a tourist brochure that described Oyster Pond as 'The safest hurricane hole in the Caribbean.'

"It will soon fill up," he said. "Why do you think this harbor is the base for the St. Martin charter fleet?" Dieter was beginning to relax now. For two hours he had been hopping about like a fellow with coals in his shorts, making his boat well-secured in advance of the storm. Sails came off; canvas Bimini, everything and anything that could create wind resistance and that could be torn to shreds. A good many boats were coming into the harbor now and the mooring field and anchorage areas were fillling to capacity. Some skippers wanted to tie up to the floating docks belonging to the charter company, others at Captain Nigel's. The dock master for each was busy running back and forth, vociferously warning off boats that tried to squeeze in. The charter company's yachts were secured to the docks, but standing off, with spider's web arrangements of lines suspending them between the floats, and there was no room for any others. I could hear the arguments getting heated. How odd, I thought, the idea of a big gale coming. One would never have suspected it. It was a beautiful afternoon with blue seas and skies full of white puffy clouds that belied no hint of trouble, a perfect day with a delightful trade wind breeze.

Dieter and I went ashore, tying up at Captain Nigel's dinghy dock. Captain Nigel's was a long-established resort at one end of the pond, with a marina and dockage area. Captain Nigel was nowhere to be seen, but I met him later, a

Frenchman with an oddly English name, a blustery, business-like, imperious fellow. Besides Captain Nigel's complex, there were shops, a snack bar, coin-op toilets and showers, two small hotels, and the local offices of Carib Yacht Charters, the company that owned most of the boats in the pond. Out through the mouth of the harbor, at a distance of several miles, I could see St. Barthelemy, or St. Bart's, a little island of peaks that seemed to rise out of the sea. At the entrance to Captain Nigel's fancy open air restaurant were a few cages housing exotic animals, one being a very venerable, colorful old Macaw; another held a stinky alligator in a green fetid pool. On the pond-side of the outdoor eating deck was an enclosure off the salt-water in which swam a captive sea-turtle and a couple of very large, quite odd-looking fish. Dieter and I sat down at the snack bar by the dinghy dock and ate burgers and fries. "Let's go into town, and check it out," I suggested. "How much is a taxi?"

"It's around twenty-five bucks," he replied.

"Can we walk, then?"

"It's a long way," Dieter said. "It's hot, and the island is hilly. No roads go through the center of the island, which is all mountainous; one must travel the periphery."

"I'm going to try anyway," I said.

"Okay, I'll go with you. But first I must drop off my reeking laundry at the laundry shack. I need some clean clothes; I'm just about out of everything."

"Good idea, I'll get mine. I think my dirty shirts are beginning to rot."

The charter company's little office, up the street from the pier, was mobbed; dozens of people, knowing that a hurricane was on the way, sought to get out of their charters and get their money and deposits back. Many were irate, as they were being refused. "Maybe they didn't read the fine print on their contracts," Dieter commented with a hint of sarcasm.

That evening, I discovered Bryan's Dinghy Dock, a bar and eatery adjacent to Captain Nigel's. Of course, it had been there, on the shore of Oyster Pond, all the time, and had been discovered and patronized by countless others, but I found it to be a good place to drop my own personal anchor, for a variety of reasons. I was drawn to it by the crowd of stranded, frustrated charter customers whose charters had been cancelled due to the storm, and now had nowhere else to go. Because Oyster Pond is some miles away from the major towns such as Phillipsburg, separated by miles of winding, hilly, dark, unpaved, difficult roads, most of these distressed folk took rooms in the three local hotels adjacent to the wharf area. They would be staying around; Bryan's would be busy, an oasis in the midst of the desolation to come, I predicted.

Bryan himself, who apparently leased space from Captain Nigel's wharf, was an American 'Ex-pat', a child of the 60's, complete with long hair and beard, loud Hawaiian print shirts, a habit of chain-smoking one cigarette after another, and effusing an endearing attitude of consummate tolerance and love of all people. Jolly, yet thin, never flustered, but exhibiting at all times a wry and sardonic sense of self-deprecating humor, Bryan's Dinghy Dock was truly the best place, perhaps the only place, within miles of Oyster Pond to get a hearty meal for short money, good cold beer, and friendly camaraderie. Every day, there were lunch and dinner specials; curried chicken with rice; barbecued pork; chili; always something good, and always served with French fries. His primitive and claustrophobic-looking kitchen served hearty portions of food as well as different styles of grilled burgers. A propane grill hooked up to big silver canisters of "country gas" was the sole source of his cooking fires.

One could sit at the outdoor counter and eat and drink, or sit at the afore-mentioned picnic tables. Behind the grill, there was actually a large room, and one gained entrance from the dock through two large sliding-glass doors. This room was furnished with round pub-style tables and a variety of types of chairs, lawn furniture, etc., and a varied collection of well-worn, dog-eared, cast-off paperback novels, some known and others obscure, Bryan's own unofficial 'lending library'. Borrow if you like, contribute if you like, read here or wherever you like. There were also an odd collection of curios, including big shells, pieces of coral, and the like, that lent an air of the exotic, and true local flavor, to this establishment that was Bryan's Dinghy Dock. Of course, there were no actual dinghies tied up there; it was not allowed in that spot; but one pulled oneself up to the bar nonetheless, and tied off one's personal painter, so that the effect was ultimately the same.

Eventually, Dieter had drunk one too many rum Painkillers at Bryan's, and decided to head back to *Two Blue* for a nap. I chose to venture into town, back to Marigot alone. I wanted to see the town again before the storm came, thinking that I might not have the opportunity to see it later, particularly if the storm was a big one and disrupted everything. So I set out walking along the hilly, hot pavement. I thought I could hitchhike my way into town, but every vehicle that went by had black faces behind the wheel, and they only laughed at me, never slowing down or stopping. In fact, a few of them rolled their windows down and shouted curses, and one tried to spit on me as his rusty van roared by. I thought it was oddly ironic that here in the Caribbean, the racial tables were turned; my white skin was now a disadvantage, an object of derision and occasional target for the simmering hatred that this black man's world held for the minority of Caribbean whites. But to be fair, such hostility was the exception rather than the rule. Most of the islanders were warm and friendly; unless, obviously, you were a white man hitching a ride. In the islands, the white man is only respected and treated with courtesy when he is willing to pay for something, which is almost all the time. If he wants something free, such as a ride into town, well that is an entirely different matter.

I mopped my brow, and continued on, looking out over the coast at the flat and low island of Tintamarre in the distance. Even from the height of land of the winding coastal road, I could see that a heavy swell was building, and the surf was rolling a long way up the beach.

At long last, a small pickup truck from the yacht charter company, with two blonde white fellows in it, stopped for me. "Squeeze on in, mate," the driver said, with a thick British accent. They were both drunk and sweaty, but no matter, they had stopped for me, recognizing me as a visiting sailor or tourist, and took me several miles to an intersection on the French side, in a low valley, but in the middle of nowhere. "We're going the other way, chap," the driver said. "There will be a local bus along in a bit; you can take that into Marigot."

"Thanks for the lift," I replied, and got out. I had no idea where I truly was. So I walked along the road in the steamy heat for about ten minutes until I came upon a local island lady in a colorful dress and I asked her about the bus. She smiled and happily told me, in broken English, that she was waiting for it as well, and that it should be along in only a few minutes. And indeed it was; a bluish-grey old Volkswagen mini-bus, full of local folks arrived in a cloud of dust and smelly diesel smoke, and the lady and I boarded it. What followed was a long, crowded, but truly wonderful ride through the winding roads of the mountainous interior, all the way to Marigot. It was wonderful because although crowded, it was a bus full of jolly people, and a driver who sang, indeed sang the whole way into town.

I remember riding by hot, dirty, flat, dusty, garishly painted cinderblock houses with corrugated metal and fiberglass roofs, the backdrop being barren volcanic mountainsides covered with green scrub but little else and rising to uninhabited peaks, all the while listening to our driver sing. He was thin and black and bearded, with a head of unruly curly hair, his arms and hands lanky and sometimes on the wheel, sometimes in the air, or mostly just one of them waving around when he was singing or making an emphatic point as he talked about life and places on the island, all it seemed for my benefit. I was seated near the front of the bus and had engaged him in conversation in-between songs. He often told humorous stories, and laughter rippled through the ranks of the passengers when he did. I remember him only as Jolly Mon, like the singing Caribbean man in the Jimmy Buffett song. The fare to ride all day around the silly island was cheap, less than five dollars, and the bus made numerous stops and eventually became packed with plenty of people as it rattled on up and down hills, around sharp curves, and even through a rain squall. I listened to Jolly Mon tell me about his extended family of musicians, a dozen of them, all singers and instrumentalists. Then he launched into full-throated song, melodious and rhythmic, filling the little bus, slapping the steering wheel to the beat, his performance punctuated always with occasional laughter and commentary. We spoke about music, and about many different things, as he drove up and over winding mountainous roads, through the spotty rain showers, and in the end I was sorry to get off the bus in Marigot.

There was a big open-air market located down near the waterfront where one could buy the most beautiful and colorful clothes and fabrics, not far from the bar where we had enjoyed our coconuts the previous morning. The whole waterfront was dominated by a great antique stone fort up on the hill overlooking the sea, Fort de France, it was known, with an oversized Tricolor waving slowly from a pole high above black cannon pointed menacingly out to sea, perpetually guarding against a foe long gone. Marigot reminded me of the Quarter in New Orleans, though much smaller, with its ornate buildings and iron balconies overlooking the streets. I found a very neat bar called 'La Bar de la Mer'. It was very French, very salty in character, and I found myself dropping anchor there for a spell after circumnavigating the Marigot waterfront. From the buzz of activity in downtown Marigot, and all along the waterfront, one would never suspect that a major storm was due to arrive in a day or so. People were going about their business shopping, dining, walking, drinking, the way they always did. There was a wide patio out in front of La Bar de la Mer, with a great charcoal grille, a chef, and numerous tables and chairs. It was an outdoor eatery, with tables around the flame-broiling grille stacked high with skewered, seasoned meats and seafoods, breads, salads, fruits, and more. This is my place, I thought, sitting down to a cold bottle of Red Stripe Jamaican beer. I looked over at a table stacked high with remarkable pale pink whole shrimp the size of small lobsters, on bamboo skewers. They looked like big prawns glowing warmly in the colorful neon lights of La Bar de la Mer's marquee.

"Those are fresh water shrimp, Ouassous we call them, farm raised on Guadeloupe," the chef explained to me, noting that I was looking them over closely. "They are a kind of prawn." The grill sizzled, and sputtered, bright flames occasionally dancing across the coals; the aroma on the air was spicy and heavenly. The menu offered me beef, lamb, pork, shrimp, but nowhere were both surf and turf combined.

"Where I come from," I explained to the chef, well into my fourth Stripe, "I would have an easier choice; for example, I love grilled lamb, but then these giant shrimp have an appeal all their own. We call it surf and turf; it combines the best of both worlds. Otherwise, I must choose one thing without ever knowing the delight of the other, and I don't have the appetite for two dinners tonight."

He grinned, and waved his hands in the air, and replied, "Sir, if it is a surf and turf that you would like, then I will make it for you, and it will be the best!" And so he did, and so it was. Caribbean spiced giant shrimp, grilled to perfection, accompanied by plump, juicy, grilled lamb chops seasoned with Herbes de Provence, piled high on the plate. And so my hunch had proven true, at least in my opinion, that no matter where one travels in the world, from icy Montreal to the heat of the Caribbean islands, if one wishes to dine well, then one can never go wrong if one dines at a French restaurant, since the French have no tolerance for bad food, generally, and any establishment that seeks to woo the business of the francophone community had best serve good food or it will soon be out of business.

Discretion being the better part of valor, due to the lateness of the hour, I hailed a cab and paid the $25 for the trip directly back to the boat. I had been warned to be wary of wandering about the streets of Marigot at night. When I returned to Oyster Pond, the hour was not yet very late, and Bryan's Dinghy Dock was awash with people whose loud voices and laughter I could easily hear from the top of the hill where the cab dropped me off. Hilarious laughter from the waterfront bar, carried on the wind gusts, greeted me as I descended the steep hill from the hotel, alternately louder, then softer or inaudible. It only made me want to get there faster, afraid that I was missing something, a good joke, or the last bottle of Carib. I hurried down the hill like a luge on dry land and nearly launched myself into the crowd. The air smelled of breath, sweaty bodies, and alcohol. The sky had become overcast, and there was a heavy dampness in the air. I looked around for Dieter, but did not see him anywhere in the crowd. The wind was sighing in the palm trees, coming in long gusts like extended exhalations, then falling to nothing.

Nearly everyone was drunk. Many of the bar patrons were from different countries, not just from the United States. I started chatting with two bearded young German guys. They spoke very good English. It was their father's 65th birthday, and they had arranged a surprise present for him; they rented a room for him in one of the small hotels up on the hill, and had sent a local prostitute to his hotel room. While he was thus occupied, they were now drinking at the bar late into the evening while the first warm unsettled gusts from the gale off-shore began to rustle the palm branches. One of the sons finished off a beer and commented how cool it would be if only a big U-boat from the days of the Reich would surface in the middle of Oyster Pond. I said nothing in reply, only put my drink to my lips, keeping in mind that everyone was feeling just a little bit trapped, after all. So everyone drank now simply because there was nothing else to do. Bryan kept a tab tally on a yellow legal pad of what everyone owed. He would be paid, he knew, sooner or later. There was a storm, some called it an early-season hurricane coming, and there was absolutely nothing for anyone to do but sit around and wait for it. Everyone knew that it was going to be bad, and that made the waiting worse, so people drank and kept on drinking.

At the bar, though, the pony bottles of Carib beer were cold and tasty and condensation beaded all over the outside of the bottles making them not only slippery but visually appealing, and each bottle was served with a little wedge of lime stuck in the mouth, just like a Corona. They also had big green bottles of Presidente beer. "Give me one of those," I said to Bryan, "I want to shake hands with the President again."

A sturdy young woman, Kelly, was in a corner talking about airplanes. She was in her mid-thirties and was an airline pilot, flying big jets like Boeing's 767s. She and her boyfriend had been on a charter and were now stuck like everyone else. She was very intelligent and serious and professional in her demeanor and did not seem the type of person who cared much for laughter or frivolity; in fact she seemed a bit severe. There had been an air disaster recently somewhere off the east coast of the United States; a jumbo jet had plunged into the Atlantic from a considerable altitude, with total loss of life; a fisherman in the vicinity had heard a sonic boom, or so he thought, and we were discussing whether or not it was feasible for a big jet in an uncontrolled dive to break the sound barrier before impact. "Not really," she replied, downing another shot of Sambuca and smoking a cigarette. "The fuselage would begin twisting and contorting; it would rip apart. They are not designed to break the sound barrier and would never do so intact." This was the sort of cheerful talk we had in the evening as the hurricane approached. Soon the wind would be shredding the canvas awnings of the closed shops along the docks.

At long last I saw Dieter toward the back of the crowd. He was easy to see because he was so tall that he stood above everyone else. He was laughing and shouting something, entertaining a group. Then he saw me.

"Nate! Captain Williams! Here, come over here! Where have you been?"

I worked my way through the jostling crowd. "Glad to see that you're awake!" I teased. "I went into town while you had your nap, I had a good feed. Shrimp and lamb chops."

"Did you bring some back for me? No, because you are an asshole. Now do you have a drink in your hand? That's good. There is a storm coming!"

I laughed. "I know!" I shouted. "Tell me something I don't know!"

"Okay Mister Williams, there is someone looking for you. I'll bet you didn't know that."

I was feeling a little drunk from all those bottles of Red Stripe. "No one is looking for me, I paid my bar tab," I shouted above the din.

"Oh yes there is." I thought for a moment. "Can't be," I said, "No one knows me here. Oh wait, Captain Carver? Is *Gleam* here? I thought he went to Antigua! He should be in English Harbour…"

"No, no no! A little lady is looking for you."

"Who? What?"

"Over there!" He pointed to a small table in the corner of the room, next to a sliding door to the dock, but there was nobody seated at it, only a chair pushed back. I felt my pulse begin to pound. I ran over to the table and out the door onto the dock, and in the darkness, I saw a diminutive dark figure of a woman standing in the blowing mist and spitting drizzle by the corner of the building. She was holding a bottle of beer in one hand, hanging low to one side. I recognized the shape of her hair.

"Amélie!" I shouted, and ran to her. She did not run away; I put my arms around her and embraced her tightly. Squeezing so hard I suppose that I might have almost squeezed the life out of her.

"Oh my God! What are you doing here? Don't you know that there is a hurricane coming?"

She dropped her bottle on the deck and hugged me, for a few moments neither of us saying anything. Then I kissed her, once and then many times, and it was seemingly a long time before we could relax our embrace or even speak. The wind was blowing harder and the occasional squalls of rain spatter were making us wet. But it was a warm rain and we did not notice or mind.

"How did you find me?"

"Don't you remember that I told you I would find you?" she chided.

"Yes, yes I remember now. But I don't think that I ever dared believe it. Or that you would try."

"I knew that you would come here, because you told me that you had been here before. And other than that, somehow I just knew."

"Why did you run out the door?" I asked.

"Because I was afraid, at the very last minute, that you would not want me here. I did not want to be rejected again."

"That wouldn't happen," I said. "But why did you come?" She thought for a moment.

"Because I had nothing back there. Nothing at all, not anywhere. So when you were there with me in Bermuda, at least I had something. And when you sailed away, I felt that I had even less than before. To have less than nothing, you have to lose something that you did not have before when you had nothing. I know that maybe that doesn't make sense. But it doesn't go back to zero. It left a hollow place. So I had to find you, to try. Just to try."

"But what about your mother?" I asked, searching her eyes.

"Mum passed on the week after you left. You remember that she had not been doing well."

"I'm so sorry," I said.

"I know. It's OK. She's in a better place now." And she hugged me tightly.

I kissed her again, and her mouth was warm, and soft, and sweet, and her eyes were wet; she sniffed, a couple of salt tears ran down her cheeks, and she hugged me harder, and I thought, I would never think that her skinny little arms could hug so hard. She pressed up against me and it was an eager togetherness, to make as much contact, everywhere, to press close, to feel the closeness, the contact, the connection, limb to limb, pressing hard, warm, caressing, trying to press against one another everywhere at once. I had not known that feeling in a long time, and now I realized how much I had missed it.

"Let's go inside," I said, "You need a fresh beer! It sounds like you met Dieter!"

"Yes, he is a good friend, he likes you. I was asking around, and he knew you, he said, and would bring you to me. He told me that your boat is here, his also, and he is looking out for you. He said that without a doubt, you would be here at the Dinghy Dock tonight."

"He knows me too well," I replied.

We went back inside. I was surprised at myself for being so happy to see her, quite nearly overjoyed, and happy not to be alone now. After all, I am a man, I reasoned, so why would I not welcome the company of a friend? I kept my arm around her when we went inside, and there was Dieter, grinning from ear to ear, jolly and red-cheeked, "Aha! I see that you found your friend!" he said to Amélie. "I found him all right," she replied.

Later, when the bar was closing, we took the dinghy through the dark and choppy seas to *Rugosa*. We sat at the dinette table in the glow of the oil lamps while the boat rocked lightly in the wind gusts and halyard lines slapped against the solid wooden mainmast. The wind whistled in the shrouds and the harbor was alive with the sounds, near and far, of noisy lines against hollow aluminum masts. Amélie sat across from me. Her eyes were dark and liquid with the glow of the lamps, the water beads in her hair sparkled dimly and she forced a weak smile. "So here I am," she said.

"You flew in?" I asked.

"Yes. This morning, from Tortola."

"Well," I said, cradling my head in my hands, "You won't be able to fly out tomorrow. I heard that all flights are cancelled."

"Stuck with me. Well not really. If you don't want me here, I can find a place to stay."

"No, no, no that's not what I meant. I'm glad you're here, with me, that is. I'm glad you came. This storm is a problem though. We can't ride it out on the boat."

"No?"

"No, remember the storm in St. George's? The wise thing is to go ashore. This is not a little blow, either. I could lose the boat. So could everyone else in here who owns one. We'll have to get a place ashore. There are small hotels up the street, maybe you saw them coming down. More like little two-story motels. Maybe we can get a room in one of them, I think there are three. We will have to invite Dieter, split the cost three ways. He can't stay on his boat through the storm either."

But she knew that I was uneasy, for she had acted on impulse, and she had no charts for the waters that lay ahead.

"I don't know what to do, really," she began. "I don't want to..."

"...Not now," I interrupted. "Please. There will be plenty of time to figure this all out later. Don't worry. We have to get through this hurricane first. Let's stay together, stay with me. We'll figure it out, no matter that we have no charts. We'll feel our way along. Toss the lead-line, go slowly. I'm glad you're here."

With that, she brightened, and came over to me, leaning over and embracing me. I squeezed her bare arms, they were warm and firm. "Come on," she said, her hands locked around the back of my neck, trying to pull me up off the settee, "I want to make love."

◆◆◆ ◆ ◆◆◆

When morning broke the next day, the wind had freshened, arriving with sheets of rain in ever more frequent squalls. St. Martin had seemed a happy, colorful, tropical paradise when I had arrived a couple of days earlier, but now there was a pre-storm tension in the air as low, scudding, dirty-gray clouds raced across the island, and the rain showers began to lash the landscape with greater frequency, blowing, slanted, soaking at times. Everything was warm, humid, and wet; clothes damp, shoes squishy. The wind whipped the coconut palm fronds around cruelly, tearing them off, fragments of palm littering the road and the stubbly Bermuda grass on what passed for little lawns. The wind was not yet strong enough to be dangerous; nothing of any size was flying about. That would come in a few hours. It was, we learned, a painfully slow moving storm. Down by the pond, workers from the charter company were closing the shutters to protect windows, and the awnings along the waterfront were bellying and flapping; they would soon tear if not taken in. Young men were zooming about the pond in grey Italian inflatables, making final adjustments to anchors and lines. The chop was kicking up even in the pond now, making it wet work for them.

A big crowd had gathered at the Dinghy Dock, all the familiar faces from the last couple of days. They had it tough; they had paid big money to charter yachts but were now marooned ashore, their deposits forfeited. So they stood around, resigned to their situation, annoyed that they were not going to get their money back just the same. As the wind rose and the humming sound of the wind in wire rigging jumped an octave, we all stood around guzzling beer and cocktails, talking, laughing, and joking while Bryan in his Hawaiian shirt kept the cold clear bottles of Carib moving and clinking. The tropical paradise of bright sun under sapphire skies, green palm trees, sea breezes, and Captain Nigel's big colorful macaw had now turned upside-down.

But for all that, we had the Dinghy Dock, a place unique in all the world, and its jolly, skinny, ageing hippie proprietor whose main goal at the moment was to raise enough money by working and then selling the business to move to the southern part of Thailand which, supposedly, had become the new chic spot for expatriate American flower children who still believed in warm climates, free love, cheap living, plentiful ganja, and the Path to Enlightenment. Bryan had been through hurricanes before, and when he heard that a big storm was coming, he set about preparing for it by purchasing and storing necessities and everything else that he knew would be needed.

The three of us, Amélie, Dieter made one last trip to our boats to bring clothes, food, and supplies in big duffel bags. Dieter, I learned with great relief, had arranged a room for us the day before at a small two-story hotel a short walk up the hill, the Ponce de Leon Hotel, a cinderblock and stucco building. Amélie and I made the last adjustments to the anchor and mooring lines holding *Rugosa*, then came ashore in the dinghy and pulled it up on the sandy shore and into the growth behind the charter company's office building. There were a lot of dinghies pulled up there too, and I took a short length of light chain that I had brought, and padlocked the dinghy with the chain looped around the base of a coconut tree. "We shouldn't lose our dinghy unless the tree goes too," I said. Dieter came in with us; we had gone over to his boat to help him make final adjustments. We carried our bags up the hill and checked into our room. We had the key; the door to the office was closed and locked and there was nobody in the place.

Once in the room, I saw that there were two queen-size beds in one room, a wicker-frame futon, a small round table and two chairs. There was a small efficiency-style kitchenette against one wall, a small refrigerator, sink, and two-burner electric stove. That will be no good, I thought, once the power goes out.

Dieter immediately turned the air conditioner on full, to dry out and cool the room "...as much as possible before the lights go out," he explained.

One entered the room, which was on the first floor, via a double sliding glass door that opened onto a patio. In the middle of the patio was an in-ground swimming pool. Off the main room there was a small, narrow bathroom or powder room, toilet and sink only, leading to a full bath with a large counter and sink, plus a shower stall, but no tub. There were tables and chairs, lawn furniture essentially, in the main room with the bed, and a little sink and coffee maker. The cupboards were empty of everything except a beat-up aluminum saucepan and some silverware.

"Don't worry," Amélie said, "I will make it comfortable in here."

"I wish we had a tub to fill with fresh water while we have water," Dieter said.

"Then let's fill everything we've got, now," I replied, "Pans, wastebaskets, whatever will hold water."

It occurred to me that we still had a couple of bags of laundry down at the laundry service shack at Captain Nigel's. "We'd better go get that," I told Dieter. "We're going to need those clean, dry clothes."

The three of us hurried down the street to the service building. Nobody was there, the girls were gone, and the shack was locked. "Shite, they've gone home," I said.

"This is a problem," Dieter said, I don't have a lot with me and some of it is soiled too."

I banged on the door. There was no answer, and the sound of my fist on the door was nearly drowned out by the rising wind gusts and its violence in the trees around us. "We've got to get in there and get our stuff," I said. "We can pay them for it when they open again."

The door was split into two parts with a shelf on the bottom half that was used for serving customers when the place was open. The top half of the door would be open and the girls came to the door and handed your laundry over to you and you paid them right there. But now it was a simple matter to jimmy the lock and hasp with my rigging knife. I could only get the top half of the door to open up. "You're small and skinny," I told Amélie, "You can climb over the shelf and onto the counter. Our bags are up there over the washers, there should be tags with our names on them."

Over the door she went, as lithe and slippery as a kid, hopped inside and reached for the clear plastic tagged bundles of cleaned, folded laundry on the shelf. It was almost dark in there with no lights. "You would make a wonderful burglar," I said. "We should try this with a bank some time."

Just as she was bringing two bundles over, a hoarse voice from behind us barked, "Hey! What are you doing there!" It was Captain Nigel.

"Your girls closed shop early," I called out, "We need our clothes! We are happy to pay you, we just need them. If we don't get them now, we probably won't be able to get them later."

"You cannot do this!" he roared, sputtering angrily. "Where do you think you are? This is the Caribbean! You cannot do this here. Too much of this happens. These girls, they work hard, this is their living, you cannot cheat them..."

"We're not cheating anybody," I replied, my voice rising. "There was nobody here to help us! We've been at sea and have no clean clothes. How much do you need? I can pay you and you can pay them!"

"You have to put it back!" he shouted. This made Dieter roar with laughter, as he turned around to face him. Captain Nigel's eyes opened wide with astonishment and recognition. "Dieter...!" The two men rushed at each other, and embraced heartily. "You are raiding the laundry room?" Nigel asked, his face now a broad grin, "Shame on you!"

"You want I should go through a hurricane in my dirty underwear?" Dieter replied, then laughed and pulled a twenty-dollar bill from his pocket and offered it to Captain Nigel, who waved it away. "Nah! You I can trust! Pay them later, I know that you will. How many bundles? Only ten dollars."

"We are good for it!" Dieter assured him. "This is my friend Captain Williams. He is all right. And this is his girlfriend Emily. They were just desperate for their clean clothes. Nobody intended to steal. Here now, my good friend, take the money now, because after the storm, no one knows where people will be."

"That's true, but you and your friends of course can stay here," and with that, Nigel gently seized the bill and it disappeared into his pocket with amazing speed. "And you must come by for a drink when this storm passes. I have good French wine. Your friends too, of course. Including your little burglar, ha? Yes of course. Keep dry and safe. I am sorry I could not offer you a room, but they were all booked up. But you have a good, sound mooring. Are you the skipper of the other boat?" Nigel asked me.

"Yes, I am, I'm Nate Williams," I explained.

"Be safe, then, Captain. Oh well, you are with Dieter, so there is no worry."

"We are up at the Ponce," Dieter said. "I booked the last room."

"Aha, my cousin Jamie's shit-hole! Well good luck there, I hope the toilets do not back up on you. Or the roof blow off. But anyway, now I must go. I have to take care of my big macaw. He is old, hurricanes upset him terribly. But I have a secure place indoors for him."

Later towards evening the wind became so strong that it was dangerous to be outdoors. A wooden shingle blew off a building and hit a fellow who was walking down the road in the cheek, literally opening his face. While a couple of people struggled to get over the roads to get him to a doctor, I decided to make one last foray down to the Dinghy Dock, with Dieter and Amélie struggling alongside against the wind in the encroaching darkness. The rain was moving nearly horizontally in gusts; Amélie's polo shirt, shorts and sneakers were thoroughly soaked, but she did not seem to mind. The hurricane was now very close to the island, and the roads were flooded everywhere with light brown-muddy water running in rivers. The wind was blowing in gusts over 60 knots, and was beginning to damage the palm trees and to rip shingles off of the hotel roofs. Brown shards of bark from the palm trees were ripping off and flying through the air. Nothing anywhere would dry. Dampness permeated all, rain, dripping wetness and tepid warmth. Perspiration did not evaporate; it simply joined the moisture from the windblown rain and ran down our foreheads and bodies under our armpits in little rivulets.

Down on the docks Captain Nigel's was deserted, and there were only a few people about, sheltered from the wind, having drinks at Bryan's. The entrance to Oyster Pond was an impossible scene of rough water, not even navigable. Earlier in the day while still light, it had been a turbulent stretch, stained yellowish brown from mud and sand stirred up by the intensifying storm. I thought about yet a day earlier, when the same scene had been impossibly blue and crystalline, with white wisps of cloud borne aloft by the trade winds, and the lovely peaks of St. Bart's in the distance. Now it was all spume and spindrift, rain and ripping wind, roiling into the harbor.

Bryan's was closing; there was no more cooking, his 'galley fires were out' until the storm passed. I thought of making one last foray to scout up some food if I could. "You two go back to the hotel," I said, "I'll be along in just a little bit."

"You be careful," Amélie said.

"Don't be too long," Dieter added, "And whatever it is you find, bring a bottle back for me too!"

I laughed, then set out against the wind, zig-zagging my way along the waterfront and up a narrow street, dodging from sheltered spot to sheltered spot, from behind one car to another. The wind gusts shook the cars parked in front of the hotel. Whenever a big gust came along, I took shelter behind a vehicle. Gradually, I made it to the portico and lobby of a stone hotel. I walked up to the owner; he was behind a counter in the open atrium, sheltered from the wind, but the rain was blowing everywhere and everything was wet. I approached the counter; the manager and an assistant were behind it, trying to troubleshoot some unnamed problem. Just then I put my hand on the copper-sheathed counter, and felt a shock; 220 volts of electricity were leaking through it.

"Holy shit!" I exclaimed as I jumped back and away from it, my arm still tingling from the shoulder to the fingers.

"Yes my friend, you see, you had better watch out," he said with a thick accent.

"No kidding," I replied. "I think you've got an electrical problem!"

"We're trying to find it," he answered impatiently. Confident, after a moment, that my heart was still beating, I then pressed my case.

"I'm looking for some food for my friend. She has not eaten anything in a couple of days. I have money to pay you."

His eyes met mine; very solemnly, he spoke quietly, "What food we have, I have to save for my hotel guests. We have a bad storm upon us, supplies could run low. But here, take this for your friend." He handed me two foil-wrapped packets the size of hot dogs in buns. I tried to hand him a soggy few bills, but he dismissed me with a wave of his hand; he would accept no payment. I thanked him, and hurried back to the Ponce, dodging flying palm branches, shingles, and other missile hazards. I handed them to Amélie; she unwrapped them. They were simple sandwiches, thick slices of lean ham and soft cheese on plain baguettes. "Where did you get these?" She asked. "At a hotel. Put them in the boat cooler with the ice; we can have them later."

"Did you bring rum?" Dieter asked. "I expect you to bring something back that is worthwhile, and all you bring are sandwiches? What good are you?"

I shrugged, "I know, I know. Useless. Useless."

Once the electricity went out, the phone soon followed. The only light in the room was the fading daylight coming in through the double glass doors. Humidity and warm moistness began to rise, and we began to be uncomfortable again. We realized that with the power out, the water would go next, so while there was water pressure, and with the help of a little flashlight that I had brought along, I filled every possible container, including a plastic wastebasket, with water. I did not realize that what I was actually doing was draining the water out of the pipes going to the upper floors; but it was fresh water, and it would be needed. I garnered perhaps five gallons, all told; with the last of the dribbly water, I took a little shower. It would be the last shower I would have for some time.

Near midnight, the wind gusts increased to hurricane force. There was no possibility of getting any sleep. The strongest gusts came in intermittent bands, and we could hear them coming from a long way off. There would first be steady wind, and in the distance, a roaring that seemed to grow in pitch and intensity as it approached, and then the full force of it would hit like a hammer, a sudden blast as defined as a moving wall, or perhaps the front of a freight train. Before each gust struck the building, the wind screamed a high-pitched scream such as I'd never heard before. The entrance to our room, the double sliding glass door that opened onto a stone patio, faced directly broadside to the wind, and as the wind increased its pitch, the glass doors began to bow and bend inward, and I was afraid that they would burst into the room at some point, imploding and thundering shards of glass throughout, cutting us to pieces. Noting the cheap construction that seemed to be the nature of most buildings on this island, I didn't think that safety glass of any kind had been used in these windows or sliding doors. If they burst, I told Amélie, we could suffer fatal injuries. "We need to move to a safer place," I said.

The three of us then squeezed into the bathroom. Amélie and I sat up on a big counter on either side of the sink, and put our backs to the concrete wall. Dieter threw some pillows in a corner and made himself a comfortable nest. This hotel, like many of the other hotels on the island of recent construction, was built of cinderblock. Most of the buildings had corrugated metal and fiber-glass over a wood frame for roofing, and some had asphalt roofing tiles. The cinderblock wall gave me some reassurance. The entrance to the bathroom was off the main room, but we figured that if the glass doors burst inward, the shards of glass would not get into the bathroom simply because one had to turn a right angle from the room to enter the bathroom. The room was laid out in some manner of European style. There was a tiny oblong room containing a toilet and a sink; the larger "bathroom" had a shower stall and a long counter with a sink in the middle. We hunkered down in this larger room with the shower. We closed the drapes across the sliding glass doors, and pushed furniture in the room up against the curtain. Now all there was left to do was wait it out and survive the storm. The idea behind closing the heavy drapes was that, should the glass doors implode, the drapes would hopefully check some of the flying shards.

At one point I realized that if the glass doors blew in, rain and water and glass would be everywhere, and it would ruin my clothes in my duffel-bag as well as any other belongings. So, in the noisy darkness, with the winds screaming all about, I dashed back into the room. I grabbed our duffel bags and dragged them into our 'sanctuary' bathroom. This took perhaps a minute, no more; but it seemed to me like an hour, and every second I was afraid that the glass doors would burst in on me. Dieter suggested that to take the pressure off the doors, we should open a couple of windows away from the wind, to let air pressure equalize with the outside. I didn't know whether he was right or not, but I opened the bathroom window, as well as another window in the toilet-room. We sat there uncomfortably in the semi-darkness, the only light coming in from an orange emergency fluorescent fixture mounted on an outside wall in an alley opposite the window. In a little while, that light failed when its battery died, and we were left in complete darkness with only the violent sound of the wind. As each fresh gust struck the building at the height of the storm, we could hear pieces of the hotel ripping off and blowing down onto the ground, pieces of roofing, and timber. Sand blew in the window; dirt and grit were in the air.

Our ears were popping constantly, as the air pressure fluctuated wildly. It was an ordeal and none of us knew how long it would last. For several hours, we sat in the humidity, enduring, sweating, well into the wee hours of the morning. Time passed very slowly. There was no possibility of sleeping while sitting up; there was no possibility of comfort, and neither of us would risk going back into the main room. It was too noisy to talk, what with the sound of the wind, and the sounds of things breaking. After what seemed an eternity, perhaps by two o'clock in the morning, the wind subsided a little, and then dropped completely. Apparently, the eye of the hurricane was directly over the island. Stiffly, we each arose and went back into the main room. The glass doors had held, and we were thankful for that. I rummaged through a bag I had brought from the boat; in it were a couple of cans of beans, soup, tuna, some crackers, and other assorted items which we immediately opened and ate, cold, by flashlight. It wasn't long before the wind picked up again, but it was from a different direction this time, quite nearly the opposite from where it had come earlier, as it would be now that the storm was moving over the island and the wind circulation was coming from the opposite direction.

Realizing that there would be no further danger from the glass doors, and there were no windows on the back wall of the room, the three of us crowded onto the single large bed and tried to get some sleep. When I awoke in the morning, I had slept a few hours, and I noticed that Dieter was gone. Outside, the skies were gray, and it was still blowing although the winds had diminished greatly.

Everything I owned was soaked or dirty. I had no clean clothes, no dry clothes, and no dry shoes. The stone patio was covered with rubble, mostly broken timbers, ripped pieces of corrugated fiberglass, and asphalt roofing tiles. Amélie sat up and rubbed her eyes; they were bleary, and she was still tired.

I found a battered saucepan in the cupboard, one of the very few utensils that the room had, and scooped some clear water out of the swimming pool to wash off part of the patio, which was now littered with ripped palm fronds, fragments of various vegetation, and roofing tiles. This pool will probably soon become a community bathtub, I mused sadly. As I was wandering about the patio, the door to the room adjacent to us on the second-floor opened, and a heavy-set older man stepped out onto the balcony. He was dressed casually in a Hawaiian shirt and shorts and spoke with a British accent. He and his wife had been staying there for some time, and had apparently come through the storm all right. She was still asleep, he said.

"Do you folks have any bottled water?" he asked.

"Not really," I answered. "I filled our wastebaskets and every pot and pan we could find from the taps before the storm hit, so we have some clean water, if you need it."

"Oh, no. I mean for you fellows. Here." He reached down and handed us four liter bottles of French mineral water. "Take care, conserve it. Trust me, chaps; you'll need it later on."

"Come have a drink with us," I offered.

"No, thank you mates, we're all set here. I have to tend to the missus. Be careful and take care. Cheers." With that, he went back into the room and shut the door.

"Decent, generous fellow," I said to Amélie, who nodded in agreement.

At that point, I decided to wander down to the dock area to see what condition it was in. "I'm going down to the dock to see what's up," I told Amélie. She flopped back onto the bed without making reply.

"Why don't you come too?"

"All right," she said, wearily, and got up. We both stepped out onto the patio, rubbing our eyes, still groggy from the nearly sleepless night, trying to take it all in. I had a small bottle of water, tepid but fresh, and poured most of it into a cup, filling it two-thirds, and the rest with Mount Gay rum from a half-full bottle that I had brought up from the Dinghy Dock the night before. I took a big swallow and handed it to Amélie. Instead of recoiling from the liquor, as I expected her to, she took it happily, and took a long pull at it, even though it was warm. I could only smile.

Bryan's was closed; and yet a number of people were standing around down there, idly gathered about the dock to observe the storm's damage, and a couple of people said that he planned to open later in the afternoon. We were all cheered by this prospect; he would rescue us, for although we could not help ourselves in any way, totally shut off from the outside world as we were, we could at least socialize and drink. Many of the boats at the dock were seriously beat up. Nylon and other synthetic lines had stretched greatly in the force of the wind, allowing boats to smash up against one another and against the dock. There was some severe damage to boats and to the dock in some places, but for the most part the fleet had fared well. For some, however, the news was quite bad. It was rather strange, how there was either a lot, or a little, damage to vessels in the harbor, with hardly any degree of damage in the middle. Some vessels exhibited only minor cosmetic damage, while others were a total loss.

The monohull ketch owned by a couple from Marseilles had moved sideways in the storm and smashed repeatedly up against a big catamaran. From the outside, there appeared to be almost little or no damage to the monohull; but inside, the cabin was totally destroyed, woodwork, paneling, and bulkheads having come loose and shattered into broken pieces and bits of wood and fragments as though a bomb had gone off in there. His boat had literally been destroyed on the inside, while sustaining no apparent outward damage. His flexible hull had literally compressed as the 150-knot winds had blown it up against the other boat. In one instance, stretching lines had allowed a big catamaran to back up against a floating dock and to chew large pieces out of it.

Rugosa was still tied securely, riding on her lines; from this vantage point I could see no damage, nor had any other boats drifted down on her. I intended to go aboard a little later after re-inflating the dinghy. I could see Dieter's boat out where it ought to be, also having escaped damage from what I could tell.

Awnings were blown away, canvas shredded; but we were greatly relieved to see that Bryan's had suffered no serious harm, and that our beer source was safe. We were relieved to know that we still had a haven where we could gather and commiserate.

Around midafternoon, a small crowd began to gather at Bryan's, and when the shutters opened, a cheer arose from the crowd. Bryan, in his remarkable and infinite wisdom, had laid in enough provisions that we would neither starve nor go thirsty.

Out of the corner of my eye, I spied Dieter picking his way along the dock, watching his footing especially where planks were broken. He had, I surmised, been to his boat. As he approached, Amélie rushed over to him and hugged his big lanky frame, exclaiming, "Dieter! We were worried about you. Is your boat okay?"

He nodded, smiling, "Everything aboard is fine." He had an air about him of rum and body odor. He had grown a stubble beard by now and his yellow tropical shirt with the dolphin prints was all wrinkled. "Yes I know, I need a bath," he said.

"Wouldn't hurt any of us," I replied. "We should use the pool before everyone else does."

We walked back up the hill to the hotel. When we arrived, we saw that while we had been down at Bryan's, a young couple had pulled up a couple of chairs and a table on the stone patio by the pool and were drinking a big bottle of wine. They spoke no English, but the tall, long black-haired woman that was the wife or girlfriend was laughing and talking loudly and animatedly and was apparently quite drunk. At least she seems happy, I thought to myself.

I looked down into the hotel's in-ground pool. The chlorinated water was still clean and clear, but the blue bottom of the pool was a crazy-quilt of black asphalt roof tiles. There were some palm fronds and a couple of small green coconuts floating in it. The sun had begun to burn through and it was growing hot.

"I'm going in," I said to Dieter. "Sounds good to me too," he replied.

"I'm going to go put my bathing suit on," Amélie said.

We stripped down to our shorts and jumped into the pool, and began removing the palm fronds and floating junk. The cool water felt good.

While we were thus splashing around, I suddenly noticed that the young woman on the patio had stood up, and, despite the emphatic entreaties of her male companion, had stripped off her bathing suit. Dieter noticed too; then I saw his jaw drop as she hopped across the patio laughing and naked and saying something very fast and very loud in French, and then swan-dove into the pool directly behind Dieter. The expression on his face was one of surprise and embarrassed amusement.

A very loud and earnest exchange ensued between the laughing girl and her male companion, who was quite upset with her, probably because there were two other strange men in the same pool with her. She was finally persuaded to climb out and put her bathing suit back on; Dieter and I were mum, of course, and did our best to pretend that nothing was happening, Dieter keeping his back to her all the while that she was in the pool, or at least pretending not to look out of the corner of his eye. Finally they stood up and took what was left of the bottle and made their way around the corner to a different hotel, presumably the one that they were staying at.

"She had very nice, long black hair," Dieter said.

"Yes, she certainly did, didn't she?"

"She gone?" asked Amélie, emerging from the room.

"You saw?" I asked.

"Are you kidding? Crikey. Well now it's my turn in the pool. At least I have a proper swimsuit on!" and with that, she dove in.

There was not much else to do but walk around the rest of the day, and later, eat from our stores of canned goods and sit around the patio drinking. Dieter and I moved a big piece of broken roof, part of an eave, out of the way, dragging it off the patio so that it would not be stepped on by bare feet or tripped over. It was a mess of splinters, nails, and jagged wood.

Across the street from the hotel stood the crest of a hill with an old naval cannon in a gun carriage mounted on it, pointing out to sea. From the hilltop, we could hear the roar of the breakers on the beaches below. White, angry surf and big swells were still rolling ashore on the unprotected beaches, while occasional drizzle and mist blew by. Down in Oyster Pond, we could see the crazed jumble of masts along the ring of the pond of all the sailboats that had blown ashore and now lay on their sides on the beach, at odd senseless angles to one another, stranded and damaged. "This island is one hell of a mess," I said.

Chapter 17

Aftermath

"However bad the storm you are in, there is still sun somewhere over your horizon."

— *Ken Nutt*

The second morning after the storm, we went down to the Dinghy Dock looking for something to eat, and were happy to see that much of the debris around the docks had been cleaned up, or at least pushed aside, and we saw, to our delight, that the Dock was once again unshuttered and open for regular hours. Bryan stood behind the bar, operating some type of propane-powered portable stove linked to a big rusty gas bottle set on the ground. It was around eleven in the morning and Oyster Pond was a busy place indeed. Boat owners and staff and crew of the charter company were working to clean up and repair damage. Some were salvaging clothing and other soaked items from their boats. I could smell coffee brewing, and the aroma was heavenly.

The little bar was nearly full; people were drinking coffee, rum, coffee with rum, beer, every variety of beverage, mostly with alcohol. Bryan had put out open cartons of Parmalat milk so that folks could lighten their coffee. There was sugar in little damp packets. Bryan was hopping around, and in response to a query from a fellow at the bar about running out of things, he shook his head and smiled, "Oh, no! I've been through this hurricane thing a few times. I know how to plan ahead." Bryan had stowed extra cases of beer and liquor, eggs, bread, batteries, bottled water, propane, ice, as much as he could cram into the limited storage space that the building afforded. Now it would pay off. Bryan had multiple pans working; he was making breakfast sandwiches for everyone.

There was no electricity, so eggs were scrambled in a pan over the gas grill. There was cheese, there was bacon, and the bread was toasted, sometimes blackened a little, over the blue flames. It was grilled bread; a little crude, perhaps, like camping and toasting your bread over a fire, but it worked, and everyone ate.

In addition to breakfast, Bryan, who was a rather decent cook, made one main dish, and lots of it, for the rest of the day, lunch and dinner. These meals were planned, their ingredients ordered in advance, and the offering changed every day, although there was nothing else on the menu. But there was no need. Each meal was a one-pot type, spaghetti and meatballs, or chicken a la king, chicken curry, or a big stew, something that involved a main dish over rice or noodles. It was good, satisfying, and filling; the portions were generous and nobody starved. Bryan kept a log on a notepad of who ate and drank what, and everyone was expected to settle up before leaving the island, whenever that might be. If you wanted to sit at the bar and drink rum, you were given the bottle, a glass, and a little notepad and pencil to keep track of your own tally. You mixed your own drinks, poured them yourself, weak or killer, the choice was up to the drinker. So, depending on what sort of a day you were having, you self-medicated accordingly.

Now I find that my memory of the next couple of days is more of a collage of images and moments, than that of a chronology. The weather steadily improved, until the last day, when the sun shone again with all its tropic intensity out of a deep blue sky. We moved back aboard our boats; all the while busy helping others with theirs. I remember the occasional visits to our little enclave at Bryan's by the South African Consul, a large, portly, and pleasant man who lived in a beautiful estate on the opposite side of Oyster Pond, on the side of a great hill. He invited anyone in distress to come over to his house for refreshment, or to make a phone call. Apparently he had the only working phone in the area, some sort of government-supported direct technological link, and he kept us informed of what was happening on the island, such as efforts to repair Princess Juliana airport so that commercial planes could begin arrivals and departures again. The U.S. had no direct representation on the island, so we Americans were stuck, without any help from our government, and we did not think that the President was going to fly in a military transport to take anyone home, despite the flurry of US-built C-130 aircraft constantly coming into the island, as well as leaving, filled with supplies and Dutch and French troops.

The hurricane had decimated the island, destroyed homes and farms and businesses, and the poor had suffered greatly. There was real fear of looting and rioting; hence the soldiers, brought in to their respective sides of the island.

We did have unofficial U.S. Government representation, a lady and her husband whose names now escape me, who were satellite consular officers. They had little or no rank or authority, as the main U.S. Consular office for the islands was in Barbados. The technical details of the connection escape me. And yet they were kind and compassionate and bought many a drink and bottle of Carib beer for their fellow Americans for whom they could do very little. They dispensed what medicines and bandages they had, made phone calls when they could get through, and in general provided moral support.

Wetness and dampness was pervasive. Clothes would not dry. Shoes remained soggy. Broken glass from windows had actually become pulverized and mixed in with the sand and the dust of the road. This broke the skin of one's feet and allowed the invasion of fungus. In the tropics, bacterial infection and fungus run rampant. On one occasion, a young fellow in his mid-20's came to the little cottage where the consular representatives lived, up the street a few blocks from Bryan's, with a problem. His sandal-type shoes, all he had brought with him and open and offering no protection, had allowed some of this glass powder to get between his feet and the sandal straps, punctured the skin, and now he had some sort of infection like 'trench foot' where the skin was literally dying and sloughing off his feet. He was justifiably concerned, but there was nothing that anyone could do about it, at least not locally.

On the afternoon of the fourth day after the storm, Philip, the dock manager for the charter company, took us with him in his double-cab truck for a ride to Philipsburg. I cannot begin to describe the scenes of devastation, of telephone and power line poles down, lying in the mud; or of houses with roofs gone. Houses were windowless, mattresses and bedding and clothing hung out on lines to dry, or simply hanging out of the blown-out windows, having been soaked by the relentless rain and flooding.

Trees and vegetation were stripped and destroyed, and the local people were standing or sitting resignedly about their yards, around their shattered homes on mud-caked streets, everything a wallowing mess, debris strewn everywhere. We passed the small airport at Grand Case where small planes had been broken up into pieces, like dismembered insect bodies, and strewn all over the airport runway and boundary areas. We saw countless yachts up on the beaches surrounding Philipsburg, large fishing and cargo craft had been driven up onto the beaches, and there were sunken vessels, some of reasonable size, in the harbor.

Driving along the rutted roads was slow, because there were many delays, military checkpoints, and blockages, but we did not at any time feel that we were in danger of being stopped and looted. In Philipsburg, sand had piled up like snowdrifts on one street that had a cinderblock wall on the side of the street opposite the sea. The sand covered cars that had parked there, burying them like snow in a blizzard, only tawny brown. We were only too happy to get back to ruined Oyster Pond, but even so, it brought scant relief or comfort; it was something akin to returning to your home after a tornado only to find that even though the land was there, the property was there, the house was blown down and could no longer be occupied. The warm feeling of being at home melts away, to be replaced by a kind of deep sadness and realization that the current reality is irreversible; there is no going back to the way the place was, at least not near-term. The island was a wreck from one end to the other.

I immediately began to feel restless. I knew that it was time to be moving on. There had been some looting of boats, a few at the other side of the pond and in the harbors at Philipsburg and other places, and of course we heard about them. There was no electricity or running water. I sat at the Dinghy Dock bar with Dieter and a group of other stranded sailors and tourists, all basically comparing notes; some of whose boats had been badly damaged. I knew that I was brooding.

"You are deep in thought," Dieter said.

"I am. I'm trying to figure out where to go next."

"I thought you were going around the world," he replied.

"Maybe. But one thing is certain; I need to get off this island. It's messed up and it's going to be messed up for a very long time."

"They will rebuild it, don't worry, down here they can be pretty quick about recovering after big storms."

"Maybe, but you know, no place is ever exactly the same again? A disaster like this changes the face of a town, an island, forever. Sure, they will rebuild things. But more often than not they will be plainer and cheaper, or rebuilt to be something else. Besides, I did not plan on staying here for very long."

"It seems that you are never one to stay in any one place for very long anyway, yourself."

"No, not lately. Are you?"

"No. Like I told you I the beginning, I am a boat vagabond. Now and forever."

"One thing we have going for us is that our boats were not damaged in the storm. We were lucky," I said.

Dieter laughed, "No, we were smart, and careful. Preparation is everything, Captain Williams."

"I want to go someplace where there has not been a hurricane or a cyclone, at least not in recent memory," I replied.

"Oh, you want some place pure, and clean, and uncorrupted, like your heart?" he mocked gently. He was good at that.

"Some place that's not a wreck is all, some place that is not a dead end," I explained irritably, knowing well enough that he knew what I meant. "This place is broken and I don't have the time or the patience to wait for it to heal."

"Well if you are looking for a place with no storms, sir, you are definitely in the wrong sea. This is the Caribbean, remember. Cyclones love these islands! Now where is the girl? Will you stay here for her?"

"Taking a nap down below in the boat, I think," I replied. "But anyhow, she's not from here, she's from Bermuda. She can go back there if she likes."

"You would send her back?"

"I can't send her anywhere," I said, "She will go where she wants. But I wanted a solo voyage, not a romance."

"That's what Popeye says, 'Wimmins is bad luck on a ship.'" Dieter quipped.

I had to laugh at this. "But it's not about luck, it's about what to do with her, how to deal with this. What am I supposed to do, take her around the world with me? What if we get two weeks out of Panama and a third of the way across the Pacific and we have a fight and she wants off the boat? What do I do, feed her to the sharks?"

"I think you actually might," Dieter replied.

For some reason this annoyed me, and I stood up and pushed in my bar stool.

"Oh don't get temperamental," he said. "It's bothering you, isn't it?"

"Yes it is, because I am not sure what to do. I mean, the sex is nice, but..."

"It's a long way to Tahiti, alone. More like four thousand miles. Do you paint? I knew a solo sailor who spent his time painting watercolors during his trip across the Pacific. He set the self-steering vane and a preventer on the boom and reeled off nearly three thousand miles that way. But I say it is better if you have someone with you. Especially if you already know that the sex is good."

I nodded, and chuckled. "Thanks for that perspective. No, I don't paint. Anyway, I need to provision the boat a bit, but there is no place to buy anything right now. But I have dry stores aboard and I can fish."

"When are you leaving?"

"Probably tomorrow, why not. I think I'll go back up to the BVI's. They were out of the main path of the storm. I think I will go to Virgin Gorda and spend some time in North Sound and go to the Crawl Pub. I liked it up that way when I was there last. But before I make any decisions or do anything, I wish I could find out whatever the hell happened to Carver and *Gleam*. They were off to Antigua, were probably down there when the storm hit. I hope they didn't take a beating."

"You will see him again," Dieter predicted. "I would bet money on it. Besides, Antigua is far enough south that he would have missed the worst of the storm too."

"He likes to hang out in the BVI's," I said. "So he might come back up here."

"So is the girl going with you?"

"I don't know," I said, "Pass me that rum bottle, will you? And some of that pineappple juice. We haven't really talked about it yet. We haven't had that fight yet. That's a big one. And it's coming, which is what I'm nervous about, as you can tell. So it'll be tonight maybe. Or in the morning while I'm getting underway. Hopefully I won't get so jazzed by it that I head out while leaving my dinghy tied to the dock or something like that."

After a while I knew that there was no way to avoid the inevitable, so reluctantly left the Dinghy Dock and went back to the boat. Amélie was having drinks, so I poured myself one of my own, and tried to kick off the conversation tactfully, but of course, as was the usual result, I did so clumsily.

It was the first time that I had ever seen her eyes flash with anger in the pale yellow light of the cabin lamps. She slammed her rum drink down on the dinette table and it sloshed out the top and onto the table and her hand. "So you want to send me back to Bermuda? Well then you do that."

"No, I didn't say that..."

"...But you meant it!"

She got up off the settee and came right up to me, her face in my face, her voice trembling with anger and tension, "You want to sail alone around the world? On your own? Fine, that's what you've always wanted I suppose. And that's all you'll ever have, as well." I kept my mouth shut, and let her berate me; I had started the conversation, and had quite obviously started it wrong. Now I was paying for it. Her British accent grew stronger, I noted, when she was angry.

"You want to be alone. Well let me tell you, I know what it means to be alone. And worse than that, I know what it means to be betrayed, betrayed by a worthless two-timing weak man from London who played the big romantic man, thinking he was simply having an innocent romp with an island girl who would never know much and never know better. Well Nate, you're no better than him, are you?"

"There hasn't been anyone else," I said.

"There hasn't been anyone else?" Her voice climbed in pitch. "There hasn't been any ONE!"

"Please, the other boats can hear...."

"Oh, other boats my royal brown ass! Now you listen to me. I came all the way down here to be with you. You don't think I can handle a boat? What did we do in Bermuda during the gale? Oh I guess that wasn't enough. Not a real test, hey?"

"It's not that. Will you please calm down a little?"

"You're not sending me back to Bermuda," she said, "You're not sending me anywhere. You want me off your boat? I'm out of here. Go sail to the ends of the Earth. I go where I want, too. Because what have I got? Where is my home? I have no home. That English son of a bitch disgraced me. But I thought there was more to you than what he had."

"Listen," I pleaded, "It's not about whom you are, but what I am. I don't know that I can be what you want me to be, and I'm not sure that I want to fit anyone else's mold that they want me to fit into. I don't change easily."

Her voice rose again. "And who told you that you needed to change anything, anything at all? Or be someone or something else other than what you are? Who said that? Don't be making assumptions. Just be who you are. Try to be more of a man than that poppycock who left me in London. You like the cookies, but what does that mean? Has none of it meant anything? I thought you were REAL!"

"I'm sorry," I said.

"Oh stuff your sorry shit in your bilge-pipe," she said, and raced by me and scurried up the ladder and onto the deck. Then I heard her stumbling footsteps on the dock, and she was gone, but I thought I knew where she might be heading. I sat alone in the cabin for a little while thinking about the things that we both had said, then went up the ladder and out onto the deck.

The little lamps on the sides of the floating dock illuminated the walkway. I went straight to the Dinghy Dock and there she was, now talking animatedly to two young sailors off the big Hylas sloop in the harbor who were buying her drinks. She was well on her way to being thoroughly drunk, and was alternately leaning on each fellow to either side of her, touching, rubbing, laughing, and being silly yet affectionate, as though she was looking to be picked up. The two sailors were playing right into it, enjoying it, obviously thinking that they had good potential here for an opportunity for a little threesome fun.

I quietly took a seat at the opposite end of the horseshoe-shaped bar, facing her, and if she saw me, she did not acknowledge me.

"Rum, please," I said to Bryan's assistant barkeep, and he pushed a bottle Mount Gay and a glass with a few rocks of ice in it over to me. I started working a drink on my own. I was watching Amélie all the while; she wanted to make me jealous, I understood that, and of course, it was working. But there was nothing I could do about it now. She was her own free agent; I had no say in what she did.

I looked around for Dieter, but he was nowhere to be seen. *I guess I'll have to handle this alone,* I remember saying to myself. She was behaving badly; the two guys focused on her were being very obnoxious, now; they were holding nothing back. One of them looked fairly strong, a big fellow with close-cropped blond hair, wearing a tank-top tee-shirt advertising a New Zealand rugby team called the 'All Blacks'. He was a lot bigger than I was, big-boned and ham-fisted, I thought as I sized him up. The other was a skinny Englishman with a goatee and an annoying nasal whine, and although I thought he would be manageable, he might end up being wiry and tough. Either way, I would still have to contend with both of them, I knew. But I also knew that I couldn't be the one to start it, no. I had to wait for one of them to break the rules; in that way, I might not be completely alone if it went badly for me. Someone might step in.

The way things were going, with the two guys getting loud and a little rough, I knew that I would not be long in waiting for my cue to get things rolling, so I swallowed my drink quickly and poured another from the bottle on the bar, and downed it in a gulp. My face felt hot. Out of the corner of my eye, I could see that another fellow seated at the bar directly over on my left was watching me curiously.

Then it happened. Both of Amélie's 'suitors' had grown drunk and unsteady, and then had become loud. The wiry Britisher with the nasal twang, who was also the more aggressive of the two, got off of his barstool and grabbed her left arm, trying to pull her away from the bar.

"Take your fucking hands off me," she shouted, suddenly changing her mood; real contact had surprised her, and she pulled away, then slapped him across the face with her right hand. It was a cracking clap that was very audible; the man reeled. The other, bigger man, who actually spoke with an odd thick drawl, as though he had come from the mountains of the Carolinas, laughed loudly, exclaiming,

"Come awn, put ayt baby, put ayt!"

209

The smaller man grabbed her arm again, this time more firmly, "You're coming with us, you horny burr-headed little kirby bitch!" he cried, but by that time I was already there, and I shouted, "Get your fucking hands off her, didn't you hear what she said?"

"Mind your own fucking business, you scummy pillock, else I'll..."

My right fist shot out very fast before I realized it, like a knee-jerk, almost as though it had a mind of its own and was acting independently of my will. It connected with the left side of his face, cutting him off in mid-sentence and jacking his head sideways. This was all happening in split-second time, and my first thought was that I could not believe that I had actually hit him so fast and so hard; I was all adrenalin, angry adrenalin. I saw his hand release her as he went right down, flat on his back, arms flying off to either side. Then I remember the angry, puzzled look of consternation on the face of the big meaty redneck with the buzz cut, but the moment that I looked away his ham fist caught me on the side of my head, smashing into my ear and for a second I saw flashes of light as I went straight down on hands and knees. He may not have been quick, but he hit hard. I recovered quickly, only two get back up and find them both standing there, the big redneck ready for more, and the short Britisher, as angry as ever and with a terribly mean look in his eye, punching out at me. He didn't hit me as hard as the big redneck did, and I gave it back to both of them as best I could, but they had four fists to my two and now there was blood and snot flying everywhere.

Then all of a sudden the Britisher disappeared and I turned to see the pummeling lightning-strike fists of the fellow who had sat to my left at the bar, a wiry Irishman, cursing the Britisher in Gaelic, laughing while he did so, and giving the guy a merciless pounding, the wiry foul-mouthed fellow stumbling backwards into a very large cactus at the base of a banana tree. I heard him cry out.

But now it was me against the big redneck, and I knew, from somewhere deep inside, that I could not win this one. He was strong and gaining the upper hand; he had already hurt me and I knew it. But he slowed for a moment and I saw that Amélie was literally up on his back, grabbing his head from behind and kicking him in the ribs like a cowboy digging his spurs into the sides of a racehorse. He turned around and threw her off, cursing her with racist insults, and then headed toward her, lifting one foot as though he were going to stomp on her face. That was the moment that I saw two very long fingers on a strong hand shoot out of the darkness and poke into each of his two eyes, at once. The redneck screamed in pain, and Dieter stood back, with blood on his fingers. At the same moment, two men jumped the redneck, pulling him to the ground, and there followed a general melee at the bar. Everyone now, it seemed, was fighting with everybody else, and I felt a strong arm take mine, throw it over a shoulder, and walk me off away from the fracas and into the island night. I had taken a serious beating, and only remember being carried aboard *Rugosa*, laid on a sheet in the forward berth, and passing out. When I awoke, there were ice packs on my head and face, and on my left ear, which had swollen up and was shaped like a bloody cauliflower. Dieter was sitting next to me reading a book and drinking a scotch. It was nearly noon.

"Ouch," I said.

"Well you should say that," he replied, noticing that I was now awake. "You picked a fight with two guys, not one guy, and one of them was a lot bigger than you. But he will not be a problem now. He is in the hospital, *abgeschossen*. The other guy went up to the village where a doctor had to pull seventy-eight cactus spines, long ones, out of his bony little ass. Oh, Bryan's bar is fine, don't worry, not much broken at all, and this morning, Bryan was out there with a boat brush and buckets of water, washing away the blood from the deck. I paid him a good tip. You'd never know now that there had been a fight there. But it was a corker, as they say, a *Blut und Rotz Faustkampf*, ha, ha. You gave back well; I'm proud of you."

"Where's Amélie?"

Dieter started to laugh. "Who, the troublemaker? The one who started it all? Or wait, I think that was you!"

"When you think about it, man, it hurts to talk and I had better not laugh, you're right, I should never have started that conversation."

"She is just up on the dock getting some ice. It will be a while before we shrink you back down to your normal size. Or at least parts of you."

"Dick feels small right now," I said.

"I'm not surprised. Different story last night. Do you still have all your teeth?"

"Amazingly, I do. Nothing broken far as I know."

A shadow appeared in the hatchway, and Amélie called down, "Well, Captain, may I come aboard? Or am I going to swing from the yard-arm?"

"You get down here," I replied, painfully but grinning. "I need that ice."

"This is for your face, not your drink," she mock-scolded.

"What if I hold the drink close to my face?"

"Well then maybe that's OK. Bryan is running low. If they don't get some electricity back soon, they will run out in a day or so."

"I'm going back over to my boat for a bit," Dieter said.

"You don't have to go," I said.

"Yes, stay," Amélie added.

"She spent a lot of time taking care of you last night with the ice-packs," Dieter said.

"We were both here," Amélie added.

"You need some time together to make up," Dieter said.

"No, we're cool," I said. "Water under the keel. Thanks to both of you for nursing me. Though you probably drank up all my liquor in the process."

"Well of course!" Dieter replied. "You don't think we'd hang around down below here just for you, do you? Besides, I have to get my boat ready. I think I am going to leave this island. Too messed up. I heard that the bridge is busted over in Simpson Bay. I could not even get into the bay now until they fix it."

"Let's go to North Sound, up to Virgin Gorda," I said. "Sail together. You'll like it there. Have you ever been there?"

"Yes, I know the BVI's well, North Sound is a good place."

"All of us?" Amélie asked.

I took her hand. "Wouldn't go without you," I said. "Besides I'm too busted up to sail this thing myself for a few days. We'll go to the Bitter End Yacht Club and pull up seats at The Crawl Pub. That's a great place."

"No more picking fights with bad Pommies," she said. "Or with big, dumb rednecks!"

I pulled her close. "Righto. No more fights with little Pommies either." She pulled back suddenly and raised her arm, "Oh if you weren't all busted up Nate I'd slap your wise ass," she exclaimed, laughing.

"Spare a little of that ice for a painkiller?" I asked. "The Mount Gay is…well, you know where it is!"

"I'll make you one," she replied. "When do we leave?"

"Let's sail out in the morning," I said. "I'll be okay. Dieter will be too. He will be ready, never wants help, but if he does, I can help him this evening. I'm sore but I can do it. Are any shops open for food or groceries?"

"No, nothing. How far is it to Virgin Gorda?"

"Might take a day or two, depends on the wind. We should be fine with the supplies we've got."

By evening, I was up and hobbling about the deck fairly well. Amélie and I had everything ready for a morning departure, and I thought I'd run over to *Two Blue* to check on Dieter's preparations and see if I could help in some way. Amélie came along with me.

As I walked down the finger pier, I could see the lights on in the main cabin of the big catamaran, and caught a whiff of a spicy Caribbean dish cooking. I sniffed, then I chuckled.

"What's funny?"

"How can it be? Dieter can mix a decent drink but he can't cook for squat. Where did he learn to cook Caribbean style? It actually smells good…"

Dieter had arranged, through Nigel, to move his boat in now to be dockside, far more convenient than sitting out on anchors, and only possible now because the storm was past. We stepped down into the cockpit and I could also smell marijuana smoke. "Whoa, ho! Dieter! What the hell are you…." I poked my head into the cabin, "…smoking…oh good God, Poppa Jon, what are you doing here?"

"What does it look like I'm doing?" he smiled and spoke slowly, drew on his rolled marijuana cigarette, then laughed a deep, slow, shaking laugh.

Dieter appeared from out of the starboard cabin. "He's coming along as the cook," Dieter explained.

"Oh, wow! Cook? Well can he, um, looks like can cook all right. You lucky bastard. But how are you going to do that? I mean, doesn't he live here? Can he sail?"

"My house blown down, Hotpeppa. I lived alone anyway. Yes I am a sailor. I was at sea many, many years, many before you were born for sure. I served as an Oiler on tramp steamers that ran all the way from South America to ports in the Gulf and the coast of Africa. All the Caribbean. Once or twice been all the way around the world. Sometimes I was the cook as well as an engineer. So you see, Hotpeppa, Poppa Jon have been many places, these old eyes are very blue, blue like the sea, because they have seen so much of it."

Nobody said anything for a minute or two; Poppa Jon handed the little cigarette around. "Oh what the hell," I said, taking it, drawing on it and then passing it to Amélie. She snatched it from my fingers while I coughed and drew on it until the seeds in it popped and were flying all around the cabin. I looked at her and her puffed cheeks, astonished.

"Like an old pro!" I said. She just shook her head. "You've got a lot to learn, Nathanael," she replied, exhaling a long blue stream of smoke. "And I like Poppa's name for you."

"Well I don't!" I blurted out, and then thinking better of myself, said, "Um, I didn't mean that, Poppa, I was just joking…"

He looked up at me from his comfortable seat at the dinette, and grinned, wagging his head from side to side, "Don't matter if you don't like it, or do like it, do'n make no difference, that's who you are. You the Hotpeppa, that's the end of it. Now, did you folks eat? I have made enough for everyone, big black iron pan on the galley. Made some jerk chicken, some nice black beans and rice. Come on and have some."

"Sounds good. I just became terribly hungry all of a sudden."

Chapter 18

Spanish Town

"The lovely thing about cruising is that planning usually turns out to be of little use."

— *Dom Degnon*

We left the harbor before sunrise, both boats motoring out into the early half-light, hulls gradually revealed to view by the transition from gray, to blue, then pink, light reflected from the brightening sky in the east. The sea was calm and glassy smooth, with only the gentle hills of a low ground swell alternately lifting and lowering us as they passed beneath. A white tropic bird circled overhead just before sunrise; a few fish jumped, startled by the approach of a hull breaking and rippling the surface of the quiet water. All was silent but for the murmur of the engines as we traveled, a few hundred yards apart, out from the channel that led into Oyster Pond, and onto the wide Caribbean Sea, with the purple peaks of St. Bart's in the distance, poking into the grey haze. Looking over at *Two Blue*, I could see the tall, lanky figure of Poppa Jon, standing on deck by the mast, holding onto the shrouds and taking in the morning as the boat made headway, Dieter in the cockpit with a coffee in hand, steering.

The sail covers were off, but there was no point in hoisting canvas until we had some wind; the sails would only rustle and luff, creating drag in the air. We were making good time, motoring together at better than six knots, and soon the island began to recede into the distance behind us, the just-risen sun illuminating the white and yellow stucco-sided houses on the steep hillsides of the island facing eastward out to sea. The further from the island we progressed, the less obvious was the damage from the storm, until at a distance of a few miles, no damage could be discerned to the naked eye, even though we knew, of course, that damage had been extensive. Like Poppa Jon, Amélie took a watch-standing post up by the mainmast, but sat on the top of the butterfly hatch with her coffee, taking in the view. It was a pretty morning, I thought, and there is no more lovely and in some ways mystical and unspoiled place to be than on a boat heading offshore at sunrise on a calm sea and a promising day.

I sat in the cockpit, trimmed the mainsail, and steered; I was always happy when getting underway again. For me, it was like a fresh breeze springing up, blowing through my soul, driving out all the accumulated dust and cobwebs that were slowly choking me the longer I remained ashore. Perhaps it was because I was simply moving somewhere, in motion, or going someplace different;

change for some is stressful, for others it is healthy, aye, even necessary. But I was never happier than when casting off from the dock, pulling away from the pier. It quickened my pulse, filled me with a sense of excitement and anticipation, like a child's emotions, and filled me with energy and lightened my step. I could barely wait to round the next headland, to see what new bay, beach, or inlet there might be, ready to be explored, and to learn what promises it might hold, as yet undiscovered by my eyes. And so we set off, out of Oyster Pond heading south, around the southern end of St. Martin, past Philipsburg, past Simpson Bay, and then bore away to the northwest, just as the breeze was beginning to freshen mid-morning. It built out of the north-east rolling along under white, puffy clouds, and we ran before it on a broad reach, an exciting, leaping run, bow plunging and throwing aside a foaming white bow-wave, running with a bone in her teeth, as the expression goes. We had all our sails set, sailing 'full and by,' and we were pushing along at eight knots; but *Two Blue*, being a catamaran, could easily do better, and she did. I watched as Poppa Jon tended one of the sails for Dieter; then they both sat back in the cockpit, and Dieter eased his boat over closer to ours, close enough that we could easily see both men, and they held up drinks and waved to us, laughing.

"You want I should slow down for you?" Dieter's voice crackled over the radio, and I could hear Poppa laughing in the background.

"Go on, get out of here," I radioed back.

"We are doing twelve knots," Dieter came back, "I can put the sea anchor over if that will help."

"That won't make me go any faster," I replied. Amélie stood up on the roof of the cabin, held onto a shroud, raised her right hand, and gave both of them the middle-finger salute.

"Going to come up and around Gorda, take Necker Island Passage, then down the channel into North Sound," I radioed back.

"I might come in from the east, through Eustatia Sound," he replied. "I don't need as much water as you do. You could probably go that way too."

"Not enough water for me, and a lot of coral heads," I said. "Save me an anchorage, will you? Out by the Bitter End."

"See you there. Call if you have problems. I will save a little rum for you."

"Roger that," I finished.

I turned to Amélie. "I would only try that passage at midday, with the sun right overhead. Otherwise you have trouble seeing the coral heads," I said. "It is very tricky in there. The channels probably have enough water but I would rather be safe than sorry."

I remember few short passages as exhilarating and enjoyable as that day, with the trade wind blowing strong and steady and *Rugosa* making great way through the water all afternoon. The sun was very strong, and so we wore floppy brimmed light-colored canvas hats with chin straps to keep them from blowing off of our heads, and dark sunglasses and sunscreen, since my boat had no shade or awning that could be rigged when the boat was sailing. We drank cool water from the tanks, filtered through a special charcoal filter that I had installed, to keep hydrated. We were sailing fast and hard, so there was no room for error and thus no room for drinking too much alcohol; it would have dehydrated us in the strong sun and wind anyway, and it would not have been good to become physically uncoordinated when the boat was very much in motion. My attitude in any case was that the drinks would taste better at the end of the day, or once the anchor was down.

Amélie made lunch below, tuna sandwiches, crackers and cheese, and bananas; we took turns steering, and I noted once again that she was a very capable sailor. From time to time we saw other sails in the distance or on the horizon, and a couple of times we passed cargo vessels that plied the routes between the islands. But in the beginning, Dieter and Poppa had pulled ahead of us, so that within an hour they were merely a dot on the horizon off the starboard bow, and by mid-afternoon they were no longer in sight.

The breeze began to moderate by late afternoon, and then slowly began to drop an hour before sunset. The sails became almost slack; the sea smoothed out as the sky began to turn orange in the west and the motion of the boat became quieter.

"Remember the three-knot rule," Amélie said.

"Three knots of speed, time to start the engine," I answered, turned the key, and the little Westerbeke diesel engine rumbled to life.

As the sun set in a brilliant blaze of orange fire, and the first bright stars ventured to peek out of the deep blue sky above, I began to see the beginning twinkling of lights through the hazy gray mist on the horizon, lights on the island of Virgin Gorda. "We'll motor up through the passage, which should take us a few hours yet, then lie offshore between Necker and Mosquito Islands until dawn," I said. "We'll just heave-to and watch the lights for a while, take turns on watch." She nodded in agreement.

We passed a quiet night, joking about how Dieter and Poppa Jon were probably already at the Crawl Pub, or somewhere, having cocktails and joking about what a terribly slow boat we were on. By morning, we had drifted perhaps a mile, no more, and less than an hour before daybreak, as soon as I could see well enough, I started the engine and headed for the narrow channel. We passed through it into North Sound, passed the beautiful but empty beach on Prickly Pear Island, and after sunrise came to anchor out in the sound within view of the Bitter End Yacht Club. I scanned the anchorage with my binoculars, but saw no sign of *Two Blue*. "Where the hell did they go?" I wondered, aloud. "They were well ahead of us; they should have been here before sunset last night." I picked up the radio and hailed them. After twenty minutes of trying, finally, Dieter's voice came back. "Hello *Rugosa,* this is *Two Blue*. We are, um, almost there."

"Say again?"

"We, er, had a little problem," he radioed back, haltingly.

"What do you mean?"

"Er, we found a little coral last night."

"You struck? Are you aground?"

"More or less. We are in Eustatia Sound, off the back side of Prickly Pear Island I think. We can see Saba Rock."

"Wow, that's nearby. Are you okay?"

"We are okay, but one side of the boat is up on a coral head. We ran up on it late yesterday."

"What happened?"

"Well, we got a little lost I think. We had some trouble reading the chart. It was blowing pretty hard and we couldn't see the shallows."

"Oh crap."

"We are waiting for the tide to rise."

"Not much tide range here, it's less than a foot between high and low."

"Then we have a problem."

"We'll have to get someone to pull you off."

"I think there is a hole…."

"Stand by one, let me try to think of something," I said. "A hole, did you say? In the boat? A big hole?"

"I don't think so," he replied, "But it does let some water in."

I put the radio down. "How bad do you think it is?" Amélie asked.

"Bad enough. They were probably toasted when they came into the sound. Dieter generally has no use for charts, uses them as placemats on the dinette. He's going to have to be hauled out somewhere and the hole patched. Hopefully he won't get fined for busting up the coral."

I began untying the dinghy. "Where are you going?"

"Ashore to find help. Coming?"

"Sure." We went to the marina at the Bitter End and soon were directed by the Bitter End's dock manager to contact a conch fisherman with a power boat across the sound in Leverick Bay. We agreed on a fee, I paid him, and within a half-hour we set off from the Bitter End dock, where he picked us up, in his big workboat with its powerful outboard engine, and found Dieter and Poppa just where we thought they might be in Eustatia Sound, high and dry on a coral head that was just beneath the surface. They weren't anywhere near the channel, I noted. There were only inches of water where they had gone up on the reef, so I went over in the dinghy and handed them the end of five hundred feet of stout anchor line.

"It's a good thing the drop-off is pretty good here," I said. "Tie this off to the hull that's floating. You guys also move over to that one and hang on to the shrouds, lean toward the water, hike out. We want to take as much weight off the grounded hull as possible when we pull."

Not much happened at first; the fisherman's engine made a lot of white water. Then Dieter and Poppa started doing a little dance, with Poppa singing, nay shouting, some lively island song as he hopped up and down, and Dieter joined in with him in unison, rocking their boat as much as they could, and it began to ease off the edge of the reef and into the water.

"There is water coming in," Dieter shouted.

"Stuff a rag down there if you can get close enough to it. Now tie the tow line off to the bow, we'll tow you to the marina," I called out, and while Dieter ran his engine and his pumps, we towed them with all the speed we could manage around Saba Rock, into North Sound, and around to the Bitter End. There was no marina there, however, or haul-out facility.

"I can run her up on the beach and fix her," Dieter radioed, hopefully.

"You're going to have to go to some place where there is a marina," I said, "So that they can do a proper repair. But for now it will probably be enough if we can get some polysulfide goop packed down in there to stop the leak until you can get hauled over in Spanish Town or someplace like that."

The hole in Dieter's boat, down at the bottom of the starboard-side hull near the bow, was no bigger than a thumb could fit through, so we filled it full of marine goop that cures under water, and he was ready to go sailing again a few hours later. Granted it wasn't a professional repair, but we figured that if he could get it fixed properly at a marina, and manage to keep off the coral heads, it would never leak again.

That evening, we ate fish that we had caught by trailing a line and lure on the trip over, grilled expertly along with green plantains, all prepared by Poppa Jon. He had set up a small charcoal fire on the beach on Prickly Pear Island and lit a smoky smoldering fire of coconut shells that worked amazingly well at keeping the mosquitoes away. Afterwards, we crossed the channel to the Bitter End and walked over to the Crawl Pub. There were rows of tourists sitting in folding chairs in a semicircle five deep, watching a sports program on a large flat-screen television out in the open air. "Let's go find a quieter bar," I suggested. "I went to sea in large part to get away from televisions." But we ended up taking the launch over to Saba Rock, the noisy, busy bar that covered a tiny island.

Conversation flowed like the Painkiller punches that Rick the bartender was making in batches of five or six. In the course of one conversation, I heard him mention a beautiful antique schooner with its Yankee captain that had been in the harbor a few days earlier. I spoke up, "Excuse me, Rick, I don't mean to interrupt, but I think I may know that boat and her skipper. Was it a staysail schooner, about eighty feet long, named *Gleam*?"

"That's the one all right," the cheerful, balding, Hawaiian-shirt-clad Rick replied. "They went down the coast a little bit to Spanish Town; I think they said they would be there for a few days anyway. I was talking to the captain a couple of nights ago and he said they got beat up a bit in Antigua. Had to haul out in English Harbor to repair a sprung plank, but other than that, they fared pretty well."

We sailed down the coast the next day. *Two Blue* caught up with us as we were rounding Collision Point, and we came to anchor in St. Thomas Bay, a stone's throw from *Gleam*. Carver's lovely schooner looked beautiful and none the worse for riding out the storm down in Antigua. We motored over in the dinghy; he was snoozing in the cockpit, only his big floppy canvas hat visible, tilted forward, under the shade of the tan-bark canopy that he had rigged over the boom. A bunch of ripening bananas hung in the canopy shade, and an empty rum bottle lay on its side in the scupper. Our dinghy was the first one to approach *Gleam*; it seemed that Dieter and Poppa were running a little bit more slowly today.   "They have yacht services here in Spanish Town," Dieter said. "We'll arrange to have her hauled out and the bottom fixed here."

"Ahoy, the *Gleam*!" I called out. Carver sat up, looked over the cockpit coaming, and waved his arm, slowly. He was wearing his sun-faded Nantucket-red button-down shirt with the sleeves rolled up and a dark blue and white print bandanna tied around his neck.

"Hey, Captain Nate! Good to see you! Come on aboard! I've got to tell you about the fun we had down in Antigua."

As Amélie climbed the boarding ladder, I could see his eyes following her cleavage. He grinned, "Hello again!" he greeted her, cheerfully, and extended his hand to help her aboard. She took it graciously and hopped over the gunwale and down into the cockpit. "Get you folks a drink?" he offered.

"Sure!" I replied. Just then, the mechanic, Jack, emerged from the main hatch. He was coming on deck to have a smoke break; Carver would not let anyone smoke a cigarette belowdecks. "Stinks up the upholstery," he had once explained.

"Good to see you again, Jack," I said. "The last time I saw you, you were in Soper's. What happened?"

"Captain offered me a berth," he replied, "So I quit the boat yard and came aboard. I was sick of that place anyway. Time to keep moving. Sold the jeep, it was ready to shit the bed anyway. But it's fuckin' good to see you too, Nathanael. You guys ride out the storm all right?"

"We did, down in Oyster Pond on Saint Martin. We were lucky, though. A lot of boats didn't do so well."

Jack looked over at Amélie. He grinned. "Whoa Nate, whatcha got here? A little brown sugar?"

"Little bit," I said. "Amélie, meet Jack. Jack, meet Amélie."

"Nice to make your acquaintance," Jack replied, seeming to be amused, in an undercurrent way that I found annoying. He wasn't sincere, I thought.

Just then we heard the approach of an outboard motor.

"Look, here comes Dieter!" I exclaimed.

"Dieter?"

"Good guy, met him in Simpson Bay. That's his catamaran, *Two Blue*."

"Who's the big fucking nigger in the dinghy with him?" Jack asked, without thinking.

"Jesus Christ, Jack!" Carver blurted out angrily, while Amélie glared silently at Jack.

Carver's angry outburst took Jack by surprise. He threw his cigarette over the side, and said "I'm sorry," roughly, as he turned and left the cockpit quickly, making his way forward up toward the foredeck to sit on the windlass alone to escape Carver's wrath and light up another smoke.

"Sorry about him, Emily, he's just clueless," Carver said. "Never learned any manners. He meant nothing by it; he's just a little bit rough around the edges."

"Nothing new to me," she replied. "I can let it go."

"Thank you," Carver said.

"He did apologize," I added. "That's probably the only apology anyone has gotten out of Jack in twenty years."

"Yeah," Carver replied, chuckling, "You're probably right."

Now Dieter's dinghy was coming alongside. Carver welcomed Dieter and Poppa Jon aboard, and I made the introductions.

While I was doing so, I saw Amélie scurry on up to the foredeck. Jack, sitting on the bitts, looked up at her warily.

"Come on back to the cockpit and have a drink with us, Jack," she began, and held out her hand. "I'm Amélie. We weren't properly introduced. Nate and I became friends in Bermuda."

Jack stood up, and grinned. "Sorry about what I said. Nice to meet you, really. What did you do, head down to fuckin' Saint Martin to find him?"

"I did. And as you can see, I found him, too."

"That's good, that's good," Jack said, finishing his cigarette and tossing it over the side. "Got to be careful. Captain John has a shit-fit if he sees ashes on the deck. Well that's good, good. Nate really needs someone, you know, more than even he knows, really. So I'll bet he's been bangin' your tight little ass like a loose screen door in a fuckin' hurricane."

222

"You could say that," she replied, smiling, and they both made their way back to the cockpit.

"Billy still aboard with you?" I asked, over a rum punch.

"Yep, he's ashore right now running a few errands with Luisa."

"Luisa? What happened to Ceci?"

"Oh that's a whole 'nuther fucking story I'd rather not get into right now. Left her in Antigua. Anyway, Luisa..."

"...Luisa Isabella. Captain's main squeeze these days," Jack interrupted. The comment made me laugh spontaneously. Carver looked over at Jack with what was becoming a characteristic look of annoyance whenever Jack opened his mouth.

"Yeah, she's a smoky little Jibaro from Vieques, you know, a Shipwrecked Mexican," Jack said. "Hot little number the captain met here in Spanish Town."

"I didn't know there was anything at all going on in Spanish Town," I replied.

"Yeah, kinda' fuckin' sleepy. But every once in a while..."

"Hey Jack, shut the fuck up, will you?" Carver said, growing terribly irritated. "Why don't you go below and swap out the RACORs or something?"

"That's my cue," Jack said, grinning, then he stood up and scurried away down the open hatch.

"Christ he can get on my nerves," Carver added. "If he weren't so goddamned good with engines and systems, I'd have thrashed and drowned his ass long ago."

We met Luisa later that afternoon when she returned in the dinghy with Billy. They were carrying a boatload of booze and groceries, and we all pitched in to help bring the bags aboard. Luisa was diminutive, with sallow, olive skin and dark brown hair, and a curvaceous body that indicated immediately, to me, what Captain Carver saw in her. She wore a mischievous smile; her dark eyes flashed with a quick intensity that belied a quick temper and her whole bearing seemed to suggest an impulsive, sharp-edged devilishness and Latin fire that gave her on one hand an almost intoxicating appeal, such that a man could not stop looking at her and watching her movements; but at the same time, I could see shoal markers in the back of my mind warning me that here was a capriciousness that could only be trouble. She was friendly enough, but she had an odd manner about her whereby every move was sensuous, sexual appeal, and deliberately and consciously projected.

She was provocative, a flirt, a teaser, probably so with all the men. Her facial features were aquiline and sharp, and she had very thin, arched eyebrows, carefully sculpted and plucked to be delicately beautiful, but I figured her for a vicious tart, the sort who causes trouble in the company of men. I was very soon to be proven correct. She did not seem interested in conversation; although I knew that she was listening intently all the time. Carver however had his eye on her always, not a critical eye, but the eye of a man who is sorely smitten. He waited on her, fetching a cushion for her when she complained that her seat on the cockpit bench was 'too hard', and mixing her a drink when she asked for one. The Carver I had come to know recently would have sent her below to make her own, and told her to bring up a round for the rest of the crew while she was at it. So smitten indeed he was.

While we were lounging about the cockpit of Gleam, I noticed at one point, and unmistakably so, that she was staring at my crotch. I caught her eye; she smiled, and looked away, and I sensed that she had wanted me to catch her staring, while pretending that I had actually caught her doing so unawares. But I knew that it was not so; and this made me very uneasy around her.

Carver's favorite spot in Spanish Town was a bar named Calico Jack's down on the waterfront overlooking the yacht harbor and the sound beyond. There was always music playing in the evenings, food grilling, and liquor flowing like a swollen stream in the rainy season. Tiki torches lit the perimeter of the deck, and although the place was a bit run-down in some ways, it was nevertheless a popular watering hole and had been so for many years. All types of flags and burgees hung from the rafters of the wood frame roof over the bar, nailed up here and there in no particular order or measured spacing; wherever one fit, it fit.

Carver liked to watch the women there, and after a few stiff drinks he was prone to get up and start dancing, with no one or anyone, as the mood took him. He shuffled around in his faded blue jeans, held up by a fat belt with a wide oval whale-tooth scrimshaw buckle, and his beat-up old topsider deck shoes, the rawhide laces of which were never properly tied, if they were even tied at all. He danced in the old '70's style that he knew, his long straw-blond hair tied back in a ponytail, and sporting a rough 'horseshoe' style blond moustache that was always in need of a trimming. But trimming was not Captain Carver's style. He liked being on the outer edge of convention in everything, refusing to bow to the constraints of full refinement. He was a rocker, deep down, and was content to remain so with total disregard for the passage of years.

On our third night on anchor, Dieter and Poppa Jon had gone ashore on a little safari, as Dieter called it, and they were vague about why they were going and where, but I figured out easily enough that Poppa Jon was out looking for a source of weed. They weren't at Calico Jack's, so I surmised that they were still scouting around, since there were no lights on in the cabin over at *Two Blue*.

Carver and I sat at the bar drinking painkillers and talking to fellow cruisers, live-aboards, casual friends and total strangers, and at one point, the Captain had assembled a group around him, telling and swapping stories and jokes, while the occasional peal of laughter from the little group of jolly tars drowned out the rest of the bar noise for a moment. Carver's face became red and cheerful, something akin to a laughing, jolly, Viking Santa Claus without a beard, if there could be such a thing. But he kept looking around, as though he were expecting someone to show up.

"Who?" I asked, correctly reading that he was searching for someone.

"Thought Luisa might show up tonight, she likes it here," he replied. "I told her that we would be here."

"Maybe she's back at the boat?"

"Well maybe. Billy's ashore, got some girl he met over in Leverick Bay of all places. Some redheaded chick who works at the marina there tending bar."

"Where's Jack? Thought he might be here tonight."

"God knows where Jack is." Carver laughed, "I think he's avoiding me! Can't say as I blame him!"

Carver was good and drunk when we left Calico Jack's, but oddly enough, he piloted the little rubber dinghy with perfect navigational accuracy and skill once we pushed it off the beach and set out toward the anchorage over the quiet, dark waters. It's the sign of a seasoned, good skipper, I thought to myself, he can pilot the Zodiac as well drunk as he can sober!

We had come ashore in one dinghy, and after Carver dropped me off at my boat, I watched the light blue phosphorescence of his wake as he putt-putted off toward *Gleam* a short distance away. Down below, Amélie was awake, listening to a station playing classical music softly on the radio.

"What, no *soca*?" I asked.

"Don't be an ass," she replied. "You think all Caribbean blacks only listen to island music? Besides, I'm not from Trinidad."

"I was only teasing you," I said.

"Well for your information," she chided, in a slightly amused, matter-of-fact tone, "Sometimes I do listen to soca music, I love it like I love calypso. Sometimes chutney soca, sometimes ragga soca. When I want to dance, when I party. Have you ever danced to Caribbean music?"

"No, but I suppose you can teach me," I said. She burst out in a giggly laugh. "Baby, there is so much that I'm just beginning to teach you. But I can't move too fast, I have to take it slow so that I don't crack the china."

"Me?" I exclaimed, surprised.

"Oh yes you. Brittle as Wedgewood. But I am starting to bend you a little bit at a time. Did you know that I can play the piano? In Hamilton, I studied the harpsichord. I can play Bach, but my favorite is Scarlatti. I'll bet you don't believe that."

"I believe it all right," I replied. "I've learned not to take anything about you for granted or to doubt you."

I was content; I lay back on the soft cushions of the berth and stuffed a pillow under my head. "I feel like getting cozy," I said, reaching my arm over her as she lay beside me. Some sounds from outside came down the hatchway but I paid them no notice.

She tensed up, suddenly. "What's that? Nate, did you hear that?"

"Huh? What...."

"Listen! It's a fight!" We both jumped up, now wide awake, aware, listening intently.

"It does sound like one!" I exclaimed, and we hurried out into the cockpit. Two men were yelling, and there were the sounds of shouting, cursing, a big fight. The sound was coming right from *Gleam*.

"Someone's attacking Carver, attacking the boat!" I said. "Quick, grab the boat hook, the fish gaff; it maybe robbers or pirates! I've got to go help him!"

"Not without me," she said, brandishing a flare pistol.

"Is that the big one?" I asked.

"Twenty six millimeter, four shells."

"We're good to go. Christ don't shoot a hole in *Skidbladner.*"

I started the engine and we zoomed off toward *Gleam*. "That sounds like Jack," Amélie exclaimed.

"Carver and Jack duking it out?"

As we approached the schooner, in the glow of the dim cabin and deck lighting, I saw Carver take a wide, wild swing that connected with the silhouette of the other man, presumably Jack. He went backwards over the side, and there was a loud splash. This was followed by a woman's scream, and a flurry of loud Spanish exclamations and entreaties spoken very quickly. I heard Carver's voice, addressing her:

"God damn you, you whoring bitch, you *Maldito Bori! Puta zorra, el engendro de generaciones de putas!*

She screamed back, *"Sucio, malo, cruel hombre, no te lo mereces a una mujer, pero un animal!"*

Then I heard a sound like a click that I knew well, and I felt the pit of my stomach go cold.

"Carver, *NO! NO!"* I shouted, as Carver's black powder Navy revolver began firing at the man in the water. Yellow-orange flames shot out of the pistol, the gun otherwise invisible in the darkness, and I could hear the sound of the gunshots echoing back from the buildings on the shore.

"Get *DOWN!"* I cried and pushed Amélie's head down into the bottom of the boat. Of course as I did so I realized what a futile effort this was, since the boat was made only of inflated rubber fabric, but at least we presented a minimal profile.

"Carver! Carver! Stop shooting! Stop!" I hollered.

He stopped, because he had fired off all six shots in the revolver's barrel anyway, and was standing, tottering unsteadily by the mainmast shrouds, holding on, unsure of himself, not reloading because he had probably forgotten to grab additional cartridges.

"I'll get you Jack, you fucking backstabbing, whore-grubbing son of a bitch!" I heard Carver yell, and it was a slow, slurred, inebriated yell.

"John, no more shooting! We're out here, me and Amélie! Stop!" I called out. "We don't want to get hit!"

"Don't help that motherfucker!" he shouted. "I'll kill him! I'm going ashore in the…and the…and I'm gonna find that treacherous bastard."

In the darkness of the harbor, I saw a figure swimming towards us. Behind Carver, in the cockpit, the woman, Luisa, was calling him terrible names and crying hysterically.

"She sounds pissed," I said to Amélie.

Jack, resembling a wet bedraggled water rat in the darkness, came up to the boat. I reached over. "Jack, you OK? I take it he missed you."

"His fuckin' knuckles didn't" he slurred, spitting out a tooth.

"Let's pull him aboard," I said, and it took both of us to get him into the boat, as he was mostly limp. "You could help too, Jack."

"Sorry. He kicked my ass."

I started the engine and headed straight toward the shore. I could still see Carver standing on the gunwale of *Gleam*, hanging on precariously. Luisa was still berating him. "He'll be lucky if he doesn't fall overside and drown," I said. "So Jack, what the fuck did you do, anyway, to get this going?"

"I bonked his little *Caco* bitch," he replied. "She'd been comin' on to me for days, you know. Thought he'd be ashore a while longer. Guess I miscalculated. We were really getting into it. You know how time flies...."

"You jackass," was all I could respond.

"Hey what the fuck, you know, it was what you call it, cosexual."

"Consensual."

"That too," he replied, wiping his mouth. His lower lip was cut and swollen up like part of an inflated toy balloon animal. "No, actually it was conditional. On condition that we wouldn't get caught." He tried to laugh.

We motored in to the beach. In the light from the marina, I could see that his face was beat up pretty badly. His nose was swollen, as was the left side of his face, and he had a cut over his eye.

"Well, it has made an entirely new fucking man out of you, Jack," I said.

"Yeah, I know. Ain't that the truth. My left eye is already swelling shut."

"I'd say come back to the boat right now, but..."

"No, that's OK. I'll go over to the boatyard. Christ I've been living in fucking boatyards since I was sixteen. I know my way around; I'll find my way into a comfortable yacht." He chuckled under his breath.

"No big deal. I been in more knuckle brawls than I can ever count. Oww, I think he cracked a rib, the big asshole. Hey, do you have any cigarettes? Some rum?"

228

"Not here, in the boat; we kind of left in a hurry when we heard what was going on, if you know what I mean."

"Well I can't go back there, that's for sure. He'll plug me with that fucking cannon of his. Didn't know he was a collector of that shit."

"Yeah, well, it's only black powder, but it's still a forty-five. You're lucky I got him drunk at Calico's."

"Wish you'd kept him there a while fucking longer. Thanks for picking me out of the water, Nate."

"Take care of yourself," I said, and with that he disappeared into the scrub by the shore, protected by the nighttime darkness, off toward the boat yard where a number of vessels in various stages of disrepair were propped up on the hard.

"He'll find accommodations," I said to Amélie. "Probably won't sleep too much tonight though. Let's go check on Carver. I've got a bad feeling about this situation right now."

As we approached *Gleam,* I shut off the motor as we neared the schooner, and I noted that now the boat was eerily quiet.

"Guess the fight's over," I said.

"Where's his dinghy?" Amélie asked.

"Oh right, it's gone. Jeez I hope Carver didn't go ashore looking for Jack. He's liable to drown on the way."

"He'll never find Jack anyway," Amélie said.

I heard the sound of another small motor, and saw a dinghy approach; I could immediately see that there were three dark figures in the boat, and Dieter's voice called out,

"Nate, is that you?"

"Yes. Me and Amélie."

"We heard the gunshots. Billy is with us. We were having a drink ashore."

"Carver and Jack had a fight," I said, as I grabbed their dinghy's painter to tie them alongside. "Also Luisa. But it doesn't sound like anyone is aboard." Just as I said that, I heard a deep, agonized moan come from *Gleam*'s cockpit.

"Christ!" I exclaimed, and climbed aboard, but Amélie was ahead of me and leaped over the rail.

229

"Nate!" she exclaimed, "Get on the radio! Call Emergency services! It's the Captain! He's badly hurt!"

Carver was lying on the cockpit floor, on his back, in a pool of blood, semiconscious, moaning and muttering.

"Bitch….knifed me," he croaked.

We gathered around him; there was blood coming from his shirt on one side and from the upper part of one leg. Amélie stripped off Carver's shirt; Poppa pulled out a knife and cut through the leg of Carver's jeans. I was already on the radio calling the local Coast Guard.

"He got to go to the hospital," Poppa said, "He's got a big, deep, dangerous wound in his thigh." Dieter meanwhile tore up a towel, and grabbed a belaying pin. "We have to make a tourniquet," he said, and began doing so, tightening it around Carver's thigh.

"Do you think the knife cut the femoral artery?" Billy asked.

"Sir, he would be dead by now if it had," Dieter responded.

"He has a knife wound in his ribs," Amélie said. "Give me a piece of the towel, make a pad. We have to keep pressure on it until the medics get here. He has lost a lot of blood."

Finally, two boats arrived, flashing lights and a siren; one of them took Carver to shore, and an ambulance carried him across the island to the small local airport and airlifted him by helicopter to the hospital in Road Town on Tortola. It turned out that the bone-handled fish filleting knife that Luisa had stabbed him with had missed Carver's femoral artery by millimeters. We knew that Luisa had taken the inflatable dinghy, and although the police searched for her, she never turned up. The dinghy was eventually found washed up on the beach at the East End of St. John. Luisa Isabella was nowhere to be found.

Chapter 19

Red Cockpits

"There is a thin line that separates life from death, but once it's crossed, it becomes as large as an ocean, and so treacherous that it's impossible to cross back."

– Federico Chini, The Sea Of Forgotten Memories

We cleaned up *Gleam*, scrubbing her spotless. Amélie scrubbed and rinsed the teak cockpit deck with a passion, putting to good use a coarse brush, detergent, and copious buckets of water for nearly half an hour. I fetched buckets of water, but she insisted on doing the scrubbing herself. She liked Carver, and there was something in her determination and energy that sparked the thought in me that her goal was to scrub away all the badness of the experience, to erase it, to make it as though it had never happened. I was glad that Luisa had not returned; I could not guarantee that Amélie would not take her apart piece by little piece if she had, filet knife-wielding skills notwithstanding.

Carver remained in the hospital for several days. He was fortunate that the knife had, miraculously, missed his internal organs and had slashed, but not cut deeply. Still, he was stitched up like an old, sun-rotted sail, or perhaps a scare-crow, or a man-overboard practice dummy, with dozens of stitches in his side and in his thigh. Jack went over to see him two days after he had been admitted. He had retrieved the dinghy that Luisa had abandoned on the shore of St. John and used it to motor many miles through Drake's Passage over to Road Town. What did it matter that he had 'borrowed' someone else's portable tank of mixed gas in order to do so?

Jack was very reluctant, even scared, he told us later, to visit the hospital, or to even go to Carver's room, but he found his courage and walked in. When Carver saw him, he waved him over to the bedside. His eyes seemed to mist; and he started with an emotional apology for shooting at Jack, and Jack began to get sniffly as well. "I'm so sorry I pounded the crap out of you, Jack," Carver began.

"Fuck, I deserved it," he replied, shrugging off the apology, "But you know what, that caco bitch fucked over both of us."

"I know that," Carver replied, "Played us against each other. I'm sorry I let her do that. She had me blinded, you know. I couldn't see what was happening."

"You were in fucking love," Jack said, beginning to laugh. Carver began to laugh too, but then winced in pain, "Owww, Jeezus, no, I was in LUST!" he chuckled, "Stupid ass me."

"Well, good thing you're a shitty fucking shot with that howitzer," Jack said, chuckling.

"I was a lousy shot. But I won't miss you next time!"

"Whoa!"

"Just kidding. I hope you're okay?"

"I'm fine," Jack said, "Been taking beatings, and giving 'em, all my life, but I will say that this was one of the better ones."

"I'm really sorry," Carver replied. "Please come on back to *Gleam*."

"You sure?"

"Absolutely. I won't let that double-crossing bitch get between us."

"Me neither. Everyone's pitching in, keeping the schooner shipshape."

"That's good to hear, I was a little worried about that. Has she come back, or been found, or anything?" Carver asked.

"Nope. I rescued the dinghy for you. That's how I got over here. Long trip, but it was a fun ride. I guess the local cops are keeping an eye out for her."

"If she's back in U.S. territory, which she probably is, that will complicate matters."

"True. But if she fucking comes back to the boat, I think tough little Emily will fucking skin her alive. By the way, she scrubbed the hell out of that cockpit."

"I'll bet she would. She's a great girl, really."

"Yeah, you know, she is. You know if Nate wasn't banging her...."

"Don't go there, for crying out loud," Carver began, laughing again while it hurt, "Jeezus crist there you go..."

"I know. Got to find someone for myself for something other than the short term. I never have a problem landing them, I just can't seem to hang onto them."

"Like fishing, you need to find a keeper."

"True. For so long it's been, well, fucking bang and release, you know?"

"Don't I!" Carver replied, amused.

Dieter and Poppa took *Two Blue* over to Road Town to pick up Carver after his release from the hospital. Dieter reasoned that the smooth ride on a stable platform, a catamaran, would be comfortable for Carver and not set him to pulling his stitches or making him wince. In fact it was an easy day with a light breeze, and the trip back took only a little more than two hours on a broad reach, with *Two Blue* slicing merrily through the light chop at twelve knots.

We rigged the mahogany and chromed rail boarding ladder with its wide, double grate platforms and rope rails, and helped Carver board *Gleam*, slowly and carefully, with Dieter and Jack on either side of him, holding onto his arms and leading him gently aboard. They eased him down into the cockpit, and helped him into a small arrangement of pillows and soft cushions piled together on the cockpit bench next to the wheel, in the shade of the awning.

"Thanks," he said, "This feels really, really good. How about a drink?"

"You can have one, John?" Dieter asked.

"I can have two if I damn well please!" Carver replied, indignantly.

"Well you heard the man," Dieter said to me, "Go mix the Captain a drink!"

"Aye, aye!" I answered, and it was my turn now to duck down the scuttle. Sure enough I found his favorite ingredients; Mount Gay amber rum, chilled orange juice, and a little pineapple juice to put in top, over ice, in the galley up forward. I made his cocktail in the largest glass I could find and brought it up to him.

"Where's yours?" he asked, grinning.

"Not far behind," I replied, "...and taking orders for the rest of you."

We had all decided that we'd had enough of Spanish Town, not that there was very much here anyway, and that it was time to move on. Nobody had a terribly pressing plan with regard to where to go, but we had spent many an evening at a beach bar or a tiki bar listening to Carver talk about heading off to the Pacific, so we essentially decided to begin heading in that direction. We were undecided as to whether we should travel together, or separately, since no one had decided on a final destination. Carver spoke of going to Tahiti, then on to Fiji, or perhaps to simply spend some time in the South Pacific, and head on to New Guinea; or even to Thailand, where he could practice every vice that he loved; he wasn't sure. It's a big world, with even bigger oceans than land masses, so he could end up anywhere, he said, but for certain, the islands of French Polynesia were high on his list.

"Did you know," he asked one evening when he was decidedly in his cups, "That when the first Europeans visited those islands in their ships, metals were so scarce that the native women would have sex with the sailors just for the gift of a handful of iron nails?" he said, and added, "Sometimes even for just one nail."

"Are you sure that was in Tahiti?" I asked.

"Well, certainly, you know, down around there. All those islands."

"Hell, I can get my hands on a whole fuckin' barrel of roofing nails before we head down there. We'll be set for a while," Jack interjected.

"I don't think that's the custom anymore," I said, shaking my head.

"Too bad," Jack muttered.

We were rafted up together in Coral Bay on the eastern end of St. John, with the discussion basically revolving around the South Pacific, and if we should all head for the Society Islands and places like Tahiti and Bora Bora. My argument against was that my boat was possibly too small, but then Carver countered that "Slocum's *Spray* was even smaller, and Robin Lee Graham's boat even smaller than that." So that was the end of my argument. But he wanted to go, and I knew that eventually he would. I doubted that Dieter would go, even though he nodded assent, perhaps, I thought, to save face. Poppa Jon did not want to go to the Pacific. But Carver had a big boat and a thirst for life and for adventure that was, perhaps, larger than that in any of us.

We agreed that we would rendezvous somewhere before heading as a group of three boats for the entrance to the Panama Canal, probably meeting in Colón.

"Why don't we meet first in the Spanish Virgins, over on the little island of Culebra?" Dieter suggested. "It's very nice there; we can anchor in Ensenada Honda, it is a very sheltered place. There is a great bar there, another Dinghy Dock like we had in St. Martin." And so we all agreed to follow that sailing plan.

We sailed over to Culebra and had been anchored in Ensenada Honda for only a few days when Dieter began having trouble with his diesel generator, or gen-set. He spent two days crawling around in the heat and humidity with wrenches and other tools, getting sweaty and black-stained with sump oil in a manner that made the poor man slippery, slimy, and stinky, all at the same time.

We tried to help him; Carver and obviously Jack knew a thing or two about engines, but at long last on the second day of trying, they stood up, shook their heads almost in unison, and Jack said, "She's going to need a re-build." We all agreed with Jack's observation that "At sea, if you can't make electricity, you're fucked." So something had to be done while Dieter could still get some life out of it. As *Two Blue*'s cabin lights flickered, dimmed, and brightened, alternately and without any pattern, a rather unsettling situation, Dieter announced that after spending some time on the Sat phone, he had learned that there was an engine shop at a marina in San Juan, and they had a rebuilt generator of the same make and model, available at a reasonable price, the only hitch being that Dieter would have to bring the boat over to San Juan to swap out the old and install the replacement.

"I'll sail over with you guys if you like," I offered. Poppa Jon could sail well enough, but he had no experience or aptitude with mechanical things.

"I can stay here and help Amélie look after your boat," Poppa offered.

"Thanks," I said, "Please do that."

Dieter asked Jack to come along, because he also knew engines well, and Jack enthusiastically agreed.

We planned our departure for the very next day, after checking the weather forecast and noting that we had a good weather window for the sail to San Juan. The distance was approximately a little more than fifty nautical miles, a full day's sail with a favorable trade wind. But the night before I left, Carver took me aside and said, in low tones, "You should bring my pistol with you. There have been reports of some robberies going on in that area, break-ins and armed robbery, often while the families are aboard. I've heard about it on the single-sideband net. They're looking for one guy in particular, an American ex-pat named Dirk Handrigan. Ex-military guy, you know, a survivor. He's already killed one guy. Robs the boats, beats his victims up pretty bad. Preys on charter boats. All in that area around the north side of Puerto Rico, Dominican Republic."

"Thanks for the advice," I said, "But you should keep your pistol aboard. Keep Jack in line."

He snorted, "Oh, stop that!"

I laughed. "Sorry Cap, just kidding. But no really, if there is shit going on around these islands, you need it. I already have one of my own aboard anyhow, well-concealed. I will bring it with me."

"Pistol?"

"Yes."

"What kind?"

"Forty-five. M-1911. Bought it from a retired Navy guy."

"Jeezus, that's some firepower! Really? Never knew you had one of those."

"Well I don't broadcast it, for obvious reasons."

"Cartridges?"

"A few clips, yes. Standard military issue."

I brought a small tan canvas rucksack with my foul weather gear, a change of clothes, a bottle of Scotch, and some other sundry items. I removed a wooden panel that formed an inset shelf next to the hull at the navigation station of *Rugosa*. I reached down into the dark cavity and lifted out a bulky, oily leather and sheepskin rolled case that contained my M-1911 .45 automatic pistol and two clips of ammunition. It felt heavy in my hand and reassuring, and smelled of gun oil and old tanned hide. I then replaced the shelf and stuffed the roll into my duffel, deep into the clothing."

"Do you always pack like you are going somewhere for a month?" Dieter asked, teasing, as I climbed aboard with the rucksack.

"I need padding for the Scotch bottle," I replied

"Ah ha!" he laughed. "How much Scotch are you bringing?"

"Never enough," I said.

The next morning, *Two Blue* weighed anchor and left the harbor before dawn. The Trade Winds were blowing steadily every day out of the east. It would be a great downwind sail, but a beat upwind to return. But right now, our main goal was to get to the marina in San Juan.

"When we leave San Juan for our return, we'll head northeast on a very long tack, maybe thirty miles or more, then turn and head southeast, to fetch Culebra," Dieter said. "We'll go south of the island and then turn back northeast again to gain the harbor here."

Amélie packed our lunch; she had grilled some fresh mahi fillets that Poppa had caught the day before, so we had grilled mahi sandwiches, and crispy plantain chips that she had fried in fresh oil. We brought bottles of water and, at Jack's insistence, a small cooler of cold beer. We sailed all day with the coast of Puerto Rico off in the distance to port as we ran downwind with the spinnaker up, ballooning out ahead of us, as we listened to the radio chatter or took brief naps ourselves as we sliced through the crystal-blue warm waters a few miles offshore. The motion of the boat running downwind was soothing and had a soporific effect. It was easy to doze off, and always a good thing anyway to get as much rest as possible, whenever possible, when sailing. As I may have mentioned before, this was always my philosophy, get sleep when you can at sea, because invariably situations arise where one has to stay awake for long hours, especially in bad weather, so it is good to have some sleep banked.

The land slowly rolled by, hilly, greenish-purple in the distance, seemingly forever, until at last we saw the bright concrete and glass downtown city buildings of San Juan and the harborfront sprawling ahead. It was essentially a quick run for a sailboat, and well before dinner time we were tied up to the service dock at the marina. The new generator would be installed the next day, the yard manager told Dieter, so we took the opportunity to head up the dock to the marina's bar and grill to have dinner and a few drinks.

We were up early the next morning; it was a warm, sunny day and Dieter had made a welcoming pot of strong coffee for us.

"How is your coffee?" Dieter asked.

"Poppa makes a better pot," I replied.

"Well fuck you then, Mister Captain Nathanael! You're welcome!"

We all laughed. "Come on Dieter, where did you learn to make coffee?"

"What are you, a coffee snob?" he asked, indignantly.

"I know what it needs," I said.

"Shot of 'Buca?" Jack suggested.

"Beat me to it," I replied. "It needs a 'stick' in it," I said.

"A 'stick'?" Dieter asked, puzzled.

"Splash of dark rum," I said. "New England sailor's expression."

"Oh-ho," he laughed, "You mean you want a EUROPEAN style coffee. Well we can fix that."

In the end, Dieter made a second pot of coffee as well. We were all very much wide awake and very much tipsy. The mechanics came over, chuckled when they saw that we were half drunk, and then began work.

"Good thing we're not working on the gen-set," Jack said.

"Amen to that," Dieter replied, "But that's why I am paying them."

The mechanical work went well and by three o'clock in the afternoon it was finished, we were sober, and the new gen-set was running smoothly, cranking out power. The cost, however, had set Dieter back considerably, and as a consequence he was low on money.

"We should go," he said, "I can't afford to spend another night on this dock."

It turned out that he didn't have a choice anyway; a sixty-foot powerboat belonging to a favored customer, a wealthy lawyer, was coming in and had reserved that slip for the night. "Just as well," Dieter muttered when informed by the dockmaster. So we cast off our lines and headed out, sailing northeastward on what would be a long overnight trip, tacking into the steady trade winds. I figured that we would be back at Culebra by morning. Before we left, however, we all went up to the marina office to shower and have a cold beer while Dieter paid his bill. We didn't lock up the boat; it seemed safe enough at this big marina.

We set out after dark, and after dinner, carefully maneuvering our way out of the harbor and out of the channel with its blinking red and green buoys, out onto the darkening Caribbean Sea.

Poppa Jon prepared an excellent dinner, a superb jerk chicken dish that he had cooked before we left and had been packed in the icebox for re-heat, I retired to my cabin, or stateroom, to get a few hours of rest. I was officially off watch, but since I would be back on deck at the assigned time of midnight, having drawn the short straw, I thought I might put my head down for a little nap. There were three of us aboard, and although *Two Blue* had technically four staterooms, the starboard side forward room was used for storage. Dieter kept luggage, spare parts, clothes, fenders, and other assorted things in there. But the three staterooms that we had were perfect for three people aboard. Of course, we would not all be in our rooms at the same time; there would be one person on watch on the helm during the three four-hour shifts that had been assigned by Dieter through the night. Jack was on watch with Dieter from eight p.m. until midnight; Dieter went to his stateroom around ten, once he was confident that Jack had control of things. I would be on from midnight until 4 a.m., when Dieter would be up again and take over after having rested for six hours.

I sat on the bunk in my cabin, which was the forward one in the port side hull or pontoon, sipped a Scotch and read a couple of chapters from a new book recently published about sailing down in the trade winds. Oddly though, I felt uneasy; I had trouble concentrating. Perhaps I am fatigued, I told myself, or uneasy simply because I was not on my own boat. But that couldn't be it; it was almost a premonitory feeling of something bad. I wondered if the weather were changing, low pressure or a change in humidity, something like a sixth sense acquired by spending so much time at sea and becoming sensitized to changes in the weather, changes that would have been imperceptible to me before I had taken to a life on the water.

I sat in a small chair by the foot of the berth and had begun to doze, feeling the easy motion of the boat slicing to windward, and had actually dozed off when I was awakened to shouting up in the cabin; the voice was Jack's, but there was also another man's voice whom I did not recognize.

"Where the *FUCK* did YOU come from?" I heard Jack roar in indignation and surprise.

I felt the hair on the back of my neck stand up; leaning across my bunk, I reached carefully into my rucksack and pulled out the oiled sheepskin pouch with my pistol. The door to my cabin was shut. I held the pistol inside the duffel bag to muffle the sound as I loaded a full clip into it and cocked it to load a round into the chamber. I cradled it in my hands; it was cool and slightly oily; it was a good piece, in very fine condition and I had kept it clean and wrapped in oiled sheepskin to keep the salt air from rusting it. Many guys did not like the .45, I recalled; too heavy, too powerful. I supposed that buying or owning one was illegal, or at least that was what a gun shop owner had told me, because it was a military weapon. I had bought mine from an old friend of the family who was a World War II veteran and collector, an old Navy Chief, a Gunner's Mate. He had owned this pistol for many years, and had readily sold it to me very reasonably when I asked him about it.

Up in the cabin, I heard Dieter's voice; "You are a stowaway! You do not belong on board this boat. When did you board us? What do you want?"

"Everything you've got," a deep, rough voice replied, loudly and arrogantly, "Or I'll kill both of you."

My immediate thought was that the stowaway did not realize, for some odd reason, that there was a third person aboard, that person being myself, even though he'd had ample opportunity to discern a third voice throughout the late afternoon and evening. I assumed that he had been hiding in the storage stateroom, with the door closed, and as such, could not hear voices throughout the rest of the boat very well, especially with the loud background noise of the boat beating to windward in choppy seas, or the engine running as we had left the harbor.

"I know who he is," Jack replied, almost with derision in his voice, "He's that fucking Dirk Handrigan that the cops are looking for. Lot of people wants your fucking head, asshole, don't make it worse…"

"Yeah that's me, and you don't know what WORSE IS! But I'm gonna show you. Turn this boat around, we're going to the Bahamas. Don't fuck with me, I'm armed!"

I heard loud arguing, and as I sat holding my gun, my nerves seemed to hum; so I took my Scotch glass back off the shelf and poured a half glass full from the jug of it next to the foot of my berth. There was no ice; it was warm; but that did not bother me. I drank it down quickly, much too quickly to appreciate it, but appreciation, and more leisurely consumption, perhaps with a cigar, could come at another time. Right now it was important, I noted to myself, to make the jangly nerves go away. I felt a light perspiration begin to break out on my forehead. I knew what I might have to do.

Suddenly there was a loud thump and banging on the deck; the men were fighting; I heard a bottle smash and then Jack's voice, crying out in pain, and shouting from him and from Handrigan. I quickly unlocked the door and burst out of my cabin and up the short stairway into the catamaran's main saloon. Dirk had Jack down on the deck on his back and there was blood all over his face; Dirk was pounding on him, punching his head, cursing and roaring, and Jack was holding his arms up, trying to block the constant, furious blows. Dirk had apparently clobbered Dieter over the head with a wooden baseball bat, knocking him out cold; but now Dirk, crouching over Jack, looked up when he heard me run up the steps of the passageway, his enraged face turning first into an expression of puzzled surprise, then rage again. He roared, "You fucking little asshole, what the Hell…where did you come from? Where did you get that gun? Well piss my ass you bastard, I'll…"

"Get off of him, now," I shouted, pointing the pistol directly at his face, steady. "Jack, slide away from under him, out of the way, stand clear."

"Dirty little Mother…"

"Back off and back up!" I shouted, commanding, again, "Or I'll blow your goddamned head off… Jack, for Christ's sake get out of the way!"

"Okay, okay!" Jack replied in a quavering voice, spitting blood and saliva out of his mouth, then rolled under the dinette, watching his attacker out of the corner of his eye. Dirk stood up, slowly, his tall, big-boned bulk intimidating. He was quite tall, late-fifties, a former Marine with Nicaragua jungle combat experience, so the news reports had said, and he was clearly a powerful and a willful man. I knew that I was up against a seasoned fighter, and it frightened me somewhat, but I held steady. He knew that the odds were against him at the moment and that he was at a disadvantage. I kept my distance, kept the pistol pointed straight at his heart, kept my eyes on him every second. He noted these things; I could see him re-examining and assessing the situation second by second by his eye movements. His hands and arms were bloody and blood droplets spattered his face. He brandished a big-bladed black combat knife, the kind I had often seen in gun shops.

"I'm going to give you three seconds to put that pistol down," he began roughly, waving the knife at me, "Or I'm going to rip your goddamned head off and shit down your neck!"

"Safety's off, Dirk. Now back up to the door. Back up. Move out into the cockpit. This is no pellet gun. You know well what the fuck it is. I qualified with this pistol in the Coast Guard. I know how to use it, I know what it can do, and I earned the Expert ribbon that proved it."

"You, give me orders? What are you, a chickenshit bosun's mate! Now put that thing down before you get hurt! I'm the Captain here now!"

"I swear to Christ I'll kill you, Dirk. Now back up. Move out into the fucking cockpit."

"Fuck you."

"Out the door! Now!" I held the pistol higher, steady, both hands. He was looking for shaking or wavering and perhaps it bothered him not to see any.

"Listen, boy. Put the gun down now and we'll forget all about this," he began in a low, steady, growling voice. Different tactic, I thought.

"I'm a combat veteran. I'm only going to give you one more chance to put the gun down. Otherwise I might forget myself and hurt you really bad. You're playing a man's game now, this is serious. Put the gun down."

I curled my finger a little more tightly around the trigger. "Dirk, you're right; maybe we can resolve this peacefully. Let's go out into the cockpit. We all need some air. Jack, you too. Let's talk. I'll put the gun down if you'll promise no retaliation."

"I already said that I wouldn't, didn't I?" he replied, irritably. "What do you want out there? Are you going to set me adrift in the dinghy?"

"No. Maybe you can take the boat to the Bahamas or wherever you want to go and we'll take the dinghy back into San Juan. Nobody needs to die."

He grinned, relaxed slightly, more confident now, reading what he thought was weakness, now crafty, planning his next move.

"That's the way to do it. No need for this way out here. Fine, let's talk..." He pushed open the glass doorway to the spacious cockpit and went out into the starlit darkness, his head turned, watching me out of the corner of his eye. He took three steps out into the dark middle of the cockpit then slowly turned around to face me. Jack was behind me.

"You'd better come out here now and throw that weapon over the side before you hurt someone with it," Dirk said. I still had it pointed directly at him.

"Not quite yet," I replied, and as he suddenly began a lunge at my feet from out of the darkness, I squeezed off the first round at the middle of his chest just as he lurched forward. There was a thunderous blast and a tongue of orange fire leaped into the night. The pistol jumped but I had it under control with both hands and then I squeezed off two more in quick succession, about a second apart. I heard Jack behind me shout a warning to me, but I had already anticipated what Dirk was going to do and had fired.

The first heavy, copper-jacketed bullet stopped Dirk and actually pushed the upper part of his body backwards in an arc, his head jerking forward, chin on chest, and arms flung off to each side. The high-velocity round smashed into Dirk's chest like a sledge hammer as the slug blossoming into a flattened mushroom shape as it blasted his sternum apart and ripped into his heart. The blunt force and velocity of the second round sent him reeling backwards against one of the dinghy davits; the third spun him around and threw him down, face down, over the side of the cockpit, head almost in the water, feet up in the air, blood every-where, flesh missing, big exit wound holes in his body, him dead as a stone, arms hanging limply over the side almost dragging in the sea.

The catamaran was still sailing, the autopilot engaged, over the beautiful night sea at about six knots, leaving behind a pale robin's egg blue glow of phosphorescence about a hundred yards astern from each of the twin hulls. "Oh, fuck, *oh fuck*!" was all that Jack could exclaim, over and over, as he looked at Dirk. I heard Dieter moan from inside the cabin. He sat up, holding his head.

"Why, Williams, why the fuck did you shoot him?" Jack asked.

"I had no choice, Jack. He would have killed both of us. Once the gun was out, there was no going back, not with him."

"I never knew that you had that!"

"Neither did he. Good thing, eh?

"Why out here in the cockpit?"

"Because I did not want to blow apart the cabin. We have a lot of cleanup to do. Here, hang onto him; don't let him fall overboard. I'm going to go help Dieter."

"I don't want to touch the sonofabitch. Why?"

"Please just hang onto him for now, don't let him fall overboard."

"Well he ain't gonna fuckin' drown now, that's for sure."

We were still heading northeastward even though we were close to the point where we should turn onto a port tack.

I gave Dieter a small bag of ice for his head, then we all had a drink and sat on the un-bloody side of the cockpit planning what to do next.

"You did the right thing, Nate," Dieter said. "I hope you're okay with it."

"Strangely," I said, "I am. But I would love to have another glass of Scotch."

"We all need one," Dieter said.

"That will be three, though, definitely not four."

Dieter laughed, weakly. "You mean Dirk doesn't get one?" he asked, facetiously.

"If you think he can drink one," I said, "I'll pour him one. But he doesn't deserve it."

"No, I agree. But what do we do with him?"

"Let's send him for a swim," I said. "Can you find some junk to weigh him down with? Maybe you can help me pick out his ballast?"

Jack looked at me with an expression of utter bewilderment; it had all happened too quickly for him.

"We're going to fucking sink him out here?"

"You want to bring him into Culebra like a trophy?" Dieter interjected.

"We're almost over the San Juan Canyon out here, "I said. "The chart says that the water is thousands of feet deep. We'll send him down to the abyss."

"How are we going to explain this?" Jack asked.

"If we do a good enough clean-up job we won't have to," I replied. "We would all be in a world of shit, especially since we're not supposed to be packing firearms in these waters. Christ, look at your face."

"It's just swelling. I think my left eye is going to swell shut. Any more ice left?"

"Sure. Maybe hold a cold can of Red Stripe against it. I know that we have some more ice. Some for your face, some for a couple of drinks. I'll get it," I said.

"No, Nate, You get the Scotch, I'll get the ice," Dieter replied. He still had his sense of humor. "I can't thank you enough," he said. "I thought he was going to kill us."

"He was," I said.

"Thank God I have a hard head," Dieter said, "But I will need a very soft hat and pillow for a few days."

My hand that had been so steady holding the pistol now shook as it poured the Scotch, with the result that a few drops spilled over the side of the deck and onto the deck. "I don't think we have and glasses aboard with wider mouths," Dieter quipped.

"We just took care of the widest mouth of all," I replied. I handed him a Scotch. "Here, we both need this." The boat was sailing on a close reach, so the wind carried any smell of blood astern and away from us. The stars and Milky Way were brilliant overhead, so much so that there was not total darkness, but faint starlight illuminating the cockpit and the sea around us. Suddenly, Jack jumped. "I saw him fucking move!" he exclaimed.

"Just your imagination," I said. "Maybe his nerves; he's as dead as he can be. Enough drink. We have work to do. We have to sink him out here, and then clean up this cockpit."

"Let's start the main engines and run the wash down pump," Dieter said. "We don't want any trace of blood in the cockpit, so we bleach and scrub. They have techniques with UV light to find blood residue that you think isn't there anymore. When we get in, nobody mentions anything. The bruises, well, we got drunk and fell down. Nobody ever saw Dirk Handrigan. Dirk Who. Jack always has bruises."

"Fuck you," Jack said, but he was grinning through his busted mouth.

It took a while, but Dieter and I found a few items, including a big pipe wrench (what he needed that for aboard, I'll never guess), some metal parts, an old water pump, and other junk. I tied these items to Dirk's legs, and filled his pockets with nuts and bolts. In all, I think I managed to load him up with almost fifty pounds of metal, tools and junk to help take him to the bottom and keep him there. It was messy, bloody work, and at one point, looking at his lifeless body, I almost began to feel badly for him, and the enormity of killing him was like having a giant grizzly bear at the door, ready to come in and raise all manner of hell, but I kept the feelings down, down under cover, like holding the lid on a boiling pot, trying to keep the steam in, or trying not to throw up. Actually, the nausea was real, I suddenly discovered, and I had to lean over the side of the cockpit to retch, suddenly, after I had finished weighing down Dirk.

"You all right?" Dieter asked.

"Yeah. Better now. Still, I would rather have sent Dirk Handrigan over the side than good Johnny Walker. But it's not to be helped. Dirk and Johnny can swim together. Here, Jack, give me a hand, let's ease him over the side."

"Should we say a prayer first?" Dieter suggested.

"You can if you like. Where he's going he'll need a fire extinguisher more than he'll need a prayer." With that, I lifted Dirk's stiffening legs and his body slid, leaving a bloody smear, over the edge of the cockpit and into the sea, sinking like, well, like a dead man with a lot of junk in his pockets.

"Jack, please throw the switch for the washdown pump," Dieter said. "I want to stay out here and get this blood cleaned up before the sun comes up and bakes it into the gelcoat. We'll be late getting in in the morning; we just say that we had trouble with the sails or something."

"So long, Dirk," I called out as the body sank below the surface. "Say hello to the hagfish for me." It has been a month of red cockpits, I thought to myself.

It seemed to take forever to get back to Culebra. Nobody spoke much; Jack got into a bottle of rum and was roaring drunk, and therefore useless, by the time we sailed into the harbor in the late afternoon. Poppa Jon knew right away that something bad had happened. When we told him the story, he just shook his head.

"Many bad, evil men in the world, they are possessed sometimes by evil spirits, who obey only the Devil himself. God decides their fate; you are only the chisel, God be the hammer. Do not trouble yourself terribly, Hotpeppa. You only answered what choice you had; you had none other. So now he is food for the fishes; that was his fate. You need not to worry, Hotpeppa, it was all in God's hands. You are blameless, and should not waste another minute thinking about it."

"But I fired the gun," I said.

"No, no, no. Your finger pulled the trigger. Your hand fired the gun. But it was not you that really fired the gun, no, no; it was your good angel, in obedience to God, to take another evil man out of the world before he could hurt more good people. Now God Almighty will deal with him, yes sir. He is food for the hag-fish and the deep sea creatures that crawl along the bottom. God directs them, too. You were only an instrument of The Lord, as they are."

"Are you calling me a bottom-feeder?" I replied, teasing.

Poppa Jon laughed. "Okay, now, that is the Captain Nate I like to see." He reached into his pocket and pulled out a fat marijuana joint.

"Oh, I don't know...." I said.

"Oh yes, Hotpeppa, this you need. Later we will have rum and I am cooking fried plantains and special grilled wahoo tonight. Very spicy. Everyone come over, we will all have lots of rum. Amélie and me, we went ashore exploring in the village, and look..." He reached into the cabin and brought forth an old, beat-up acoustic guitar. "Your sweet little honey Amélie bought it for me. It is old but plays very nice and holds its tune. We put new strings on it." He strummed it a couple of times, and it sounded good. "Tonight we will make some music," he said. "I can play, and I can sing, not too bad either. I will play you some nice Trinidad songs from my youth, from the crazy old days. But look now, I see a boat coming."

Sure enough, the crew of *Gleam*, and Amélie from *Rugosa*, were approaching in Carver's old inflatable, and we gathered in the spacious cockpit of *Two Blue* for drinks and Poppa Jon's wahoo dinner. The Caribbean-spicy aroma of the wahoo sizzling on the charcoal grill was tantalizing.

"Amélie, that was so kind of you to buy that guitar for Poppa," I said.

"Oh, gosh, it was only a few dollars, and he can play really well. So I got it for him. You should hear him."

"That will be great," I said.

We all sat and passed a big bottle of amber rum around. There was plenty of ice, now that Dieter's generator was fixed and we could run the ice-maker.

By turns, Jack, Dieter, and I began telling our versions of the tale, each one, in his eagerness, stumbling over the words, and one another, in a bid to get the story out and shared, to purge our souls and conscience, because talking about it eased the pain of remembering the trauma of the battle, and it really was very much a battle, and the subsequent shooting and killing of Dirk Handrigan. We needed to get it off our chests; and in the course of doing so, the three of us became very drunk, which only served as an encouragement, I think, for Amélie, Carver, and Poppa Jon to follow suit. But Jack's telling of it was the most emphatic, passionate, and colorful.

"Then Nate here, he had this big fuckin' cannon that nobody knew he had," Jack said, waving his arms as though he were trying to illustrate the size of a big fish that he had caught, "...And he pulled it out and Blam! Blam! He blew the livin' FUCK out of this sonofabitch Handrigan."

"Jack, *easy...*" I began.

"No! No! I mean, there was fuckin' blood and shit fucking everywhere, like you wouldn't believe, sticky and warm and stinking like someone hit a deer with an RPG or something, Jeeezus..."

"It took us the whole night, lots of washdown, and all the bilge cleaner and soap we had on board to scrub the cockpit down," I said. "Looks really clean now, don't it?"

Then we explained how we weighted Dirk down so that he would go down to the bottom of the trench and hopefully stay there.

"Good three or four miles," Dieter said. "Probably still sinking, the asshole."

"And may he fuckin' stay there," Jack replied, taking another pull at the bottle.

"There's no need for this to ever go any further than this cockpit," Carver spoke up, authoritatively and with a dead-serious tone. "Consider the matter closed."

"A 'Dead' issue", I said.

Carver chuckled. "Yes, absolutely. Look, Nate, you had no choice, you did what you had to do, so now let's put a stop-water in it permanently and fill the sails. Move away from it, eyes ahead."

Then it was time for Poppa Jon to light up and pass around his 'after dinner smoke', "Only proper," he said grinning, showing his big white stained teeth and laughing from deep down inside. Then he picked up his guitar and began playing and singing.

"Now we sing my favorite, all the time favorite when I was growing up, it's called 'Mangoes. You know mangoes? This one called 'Mangoes, Mangoes, Mangoes, and it go like this:

Mango vere, mango teen
Mango vere, mango teen
Ah want a penny to buy mango vert mango teen
gimme ah penny to buy mango vert mango teen
Mango doudou sou se matin
savez-vous all for me
Mango dou dou sou se matin
Savez-vous all for me"

In a moment, we were all singing along and following Poppa Jon sing the Mango song. We were laughing and singing with him and it seemed like all the troubles behind us had been nothing but a very bad dream, like a dark apparition hidden away in a rock cave somewhere.

Chapter 20

The Margin

For always roaming with a hungry heart......I am a part of all that I have met; Yet all experience is an arch wherethro' Gleams that untravell'd world whose margin fades, For ever and forever when I move. —Tennyson, 'Ulysses'

After repairing the refrigeration unit, we returned to the BVIs and rendezvoused with *Gleam* and *Two Blue* in Soper's Hole, Tortola. It was decided, or rather undecided, by a consensus of uncertainty that we should all do nothing together for a while, but rather each of us should go cruising around the Caribbean for a month or so before moving on to somewhere else, together or separately. In essence, it was time to split up for a while. That is the way of vagabonds and people who are used to traveling or living alone. They thirst for social interaction and camaraderie, like moths drawn to a lamp at night; yet at the same time, they fear the lamp, and cannot stand its brilliance for very long, for they know that they will ultimately be burned by it. In a sense, we are all moths, and all have been burned by the heat of social interaction, emotional attachments, and relationships; some have been burned badly enough that they will never approach the lamp again; but most people simply recover, get back up on their feet, and madly wing toward the light once more, knowing full well the inevitability of the result, but not fearing it, or at least realizing that we cannot live without it. It is better to be burned by the lamp's fire than to languish in lonely darkness, one rationalizes; and so we carry on like individual comets, speeding into close orbit and then veering off into the cold, dark, distant depths of space until the time comes when we return again in a seemingly endless and predictable cycle.

And yet there are those who, having lived alone long enough, become accustomed to the darkness and even find a comfort in anonymity and solitude. To them it is a preferred state of being, long after the memory of whatever pain caused them to flee the light in the first place has been forgotten. These are the boat bums and solo cruising people who find the pressures of society and social interaction on a daily basis to be too overwhelming; they seek solace in the empty places, where nature's stark beauty stands in simple full revelation, always true, never ambiguous, and never malicious. Like Jason the solo sailor who had been allowed to pass, there were truths and epiphanies out there, but you had to find them. And it was possible to become obsessed with seeking them, as a man once maddened by the glimmer of gold, spends the rest of his life searching hungrily for the yellow metal in streams and in holes and crevices in the earth. Jason's world had been closing in around him and in bursting his way out into the openness of beyond, found in the end that it was not an empty place at all, and turned his empty soul inside-out and the wide spaces became him, and filled him.

Despite all that his voyage taught him, it had ultimately not equipped him to live in the world among so many people, or to recapture his former life and cope with it successfully and adapt. He was and would always be an outlier. The sea had changed him in some ways, but left the whole cloth of the man intact. After his joyful return to family and friends, who had celebrated the end of his voyage at the island, in a few months his reconstituted marriage fell apart, this time for good; he had no income but from the sale of prints of his paintings done at sea, and he chomped and chafed at life ashore and the walls of life that were once again encroaching. He was a loner, and would always be. He would forever be different, a man apart, the square peg. For the sea had indeed changed him; it had given him serenity, but that serenity came at a price, and that price was the inability to ever adjust to living ashore again. It was now worse than before. He longed for, and often spoke of, the almost transcendental time that he had spent out in the middle of the Pacific, in the lagoon of Minerva Reef on the way to Tonga. It was a place, he said, with almost no solid land around, no greenery, and yet the coral ring breaks the seas so that, having threaded the needle-like opening, he could now anchor in the middle of the broad Pacific in flat water and contemplate blue skies, fluffy clouds, and an endless watery horizon in every direction, protected almost magically from the turbulence of the surrounding ocean. He anchored there for a week or more, swimming, fishing, and lying on the brilliant white coral sandy beach. The water is so clear, he said, that the boat seemed to be suspended in space above the bright coral sand bottom; looking over the side of the boat in calm water gave him vertigo. It was, he said, the purest place on earth, and he thought he might stare for hours down into the water, and when he did he saw his own face reflected in it, and this began him thinking about himself; could he not learn to love that image? Could not others? But perhaps he had not read Melville, or even the first chapter of *Moby Dick*, where he would have read, "And still deeper the meaning of that story of Narcissus, who because he could not grasp the tormenting, mild image he saw in the fountain, plunged into it and was drowned. But that same image, we ourselves see in all rivers and oceans. It is the image of the ungraspable phantom of life; and this is the key to it all."

So Jason readied his boat for sea once more, and set out on a second voyage in search of that elusive phantom, this time without the blessings of his family or their help and resources, and without the knowledge that a wife would be waiting at home this time. He sailed in search of that opium of peace, solitude, and communion. He sailed off once again with his mind's chart laid out across his consciousness, heading back to Minerva Reefs while seeking to recreate the peace that he had found, and to regain the the innocence of his first voyage.

But the sea, without malice and yet an unforgiving mistress, can be fickle; whether or not Jason made it across the Pacific to Minerva is not known, only that after many months without contact, his family reluctantly began searching for him, but he had not been seen down in the islands, and never, as far as anyone knows, made landfall, unless it was to a yet-undiscovered island, or an uninhabited one, or perhaps at last that insular Tahiti in his soul, that peaceable little corner of paradise that had for so long eluded him.

Captain John Carver wanted to go to the Pacific; he had the will, the means, and the boat to do so. Dieter, on the other hand, was not so sure that he wanted to leave the Caribbean, but he was most assuredly not going back to St. Martin with the place in its current state of storm damage. But he thought he might sail down through the Windward Islands, the Lesser Antilles such as St. Vincent, Martinique, and the Grenadines, and even beyond, to explore Trinidad, and eventually end up on the coast of South America. Poppa Jon wanted to revisit his old village on Trinidad.

I was happy to stay in the Caribbean for a while before moving on elsewhere. After all, I had all the time in the world; I was not on any schedule. Life was as I had predicted it would be. There was nothing to do, and everything to do, depending on what one's individual idea of doing something was to be. The primary things to do in the islands were to sail, explore, lie on the beaches, and drink. These are all attractive things when you are preoccupied with something else, such as a full-time job in a cold climate. But once you are down in the islands and these are the only things to do, then all of a sudden, they take on an unforeseen monotony. It's wonderful for a few weeks, or a few months, but when that time begins to stretch into years, it becomes an issue of asking, 'Is this all that there is? Is there no forward progress to be made?' But of course it is, and *you knew that before you came down here*, I told myself on several occasions. It is too hot to work hard; there is no money to be made without working hard; and the types of traditional business models that work in the northern countries don't work as well here, if at all. You can run a bar, run a charter business, be a vagabond musician in an already competitive field, manage property and rentals, and do many other things that thrive in a tourism-based economy, maybe. All the while, you hope that the northern economies that are so different will continue to thrive, and not tank, so that the people who want to travel here will have the disposable income to continue doing so. There is little money to be made for the visitor or vagabond seeking to relocate; the entire economy is based on other people visiting and spending their money. All you can do is spend, the money draining out of you like blood oozing from a wound that never heals. But if you have no money, you have nothing; you're worse off than the most impoverished native. To be poor is bad enough; to be a poor white foreigner is practically an impossible situation, for there will be no jobs or opportunity for you to earn enough to eat. There is no sympathy for you from the locals. They actually expect you to have money, and lots of it; there is a vast gulf between you and the native population, even though we are all, if distantly, brothers and sisters. If you were to walk around asking for assistance, and saying that you have no money, the locals will look at you as though you have just descended from the moon; there is no such animal as you, so you must be a fraud, or worse. You must have money, because you certainly don't know how to do real work, people of your color, or lack thereof, never do. This is why the rich love the Caribbean. They have an inexhaustible supply of money for basic needs and to enjoy themselves, and any 'foreign' workers here are tag-alongs, employed by the rich, living off of their largess. The rich know this, and take full advantage of it. The price of visiting the Caribbean, for the young white northerner, is to clean the rich man's toilets aboard his superyacht. Don't like that duty? Go home, if you still have enough cash for a plane ticket.

And yet I had found my own way, as I always would, that did not require much money, only my boat, as my shelter, my kitchen, my bed, my transportation. The only toilet that I was required to clean was my own, and I was perfectly satisfied with that.

"Let's sail back over to North Sound today," I suggested to Amélie the next morning. "We can go to the beach on Prickly Pear, and then hang out at a beach bar. Maybe we'll go over to Leverick Bay." She agreed. We sailed all afternoon and then anchored near the Bitter End in North Sound, with the westward-facing shoreline and Saba Rock resort catching the last golden rays of the setting sun.

It was just before sunset, and now the steady breeze that had blown all day out of the northeast dropped down to barely a breath. We anchored in the shade of the long shadows cast by the rounded, verdant mountain tops of Virgin Gorda that lengthened as the sun sank behind them. The surface of the harbor became still and smooth like a warm glass mirror and we sat under the cockpit awning on the soft cushions and drank rum punch 'sundowners' while the occasional small fish jumped nearby, breaking the surface and creating ever-widening small intersecting circles of ripples. We were now floating gently in quiet and restful contemplation of the day that had just passed, the mooring pennant dipping in a slack curve as we took in the pleasant, tranquil view of the widening passage leading out to the sound. The last of the day's sailboats were going to and fro in the distance, seeking an anchorage for the night, much like a cat or a small dog that paces in circles until it finds the ideal choice of a spot to bed down and settle. We watched the colored lights of the channel buoys begin to blink, stationary, while the red, green, and white steady lights of the boats crisscrossed our line of sight in their determined search to find just the right spot to drop the hook before dark.

We were not anchored very close to the shore, because we needed the depth; and yet we felt close to it, to the darkening shade of the cool beach beneath the leaning palm trees, their fronds bowed lazily, almost sleepily, toward the water; and we could almost feel the coolness of that shade now that night was falling. With the fading twilight, and the faint twinkling of the first stars peeking out of the deepening mauve dome overhead, came the first night-sounds of the birds chirping unseen in the dark green, shiny-leaved succulent tropical growth along the beach.

From somewhere in the distance, a voice, then more voices, sporadic, unintelligible, echoed faintly across the water, distorted by the air. Then we heard music, bright, cheerful, boisterous melodies and energy just barely within earshot, and more sounds of merriment ashore. A cat's paw of a breeze wafted the incense-like tang of wood smoke and charcoal, in occasional tantalizing waves, to our sharpening senses; then came also the aroma of food grilling somewhere over charcoals, and I felt my belly grumble. Here in the islands, there was time, all the time in the world, it seemed; time to overcome the sleepy inertia of the cockpit, and I was suddenly possessed of the urge to take the dinghy through the darkness ashore, to find that grill, those voices, that music, my ear aching for it. At the dinghy dock, the spotlights would shine down through the nearly transparent, crystal sapphire-blue water all the way to the coral-speckled bottom, and the big fish would swim and circle darkly in figure-eights in the light, suspended between the surface and the bottom, mesmerizing to watch in their warm tropical sea. At the Pusser's café bar they made 'painkiller' rum punches dusted with ground nutmeg, the spice of the islands. I thought about it; I saw one in my mind's eye. There would be food, friends, drink, and companionship, a clean, well-lighted place.

"Time to go ashore," I said, "I need some nutmeg in my punch."

"Is that all?" Amélie asked.

"No. Also I want to eat. There will be grilled good things. I grow weary of brown bananas and cans of tuna."

"And...?"

"And then I'm going to get crazy drunk and dance with the Moko Jumbies,"

I said, draining the last of my cup. At first there was no response. Then she sighed, "Again?"

"Yes," I said, "You come, too." I heard her laugh as she finished her drink.

The main scuttle leading below was a square of darkness as I sparked the anchor light, watching its blue flame grow to a yellow tongue as the kerosene, fed by the wick, began to burn. I hoisted the lantern up the mast on the messenger line, watched it flicker for a few moments, and then we climbed down into the dinghy and began the short trip across the night-enshrouded harbor toward the bright dock lights of the café bar and Leverick Bay resorts.

It felt good to relax over a few drinks at the bar while the aroma of grilling steaks and rum-butter sauced lobster broiled over the hot charcoals in the big black cast-iron barbecue grill. We were drinking Painkiller rum punches and talking quietly, and Amélie leaned over and rested her head on my shoulder. I could smell the mild flowery perfume in her hair.

"I need to ask you, you know, about what happened on that trip to San Juan. You are awfully quiet sometimes, and that makes me worry about you."

"Haven't had a lot to say, really," I replied, "Mostly thinking."

"Does what happened bother you very much?"

"Sometimes," I said. "Not as much as if I'd had much choice about it. I mean, you do what you have to do. But it still feels horrible sometimes when I think about all that it means. There is a terrible finality about it for him, whether justified or not; and yet for me, it lives over and over again, it is etched into my soul, into the pages of my life's chronology, and it won't go away. Perhaps it never will."

"Will you be all right?" she asked.

"I'm already all right. Sometimes I think that we are all, you know, puppets, with someone else pulling the strings. I didn't ask for that scenario to happen. And yet once I was in it, I had to find my way out of it. I don't blame myself at all; it was an innocent thing; I was helping out a friend. What if, in fact, we are all God's puppets, then, after a fashion? If He is pulling the strings, I can't punish myself for the way the play ends up. That's not an excuse to get out of accountability; on the contrary. If I had committed a deliberate crime, or done something out of wickedness, a bad judgment call, then that is different. But that guy Dirk set his own fate in motion. It's like the desperate criminal who commits 'suicide by cop'. Well we were the cop surrogates, I guess.

Anyhow...so where are the Leverick Bay Moko Jumbies tonight?"

Amélie laughed. "The Moko Jumbies are just for tourists!" she said. "It's just a lighthearted show."

"Which is precisely what I need right now," I replied.

"You poor Nate. I also think you need another Painkiller. There is a reason they call them that, you know."

"Amen to that," I said, and ordered another round.

Eventually, our talk turned to future plans.

"Are we going to the Pacific?" she asked.

"We? Are you going with me?"

"I will go with you whichever direction the wind blows you, like the song goes, my 'man of strong mind.'"

"I like that," I said. "But as you have learned, I don't plan terribly far ahead. Perhaps I will just keep sailing. I'm not much for house, home, and hearth. Maybe I will sail off the end of the earth, or like Ulysses, beyond the sunset, and the baths of all the Western stars. If you're into settling down, I am not ready to even begin to think about that sort of thing yet, and I'm not sure that I ever will be."

"There is no need," she replied. "And may never be. I am content for now, and for all of the future that I can see, to sail along with you."

"That makes me happy," I answered. "But for all you know, you might be sailing into the Mouth of Hell."

"Then you will need someone by your side," she replied, "And that will be me. You know by now that I take my life one day at a time. I have now for a few years. So that is just fine, because that way, whatever comes over the horizon is always unexpected. If you expect something and don't get it, there is disappointment in that. You will never be happy. But if you keep your mind and heart open, well, you take things as they come, with no expectations. Then you will always be alive, sometimes surprised, and more often happy."

"We'll see," I said. "I'm not the warmest or most open soul you will ever meet."

"I don't agree," she replied, flatly. "But you know," she began, "You have never really told me about your situation, how you got here, and why."

"It isn't something that I much like to talk about," I replied.

"Well, I think that if we are going to be together, you owe me that explanation," she said.

"I owe nothing to anyone," I replied.

"That isn't true. Are you married? I always wanted to ask. I had a suspicion."

"I'm not sure," I replied.

"What's that supposed to mean? Either you are, or you aren't!"

Okay, fine, just let me pour myself another drink first."

"You are, or you aren't!" she exclaimed, a little more dramatically. "I told you everything about me..."

"I WAS, I interjected strongly, the pitch of my voice rising.

"Yes I was." I poured myself a strong rum drink.

"So what happened?"

"It's a long story."

"I have time."

So I began, "In the end, there isn't a lot to tell. I worked on fishing boats out of Point Judith and Galilee when I was young. We would sometimes go in to Block Island when bad weather was breaking and one time while our boat was in overnight for a storm, I met a girl at a hotel bar and we more or less hit it off. She was from the island, raised there, and was as wild and crazy as you would expect someone to be having been raised on those empty moorlands and cliffs. She had flaming red hair and her wildness appealed to me. I met her in a locals' bar in the center of town. It was a place where the fishermen drank. There was a pool table in there and people brought their dogs in and the dogs slept on the rough wooden floor and sometimes there were people-fights and sometimes there were dog-fights."

"I remember the place being called the 'Long-liner.' The owner was also the bartender. He had only one eye, the other one was just a blank white ball, got it injured on a fishing boat, he said. Some big hook caught it or stuck into it or something like that. Anyhow, I met her there one drunken night. I'm talking to her on one side of me, and on the other side of me stood some drunken fisherman in hip waders and a buffalo plaid flannel shirt. He had a huge brown beard and was making no sense, blabbering, and he opened his fly and peed down into one of his hip waders because he was too drunk to walk to the bathroom. They just let him stand there and keep drinking, didn't even throw him out, that's the kind of place it was."

"But anyhow, that's where I met her, and it seemed to click. So we stayed in touch and ended up spending some time together over the next few months when my boat docked there and sometimes she would take the ferry over to meet me in Galilee. I was twenty at the time and she was eighteen and before we knew it she was pregnant. It was springtime and it seemed like such a wonderful, positive thing, I guess we were young and had no idea how people could be about such things."

"Once they found out, my parents, whom I had never had a terribly close relationship with, disowned me and her family kicked her out too, so we basically said 'fuck them all' and we went to the Kent County courthouse and got married. We set up housekeeping in a rented beach cottage in Matunuck and it was a tough, cold first winter. We burned driftwood that we collected on the beach in a wood stove, but the place was drafty and there was always a strong wind coming in off the Sound, cold and damp and bone-chilling. I was away a lot on the fishing boats so we basically ate a lot of fish, whatever I could bring back, plus what I could afford with the money I made fishing. I mean, we didn't do too badly; there was always bread, milk, staples and basics, we ate a lot of chicken and pasta. But all the time she was in this spare, bare, small three-room one-story place that seemed always cold. And she could look out the front window and through the daytime fog she could always see the gray shadow of Block Island, and at night time the glowing lights, and it made her homesick for the island that her family had basically thrown her off of. She didn't have a job, all she had were the daytime soaps on T.V. There wasn't a lot of work to be had down in South County in the winter time. And there was nothing to do out on the island in the winter; if someone didn't have a place over there for you, you just couldn't be there. So she would look out the window every day at this tantalizing image of the island, the place where she wanted to go back to, but she couldn't, and there it was in plain view on a clear day, taunting her."

"That's terrible," Amélie said.

"But she had a bright spot in her life, and that was the thought of having our baby. But like I said, it had been a rough winter and she had been sick a lot. So one day we got a radio call on the bridge and the Captain said that we had to go in, that Eleanor was having a baby but that she was sick and had to go to South County Hospital. We were only a few hours out and the crew didn't care if we went back anyhow because it had been rough and we hadn't caught much of anything for two days. A few hours later we were at the dock in Galilee and I drove like a madman to the hospital. It was three o'clock in the morning, and I was too late. The baby, it had been a boy, was dead, something was messed up and he got strangled by his own umbilical cord and the doctors didn't realize what the problem was until it was too late. They operated, to do a Caesarean, but still they were too late. I mean, I remember seeing her in the recovery room, she was wide awake and wearing that clumsy oxygen mask and the tears were just running like a stream down the sides of her face and soaking the pillow. We both cried there together, and I think it was the most horrible few hours of my life. That was the first time I had ever seen that empty look in her eyes that I would see so often later on, before she left me. And that's why I hate every March so much. It became the month that I came to hate and always would." Amélie said nothing; she knew what the rest of it could be.

"Anyway, it didn't take long. Somehow the baby's death was my fault. If I hadn't been away on that fishing boat, I could have driven her to the hospital sooner. She had been having pain for two days. She could have gotten to the hospital, she had our car, but why she didn't just go I'll never know, she said that something was wrong with the car but I think she was afraid to drive herself to the hospital, or was maybe hoping that she could wait for me to get back in. We didn't have any health insurance and no money to pay for a hospital, so maybe that made her hesitate, but anyhow in the end it was my fault, just as her being off the island and rejected by her parents was my fault, my doing. So one day I came home from a trip and she was gone. She didn't even take the car. Her family on the island wouldn't talk to me, but eventually I found out that she took a bus out to Ohio where an older cousin lived with her husband and their family. They too had been on the outs with the island family members for many years. So I guess she moved in with them, I say I guess because I never heard from her again. Never again, over these many years, and I wouldn't know where to start looking for her if I wanted to find her. Maybe she remarried or something, or who knows. I never got any divorce papers or anything. It was just as though it had never happened."

"She shouldn't have blamed you," Amélie said. "And you know there must be records somewhere, at the very simplest at the courthouse. It wouldn't be much trouble to get them if you went back there."

"I don't know, I have just never wanted to dig it up, like opening an old wound," I said. "We were kids, basically. I was just doing what I knew how to do. It was hard work in all kinds of weather but I was young and it didn't bother me. I always brought a paycheck home, sometimes smaller, sometimes larger, but always a pay, and a bucket of fish. We rarely went out anywhere at night unless it was to a local fishermen's bar where the draft beer was cheap and we could play darts or pool. That was our life. What's she doing now? I have no idea. I hope she found another guy, I hope she's happy, I guess that's all. But for a long time I questioned whether or not I was any good at all, whether or not I was worth keeping. I felt as though I had failed at the most important thing that there is, building and growing a family. I was young and full of energy and had big dreams. I was strong, too, and could lift the tubs of fish like they were nothing. I could steer and handle the boat in the worst weather, and hold my own on a fight down at the Crusty Dragger bar in Galilee. But I couldn't keep Eleanor happy. We often fought about money, or how she felt trapped, or wanted to get away, or missed her parents, even though she was never really close to them. But you don't seem to mind the way I am; I seem all right to you?"

"So it's possible that you're still, technically, married."

"If you say so. Maybe she divorced me in absencia. Maybe we've been separated for so long that we're Common Law Divorced, or something."

"I don't believe there is such a thing. But it's no matter, it doesn't really affect us."

"Doesn't change the way the wind blows or how we trim our sails," I said. "But you don't have to keep me with my baggage, or the way that I am."

"If I didn't like you the way you are, I would not be here right now," she replied, with an air of finality about it. That settled me somewhat, as I had become somewhat agitated, and I finished my drink, hoping that I would not be called upon again to recall such a terribly sad time in my life.

Just about then, we heard the approach of louder and louder music and laughter and singing, and yellow torch-light was beginning to illuminate the trees around. Drums were beating in excited, fast-pulsing rhythms. This sudden appearance of sound, color, and light brought me back to the present, in both time and location, and banished my past memories to the place where they had been safely stored before.

"It's the Jumbies," I exclaimed, and then stood up, rather unsteady, and went over toward the site of the hubbub. It was all sound and light and color and joy, with vibrantly costumed people lurching around oddly on tall stilts, and I went into their midst and began dancing joyously with them, and all of the other people who were part of the crowd, until everything inside of me had become loose and careless and happy without any specific or identifiable reason. It was like steam blowing out of a kettle and it felt better the emptier my kettle became.

In the morning I awoke in the sand under a bush of dense, fat green succulent leaves, with Amélie curled up next to me. I was thirsty and my clothes were full of fine coral sand and my head hurt. I did not wake her up, but just sat there for a while staring out across the beach at the water and across the Sound. The sky above was broken overcast and low, grey-bottomed clouds were scudding across it from the southeast. A few fat raindrops fell; I could hear them slapping against the dry fronds in the coconut palms above. After a few minutes they stopped. The weather is changing, I observed, to myself. I could see my *Rugosa* out a few hundred yards offshore, swinging obediently on her pennant, safe and secure. The oil lantern was still up the mainmast. Got to remember to take that down first thing, before it runs dry, I reminded myself. Then Amélie stirred, uttered something of an uncomfortable moan, so I reached over and drew her skinny, sandy warmth up against me, like a warm, pliable bag of soft flesh-padded limbs loosely connected at the joints.

"Good heavens," she muttered, "How much did I drink? I feel awful." She reached under some leaves and drew out a half-empty water bottle. "I'll share," she said. "God, I feel like I need a shower, or at least a swim, first."

"There's the water," I said, "And I think the bar is open for Bloody Marys."

"Oh, not more!"

"I'm having one. The key is to stop after one or two, then have a nap."

"Uh-huh."

We swam first. The water was warm and clear, with a constant flow of light and steady surf rolling in onto the beach. I watched her, remembering how she looked in the water when I first saw her swimming on Bermuda, and it was much the same, I thought. She turned to me and smiled, as if she knew what I was thinking. A couple of charter catamarans were coming into North Sound, and were working on setting their anchors. The swim refreshed us and we then sat at the bar for a couple of Bloodies. It was now mid-morning. Jimmy, the bartender, an island lad, understood completely; in fact we were far from alone; other bleary-eyed cruisers had already 'dropped anchor' at the bar. We were wet, but at least we weren't covered with sand, appearing to have slept on the beach or in the bushes. We were both a little stiff, but soon everything was, once again, flexible and loose.

That night, I had a disturbing dream that we were crossing the Pacific and that a gale had come up and carried away the rig. Then I awoke to the slap-slap-slapping of a loose halyard against the mainmast and it was loud enough to wake and annoy me. The sound travels right down the solid mast and into the hull and when I awoke I was startled a little bit and disoriented from my dream, although of course I had heard the sound many times before. I got up silently in the warm, humid darkness and went to the ladder to look out on deck. The wind was up and the harbor was dark as hell. But I was still securely moored, with dinghy still obediently riding at the end of her painter.

I donned my headlamp and went out on deck check the lines and tighten the halyard. It was windy and I got slapped with some fat rain drops so I knew that a front was coming through. I was careful not to stub a toe on the deck hardware. It was a clouded-over black night but for the shore lights. I was moving around the deck in my underwear and getting rained on, hooking up bungees to the shrouds to pull and hold the halyards away from the mast, keeping them outboard toward the shrouds so that it would be quiet at last down below. Finally, with everything settled, I went back down into the cabin and pulled the sliding hatch cover closed to keep the rain out. The wind, from the north, raised small waves in the bay and I could hear them slapping against the hull, but only for a few minutes. The wind blew strong as the front came through, the gusts whistling in the rigging and rudely pushing the boat around on her anchor rode. I tried to go back to sleep, but the dream still bothered me and with the rain spattering down I sat up again and lit a candle and poured myself a glass of dark Brugal rum, one of my favorite rums from the Dominican Republic. Then I took it over to the ladder and went up two steps and stood there for a while looking out through the open hatch. It's one of my favorite 'perches' when I am having a little drink alone; my head is framed by the hatch, protected from the weather like a cowling, and it feels like a secure place with a window on the world, so to speak. I could not sleep, so what the heck. I saw some heat lightning in a bank of clouds astern so I watched that for a bit until it faded and I was starting to feel a little woozy and tired. Thought of mixing another, but by now it was after 2 a.m. Then I felt a warm hand against my arm.

"Remember when we sat together in front of the Casuarina log fire in the cottage in Bermuda, and sipped dark rum while the rain was falling?" Amélie asked, softly.

"Back in the beginning," I said. "Can I pour you some?" She squeezed my arm.

"It seems so long ago," I said, "Even though it was maybe a year ago."

"It was a good beginning," she replied. "Let's re-live it, again. Now."

"We have no fireplace, and no fire. Well I suppose we have a candle."

"That will do just fine," she said. "We can supply the rest. I want the intensity, just like it was that first time." In the candle light I could see small beads of perspiration breaking out on her forehead; she was warm to the touch, now. "You're glowing," I said.

"It doesn't matter if we don't sleep all night," she added, "There is always tomorrow, we'll have all day if we want."

"If we want." And with that, we wasted no more time, nor even a word, but made love with a feverish intensity, all limbs, all touching, in contact as much and in as many places as possible, energy expended, breathtaking, breath taken, until at last we rested, damp and cool and limp-flat and expended, tranquil and at peace, for having given everything, taken everything, until all had been shared in a perfect blending and melding of feeling from the very depths of our being, or so it seemed. I lay on the bunk wondering, 'Where did that come from,' and was able to fall asleep, finally, the candle having burned down and out in the brass socket of the candlestick, and Amélie beginning to snore ungraciously as the first gray light was appearing in the east.

When I awoke, I knew instinctively, as soon as I opened my eyes, that it was the right day, the right time, to move on. There was no reason to wait any longer. The sky was bright overcast with gusty, fitful winds and scudding clouds. Light rain showers splattered on the deck, occasionally. I made coffee, and checked the two small lines that I had baited and set over the side the night before. To my surprise, they both had fish on them, two small jacks. I hauled the lines in and drew my knife, then cleaned them quickly. "We have breakfast," I said as I descended the ladder. Amélie clapped her hands. "Excellent! Let's fry those babies up!"

We fried them in a skillet, along with sliced plantain and some left-over spiced rice and beans, and ate them with molasses-baked brown bread from a can, the bread sliced and toasted over the blue galley flame. It was a good meal with the hot coffee whitened with the last of a cool box of Parmalat milk. "It's time to go, isn't it?" she said.

"Yes," I answered.

Chapter 21

English Harbour

Is there something we have forgotten? Some precious thing we have lost, wandering in strange lands?

— Arna Bontemps

"I am not ready for the Pacific yet," I told Amélie as we sat in comfortable chairs on the beach in front of the Soggy Dollar, sipping rum punches. We had been in the water for a morning swim and now the day was warming up, the trade winds had picked up, and with the approach of the noon hour, the sparkling clear water off the beach was churning into light surf as it rolled up the white-grained strand. "I need time to think about this."

"We don't need to go anywhere; we have no schedule, at least I certainly don't," she replied.

"Let's maybe head down to Antigua, Grenada, for a little bit. I need to think this thing through."

I had an itch to stay put here in North Sound, to relax for awhile in this peaceful anchorage, surrounded by the mountainous hills of the island.

After breakfast the next morning, I sat in the cockpit alone, considering my options. It was a beautiful morning; the rain showers and clouds had departed, opening up a bright blue sky and a brilliant sunny day, with an easterly trade wind blowing gentle and warm. To me, this was one of the most beautiful places to sail in the world; Drake's Channel, or Drake's Passage, call it what you will, it has always seemed to me to be the place where good sailors go to experience a bit of heaven before they actually die. "Let's just go for a day-sail up and down Drake's for the day," I suggested.

So we hoisted anchor and sailed all morning down the passage back toward the west end of Tortola, then sailed back in long tacks between Tortola and the distant islands on the opposite side of the channel, including Norman Island and Salt Islands, near the sad place where the wreck of the great iron steamship RMS Rhone sleeps in shallow waters more than a century and a half since her tragic shipwreck during a hurricane. Sailboats darted back and forth across the sea-sweet breeze as we beat our way gently across the sun-dappled, sparkling turquoise-blue Caribbean. It was easy, steady sailing, like a dream; with my floppy straw hat and bottle of water, I was content to tend the wheel lightly as we moved along, savoring every moment, every freshening puff that lifted my *Rugosa* to lean into and greet the next succession of small waves. At one point, a small gray whale surfaced barely twenty feet away, swimming in the same direction that we were, and as quickly sounded without taking the time to exhale.

Later in the afternoon we were within view of Spanish Town and heading up the passage between Virgin Gorda and the Dog Islands, when the wind became variable and nearly died, so we furled our sails and motored the rest of the way to North Sound. My nose caught the faint odor of wood smoke, as if, perhaps, someone had a beach fire going somewhere in the lengthening cool shadow of the mountainous green island, its sides sloping steeply down to the water, and it reminded me of camping in the mountains of New Hampshire, by a river perhaps in the White Mountains, and the deepening quiet of dusk and the evening.

We motored around to the entrance channel to North Sound, then in past Mosquito Island and Prickly Pear, to come at last to anchor within view of the red-roofed Bitter End resort buildings, the bar and restaurant resort of Saba Rock, and the quiet calm of evening in a harbor of moored and anchored sail and power boats of all sizes.

Once we were back in the Sound and on our anchor, it was time to pause, relax, and rest. The sun was going down beyond the hills in the direction of Leverick Bay; but we would not be going to see the jumbies tonight. Instead, we took the dinghy in to the little dock in the shallows in front of the Crawl Pub on the Bitter End side of the harbor as the lights along the shore came on, and made a dinner of pizza and beer. We were tired from our sail up the passage, perhaps less tired than satisfied and deeply fulfilled. Amélie and I sat quietly, saying little, our minds each filled with so many images to wade through and appreciate after a long and full day of wind, light, color, and motion.

"What are you thinking about?" Amélie asked.

"I was thinking about the view of the tops of Virgin Gorda as we approached Spanish Town, and of the deserted island called Fallen Jerusalem, and how it became that way, just a jumble of giant boulders. And I remember that one gray whale that surfaced near us, how strange, and the small planes coming into the Beef Island airport, and taking off again, as we sailed by. And you?"

"I was just thinking about how lucky we are, how lucky I am to be here. Even though life is harder sometimes, living in a small cabin on a boat, no washing machine, no television, we have to take showers ashore. And yet I would not want any of those things like televisions aboard. That's precisely the stuff that we escaped from. I know that it's a little bit primitive in some ways, but I love the life on a boat. It's a little bit like camping, and that helps make it feel like an adventure."

"It is an adventure. An adventure in paradise or at the very least the closest we can get to it on earth. Sailing today was like heaven, I wish it could have been a thousand miles rather than thirty."

We live an adventure like this, I reasoned, silently to myself, because I know that as we grow older, our days become more repetitive, mundane, and unremarkable. Life skitters by ever more quickly and unnoticed. This is a tragedy, because every minute, like every stroke of the club in golfing, has equal value, regardless of the distance the ball travels. Life's experiences are cumulative; the mind knows this, and quite efficiently does not preserve, or write over, that which has already been similarly written. So to avoid stagnation, we must seek ever-newer adventures and experiences to write fresh in the book that has more blank pages than we will ever know, and slow the passage of time by filling these pages with richness before it inevitably goes out of print. Our enemy is the encroaching and insidious lethargy of comfort, with its soothing yet malevolent Siren's song growing ever more irresistible as it whispers insistently into the ear of advancing age.

Because it was warm, I left the main hatch open for ventilation, but in this enclosed bay, there were more mosquitoes than we had experienced in Tortola. So I draped an Army-surplus mosquito net over the entrance to the hatch as good insurance against the Yellow Jack, Dengue, or Malaria. Yes there are mosquitoes down here, I noted, and they are not like our gentle New England summer mosquitoes, no. They have a very high-pitched, nasty, threatening whine, like little Stukas, and their sound is alarming, suggesting that they mean business; Death on the wing. Sure enough, after Amélie had fallen asleep, and I was ready to drift off myself, I was awakened by the sharp single-engine whine of a lone mosquito loose in the hot, stuffy cabin. I became quite alarmed, put the light on, and searched frantically for it for a few minutes, but then oddly heard no more of the insect. Perhaps, it is gone, I said to myself, but in my heart knew better; it is waiting for me to fall asleep, I thought, it will get me then and quench its thirst. Hopefully it will leave me with nothing more than a small deficiency of blood.

In the morning, while Amélie slept in, I quietly took the dinghy ashore and walked the beach around the back of the Bitter End. Sailboats were heading out onto Eustatia Sound, and a gentle but fresh morning trade wind was blowing in. A big brown pelican fished in the crystalline shallows; at one point I watched a couple of rays leap from the shallow water, their white undersides flashing brilliantly, as perhaps they were startled by a predator. The green-leafed bushes growing full and high along the hillside were alive with flowers, beautiful red, pink, orange, and fuchsia blooms that splashed color everywhere they grew, punctuated with and shaded by tall coconut palms. The beauty of the scene, and the life that seemed to be bursting everywhere from fish, birds, and flora, cheered me. This was the essence of the tropics that I loved, and had so long sought. It was life, life that thrives and continues on in a long succession from the misty origins of time, into the present, and hopefully will persevere into the future.

Back at the boat, as I swung the dinghy downwind and came up under *Rugosa*'s stern, I caught a lovely whiff of the aroma of fresh-brewed coffee. "I am baking bread, too," Amélie called up from the cabin as I tied off the dinghy painter, "But it won't be ready for a bit, the loaf has to rise."

"I brought you a gift that we can have now," I said. "I bought a small rum cake at the little store." So that was what we had for breakfast that morning; a golden, vanilla-rich, aromatic Caribbean rum cake and fresh, strong coffee. By noon, we were once again on our way, with the delightful aroma of a couple of loaves of yeast bread baking in the propane galley as we sailed down passing Spanish Town to port and out past the BVIs headed south.

After several days of beating southeast and south into the trades, tacking back and forth on long tacks between the Leeward Islands, we sailed through rough, roiling waters to the south of mountainous Antigua, and then turned north to seek the shelter of English Harbour, in past the sea-sculptured cliff caves known as the Pillars of Hercules, to the ancient dockyard where Nelson and the British Navy used to repair and refit their wooden warships. We docked stern-to the wharf, Mediterranean-style, as were all the other boats, resembling an array of sardines on a giant fishing hook. We were docked alongside mostly larger, classic, beautiful sailing yachts, all well-kept up. At first I felt small, and cheap, somewhat intimidated; but this wore off quickly after Amélie and I rigged the awning and sat in the cockpit in the shade, in the late afternoon, with a couple of rum punches. "I hate the rich," I said.

"I know you do," she replied. "But they have such beautiful classic yachts."

"They do and they are. Let's go ashore later and walk the perimeter of the wharf and have a look at them." Nelson's dockyard seemed to be situated in a great bowl; high, green hills towered over us from across the crescent-shaped harbor on either side. It appeared to be a very sheltered place.

We were docked practically adjacent to a café that served breakfast every morning, from coffee to juices to eggs to fresh-baked croissants. There was a patio with small tables and chairs, shaded by a randomly tilted assortment of umbrellas. This slip location was a fortuitous coincidence, I told myself. On the opposite side of the small building was a liquor store, with shelves stocked with rum and wine and cold beer in chillers. "I could live here," I said to Amélie.

We went ashore an hour or so before the sun sank behind the high hills to the west. We walked through the dockyard complex together, with old cannons half-buried vertically in the ground to serve as dock bollards, and anchors and massive old iron hardware lying about everywhere. All of the buildings were very old English-style, constructed of antique brick. Blacksmith-forged long-strap iron hinges, holding the warped thick panels of weathered wooden shutters together, creaked on rusted pintles. I already loved the place.

"You like this place because it reminds you of your New England," Amélie said.

"It does, but strangely different, being situated down here in the tropics. Does it remind you of England?"

"Oh yes, in many ways. And I love brick."

"That's the neat part," I said. "There is surely no clay on this island. These bricks had to be brought here in the holds of English ships. Probably came here as ballast. All in the 18th Century. Imagine shipping all the materials needed to build a village, practically, in wooden ships from thousands of miles away, and back then."

We explored the Dockyard and the surrounding area. There were two hotels, each with a bar and a restaurant and rooms to let, a bakery, showers and laundry, some shops, a place called the Galley bar down by the wharf, a museum, and if one walked out of the dockyard complex, past the guard in a little gatehouse, there were more shops and a quaint little Caribbean village named Falmouth that was very much like a lot of other run-down Caribbean villages. It also had a few native-run cottage bars by the side of the road where one could drink cheap liquor in a setting that was very much that of a too-small, run-down private dwelling shack where someone lived, presumably the proprietor. They didn't look safe, which was what I found attractive. Amélie did not like such places at all and refused to go into any with me, despite my entreaties. I teased her, suggesting that we should go into one here, or there, and finally she pulled hard on my arm and became annoyed with me and exclaimed that "We are not going to venture into any of these ruddy low houses or Rasta-shacks!" And that was the end of the discussion as well as my teasing.

The next late afternoon we followed a path snaking up and along the hillside on the west side of the dockyard. The well-traveled trail wound its way out toward the entrance to the harbor, over brown dirt and rough rotten stone, and past some foundations and ruins. Round barrel cacti were growing in among the rocks, and I noted with some pleasure how we seemed to be surrounded by darting geckos and the rich red blossoms of flowering hibiscus. The path led out along a row of stone battlements and old, massive, rusty cannon, a place actually called Fort Berkeley. The road between the battlements was built upon a natural peninsula that led out to the mouth of the harbor. There were two old buildings out there, both long empty ruins, a powder house on the slope down near the water, and a small square stone block guard house with a pyramid-shaped roof. The guard house was out nearly at the end of the pier. It was also empty but for a few bags of concrete or plaster in one corner, bags that had long ago become wetted and had solidified into bricks of their own. The floor was covered with stone dust and rubble, and the roof above, built over sturdy gray weathered rafters, was full of openings and small holes through which the blue sky beyond was plainly visible.

"Not going to stay very dry in here in a rainstorm," I said. Open windows in the walls stared blankly out in all four directions, with only half-open warped old wooden shutters to keep the weather out. I pulled on one, but it wouldn't move; the hinge had become so rusted over the years that the shutter was frozen in a half-open position. The east-facing casement had no shutters left on it at all. We looked out through the windows, but as I was ready to walk out of the place, Amélie put her arms around me. "We're all alone out here," she said, hinting at intended mischief.

"I'm good with that," I said, and we began kissing, and I ran my arms and hands over her smooth body, caressing her as she caressed me, and eventually reached down behind her to run my hands beneath her shorts and caress her buttocks.

"Oh my goodness!" she exclaimed, startled. "Not here!"

"Why not?" I asked, warming to it all. I began pulling at her clothes to loosen them. She did not resist. "It was your idea, wasn't it?"

"Yes, in a way, but...what if someone should come down here and discover us?"

"We'll see them coming down the path from a distance. Plenty of time to pull your shorts up."

"I don't think we should," she replied, but her tone was not one of firm refusal, but belied a resistance that was quickly weakening.

"Oh sure, come on. How about out there, over one of those big cannon?"

She gave me a gentle slap. "You're crazy!"

"They're warm from being in the sun all day," I suggested.

"Out there in front of God and everyone? Don't be crazy. Spread-eagle me over a rusty old cannon. You're out of your mind."

"Here, then."

"I'm not doing it on this awful dirt floor."

"No of course not. Standing up. Against the wall."

She laughed. "We've never done it standing up before," she said. I pulled her shorts down to her knees. "Tippy-toes," I said.

"I'm just a little nervous. I want to keep my top on."

"Up around your neck, then." I pulled it up until it was around her nose. "Oh good God! What's with you today? Suddenly so horny!" she remonstrated.

"Horny sailor," I said.

"Fine!" she replied, and by now we were up against the stone-dusty wall. There was something very primitive feeling about it and it made me very aroused and excited in a strange and primordial way. It might have been a little rough, because at one point she gasped, "Ouch! Not so hard! These rocks are not soft behind me. Don't bruise me!"

"I'm sorry," I replied, without pausing.

We were both breathing hard and paying absolutely no attention at all to whether or not anyone was hiking down the path to the guard house, and it was good that no one actually did, because they would have caught us 'In flagrante delicto.'

Then once again, gasping, she exclaimed, with a little more urgency, "I swear to God Nate don't bang me so hard against this wall. If you fucking knock this place down on top of our heads I will goddamn kill you!"

But the wall didn't give way, and she reached around the back of my neck, around my shoulders, and then hoisted herself up suddenly, wrapping her legs around my waist and squeezing me with her thighs. She seemed remarkably light, I remember thinking, and it was very intense and seemed terribly naughty but at the time we were so absorbed in the moment that we did not care a whit about anything else in the world, and when we were finished we were glossy with perspiration. I'd given her a good rogering, I thought to myself, a bit rascally and it would have seemed almost comical, had it not been for the sincere enjoyment of it, quenching need, and then the playfulness of being in the old stone guard house, in what would have been a disconcerting sight for a perfect stranger to stumble in upon. But we were past care, in the heat of our passion, as it surely goes, I thought, with most people our age.

When we had finished I wiped the stone dust off of her moist buttocks and shoulder blades while she fixed her clothes, and she just smiled knowingly at me as we stepped back out into the late-day golden sunlight. I began to question, albeit momentarily, what we had just done, but only momentarily. There could be no wrong time, no wrong way, I thought, here in paradise. This was a pure place, outdoors, natural, and clean. Was it profane, measured against the sacredness of the realization of this dream? Did it spoil it? No, I concluded. It was appropriate and right and fine to do, and we each felt good about it afterwards. There is nothing dirty about making love to someone close to you in a beautiful place where you want to be. Nothing incongruent or inappropriate about it at all.

Later, we were having a drink at the Galley Bar, a moment's walk from our moored boat. This is so much like home, and yet it is not, I kept thinking to myself. Home, if home could be lifted up like Dorothy's farmhouse in The Wizard of Oz and dropped, suddenly, into paradise, into the middle of the Caribbean. But then, no; this is not New England, it is not even England, it has not been England in two centuries. Those people are all dead and gone. These black faces here are Antiguans. They are not English, I observed, yet they keep the place up, maintain it with almost a loving and reverential attitude. Perhaps because it brings people; it brings the big yachts, and it brings money.

We learned that a sailing event had begun just a couple of days after we had arrived. Very large, elegant sailing yachts began arriving a few at a time, and tying up alongside the very long slips at the west end of the harbor. They were there for the annual Superyacht Challenge, week-long race of big, modern sailboats worth millions of dollars, with skyscraper-tall masts and hulls a hundred feet long or more, going out every day to compete for a few hours in the broad waters off the south end of Antigua.

At night, the young people crewing on these boats would gather on the beach for pre-arranged parties. Temporary bars were set up and big charcoal grills were trundled in to grill chicken, shrimp, and lobsters, sending clouds of aromatic smoke into the night air. Hired chefs plied their trade over glowing coals and upward bursts of flame as they turned their sizzling fare over, crowds of young sailors, drinks in hands, standing around and waiting for their turn to garnish a plate. Socializing was intensive; these were young people from all over the world, mostly pale skin from northern latitudes, signed on to these boats to work like dogs for a week and sleep in cramped quarters, all for the opportunity to experience the exciting adventure-trip of a lifetime, toiling about the tilted decks of these behemoth sailboats as they came to life in the brisk winds and high seas in the waters south of Antigua. Who would not want such a thing, to be young and in your early twenties and have the opportunity to do such? We never had such opportunities when I was in my twenties, I noted to myself, with a twinge of regret, and perhaps a touch of envy; such opportunities were not available to young people growing up in cold, clap-boarded New England. But would I begrudge it to these kids? Not at all. Of course, I call them 'kids', but I was no more than thirty-eight years old myself, and yet I felt in some ways so much older than they, not knowing why, perhaps due to my frame of mind, or upbringing, or culture; I knew not which. All I knew was that I felt very different from them, very far apart, and could not say why.

On a Friday morning, and I say this because happily I knew that it was indeed Friday, since most of the time I really paid no attention to what day of the week it actually was, living, as we were, literally on 'island time', Amélie came up the ladder from down below while I was sitting in the cockpit, enjoying my morning coffee with a splash of English Harbour rum in it. This rum, distilled on Antigua, was nicely smooth and floral and came in a fat green 18th Century-style bottle and had become my favorite sipping rum. The bottle was empty and I knew that I would have to acquire a new one, but happily a little bottle shop on the opposite side of the little building that housed the breakfast café had plenty more.

"I have some bad news," she began.

"How bad?"

"I have to leave. I noted last night that my passport will soon expire and I have to go back to Bermuda to renew it."

"Is it a Bermudian passport?"

"Unfortunately so. I have to go to Hamilton. It's not a big deal, I just can't do it from here."

"How much time left on it?"

"Weeks," she replied.

"You've got to be kidding me!"

272

"Nope. I have to catch a flight. It's going to be expensive, but I have the money. There will be a layover somewhere on the east coast, it seems, there is nothing direct. Hopefully it can be done in just a few days."

"When do you go?" I asked, taken much aback by this sudden revelation. Amélie seemed sad; she hung her head, gazing downward, obviously feeling down but at the same time resigned to what she had to do.

"I leave tomorrow," she said, "Taxi in the morning right from the front gate. If I don't do this, we will never be able to go to the places we want to together. Every goddamn rock down here that we want to stop at, we have to clear into. It will be the same for Panama, any place around the world, so many different countries. I can't live my life stuck on the boat."

"Do you have to go so soon?" I asked, "I mean, would you get a better ticket price if you waited?"

"I've already waited too long," she replied, "Didn't keep up on it. I should have begun the process a couple of months ago. So it may complicate things that it is so close to expiration. I hope I can get this done without delays, but I cannot wait any longer."

"Oh, there's no issue with it then," I replied, "You just have to do it."

That evening, Amélie was upset. She turned in early but did not sleep well and did not want to make love. "I just want to get this over with and be back here with you," she said, at one point. "Let's have a drink, can we?"

"Let's walk over to the beach party," I suggested, "It's not really that late. A little revelry might perk up your spirits. I want to drink from a plastic cup tonight."

Of course we drank too much, and I had to almost carry her back to the boat and put her aboard, but going to the party had made her feel better. She was laughing and giddy and silly and she put her arms around my neck and clasped her hands behind and almost pulled me down with her when she lost her balance, but she seemed happy. "We'll be able to go wherever we want," she giggled, her breath heavily aromatic with gin, "And it'll be years before I have to go back to Bermuda. If you marry me, you can live there and be a Bermudian."

This made me smile, and laugh myself, "And keep *Rugosa* in the harbor at St. George's," I said.

"Oh yes, oh yes you can!" She laughed again, and then burped hard, and it smelled sour and I was afraid that she would throw up. "You'd better take it easy right now," I said, "Let me help you to the berth. How do you feel?"

"I'm fine, she stammered, then giggled and laughed again, seemingly for no reason, but I knew that it was simply because she was thinking about returning, after the bureaucratic rigamarole was finished, and the thought of coming back made her happy, as did the thought of continuing the voyage, perhaps around the world, or wherever our charts led us and the winds of the earth blew us, and with the possibility that we would live happily ever after back on her home island of Bermuda.

In the morning, she was groggy and she smiled weakly at me as she sipped her coffee and I helped pack her bag. Then I stood at the front gated entrance to Nelson's Dockyard and I watched the small, smelly, smoky taxi drive her away on her half-hour ride to the airport, and as the cab disappeared around a corner, I once again felt very much alone and there was a sinking feeling in my stomach, something that was not really a bad feeling, or premonitory, but just a not-so-good feeling overall and I wondered what, after all, that it meant.

We shared one last embrace before she climbed into the taxi. "You behave yourself, now, for me," she admonished me, with gentle humor.

"I promise I will, I'll be good," I replied, with a smirk.

"Don't say that unless you really mean it," she teased, and then waved through the open window as the cab drove away.

I passed the day by being busy, in an attempt to take my mind off her leaving, and so I drank some beer, donned a pair of cutoffs and a mask and went swimming around the boat with a scrub brush, doing my best to give *Rugosa* something of a bottom job. It would have been a lot easier if I had taken the trouble to rent scuba gear, but I didn't, and as a result it was an exhausting couple of hours, after which I had done a fairly passable job, but after I rinsed off I simply sat around the cockpit for a while in the shade, nursing a few scrapes and scratches from barnacles and sea growth that I had brushed up against on the hull, and sipping a cold rum punch, watching the activity on the nearby boats and in the harbor. Eventually I dozed off and when I awoke it was late in the day and the sun was setting.

In the morning I awoke early and my first thoughts were to wonder if Amélie had arrived back in Bermuda yet; how she had found the apartment, hopefully intact as she had left it, and a few other thoughts; but then my mind turned to work that I needed to do on the boat, to repair this, change that, check my running rigging for chafe, and attend to other small matters. I knew that I could always focus best when I was alone, for then there was only me and the boat, and no one else to present a distraction. I had some laundry to do, but first I thought I would walk over to the shower building with a towel, clean shirt, and

274

bar of soap, and have a clean and refreshing shower in the morning air before the day commenced to grow hot. This I did, but forgot my towel, oddly, but it was no matter; I walked around afterwards without my shirt on in the sun, until my upper body had dried, and then was able to don my shirt. The early morning air felt good and there was a slight breeze freshening, rustling the tops of the tall palms. The superyachts were still at their piers, and there was much activity about them. They would not be heading out to race for an hour or two yet.

I stopped at the bakery for a spicy hot meat pie on my way back to the wharf, and remembered that I needed to replenish my supply of English Harbor rum, so I went into the little store to grab a bottle. As I maneuvered into line to pay, a young woman in her twenties dressed in a white pullover sport shirt and faded denim shorts, who had obviously not seen me, stepped in front of me. When she realized this, she then turned, surprised, and with a slight British accent, exclaimed, terribly politely, "Oh! I am so sorry; did I cut you in line?" She was thin, blonde, and very fair, her light skin sunburned pink on her face and neck and places where the sun had peeked in; her eyes were light blue and she could have been no more than twenty.

"Oh certainly not, go ahead, please!" I replied. "Racing today?"

"Oh yes!" she responded, enthusiastically, if seemingly a little bashful. "We've done well this week! We're the *Avantia*, you know, the big one at the end of the dock. Yours?"

"Just a visiting cruiser," I said. "Good luck today to *Avantia* and her crew!"

"Thank you! You too!"

Another girl from the U.K., I thought, but then I noticed that her cloth belt was imprinted with the familiar logo of Oldport Shipyard, a very familiar big-yachts shipyard up in Rhode Island. She isn't British, I thought, just affecting an accent. She's a Yankee from Rhode Island, probably her first time down here crewing on a superyacht. People sometimes affect an accent of sorts, I've often noted, when they are in an exciting, new environment full of other people like them from different and wonderful places. They affect an accent because it helps them do one of two things, and perhaps both; they want to stand out, individually, whilst at the same time feel as though they are a part of this group and not just so ordinary, coming from this place or that. Of course, if you are young and in a group of peers from exotic places where you have never traveled, the place where you are from tends to feel as though it's ordinary to you, even though it actually is not and others may not think so. But if, after all, you're sailing with a bunch of other kids who happen to be from the UK, sooner or later you start unconsciously to talk like them too, at least a little bit. It's a way of fitting in, and perhaps, sounding a little bit sophisticated so that you will hopefully be accepted more readily and better regarded.

There was something about her slim, young figure that caught my eye. She was someone who must have sailed a good deal, for she seemed lithe and athletic, with a form that was pleasant to look at, yet graceful as she moved. Her blonde hair was tied back in a ponytail behind her ball cap, and her cheeks were lightly freckled. She had a small, freckled nose and her eyebrows were such light blond that they were almost invisible. I felt myself smiling as I left the store, heading back to the boat with my provisions. There was something fetching about her, I noted, remembering the old term, and for some reason she stuck in my mind's eye. I had become suddenly taken with her; why, I could not be sure; no doubt it is just whimsy, I reasoned, and yet perhaps it was because she came from my country, my culture, my color, my boating neighborhood, so to speak. She was like me, in some ways, and loved sailing and being out on the sea. Opposites don't always attract, I noted. Sometimes you want to be close to what feels like home, like comfort food. Yes, this girl felt like home, like comfort food to me. Could that be dangerous?

Later in the morning, I was able to get through to Amélie. She did not sound happy, but her voice reflected a mixture of sadness and anger, both at the same time. "There are some problems," she began, "too complicated to elaborate here, all government stuff. I'm afraid I'm going to be stuck here for a while."

"How long? Any estimate?"

"Could be a week, could be several. Don't know yet. But it's going to go through. Damned bureaucrats."

"That's government for you."

"That's British government, especially."

"They're all that way. Look at the shit we have to go through just to clear in at Tortola. Then sail over to St. Thomas and go through the entire ordeal again with the U. S. customs."

"I'm depressed," she replied, "Don't want to talk about it. Promise you will call me? Not just e-mail?"

"I promise," I replied, albeit half-heartedly, because staying in touch, or making small talk on the phone, is not something that I am very good or consistent at.

"I know that you're not a very chatty guy," she continued, "But try for me."

"Stop reading my mind," I said, "You're already making me feel guilty for something that I have not yet failed to do." I heard her laugh at the other end of the line.

Around noon time a front came through, dark and squally, cool and wet. I got rained on while walking about and for the first time in many months I shivered and felt cold. But then the sun came back out, bright and strong, and I soon dried out. It rains nearly every day down here, I noted, usually briefly. But on the plus side, if you get rained on, you'll usually dry quickly. Everything does, even with the humidity, perhaps because the sun is fairly intense, even during the winter months. And because of the strong sun, I made liberal use of sunscreen on my bare flesh, since I had already become sunburned in places that I ignored.

Later in the afternoon, I was surprised and delighted to see *Two Blue* sail into English Harbor. Poppa Jon was up on the foredeck, tending the sails as they dropped, while Dieter was at the helm, motoring in. I hailed them on my hand-held VHF, then ran down to the wharf to help them dock, securing the dock lines as they moored. I was no longer alone; friends had come into the harbor.

We found ourselves seated around a table at the Galley bar. Dieter and Poppa Jon had been as far south as Grenada, where they had stayed for a few days watching the Sailing Festival. "They have the most wonderful little wooden boats," he began, in wistful remembrance. "They are beautiful, in bright colors, small boats, painted so handsomely, very shiny and smooth hulls, bright reds, yellows, greens, with cool names lettered on them," he recalled. "So many young people in daily races, crowds standing on the beach, taking photos, cheering on the different boat teams, I felt young again just watching them."

"He did more than that," Poppa Jon spoke up. "He went sailing with them."

"How did you do that?" I asked, surprised.

"He got a snoot full of his gin," Poppa Jon replied quickly before Dieter could speak, "And then he talked them into letting him go in one of the boats."

"I did all right though, didn't I?" Dieter asked.

"Yeah, you did all right, grandpa. Then you fell down while trying to jump into the boat, going off the beach, and another boat ran over you and almost broke your leg."

"Well, hey, that wasn't my fault!"

"Hmmm, no, maybe the gin bottle's fault. Should have seen it, Nate, some twenty boats all starting the race, like four or five of these kids in each boat, all teenagers, all native island kids, you know, like me, and then there is this great big old German guy here wanting to jump into the boat and sail with them."

"How did he do?" I asked.

"We took second place, twice, out of twenty-five boats!" Dieter exclaimed, proudly.

"Did he?" I asked Poppa.

"Well, the boat did," Poppa replied. "He did look a bit out of place, mon."

"Did the kids mind?"

Poppa Jon let a go a deep, shaking laugh. "Well, they didn't throw him overboard," he replied. "They suffered him."

"Oh bullshit," Dieter replied, and laughed. "They knew that I am a kindred spirit. In my heart I am Black too, just like them, and they knew it."

Poppa Jon grinned and rolled his eyes. "Yah, Captain Dieter, you just go ahead and keep thinking that," then slowly shook his head.

"You don't think so?" Dieter asked, as though offended.

Poppa Jon stood up. "I have to walk over to the Men's Room," he said, and walked away chuckling to himself.

"I could live there, I swear. I love the beautiful little boats with their strange sailing rigs, odd little bowsprits and clipper bows, of all things. And they pull them right up onto the beach. The water is so full of color itself, blue, yellow from the sand beneath, green and blue in the shallows, warm and pleasant, I wished that I could live there, stay there forever. Time would stand still for me there."

"Stands still for no one, Dieter. That is not your world, really. But you can always be an observer."

"Yes, I can."

It was after sunset now and Poppa Jon returned just as a small crowd of young sailors from the superyacht races, now concluded for the day, came into the bar and occupied a couple of tables at the open end of the deck. I saw a familiar face; it was the girl I had spoken to in the bottle shop that morning. "Excuse me for minute, guys," I said, and walked over to her. She was sitting with a group and did not seem to be preoccupied with anyone in particular. I tapped her on the shoulder, and when she looked up, she recognized me immediately, and I asked, "How did your boat place today? Did you have a good race?" She grinned, her face was flush from sun and drink, and she was beaming. "Oh, we did great!" and she proceeded to tell me all about it. I sat down for a moment, pulling up an empty chair, and somehow worked in the usual getting-acquainted talk. Her name was Jenna; her faux British accent disappeared when she spoke to me; I was from her neck of the woods, after all, and now I knew it. I lied and told her that my name was Dan, and then all about my boat, how I had fixed it up and decided to go adventuring on my own. "Oh, I'll have to see it," she exclaimed, as I bought her another drink. "There's a party on the beach tonight, like last night, you're welcome to come along with us in a little bit, Dan, if you like." In the course of telling my story, I neglected to mention Amélie. But we were talking about boats and sailing, not lovers, or revealing secrets about our lives; this wasn't that kind of conversation.

"I sure will," I said.

"Are those guys your crew?" Jenna asked.

"No, they're cruising friends on another boat that came in this afternoon. I met them some time back on St. Martin. That's how it is with cruising live-aboard folks; you keep running into one another in different harbors." We both laughed. "I'd like to have a nice boat and live aboard it too someday," she said. "Right now though I just work on boats, all summer and nearly year round at Oldport. But that's what I want to do, just be around boats. This is the second winter that I've really gotten away from Rhode Island to the tropics for any reasonable amount of time."

I'm not sure why I gave her a false name, other than, perhaps, I had spur-of-the-moment ulterior motives. Amélie had popped into my head at the moment that the conversation began, a little brown angel-image of my conscience in my mind's eye reminding me of my moral responsibility to behave myself, and also of my promise to do so. But, I rationalized, I haven't done anything wrong yet, have I? I'm just having a conversation. And what's in a name, anyway? I wanted to hedge my bets and keep my options open in the event that I chose to misbehave. It was a game and this was all in fun; giving a fake name was part of the game, and if I played, I did not want it getting back to Amélie whenever she might return. I was intending to cheat, but I was putting the whole issue out of my mind for the moment. I was fishing, and I had to concentrate on landing my fish. I wanted to play without consequences.

I re-joined Dieter and Poppa Jon, who of course inquired about my 'new friend'. "She's young," Poppa Jon noted. "She's on one of the big boats?"

"She probably has a boyfriend on one of the boats," Dieter added.

"Oh pipe down you guys. I got invited to the beach party." The young sailors were standing up from their tables and pushing their chairs in. "...And it looks like it's about to kick off."

"Can anyone go?" Dieter asked.

"It's a cash bar," I replied, "So if you've got a pocket full of E.C. dollars, you're welcome."

"Well then, what are we waiting for?" Dieter asked. "Let's finish our drinks and then go to the party!"

"I'll meet you over there, I need to stop by the boat," I said, and went below where I hastily searched for and hid anything belonging to Amélie that she might have left out in plain view. I knew what I was doing, and already felt guilty about it as I did it, and was doing it automatically, all on the intuitive hunch that something might just happen between me and Jenna later on. I just had a feeling, a gut thing I might call it, but it was real and while I could not put my finger on where it came from, exactly, I knew that it was thoroughly authentic in a way that a man smells opportunity with a woman even though there are no outward signs. It is, I suppose, akin to a shark smelling blood in the water and going into hunting mode; it just happens. I knew that it was wrong, too, but I was rationalizing at lightning speed in my head and simply ignoring any stop signs in the road. I was focused. I was going to do my best to get that girl in my bunk, or her bunk, and how I did it, through charm, strategy, and drink, it did not matter. I rationalized in many ways; I reminded myself that after all, I was not married to, or engaged to, Amélie; but as I thought this, I momentarily laughed at myself. Who are you fooling, I asked myself. You know what you're about, and you know that it isn't right, it's betrayal, but you're going full steam ahead to do it anyway.

I met up with Dieter and Poppa Jon on the beach at the edge of the loud party crowd. "That was fast," Dieter greeted me.

"Yup. Let's get a drink. Damn, I'm hungry. Can we get into that grilled stuff? Buy a plate? I'm watching the leaping flames on the grill and can smell the steak or chicken or whatever it is and the lobster and shrimp. Dinner is calling."

I moved through the jostling crowd, finding my way back to the water's edge from the little bar set up on the beach, and as suddenly, ran right into Jenna, who had just turned away from another conversation. "Oh hi, it's you! Dan, right? I hoped I'd see you here," she said. She had a full drink in one hand and she seemed tipsy. We talked for a little bit.

"Come on down the dock, I'll show you *Avantia*," she said.

"Looks like they have a guard and gate on the dock," I replied.

"You're with me, it's OK, and I've got the I.D. needed to get us aboard."

So then it was no trouble, and she brought me down the dock and aboard the magnificent new yacht that she was sailing on, more than a hundred feet long. Jenna was stumbling occasionally and on one instance, I had to catch her to prevent her from falling, to which she replied, "Oh, I'm so sorry for that, thank you," once more in her revived faux British accent.

She showed me the bright and luxurious cabins belowdecks, as well as the tight, uncomfortable-looking berths where the crewmembers stayed. "It's worth it though," she commented, "to be able to be on an adventure like this."

Once we had returned to the party, and she had refilled her drink, she asked to see my boat. "It isn't anywhere nearly as impressive as your *Avantia*," I said.

"What's your boat's name?" she asked.

"*Serenity*," I replied, lying again.

"Oh, that's pretty. Pretty common, though," she stuttered.

"Well, I'm a pretty common guy," I said.

"Obviously, you're not," she laughed.

We zig-zagged along the wharf until we came to my boat, and I helped her aboard. It was dark down in the main cabin. I knew that now, something was about to happen, and it did. Without much of a word spoken, we fell hungrily into each other's arms, and began pulling one another's clothes off in the darkness. I was drunk, too and I should never have allowed it to happen, but we had sex, strong, fast, eager, and intense. She made love as though she had been deprived for some time, but I knew that it couldn't be so, but rather a characteristic of strong-willed, adventurous, athletic girls her age, impulsive, burning like a sudden burst of flammable liquid, then going out as quickly once the fuel is exhausted.

After we were done, we were both sweating profusely and breathing heavily; she seemed quiet and a little unsteady as she struggled to pull her clothes on, then I helped her back onto the wharf. I wanted to lead her back to her party and to her boat, but she refused. Something seemed a little bit wrong. I tried to make small talk, but she did not want to talk. I thought that perhaps she was embarrassed for having such a sudden and intense release of passion. Maybe a little guilty, I thought. Must have a boyfriend somewhere.

"I can walk you back to the dock," I said. She was headed in a direction that led toward the entrance to the Dockyard.

"No, no, I'm OK, really."

"This isn't the way..."

"No really, it's fine, I'm OK," she insisted, a little more forcefully, seeming annoyed. I could tell that she wanted to be alone, and at the same time, it was fairly quiet in the Dockyard. Security was good here due to the many expensive boats moored about. She couldn't get into much trouble unless she walked off the end of the wharf, which, I thought, was in fact a real possibility.

"Are you absolutely sure, Jenna?"

The mention of her name seemed to irritate her. "Just let me go, OK? I mean it."

"Fine. Good night," and I walked away, turning around a couple of times to watch her stumble aimlessly away around anchors, cannon, and buildings in the Dockyard.

I went back to my boat, feeling guilty as hell now myself, and put my head down on my pillow. In a few moments I was deeply and drunkenly asleep.

I would have slept later, except that I was awakened shortly after sunrise by Dieter, alone. He had come aboard, and he shook my shoulder gently but urgently to awaken me. "What is it?" I said.

"Missed you leaving the party last night," he answered.

"I sort of got sidetracked," I said.

"There is a problem," he began. "You need to leave."

"What do you mean? Leave where?"

"That girl from the big boat. Last night. What did you do?"

I was rubbing my eyes. "I brought her back to the boat. Okay?"

"Not okay. The police were down at the dock this morning, asking questions. The word out there is that she is claiming that she was raped."

I stood up, now wide awake all of a sudden, and felt my face turn red. My pulse began pounding with the adrenalin release, as my mind fought to get up to speed. "That's not true!" I cried. "Sure we were drinking. But it was completely consensual. I even offered to walk her back to the boat..."

"Maybe you should have. Yes, yes, consensual with you. But not with someone else."

"What?"

"You were the last one seen with her at the party, but of course nobody knows you. Which way was she going when you saw her last?"

"She was going in every direction but her boat," I answered.

"That's where the trouble began. Two other guys found her after that, I guess she walked out the front gate or something into the village. They probably weren't from the Dockyard. Scuttlebutt I am getting is that they were from the town, maybe had been at a Rasta shack. Dark boys. Got her aside and had their way with her. But she does not want to admit that, and besides, the locals here would protect them. So it looks like you get to take the fall for them. Word gets around quickly down here on the docks, like lightning."

"I don't believe this."

"Did you know that she is engaged to some guy back in Rhode Island? Co-owner of that shipyard she works at."

"No, she wasn't wearing any kind of a ring that I could see."

"Was probably in her seabag. But he's outraged, going to fly down here. She's now at the medical center in St. John's. Police drove her there. Not good. She will never tell her fiancé that she was raped by two black boys from Antigua who smoked dope with her and then got into the rough stuff. She does not want to lose her boy back home. And he will be here I guess as soon as he can get on a flight."

"What should I do? I didn't do anything wrong. I had sex with her, and she wanted it."

"Doesn't matter; no one will side with you. Clear out of here as soon as the Customs Office opens. Lots of people will be lining up this morning now that the last race finished yesterday. Just go. I hear that she didn't even remember what boat it happened on. So it could be awhile before you're fingered unless someone from the boat or the party recognizes you. But it was very dark. And you talked to her in the Galley bar with other people around."

"Nothing uncommon about that. Shit. I wanted to wait until Carver and *Gleam* got here."

"They aren't even coming here," Dieter said. "They've already begun heading back to the B.V.I.s. They were way the hell down in St. Vincent and the Grenadines. I talked to him on the radio down there. Now you need to get underway. I'll help with the lines and anchor, you get over to Customs."

"Where will you go?" I asked.

"I think Poppa and I will head back to Grenada. I liked it there. Then, who knows. We may go on to Trinidad so that Poppa can visit his old haunts again."

"But you came all the way here!"

"Because I knew that you would come here, and besides, I like this place now. Carver told me when we radioed that you would probably be here. This has for some years been a favorite anchorage for him and his *Gleam*. But I think he is headed for the Pacific. That's not for me. So when you see him again, say hello for his old friends Dieter and Poppa Jon, and wish him fair winds, wherever he goes."

Poppa Jon had come aboard now, and I embraced both of them, for I suspected that I might not see them again soon, if ever, and then sadly, but determinedly, made my way across the Dockyard to the Customs Office. It was nine o'clock now and the office was just opening. I let a couple of other people get in line in front of me, for I did not want to be the first in line, nor did I want to seem to be too eager. I had a horrible hangover, which only made everything about the way I felt much worse.

The Customs Officer was a very short, heavy-set black woman in a starched, cleanly pressed uniform shirt, with very dark skin and her face glistened shiny in the morning light. She was sour and unpleasant, as many of these islanders tend to be toward lighter-skinned off-islanders, but she stamped my passport and papers promptly without much question.

"Did you have a nice visit?" she asked.

I smiled pleasantly. "I've had a great visit," I said, "Can't wait to come back to watch the Classic Regatta." I paid my departure fee in cash.

"Yes," she said, waxing friendlier, now, "That's a great event." There was a line building behind me. "Next."

Within the hour *Rugosa* was underway and heading for the open sea, out past Fort Berkeley to starboard, and the Pillars of Hercules off my port beam. I kept my head low, leaving the harbor, and once I was out past the Pillars, I looked back at English Harbor, with mixed feelings; I was angry and indignant, and yet scared too, and kept my eye on the harbor entrance for a while, expecting at any moment to see a police boat come roaring out of the channel, lights flashing, pushing a white bow wave of foam. But there were only three other sailboats leaving behind me, innocently enough.

Well, I told myself, you liked that place, but you screwed it up. If you had left that damned drunk sailing chick alone, and not played the horny goat, you would be having coffee and a croissant at the café right now.

For the sake of a little feel-good, the one-night stand had not been worth it, not worth it at all. I had proven nothing to myself other than that I could seduce a young woman, nothing that I had not done before. And now there were consequences, borne out of lies. But then, like the fox that turned his nose up at the sour grapes, so did I, the practical sailor, rationalize. It was time to leave, anyway; I had been there too long. But I did not stop at the fuel dock on the way out, no, I just wanted out of there with as little contact with anyone as possible. I knew that I would have to sail, then, most of the way back to Tortola. That's where I would get more fuel, and stay for a few days before moving on. From now on, I told myself, I must behave. Go to Tortola. Try to reach Carver and *Gleam*. Keep a low profile. Arrange to meet up with Amélie. Be a good boy from now on. Time makes many things go away, or if they do not go away, pushes them far enough into the background that you can ignore them. Truly bad things never, ever go away. I would learn this yet again, soon enough.

Chapter 22

Change of Course

It's out there at sea that you are really yourself.

—Vito Dumas

In my mind's log-book, I write, *"I am sailing along full and by, in the middle of the night, under a full moon, north-westerly from Antigua. The trade winds are blowing gently at a steady fourteen knots; all of Rugosa's sails, main, mizzen and the two foresails, are up and they drive her on a broad reach toward the British Virgin Islands and tomorrow."* But for the present, I savor the moment; *Rugosa* steers easily, responsive to the slightest touch, moving along as smoothly as though she were sliding through a sea of cream. The moist wind caresses my shirtless skin, bathes me in comforting cool, and I consider, for a moment, these storied waters, and how the British, French, Spanish, and others, not to mention the pirates of old, fought for control of these sea-lanes once upon a time. Now I cross their wakes. I left English Harbor, Antigua, before ten o'clock in the morning. Some hours ago I watched the sun set in a fiery bronze disc over the silhouetted mountains of the islands of St. Kitts and Nevis to port. Eventually their lights began to gleam, a few at a time and then they were all glittering as darkness fell and I could see them sparkling and glowing in the distance until I finally put them astern. I am doing the one task I love best, hand steering my boat. *One does not tire of such duty,* I reflect.

On a broad reach, heading downwind, *Rugosa* rolls slightly with each swell passing under her starboard quarter. Her long main boom, extending out to port, enhances this roll; but it is a steady, regular rhythm, and my body has become accustomed to the gentle motion as my boat surges ahead. There are, of course, the sounds of the sea, the waves passing by, the water swishing by the hull, foaming after the bow wave and as quickly passing astern. There are the regular sounds of the rigging working, the chafe leathers in the boom and gaff jaws grumbling against the wood of the masts, tight running rigging lines, and wind through them at times. It is a steady symphony of sounds as my boat works its way across the Caribbean Sea through the silvery moonlit darkness.

For a while, after the sun had set, I slept. I set the auto-steering and let it guide her for a few hours, the radar setting for a two-mile alarm radius, but no other vessel came near. I slept uninterrupted for perhaps four hours, feeling refreshed when I awoke in the cockpit, with the island of Saba falling just abaft my port beam. I had watched the full moon rise in the east as the sun set, but now the myriad sparkling lights of St. Kitts had passed many miles astern, and the great mountain of Saba loomed off the port beam in the darkness. I saw what appear to be strings of yellow lights outlining its dark, steep mass. I took a pull at my water bottle; *I am sailing back the way I came down here,* I said to myself, *northwestward along the Leeward Islands chain toward the BVIs and Tortola.*

At dawn, the sun rises, opposite the sinking full moon. Fair-weather tropical skies with a smattering of fluffy color-splashed clouds lighten overhead; *I had a great run bowling along through the night,* I say to myself. Flying fish are darting everywhere this morning like flakes of silver, or perhaps loose handfuls of shining pieces-of-eight flung wide; they are skipping across the waves as *Rugosa* and I greet the new day.

I am back in my element again, sailing alone just as I had started out, and feeling good about it. Once again, I reminded myself why I love this; because life at sea follows a set of unchanging, rigid rules. They make the unpredictable sea in some ways predictable. You follow the rules. Sometimes even when you follow the rules, you are overpowered or overwhelmed by the sea, and you die. But the sea is trustworthy in the sense that it is governed by the laws of nature, and no others. It has no evil intent or malice; only mankind is capable of that, which is why I always ultimately prefer the trustworthy company of the sea. At least the sea will not unjustly accuse me of a crime that I did not commit.

Clearing in at Customs in Soper's Hole at the West End of Tortola was no issue, and although I was slightly nervous, and did my best to disguise it, there were no problems or questions that suggested anything more than a routine clearing in or out and indeed, one of the clerks was beginning to recognize me and he smiled and welcomed me back to the BVIs. I relaxed somewhat; the whole Caribbean wasn't hunting for me, after all. I went back out to my dinghy only to be cheered by the sight of *Gleam* coming to anchor only a hundred yards away from my *Rugosa*. I putted over in my beat-up old *Skidbladner*, my patched and leaking inflatable dinghy. I hailed Captain John with a boisterous "Ahoy!" and was promptly invited to tie up and ascend the boarding ladder for a drink as he and Jack put the boat away, as they say. Carver shut off *Gleam*'s engine, mixed a couple of drinks and then settled down in the cockpit as Jack and crewman Billy finished rigging the awning. They had been cruising around the islands, most recently to Norman Island, often considered to be the model for Stevenson's 'Treasure Island', and where Carver, like many others before him, went poking around in the rock structures known as the 'Treasure Caves' where a chest of money had actually been found one hundred and fifty-odd years before.

Carver poured me a drink, and I told him my story, and then asked him if he had heard anything in the past few days. He had; he had spoken to Dieter at the Pirates Bight bar on the beach over at Norman Island. "And I think he's still there," Carver added, and laughed. As for the girl, Jenna, "Oh, hell," Carver replied. "She's already back in the states. Dieter told me. The skipper put her on a plane as soon as she was released from the hospital the next day. She won't be sailing on *Avantia* again. But she stuck to her story and the authorities are looking for you, well, not you exactly, because she couldn't remember your name, and then finally she remembered the name of the boat, '*Serenity*', and actually there was a '*Serenity*' in the harbor but it's a 90-ft. power megayacht and they knew that wasn't it. All she remembered was that it was a traditional rig but of course there are a dozen like that in the harbor at any given time. So it seems to be a cold case right now unless you run into her again at a Newport bar. Or she tells the truth, which is pretty unlikely. But you know, it's the whole court business and notoriety that ruins you, financially and every other way. When a woman cries 'Rape!' today, even if it's proven to be a lie, your life and career are destroyed no matter if you are innocent of the crime."

"Fuckin' right about that," Jack chimed in.

"Ever been accused of that?" Carver turned to him and asked, teasing.

Jack grinned, stared down at his drink and his cigarette. "I've been with lots of women; older women, younger women. It's all been good, always a two-way street. Never had a complaint either. Sometimes I paid for it..."

"...Not the Chicken Ranch!" Carver interrupted.

"Yes, absolutely," Jack laughed a snarly laugh, "And let me tell you, I am a great fucking believer in education and experience, yes sir, it was some of the best I had. A man gets his money's worth when he's paying a professional."

"Jack," was all I could say, shaking my head, "Jack..."

"...But it was always, always fucking conceptual," he added.

"Consensual?" I asked

"You know what I mean, wiseass. Never forced, I don't believe that's right, never."

"You're a lover not a fighter, you're saying," Carver said.

"Fucking right. Why they call it love-making, not just fucking."

"Love-making with whores?" I asked.

"It's all the same, buddy Nate. You put your cash on the barrelhead one way or the other eventually. So says I, it's better to pay at the Point of Purchase. Then you're done with it."

I could only nod at his practical wisdom, after all. "Not the marrying type," I replied.

"Fucking A," he said. "Never wanted no part of that arrangement."

"Life gets lonely though," Carver countered.

"That's bullshit, I mean, pardon my saying Captain, but a man can find companionship, if he knows how to look for it. But it's all about what you're fuckin' looking for, which is not always the same thing as what womens is looking for. They want a man to bind to and seed a family. And then the poor stiff spends the rest of his life pullin' in the traces until he retires and dies. Once the family starts the sex stops, and you can't just fucking go out and get some elsewhere 'cause you're feelin' a little deprived and the old lady won't give you any. No sir, I seen that too many fucking times. Rich man can have a mistress. Poor man gets Mary Palm unless he wants a divorce, and then he still has to pay. Nope; I don't want no part of diaper changin', screaming babies, coming home to questions like why you've been out so late, and where, all that bullshit. No sir, I'm a batch man, dyed-in-the-wool, and always will be."

Before sunset, Dieter and Poppa Jon sailed around the point and into Soper's, anchoring not far away from us, and soon were aboard. Carver made dinner; he had a large black cast-iron frying pan, and old one that had been in his family for many years, and was a favorite of his for cooking. He cooked his favorite one-pan chicken dish, with boneless chicken, onions, bell peppers, olive oil and pasta, and the five of us sat in the cockpit with 'boat drinks' and ate ravenously until the pan was completely empty, and time for those who smoked to do so. I slept right there in the cockpit that night; we were up drinking and laughing and talking loudly and well-lubricated until the wee hours. The next day, Amélie arrived at the Beef Island airport at the opposite end of Tortola, and I hired a taxi to go pick her up. She greeted me with an impossibly strong, tight embrace, eager kisses, and even a small tear down one cheek. I felt my body go into a cold sweat, the cold sweat of guilt. How am I ever going to be able to live this secret down, I asked myself. She looked searchingly into my eyes. "Everything OK?"

"Yes," I lied, "We were all up really late last night on *Gleam*, and I'm hung over as hell." *I must never, ever mention a word*, I told myself. *Not even on my death-bed.*

"Hmm, you don't seem quite yourself, for sure. Well then let's get back and go to the Pusser's Café first and get you some hair of the baboon," she said. "That will straighten you out!" She giggled. "Now look at this!" And she pulled out and showed me her shiny new Bermudian passport. "We can go anywhere, now!"

"We can start with Tahiti. Or Bora Bora. Or someplace like that."

"I can't wait. How was your sail up here from Antigua?" she asked.

"Pretty easy," I replied. "But it was time. Everyone was meeting here in Soper's, and I'd had enough of that place, it was getting stale."

"Well of course, I wasn't there!" she teased. I felt myself cringe, inside. "Now where? Off to the Pacific, at last?"

"Looking that way," I said. "But just us and *Gleam*. Dieter and Poppa Jon have decided to head to St. Croix for a bit, then to meander their way south, probably down to Trinidad to see Poppa's relatives."

"I will miss them," was all she replied.

The last evening before we all went our separate ways, we gathered aboard *Gleam* for a final party, just the seven of us. We would meet up with *Gleam* at the Panama Canal, then around four thousand miles later, in Tahiti. From there on, we had no specific plans; perhaps we would then go on to other islands and maybe end up in the South China Sea; Carver was still undecided and occasionally mentioned the possibility of going to Thailand.

Parting ways with Dieter and Poppa Jon was difficult, as I knew that it would be; it is always that way with friends with whom one has become close, especially with fellow vagabonds in the world of sea people. As the last evening together drew to a close, there were many hugs, and many tears. Amélie hugged Dieter and Poppa Jon and wept, saying that she did not know if she would ever see them again, and how this made her very sad and pained her greatly. Dieter told her to take good care of me, and to not let me out of her sight, not for very long at all, meaning so in a mischievous and humorous way, hoping to lighten her up a little. Then Poppa sat her down and said something quietly into her ear, speaking softly in his native patois, and as he did so, I saw her brighten up and laugh, and they both laughed now as he wiped away the tears from her wet cheeks with his soft cotton bandana. Then he turned to me and grinned, and said, "Hotpeppa, now you will no longer be a hotpeppa, but you have graduated now to Captain Nate, so you are a captain, even if you are still maybe a hotpeppa a little bit but we will not call you by that name anymore. So now you need to take care of this little girl, hey? And you must not let any harm come to her. I know you are a good man, now, strong too, and I believe that you will protect her, hey? There is a lot of love between you."

"Oh, Poppa..." I interjected, a little embarrassed,

"No, no you listen to me. Because that is what a Captain does, he listens too as well as gives orders. Remember that the man who cannot take orders cannot command, and the man who cannot listen has no authority to speak. OK? This is what Poppa Jon says, to you. So now sit down, before we go, I have something for you." He went into the cabin and brought out his guitar.

"Are you going to play us a song?" Billy asked.

"I have a little going-away song, yes. It is another old song from my youth. My song is my gift to you, but it troubles me a little bit. It is a strange gift, sweet and sour, happy and sad."

"Why is that?" I asked.

"I have had a dream for a few nights, and in this dream, I am always sitting on a rock down by the beach at night, under a big coconut tree, playing this same song; it is called 'Salt Fish Water.' I do not know why it is always this song, since I know so many. But perhaps it means that I was meant to sing it for you." And with that, his deep, sonorous baritone voice began the old song:

"Salt fish water kill me daughter
Pam panam, na-kam, panam
Salt fish water kill me daughter
Pam panam, a-na-kam, panam

Oh a-heave and a-ho, look-e kill me daughter
Pam panam, a-na-kam, panam
Oh, Salt fish water kill me daughter
Pam panam, a-na-kam, panam

De gal run home an she swallow de water
Pam panam, na-kam, panam
Salt fish water kill me daughter
Pam panam, na-kam, panam

Oh a-heave and a-ho, look-e kill me daughter
Pam panam, a-na-kam, panam
Oh, Salt fish water kill Annie daughter
Pam panam, a-na-kam, panam"

Poppa had been staring at me during the entire song, and there was sadness in his eyes that I could not understand nor fathom. Some of us sang along with some of the verses, but it did not seem to be a happy song, and we were glad when it was over, even though we clapped and told Poppa how wonderful it was. A new round of rum drinks lightened the mood somewhat, but it was getting late and nearly time to turn in, with everyone being emotionally spent from the hard good-byes.

Carver invited all of us to stay aboard; there were plenty of berths below. As we began to gradually disappear, one by one, belowdecks, I took a few moments to steal away in the darkness to the foredeck of the big schooner for a few moments of reflection. I remember precisely what it was like; the moonlight was tracing a path of silver across the quiet harbor; up forward on the bow, standing next to the bowsprit and steadying myself with the thick metal cable of the forestay, I felt my bare feet cozy against the still-warm teak wood of the antique schooner's deck, and the cool zephyrs of the last of the day's trade wind breezes were softly cooling and caressing my shirtless frame. My body was relaxed now that the heat of the tropical day was gone. It is a time for quiet contemplation, I told myself, and personal space; hold onto the steel shroud, and sip your rum punch, and take it all in. The cheerful sounds of distant shoreside music, and the smoky aromas of charcoal, wood smoke, grilling shrimp, and beef somehow made their way across the water from an outdoor restaurant, and I could feel my appetite sharpen with each wafting scent, faintly captured. The rum warms your insides, and sends your imagination drifting off the mooring and steering away downwind to the waypoints of random dreams, I noted. I was too tired to try to figure out what Poppa Jon had been intimating with his song; that analysis could wait for the morrow. I looked down through the open butterfly hatch on deck to the main saloon from whence the muted golden glow of the lamps emanated; then I went below to join them, so that we could all enjoy our night-caps and final toast together, and well-wishing cheers for a pleasant sleep for Captain and crew before each one of us headed off to the soft bunk assigned, where a pillow awaited our weary and sun-tanned heads.

As we drift off to sleep, I thought, quietly tethered to the circumscribing scope of the anchor rode, dreams take each of us back across the wide Deep that we have ventured upon this voyage, across the warm turquoise waters dotted with green islands, places of wonder, palms, and Siren-alluring beauty. Through the wavy, ancient thick glass panel in the cabin trunk above, I glimpsed a single watery, bright star as I lay in my bunk; Amélie was already asleep beside me. This image of the star was the last image I saw before I sank into unconsciousness, dreaming that I was now rising above the harbor as a weightless spirit and following that blue-brilliant white flame in its nightly path across the tropic sky and sea below. It is after all an adventure of journeys, journeys unending, which is as we would have it be.

Chapter 23

To a Newer World

The voyage of discovery is not in seeking new landscapes but in having new eyes.

—Marcel Proust

Our plan was to meet up with *Gleam* at the same rendezvous point, ultimately; it was a place with the oddly unappealing name of 'Colon Flats', and it was a bay where pleasure boats are supposed to wait to transit the canal. We provisioned the boat well with food, fuel and water before we left, sailing over to Road Town where provisioning would be hopefully less expensive than in the small harbor of Soper's Hole. We did not want to stop on the way to Colon Flats, but there was always that possibility that we might need to. I told Amélie that I would not be surprised if we were to meet up with Carver somewhere as we converge on the ditch. "After all, you don't just go through it once you get there," I said. "Boats have to wait, for days, weeks even, and then they call you to go through, often in groups. So we may find *Gleam* at anchor if they are already there. She is larger and faster than we are."

It took us a few days to prepare the boat, load supplies, and make certain that we were ready. I did my best to obtain a long-term forecast for my route. I gathered information from several different sources, and then put it all together, looking for consensus at certain points, and the results gave me confidence. So on a bright Thursday morning we cleared out of Tortola and sailed south to southwest, around the underside of Puerto Rico.

The easterly trades were healthy, but I wasn't anticipating a terribly rough ride, but I knew that it could well turn out to be one, once we were a few hundred miles along and approaching the Colombian coast.

"It's more than a thousand nautical miles," I told Amélie, once we had left the Virgin Islands behind us and had settled into the routine of the passage. "There is a lot of open water to cross. The steady trades will, after a while, build some significant seas over time because the fetch is so many hundreds of miles. But we should be used to it by then. I expect it to take us close to ten days, maybe less. The advice that I have been given is to stay away from the gradually shallower waters off the coast of Colombia, because the lessening in the depth will allow the seas to become steep and it could be dangerous if they begin to break. On the up-side, it will be good practice for sailing westward across the Pacific."

"Why would it get so rough here? This is the Caribbean," she replied.

"We're at the height of the trade wind season, when the constant easterly winds pile up the water in the western Caribbean, sometimes making sea conditions hazardous. I've heard that many boats have been knocked down or pooped by the steep following seas, while others have been lost on the coast of Colombia after having been set off course by the strong current."

"Well, you had better not let that happen to us," she said.

"I won't. We sail in a slight curve around Colombia, because there is an area of ocean to the north of the coast where the significant wave height is higher than elsewhere. So we will avoid it and head for roughly 13 degrees north, 77 west, and then turn and sail more south directly to Colon. On the plus side, it's almost all downwind sailing for us."

Now the days flew by, a week flew by, and we rolled along under bright blue skies with steady, strong trade winds from behind. The deep sapphire-blue seas built up into long, high, but benevolent swells, and we rose and fell with them, with *Rugosa*'s mainsail triple-reefed, run out on the port side, and the jib held out to starboard, wing and wing, with an old spinnaker pole. *Rugosa* rose and fell as though on a roller coaster, the quartering seas sliding gently under her as we left a wake of foam, averaging nearly seven knots the whole time. Sun-block, floppy hats, loose-fitting white clothing and sunglasses were the rule. We drank a lot of water, and ate bread and peanut butter, fruit, and occasionally, fresh fish. We rarely cooked on the galley, except to carefully make coffee, due to the pronounced motion of the boat. Although the sea was warm, and the temperature nearly eighty degrees Fahrenheit, the constant breeze from behind kept us comfortable, and the spinning prop and generator kept us supplied day and night with all the electricity that we needed for our lights and instruments, and most importantly our reefer unit, keeping our food cold, some of it frozen, and of course our few bottles of beer keeping cold as well. They were long gone by the time we reached the coast of Panama.

I had purchased a small electric water-maker, a reverse-osmosis system that produced only a gallon or two an hour; but since my electricity was free, I did not care, and I kept it running, supplying our daily needs for washing and cleaning, even though we were very economical about our use, and in a few days we had topped off our water bladder-tanks. "We will be happy to have full tanks when we get to Panama," I told Amélie. "It will be hot, we will be on an anchor probably for a few days, so the only way to get water is, well, to go get it ashore." Amélie then began scouting up extra containers, including a couple of collapsible vinyl water bags, saying, "I'll fill whatever I can find, then, and stow it where I can. We aren't burning a drop of fuel right now, so why not, better to have it in reserve."

We sailed almost the entire distance, and in the early gray light of morning, I rejoiced at the distant sight of a long, bluish coastline stretching forever in either direction. We had been passed by cargo ships heading into Panama the past couple of days, and now they were anchored everywhere, massive tankers and freighters, all waiting to transit the canal. We motored in carefully around them, and anchored at the 'Colon Flats,' a designated anchoring area for small vessels just outside of the Panama Canal channel. As we were choosing a spot to drop the hook, I saw *Gleam* about a quarter mile away, anchored among a small group of boats. "Let's head over there and see Captain John," I said.

Carver was surprised and happy to see us; he had only been there for a couple of days. Jack and Billy were aboard and seemed to have weathered the trip well. They were both cheerful and eager to see the broad Pacific lying invisible beyond the isthmus.

Carver invited us aboard for cool drinks; we agreed to do the canal transit together, since we were now all together. "There used to be a great, cool place to hang out here, the Panama Yacht Club. But a few years ago, there was some sort of legal wrangle, and the ports company ripped it down out of the blue one day when it was closed for a national holiday. There's no other good place around here, either."

"It's a pain in the ass, expensive, and time-consuming to do this canal trip," he said, having done this before but on merchant vessels. "There's a long list of formalities to clear through customs, quarantine and immigration. There is no quick way to do it. You need all your ship's papers and your passports, and you have to do the trot back and forth between the offices of banana republic bureaucrats. And it's hot and humid. When it's all done and you're through the canal, your wallet will be empty, but at least you will have the whole broad Pacific in front of you."

"Remember, we're probably going to go through with other vessels. It's about 50 miles all told. But first we need to locate a bunch of old tires to line the hulls with so that we don't get damaged by the walls of the locks or by other vessels. We're also going to need to pay for local line handlers. They will be aboard our boats when we transit the canal. So by the time we're done, we're out about a grand and a half for each boat. Lastly, once you pay the fee, you'll need to phone the Marine Traffic Scheduler for a transit date assignment. It could be a week or two before we actually transit the canal. Go really light on your fresh water; the only way to replenish what you've got is to trek ashore with jugs. Avoid poking around ashore, too. You'll get rolled in an alley, or worse."

As expected, we had a few days to wait for our trip through the canal, so we ended up spending the time at anchor, lying around in the shade on *Gleam*, her wide canvas awning rigged to shelter us from the sun. In the meantime, we drank cool rum drinks, watching an endless convoy of ships of all kinds entering and leaving the canal. Two days before our transit, we were happily enjoying our afternoon aboard *Gleam*, well into rum cocktails, now with ice, because Jack had tinkered with, repaired, and recharged the Freon in the old ice maker. Carver had generously squandered some precious fuel to run the generator to recharge the house batteries, and also run the ice-maker, so we were all getting pleasantly drunk while he began to ramble a bit, baring his soul and sharing his thoughts about the future.

"There are times," he began, "When I grow tired of this seagoing life, and yearn for a change. As wonderful and adventurous as it is, I have often thought that I would like to go out west, to ride horses and live a cowboy life, or on a dude ranch, you know? "

"That's a long way from the water, skipper," Billy said.

"It's a one-eighty, really, I know," Carver replied. "A complete change. I would get a rifle and go out there and ride, shoot, travel through the mountains, the high desert, the plains, the badlands, wherever. And there are times when I would just rather be on the porch of my little old family summer cottage in Mattapoisett, watching the distant sails on Buzzard's Bay on a summer evening as the sun sets behind the oak forest off to the west. In the purple evening the big dragonflies are circling over the marsh, picking off the mosquitoes, and the bats come out in the twilight. The water gets very still in the marshy inlet, like a pane of glass, reflecting the deepening sky. Yes, I've sat many evenings in a porch rocker there with a drink in my hand, feeling like there was no greater place to be in the entire world. But the sea keeps calling me back."

"The Caribbean seems to be getting a bit crowded," I said.

"Crowded? You're not just kidding. It's way overcrowded. It's getting ruined. Back in the seventies when I first started coming here, it was neat. Lots of vagabonds, crazies, sailing people, but then it got discovered. So some years ago those original authentic crazy people weighed anchor and headed off to the South Pacific. You'd be surprised how much a couple thousand miles of water can do to keep the riff-raff out. Only real cruisers went out there, spending weeks at a time at sea. They escaped the crowds; it was an open enough place that you could find your own little personal motu. But even now the crowds are filling up the good places and the hard-core sailors have once again begun to shove off for remote places where the tiki-bar tourists don't gather. Some of them are going well outside the tropical zone, to cold-water lands and the high latitudes, but that's not for me."

"The Pacific is a place of legends," I said. "Captain Cook, pirates, all that sort of thing, Tahiti, Papeete, French Polynesia, the Society Islands."

"Which is why I want to go there, take *Gleam* there. And I have a good mind to do that, once we're through the canal, then out into the broad Pacific. Who knows where I will end up? I'm thinking of going to Thailand, but I already told you that." He had sparked up, and there was a sparkle in his eye, an old sparkle, perhaps, like a kid's delight, like a young man's enthusiasm. Carver was a young man again in his mind and heart, dreaming of adventure, addicted to the dream, and it was good for him, I thought to myself.

But all in all, I was anxious to move on as well. The cabin of *Rugosa* was too stuffy and hot for sleeping below most nights, so we slept out on deck under the Lord Jim awning and the aforementioned army surplus mosquito net that I had acquired some years before.

"I'll be happy when we leave this place," I said. "I don't like it. We sleep out on the deck and I can hear the sounds of the jungle on shore at night."

"The jungle doesn't sleep," Amélie replied. "In fact I think it is mostly awake at night."

"I hate the sounds of the monkeys screaming in the jungle," I said. "Or they howl, or roar, and make all kinds of nasty sounds. You can hear death in the jungle at night."

"They say that those are the souls of the men who died digging the canal," she added.

"Nice, yeah. Something on the order of twenty-five thousand all told. There is a lot of sadness buried in that ditch. On top of that, I'm always concerned that some mosquito is going to bite me and give me the Yellow Jack. Not only is it hot and stifling down here, but it's a damned unhappy place. You go ashore and you know that they don't like us here. All these cops on scooters running around carrying assault rifles all the time. The sooner we can move on from here, the better I'll feel."

"From here, French Polynesia is pretty much a westerly run," Carver said. "It is going to be a long leg. But with good weather, we just keep roaring along, day after day, until that day comes when you see a cloud on the horizon in a clear sky, a cloud that doesn't move for hours at a time, and you know that there is an island under it. It fills your heart with joy to suddenly realize that. And eventually a peak appears; it is the very high top of that island, an island that slowly emerges from the sea as you close in on it. It is a beautiful thing to watch unfold."

Suddenly an old weather poem came to mind, and I recited it aloud,

"When mountains and cliffs in the clouds appear,
Some sun and violent showers are near."

"Thank you for that happy thought," Carver snorted.

Two weeks later, we were a hundred miles or more offshore after exiting the canal. The waters were still quite warm, and the weather was rough and squally, with an endless succession of gray, wet, windy days and then occasional sunny days that allowed us and the boat to dry out, and the warm sun made us feel cheerful again. But we were beset by calms and counter-currents that made our progress slow and uncertain for days on end, tacking back and forth and sometimes motoring, and it was very frustrating. In the heat and humidity, all of our fresh fruits and vegetables began to spoil, and spoil quickly. Amélie came up the ladder from the cabin with a bowl full of slimy, rotting green bell peppers. "Got to chuck these," she said. "These were the first to go, and there's not a one of them in the lot that I can save."

We had high winds, no wind, rain and bad weather, never predictable, so I was constantly adjusting the sails, reefing or shaking out a reef, and it seemed like it would go on like this forever. I wanted to stay well offshore of the coast of Ecuador, and we had no plans to stop in the Galapagos, but basically follow a middle course between them until we would work our way out into the open Pacific. We saw many native craft, even the small wooden open sailing craft of fishermen, at what would have seemed impossible distances from shore. I was much surprised to see them so far out away from land.

While we were still perhaps one hundred nautical miles or so off the coast of Colombia and Ecuador, we continuously had to dodge the fishing lines of long-liners, else we would get them caught in *Rugosa*'s propeller. One morning, right after first light, to my great surprise, I saw a small panga with a noisy outboard engine approaching with what appeared to be four or five men in it. The winds were light, we were moving fairly slowly, and so their lightweight boat closed the gap quickly.

I called down to Amélie from the cockpit, and the tone of urgency roused her from her drowsy napping. "Amélie!" I called. "Bring me up the forty-five; you know where I keep it!"

I heard her sputter, "Oh, my God," but she was quick about it and handed it up to me. It was still early in the day and the sun was not up yet and I could not make out exactly what the dark figures in the Panga were up to. They approached us, keeping with us but keeping a respectable distance off, and in broken English said that they were fishermen and needed some water. They kept asking for water, and then began to close in, but I brandished the pistol, and when they saw it, the expressions on their faces changed, they seemed to look at each other and speak quickly and in low voices that I could not understand. I began to see their faces now as the sun was peeking over the horizon, and they stopped closing in on *Rugosa*.

Amélie brought up a liter bottle of fresh water from below. I motioned them to approach us. "Toss the bottle to them when they are almost alongside," I said.

The boat approached as I waved them in, all the while standing, bracing myself against the mizzen shrouds and keeping the pistol pointed their way and plainly visible. When they came near enough, I saw one man's arms outreached; Amélie tossed the bottle, and he caught it, heavily.

"We are going to Tahiti," I called out, "So this is all we can spare right now." They nodded and waved, a sort of 'thank you', and then pulled away quickly, looking back at us and my pistol, which was still plainly visible in one hand while I waved back with the other.

"The scary thing is that you never know, in a situation like this, if the fishermen really just want some more water or if they are just trying to get in closer, even onto our boat, hold us up and rob us," I said to Amélie. "Carver told me that he knew some guys who had a bad experience in Cartegena, when their boat was approached upon arrival by four strange men in a panga who held him and the crew up at gun and knife point. So please don't wonder why I get on edge when strangers approach in a small boat especially out in the middle of the ocean."

"I understand completely," she answered. "This new ocean feels much different from the other. And this does not feel like the friendly Caribbean where we have been spending so much time."

"Nor is it like Bermuda?"

"No!" she exclaimed, "Nothing like Bermuda! Rarely does much of anything amiss happen in Bermuda!" Later, when the panga was long out of sight, she stowed the gun back in its hiding place below.

At last we worked our way out into the trades; the winds were mostly light and uncertain at first, but after a few days they grew stronger and steadier. The seas were beautifully blue, clean and clear, and occasionally we passed floating strands of giant kelp many feet long, drifting with the current. I knew that our trip would be a long one, but I didn't mind because we had plenty of stores and we had brought some new books that we had bought at shops down in the islands. And although we had thousands of miles to go, I was happy to be at sea again after the stifling, buggy, humid, unhealthy weather in Panama. There was no escaping the heat and humidity there, or the awful howling of the monkeys; sometimes I could have sworn that infants in distress were just out of sight within the perimeter of the jungle. It was unnerving; *their voices are too much like ours,* I thought.

We sailed along for thirty-eight days, having great luck catching small tuna and dorados to supplement our diet. The further along we got, the steadier the weather conditions became, and it became almost boring to be sailing along in the trades. Each day had the same routine, and I began to realize why the old sailing ships followed regular routines for the sailors; it made the time pass more quickly with everyone busy doing his job, whether it might be handling sails, standing watch, cleaning, or making repairs, with idle time spent carving and whittling and making small objects for a loved one back home.

Amélie and I spent a good deal of time reading the books that we had brought, and working on small things around the boat. She cleaned down in places that had never been cleaned, so that the boat below was fresh and spotless. She was very good at macramé, and wove Turk's Heads and many other beautiful things out of white cotton three-strand 'small stuff'. Sometimes she sang, and played her harmonica, which she was very good at. Sometimes I sang along as well once she had taught me the song.

But there were things that *Rugosa* needed now, things that we simply could not do while sailing across the Pacific. Our sails were in good shape, but some of the seams were becoming sun-rotted and pulling apart. I took the staysail down for this reason, but in a single afternoon, Amélie plied her sailmaker's needle and twine, plus her leather sailmaker's palm, and stitched it up in great style so that I could hoist it once more. Varnish was peeling and needed touch-up;

the sun had a way of eating up everything, and I noted that some of the running rigging looked worn and frayed in spots, and would eventually need to be replaced.

Day thirty-nine began like any other, with a beautiful sunrise, an empty horizon, and a freshening breeze. Amélie sat on deck in the morning, reading, and suddenly called out, "Look! Dolphins!" and indeed, a pod of small bluish-grey porpoises were swimming in close on the starboard side of *Rugosa*. "They bring good luck," she said.

"Let's hope so," I answered. We were now beginning to approach the Pacific islands, and we were both anxious for the first sight of land after so many days at sea. In the back of my mind was the nagging thought, "What if there is no land? What if this is all an illusion?" And I laughed at myself for having such a silly thought, but nevertheless I wanted to see something.

"When will we see an island?" Amélie asked, handing me a mug of morning coffee with my usual shot of black strap rum in it.

"I have plotted a course for the island of Hiva Oa in the Marquesas Islands, French Polynesia. That will be our first stop; we should be there in a couple of days. You can see my plot on the chart. There is a village there named Atuona, and a nice harbor appropriately named Atuona Bay, a good anchorage. We can rest up there and take on some supplies before heading off again to Tahiti."

Evening came; I was grilling a small dorado, or mahi-mahi, that we had caught for our dinner, when I heard a familiar sound, though it was one that I had not heard since leaving the isthmus; it was the whining drone of a small single-engine plane, approaching from the sky directly ahead. It was flying low and appeared to be descending, heading directly toward us. Perhaps he wants to have a look at us, I thought to myself.

"Be sure to wave to them!" Amélie, called out, cheerfully.

"Land must be getting closer," I replied, "I'll check our position on the chart after dinner."

The drone of the plane's engine grew louder, and in a couple of minutes I could see it completely, and it seemed to be vectoring in on us, flying even lower.

"I hope he realizes that we're not an aircraft carrier, that he can't land here," I said.

Amélie seemed suddenly alarmed as she watched it approach. "It looks like it's going to dive right into us!" she exclaimed, and at that moment, the plane buzzed us, passing only a few feet above our mainmast.

"You ASSHOLE!" I yelled out, shaking my fist at the pilot, but he was already gone, his plane disappearing into the sky astern as he climbed back into the sky. He had passed above us so quickly, diving and then ascending on a steep angle, that I could not read the plane's markings or numbers.

"What the hell was that all about?" she asked.

"I have no idea. Hot dog. Jerk."

"Do you want the pistol?"

"For what? I'm not going to shoot at him, even if he is an asshole cowboy."

We had all but forgotten about the plane when, less than an hour later, after dark, we saw a single white light on the horizon ahead. As the minutes went by, it seemed to be drawing closer. "Thankfully that's a boat or a ship, and not a plane," I remarked. I had no idea then, nor did I suspect that the two might possibly be linked.

"Is the radar on?" Amélie asked.

"Nope. But you're right, I should fire it up."

After the system had warmed up, it showed a vessel approximately two miles away.

The light grew brighter, and it appeared that the vessel, a motorized vessel of some sort, was approaching at speed. I also observed, with some annoyance, that she was not showing any type of running lights, only the single bright, white light that seemed to be more of a spotlight than anything else.

"Do you think they see us?" Amélie asked, tension and puzzlement, at the same time, showing in her voice.

"Oh hell yes they see us," I replied, "I'm going to hail them on the VHF." Before going below to turn on the radar set, I reached down in the cockpit to the engine panel and cranked the Westerbeke diesel to life.

Once the VHF radio was on, I hailed the ship on all the known channels, international distress, ship working channels, but there was no response. I was yelling into the microphone, keyed. Still, the vessel approached in what appeared to be a head-on direction. I could make it out now to be, perhaps, some sort of a steel vessel, a beat-up fishing trawler, large and heavy, maybe one hundred feet long, with masts and gear for fishing, and what appeared to be Chinese characters or lettering on its hull.

"Goddamned fishermen," I sputtered, "No radio, no proper running lights."

I drew the flare gun from out of the nav desk drawer, and was about to fire a flare overhead, when I saw that the vessel was slowing as it came within a hundred yards of us.

"What do you want?" I shouted out. I held up my hand-held VHF radio in my hand, pointing to it, in the white glare of their spotlight. I heard voices, but did not understand the language; they were clearly Asians, though. The ship drew closer; again I waved my radio and my arms, as though to convey "I don't understand," and then I heard their voices grow louder; several of them were arguing, and the argument, I sensed, was a heated one. I whispered to Amélie, "I'll need that pistol, now."

"Don't," she said, "They're probably armed; they'll blow us to pieces!"

At that moment, I saw the vessel turn toward us. There was a man up on the foredeck standing next to something that looked like a machine gun mount, and swung the mounted gun in our direction. "Oh, my God," was all I remember uttering an instant before the shooting began. "Get below!" I screamed to Amélie, and as she stood up to race for the main hatch, I saw her jump as a high-caliber round tore through her chest. She made no sound but collapsed in the cockpit, killed instantly. I sat for a moment utterly stunned with disbelief.

They were all firing now, and the big slugs from the machine gun were making a horrible racket; it was pandemonium. Wood was splintering and the spars were exploding as the big rounds hit them. Bronze fittings and other metal parts of the boat were ringing like bells as slugs hit them; the portholes exploded in showers of glass, the wheel was blown away along with the compass binnacle and stand. I felt shards of glass, splinters of wood pierce my skin as I dived below to take shelter, and I heard the mortal thuds as machine gun rounds pierced the hull below the waterline. Water was coming in fast; I searched for my pistol frantically in the dark, while crying, shouting, and cursing at the same time. But while I was groping for it the firing ceased, the ship gunned its engines, and quickly pulled away. When I finally found the gun and came out into the cockpit, they were already out of effective range, but I fired anyway, until all the rounds in the clip, and all that I had, were spent; then I held the pistol uselessly in my hands as my boat, in the darkness, was quickly sinking under me.

I was numb; I was bleeding from splinter wounds, but I paid them no notice. I picked up Amélie and cradled her in my arms, sobbing, holding her motionless body close to mine. She was limp and warm and covered with blood but completely lifeless and her blood was everywhere in the cockpit and all over me, not that I cared, I was just in terrible shock to see her small form so quiet and loose as though asleep, her vital spark completely gone and I held her for a few moments, as long as I could spare the little precious time afloat that I had.

Through the glass, shattered sharp shards of fiberglass and wood and torn metal, I brought her below and laid her in our bunk which was gradually sinking to the level of the rising water filling the hull. The water had already risen above the cabin sole.

They had shot up the cabin especially with the small arms, taking out all electronics and shattering the EPIRB, parts of its battery scattered all over. I laid her down on the bunk and covered her with a sheet and then wrapped her in a blanket, covering her face as best I could see in the darkness, my vision blurred by a running, flooding river of tears, and I kissed her forehead for the last time as I heard the engine sputter and die as seawater flooded it.

Now there was only silence and I stood in the utter darkness and rising water and knew that she was gone, completely gone, and that there was nothing left for me to do than to go up on deck and save my own life, even though at that moment, I did not care one way or another whether or not I lived or died, my soul was so completely devastated. There had not even been time for a final word or a good-bye.

Skidbladner, on the foredeck, had been punctured in a few places but I could still inflate parts of it, and after working desperately, at last I launched her, having the presence of mind only enough to grab a few bottles of water and a ball cap. I was not thinking straight and my boat was sinking. *Rugosa*'s decks were already awash as I eased the dinghy into the sea; the big Chinese vessel had disappeared into the darkness with no lights showing; for all I knew, and for all the world, she was gone, almost as though she had never existed. Only the damage that they had done remained as a stark and horrific testament to the reality of it.

There passed some days of pain, heat, chill, hunger, and terrible thirst, and at last, dreams and hallucinations, half-waking, mostly delirious. I dreamt quite a few times that we were sailing again on *Rugosa*, and that she was whole and that Amélie was there beside me, very much alive, and it was so real that I believed that it was so, and had no memory of what had happened. Then in broad daylight the Chinese fishing boat appeared again and it was right up close to us and the scowling crewmen were standing there on the deck, facing us, with AK-47 rifles in their hands, under the hot Pacific sun. They were stopped and we were stopped and nobody spoke a word. Some sort of a pirate flag was flying from one of their steel masts.

"Leave us alone, please," I called to them, "We are going to Tahiti. You can take whatever we have, whatever you want."

They made no motion, nor spoke, but simply stood there facing us, their guns trained upon us. I remembered where I kept my .45 pistol down belowdecks. Amélie can sneak below and fetch it, I thought, and then we might at least have a fighting chance, if I can get off a few shots from the cover of the cabin trunk.

"Don't shoot us; we're unarmed!" I shouted to them, hoping to trick them into holding their fire, or sparing us, until such time as I could get my automatic pistol in my hand. "We have no guns!"

"Don't say that unless you mean it," Amélie said to me, looking up at me with a devilish twinkle in her eye and her mouth in a coy grin.

I looked down at her in total puzzlement at her cryptic comment, and all of a sudden we were back in Antigua and she was in the taxi heading off to the airport. But now I was seated in the back with her as well and we were both trundling at very slow speed down the long, dusty, bumpy road to the airport a half hour away. The road moved and undulated like waves on the sea and the taxi seemed to move up and down with them as it slowly rolled along.

"Good God, it's hot," I said, "And I am terribly thirsty. We should stop for water soon." Then, "I didn't realize that I was going with you!"

She turned to me and looked into my eyes, and her face was very sad.

"That's because you're not," she replied. "You have to stay."

And then I awoke. I was lying in the sloshy bottom of half-sunken *Skidbladner,* and my skin was burned red and peeling in the hot sun where I had no clothes to cover certain areas of my body. I was terribly thirsty and in great pain and I thought that perhaps I might die, and thought how much of a relief it might be to actually do so. Then I remembered the dream with Amélie in it and I began to cry, to sob loudly and uncontrollably, but there were no tears, my body was so dehydrated, so I rubbed water from the bottom of the dinghy, water that was flowing around my body, in my eyes and it stung so badly that I wished that I had not done so. I felt utterly wretched and weak; I became weepy and emotional easily, as if I no longer had any strength of spirit. I realized that sores were developing all along my back, legs and arms wherever they were submerged in the salt water at the bottom of the boat, and especially around cuts and scratches where glass, splinters, and other sharp things had cut me. I wished that I had been shot, too; I did not know why they had opened fire on us, or who they were, or what they wanted, other than to kill and sink us. Before I had left the boat, I had thrown my now-useless pistol into the sea; I had not been thoughtful enough to have even saved a single round for myself.

In my delirium, I imagined the sea teeming with sharks, and at one point, a very curious shark bumped the bottom of *Skidbladner*, but my tough old Achilles inflatable withstood the assault and did not tear, and the shark eventually lost interest and swam away. But I also was taken, at times, with the almost overwhelming urge, in my pain and sorrow, to simply crawl over the side of the dinghy and let the sharks finish me off; but I had known a friend in California who had been an avid surfer in Malibu until a shark bit off one of his legs and he nearly died, and would have had it not been for the quick assistance of others nearby and a rubber tourniquet; but the way that he described the excruciating agony of the attack dissuaded me, even now, from taking that way out.

I had a waking dream one night where I seemingly awoke to see my father sitting opposite me in the dinghy, leaning back against the half-deflated bladder on one side of the boat. It was a cool, clear, brilliantly starlit night and the sea was quiet. I felt a sudden overwhelming flood of emotion pour over me at the sight of my father, as though a huge wave had boarded my boat unexpectedly and had drenched everything. I began to cry, in my dream, and I apologized to him for my outward show of weakness. "I'm sorry," I said. He seemed so terribly real, and he ignored my apology, and spoke:

"You're not going to get anywhere unless you start rowing," he said.

"What are you doing here?" I laughed, happily, now, "You don't even like boats, and you don't swim!"

"Doesn't matter. Now, Nate, are you going to row?"

"I can't," I said. "I'm too weak, and besides, the oars are gone. Dad, they killed Amélie. Why? What was that plane, that boat?"

No matter that for days I had been trying to figure out, exhaustively, what the incident had all been about; I had theories, of course, and by process of elimination had narrowed the list down in my mind. But now the explanation came from his mouth.

"Spotter plane," he said.

"I figured that much, Dad."

"Lots of drug trade going on down here in that area that you don't hear much about. A lot of meth, other stuff too. That boat was a floating meth lab."

"Not a fishing boat?"

"No. Just looked like one. Intentionally."

"But why did they shoot at us?"

"Case of mistaken identity. Thought you were encroaching on their trade territory. Thought you were someone else."

"Someone else? Who?"

"Another smuggler from the competition. Similar boat."

"Good God," I replied. "But I think I'm toast now, though."

"No you're not. Remember the snow bank? The sled?"

I brightened. "Dad, you remember that!"

"Of course I do. And we came out of that, you came out of that, remember?"

"Yes...I do."

"And what was on the other side of the snow bank, when you came through it?"

"The sun. I remember seeing, through my tears, the brilliant, bright, sparkling sun, after the snow fell away from my face."

And then I awoke then to the morning sun in my eyes, growing hot, and the raft full of smelly, salty water. To my great surprise, a sizable flying fish was flapping about in the water in the bottom of the dinghy. Although it was slippery, I managed to catch it, shouting and gasping at the same time; then holding it tightly, I ate it, slowly, every last bit of it except the largest bones and fins; it made me nauseous, but I ate it as slowly as I could restrain myself, and forced it to stay down, and after an hour or so, I was all right. I chuckled for a moment as I remembered the dinner of goat vindaloo at the Indian restaurant, with Dieter, on the island of St. Martin. "Well," I spoke to myself, aloud, "Now I know that if ever I am rescued, I won't ever need to eat a flying fish, cooked or raw, ever again." And at the same time, the thought of a plate of goat vindaloo seemed pure ambrosia, and I wished that I had a big plateful in front of me, so much so that I could almost see it dance before my eyes, and smell the heavenly aroma of it.

The seawater in the dinghy had become concentrated from evaporation in the sun, so it was very salty now and where it wicked up the shredded clothing that I still had on my body, it grew white crusty salt crystals in a frosty rime at the frayed edge where the cloth met the water. I lay on my back and wished for death; in an instant, it seems, everything good had gone wrong, and it had not been from the fury of the sea, no; it had come from the cruelty, treachery, and mindless, Godless darkness in the heart of Man, the only place in the world where true malice and calculated cruelty find a welcome harbor.

I lay there for some time, on my back, not quite sure whether I was actually awake or asleep, staring up at the sky. I could hear myself breathing, raspy but steady and slow. I had what was left of a ball cap placed on my forehead, with the shredded visor barely shading my eyes. I watched a white, puffy cloud in the great distance grow, with abstract curiosity, as there was nothing else to watch and I felt too weak to raise myself up. The two intact inflatable sections of *Skidbladner* still held air, since the rest had been punctured, and this kept enough of the dinghy above the surface of the ocean that I had some protection from sharks in that my body was not in any way submerged naked in the sea. But I knew that predators must be out there, in the vicinity, circling and waiting no doubt.

As I pondered these things, I noted that the cloud, as it was approaching, was growing quickly and had acquired a dark underbelly. "Send that cloud my way, Dad," I heard myself whisper. The cloud continued to grow, until at last it was overhead and shadowing me, and I felt a cool puff of wind blow across the dinghy and me, soothing my body, carrying away the heat, raising dark ripples on the ocean swells all around. Then I felt cool, fat droplets of rain begin to fall on me, faster and faster, and as they fell, I cried again, this time weakly but joyfully. The rain began pouring down in a relieving, hydrating deluge, and I shivered and shook with chills so violent that I could not control them. And then I remembered the few lines from Coleridge's Rime of the Ancient Mariner, when the rains come to soothe his parched body and soul,

"My lips were wet, my throat was cold,
My garments all were dank;
Sure I had drunken in my dreams,
And still my body drank."

And so did I, as the dinghy filled with rainwater, I found strength to come to my knees and scoop and splash as much of the salt water out as I could, which was most all of it, using my hands, a bit of clothing, whatever, and then the continuing rain from the squall filled the dinghy to a depth of two inches before it stopped. It was this water that I lived on for two more days until I was seen by lookouts on a passing freighter, a Malaysia-flagged container ship, and rescued, having lost some thirty pounds in what seemed to be no time at all. But I was completely numb, in shock mentally and physically, and although I began to take nourishment from my rescuers, I feigned amnesia; I could not speak, and I seemed to be drifting through a haze rather than real life, like watching my own life going by like a movie or a television show, distant, detached, not really a part of it anymore, and not really wanting to be, after losing so much that had been important to me, escaping with barely my life.

Chapter 24

Landfall

In a land of immigrants, one was not an alien but simply the latest arrival.

— Rudolf Arnheim

After nearly a week at sea, the ship docked in San Diego. I had not left my cabin or berth the whole time that I had been aboard since my rescue. There was a porthole above my bunk through which the gray light shone, and sometimes the blue of the sky could be seen on sunny days, along with occasional white, fluffy, cheerful clouds. Sometimes even a slanted beam of sunlight penetrated the semi-darkness, the shaft falling on the cabin bulkhead down by my feet as the day was drawing late and the sun was sinking in the sky. But I never stood up to look out of my porthole, for I did not want to see the sea, not even to glimpse it, nor to show it my face. When the medical corpsman visited me twice each day to check the bandages on my superficial flesh wounds, and to bring me some soup, or a sandwich and some coffee, I feigned the inability to rise for anything other than to visit the toilet, and so the officers thought that my condition was in fact worse than it actually was. I did this for a reason, because they were watching me and I did not want to be turned over to detectives, customs people, or police once the ship had docked. I don't think they quite knew what to do with me, but they apparently had swallowed my story and did not think that I was any sort of criminal, or fugitive, or security risk, and perhaps I was not even well enough to go anywhere or escape on my own.

They were sympathetic to my plight, and actually quite kind; they did not attempt to bind me, nor lock my cabin door, but told me that if I should be able to walk around a little, I was welcome to join them on the mess deck for meals, even to come up to the bridge if I chose. I was simply a storm-shipwrecked sailor who had sustained serious injuries in the tragic loss of his vessel, and beyond that, I had told them very little. Because of the abrasions to my head, I was able to feign partial amnesia, and this they did not question, which served my purposes well. I was essentially left alone, though always kindly treated and showed the greatest consideration.

But the first night that the ship had docked in port, and we docked around sunset, I quietly made my way ashore right after dark by hiding atop a container as it was being unloaded by a dock crane. I slid down the opposite side of it when it was placed on the pier, and eased myself down to the pier by means of a short length of line that I had cut from a throw ring on deck. Although it was a high container and easing down by the rope was painful to my hands, knees and feet, I was able to walk away, albeit hobbling and hopping at first. Then I turned my back to the sea and walked away from the port, through an open gate, and toward the town. There was a chill Pacific rain beginning to fall, so after about a half hour of walking, and becoming thoroughly damp, I took shelter by sneaking aboard an antique iron sailing ship docked at the Maritime Museum at the docks downtown. I did things this way because I did not want to talk to anyone, or answer questions. I wanted only to be by myself, in my own mind, to try to sort out the meaning of all that had happened, if there was indeed a meaning after all.

The museum foundation had been making repairs to the old Cape Horner bark *Star of India* and there was nobody aboard, it was well after hours, and I was able to climb aboard undetected, as the ship was moored alongside a busy street and sidewalk, by walking tightrope-style along a mooring line while bracing against the hull. I slipped under a blue tarp in a roped-off section up on the foredeck and found easy entry through a hole where rotted deck timbers had been cut away as part of a restoration job. I felt my way below carefully in the dim light, and fortunately found, on the middle deck, a museum display cabin and berth where I curled up in the bunk on an old straw-filled mattress. The bunk was short, I suppose because, as I have heard, people were generally shorter and smaller back then, and to keep warm, I gathered up and slept under two dusty woolen blankets, both about a hundred years old. But I was warm now and I slept well for a few hours. When I awoke, it was of course still dark in the hold, but my clothes were mostly dry now and something inside me told me that it was time to get moving and get off the ship before my 'stow-away' status was discovered.

My stomach was growling and all that I had to eat was a small block of hard cheese and some biscuit that I had taken from the container ship and stowed in a small rucksack that I had found in the sail locker. I did not know whom it might have belonged to, but it had seemed abandoned, the same way that I felt, myself. I ate the cheese and biscuit and wished for some water, or even better, a cup of hot coffee, so I retraced my steps topside and found myself on the black, wet wooden deck of the big ship under gray, cool skies in the early dim light of pre-dawn. Shouldering my rucksack, I walked quite unmolested and unnoticed down the gangway to the pier, ducking under an ineffectual chain-link gate, and onto the concrete pier that ran along the broad main street that ran along the perimeter of the harbor. Bleary-eyed, I stepped into the path of a couple of early morning joggers who took no notice of me, but simply avoided me and continued on past. I was still hungry, since there had been no food to be found aboard the uninhabited old clipper, so I went looking for a coffee shop. I noted, in passing a store front window, that my beard had grown in full and dark, a bit long and wild; this amused me a little, and gave me cause to chuckle at myself, at my own rough and unkempt appearance, if only momentarily, because in the wet pane of wavy, dirty glass, it seemed to me that I was gazing into the face of a stranger.

But now it was a new day; it was San Diego, a place I had visited in the distant past. I was completely alone and I felt it keenly. My shirt, pants, and shoes were odd and loose-fitting elements of personal clothing that the crewmen had donated for me to wear; but I had no complaints, only feelings of gratitude. I even had a small amount of money in my pocket that they had given me if I should like to use the vending machines on the mess deck or the ship's commissary. It would be enough to buy a coffee and some breakfast, and a cheap disposable razor at the drugstore. Once I had eaten and purchased the razor, I went down to the seaside park, found a public bathroom, and cleaned myself up as best I could.

I was by myself and without her, she whose name I could not even whisper, and without my boat, now and forever. I did not turn to face the sea, for I wanted only to be as far away from the sea as possible, in a place very different and devoid of the salt air and the cloying smell of sea-wrack and the tide, and yet I wanted a place as open, bleak, and empty as the wide, wide ocean that I had so many times crossed over. So later in the morning I went to a west coast branch of my own bank, and spent a couple of hours explaining how my wallet had been stolen, and going through the many difficult and contorted perambulations necessary to prove my identity and gain access to my accounts and my money. At one point, the oddly suspicious and nosy 'customer care representative' asked me what I was doing so far west, in San Diego. I looked back at him and smiled.

"I'm going to hike the Pacific Crest Trail," I replied.

"But that's way, way to the north, at the other end of the state," he replied, with an interrogative air.

"Well obviously I'm not there yet. Which is why I need access to my account!"

Once I was equipped with my paper-temporary-everythings, I drew money from my old account, bought a few things for my pack including a clean change of clothes from a Salvation Army store, booked a motel room and after cleaning up, set out to walk about the town. I had shaved my face clean not only to look less like a castaway to the bank personnel, but also so that I would not be recognized easily had the ship's officers decided to report me missing to the police and customs officers. I changed my clothes and gave the ones I had been wearing to a homeless man who had slept all night in the park down by the USS Midway with his rusty shopping basket as his portable home.

Two days later I bought a vintage running 1929 Indian Scout motorcycle that I luckily had seen at a roadside estate sale, and grabbed it before someone else did. It was the model bike that I had always admired as a kid, and after all of the necessary details and paperwork were complete, I turned in my motel room key, gassed up the Scout, gave it an oil change, and set a course for the Nevada desert, not toward any destination in particular, just some place different where I might find solitude, solace, and healing.

Chapter 25

The Bear's Paw

The devout have laid out gardens in the desert.

— *Robert Duncan*

The stony trail led steeply up the mountainside from where it began at the lodge, which was already halfway up Mount Charleston. Looking down from an outcropping of ledge, I could see the roof of the lodge far below, and the wisp of blue pinewood smoke snaking upwards into the early evening air from the lodge's central chimney. It was late in the day, and late in the season, and the desert-dry air at these altitudes was quickly growing mountain-cool. The path snaked around the wide bases of ancient Ponderosa pines and redwoods, their trunks covered with rough, deeply featured reddish-brown bark. I crossed a dry creek bed, and noted the last glint of sunlight beaming down through the upper branches of the pines. It would be setting over the mountains to the west soon.

The path leveled out, and crossed a curious flat plateau, not more than a couple of hundred yards across, covered almost exclusively by a dense growth of small quaking aspen. They were young trees, I guessed, no more than ten feet tall at most, and their leaves glowed like burnished gold and fluttered rapidly and fitfully in the light breeze that was occasionally gusting down the mountain slope. It was like watching a sea of fluttering gold motion that came and went, in startling fashion, with each puff of wind. Looking up, I could see patches of snow on the heights in the shadows of the trees, and I heard a rustle and saw a small goat with shaggy white hair, high up near the tree line. The wispy incense-like aroma of pine logs burning in the lodge's fireplace reached my nostrils; I was in a wild place, and I knew that I was alone, as much as I had ever been alone on the wide sea.

From an open spot at the edge of the aspen plateau, I could see many miles out over the high desert, all the way to the intensifying glowing neon of the city of Las Vegas many miles away. It was an island of brilliant light surrounded by the blackness of the dusk-enshrouded desert, and rising air currents disturbed the lights and made it seem to be a great stationary orange brush fire. It was an everlasting, ever-changing fiery mirage, burning without a sound, for there were no sounds to be heard from the city or from human habitation way up here on the mountain. The air was thin and growing crisp, and I could hear my own pulse pounding in my ears, such was the silence. Every once in a while, though, the wind would rustle the aspen leaves once more, and it was a comforting sound, just because it reminded me that my ears were still working, and it gave me a sense of place.

I gathered some evergreen brush and made a simple half-shelter, and built a small fire within a circle of stones from the deadfall around me, gathered while there was still a little light. I unpacked my gear and my warm sleeping bag, and listened to the fire crackle, lying on a bed of spruce branches with my lower body halfway into the bag, my wool lodge shirt keeping my upper body warm. From somewhere in the distance came the furtive sounds of small animals in the brush, and the voice of a bird calling out its evening song. I stared into the glowing coals for perhaps an hour, thinking of many things, entranced by the vision of the embers constantly changing, an image of hell, perhaps, though in miniature, and my mind drifted back many months, playing slowly like an old home movie on a reel to reel projector.

In the end, I asked myself, what does a man have? What do you get to keep, when all else is taken away? You get to keep what you came into the world with, that being your life, at least for a while; that is the last thing to go. But then I thought, that when all else has been taken away, friends, lovers, family, money, goods and possessions, there is still a man's dignity, and no one and nothing else can take that away from him; he can only throw it away or destroy it of his own volition. Everything in the world and life changes, albeit some things, like mountains, more slowly than our lives; nothing stays the same, and nothing lasts forever. We grow old, and have but the richness of our memories when all else is removed, and that is only while our fragile and temporary minds last. Only our souls go on forever, I said to myself, and every man knows that he has a soul, but it is a stranger to him rather than a familiar companion.

I still had my flask, and had re-filled it with whisky down at the Lodge earlier. I had taken a chance and asked the bartender to refill it for me.

"What's that?" he asked gruffly, then, "Oh." He was a tall, older man with a long, deeply-lined face, thinning black hair, and a bushy moustache.

"My hiking flask," I answered. "It's for the trail."

"I'm not supposed to, but OK. Anything special?"

"How about that Colorado Mountain whisky brand up there?"

He chuckled. "Oh that shit. You got it, buddy. How much does it hold? Heck, I figure five dollars ought to do it. And that's being generous."

"Sure," I said, pushing the money across the bar.

Now I had the flask and I took a long pull at it, it was still warm from being in my shirt pocket. It tasted fine, not harsh, so I had another pull and still another until I could feel myself growing mellow and woozy. Then I stared into the fading fire until at last my thoughts didn't make any sense anymore, and I was asleep. I slept hard and did not dream, and when I awoke, it was morning, the air was biting cold, and the sun had risen in the distance on my side of the mountain.

I hiked all that day and by early afternoon, when I returned to my bike parked and chained at the Lodge, I was gnawingly hungry. There was a filling station down where the end of the long, winding mountain road met the highway, so I topped off my Indian 101 Scout's fuel tank and bought, on a lark, some small brick-like chunks of orange stuff wrapped in waxed paper, something that the lady behind the counter called 'Mexican candy.' She was a short, plump woman with jet-black hair, a round face, and a lot of dark moles, and her eyes sparkled with jolly humor so I bought the stuff even though it did not look especially appetizing. "It's made with squash, or sweet potato, and sugar. It is very dense, but not hard, and very sweet. You will want a bottle of water," she added.

I gnawed at it while riding down the road and in a little while I wasn't hungry at all anymore, it was something like hard sweet potato fudge.

An hour before sunset I rode into Red Rock Canyon and it was like being on Mars, as I had imagined that it would be, but while being able to breathe. The canyon was silent and the rock walls brilliant, stark, crisp, glowing red, ochre, and orange in the setting sun and the shadows deep purple and the edges hard, sharp, well-defined and angular. The nearly full moon had risen earlier and it hung pale and translucent in the eastern sky above the canyon rim, in a cold, dry, and cloudless blue sky, as blue as deep space with a red tinge that was reflected up from the canyon. There was very little scrub, only some down off the road in the deep gullies, and not a sound but the growl from the old bike's engine, odd yet smooth, sounding like history. After I went around the loop and exited the canyon I felt as though I had made a visit to another planet.

As the sun was setting and blue shadows were advancing across the land, I sometimes saw wild burros out in the desert away from the road. There were a curious number of small oases, probably the location of small springs or water sources, and the gentle burros would always be near them, usually one or two. The oases were simply marked by the concentrated growth of a cluster of bushes or shrubs with green leaves, a sure sign of water below the surface.

I stopped for the night at a motel and biker saloon complex out in the middle of nowhere, a wild-looking place and I would not have stopped there except that it had a grill. The grill was working and the drifting blue-smoke aroma of meat with chipotle seasoning being barbecued caught me as I was roaring by and it pulled me in just as effectively as a big reel with wire line will turn a marlin's head and haul him in right smartly with no chance of escape. The aroma was driving me half mad as I pulled into the dusty dirt lot. I went in to the bar with all the other riders and ordered a tall, cold beer and then the steak plate, and I ate eagerly and then sat out back beside a small bricked-in artificial pond with a little water fountain and a family of ducks swimming around in it. Cane and bamboo had been planted around it, as well as other greenery, and I marveled at this watery place out in the middle of the desert, a small-scale oasis fed by mountain springs, as a sign indicated, complete with green cane and ducks, and a sweet-smelling open fire of split Ponderosa logs and mesquite, plus chairs to sit in to enjoy it with a whisky on the rocks in my hand. There was a certain Oriental quality about it that had the effect on my soul of a little bit of oil on a stormy sea; it smoothed the rough tops and made the gale more bearable, at least for the moment.

It was growing darker now and as I sat staring at the fire, my tired and dry mind wandering, I noticed, rather suddenly, a man sitting across from me, on the other side of the little fire pit, and he seemed to be looking up at me on occasion, but not staring impolitely. He sat on a wooden bench, leaning forward, dressed in worn, heavy leathers and he wore his jet-black hair long and stringy down on each side, and a dark red bandanna or sweat band around his head and forehead. His face was long and thin, his features chiseled, and the firelight played on the deep folds of his face and his prominent nose, and I thought that he was the very image of the stern warrior Comanche from the old Westerns. His skin was darker than mine, and weathered like a rock outcropping of ledge on a mountainside, and he had only a slight, scraggly wisp of a beard, more like the odd bristle here and there, and he did not smile, but only stared, not directly but obliquely, until I met his eyes with mine, and I did so because I wanted him to know that I was looking back, and that I was unafraid of meeting his gaze.

At last he spoke to me. "I like your bike, friend. How long have you had it?"

"A few weeks. I was lucky to find it."

"Yes, you were."

"They say that of all the Indians, that was the best one," I said. He looked down when I said this, and seemed to smile with amusement as he did. I had left him an opening.

"So you found a good Indian then? Good for you. They are extremely rare. Most all good Indians are dead Indians, as you may have heard."

"Well that isn't what I meant...."

"...So be careful that you do not find a bad Indian. They are actually everywhere." He grinned.

"Thanks for the warning," I replied.

"Where are you from?" he asked. "Not that it matters terribly. You are not from here; you seem like a fish out of water."

"Appropriate, actually. But is it that obvious?"

"Yes," he nodded. "You have that flopping-around-in-dry-dirt air about you. What are you running from?"

"I'm not running from anything," I replied, firmly.

"Everyone is running from something. When a man is in a place where he does not feel comfortable, or believes that he does not belong there naturally, it is because he is running from something, usually something that is in a place where he once was comfortable."

"I've never been comfortable anywhere," I said. "But this little oasis seems benign. It's like a little island, where one might stop for water, or rest, or a quiet night's sleep on a bed that doesn't move."

"That could be. You have the smell of a water rat."

"Nicely put. I do wash when I can."

"No, no. It's like coming up on a hidden pond or a lake. You can smell the fresh water from a distance even if you cannot see it. It's not unpleasant, certainly."

"I see. I have spent much time at sea. When you have been at sea for some time, you can smell the land when you are approaching it at night from many miles away. It's different. But I'm not a fugitive from anything, unless I suppose it is Death. I suppose that I am running from Death."

"Every man runs from Death," he replied quickly, "Or thinks he does. But life is very much like a round room, or a fort, or a crater. It is a circle. So the faster you run away from something, the faster you are running toward it again. That's a thought that never comes into a man's head most of the time because his head is turned around; his eyes are perpetually looking backwards as he runs

319

away. So he never looks ahead to where he is going. And the worst part is that everything, including the universe, is a circle. He ends up running smack-dab right back into the thing that he is running away from in the first place."

I took up a small stick, and began scratching shapes into the dirt by my feet. He focused intensely on what I was scratching. "Not running from my own. I have never been terribly afraid of it for myself, really. *Cuando viene, viene*. But I lost a dear friend during my journey," I said, after a pause. "She was killed by pirates in the Pacific. Shot. They sank my boat. Why I was spared by fate, I'm not sure."

"Perhaps to tell the story," he offered. "But that is terrible indeed. I am sorry for your loss," he added, not unkindly. "But you hold her in your heart, she lives there still. And you cannot let her go to rest."

"I don't want to," I replied.

"In time you must," he said. "It is unkind to hold a spirit here on earth, tied to your heart. The dead need to move on, and we must let them go, even though it hurts. We do not understand this at first. But to hang onto them is to keep them here, and until we let them move on, they are unable to move onward to final peace."

I nodded, not believing, but not inclined to argue.

"We have all known loss," he continued. "But no more of that for now. Will you show me your bike? My name is Noconah. I am a Comanche. Noke will do. I also have a vintage Indian bike."

"You have a Scout, too?" I asked, surprised.

"No," he broke into a broad smile, "Mine is a Chief!" He laughed heartily.

"Should have known," I chuckled.

"You have to understand, for some odd reason, I'm partial to the brand."

"I get that!"

We went to the bar and drank cold beer from long-neck bottles. Noke had been an Army Ranger during the Gulf War. He had seen a lot of combat, he said, but added as a cautionary caveat that he was not much inclined to telling war stories. "There is just too much," he said, "My heart is very full, but there are many things that don't translate well into words. You can feel them, but you cannot always communicate them properly. I lost many friends for whom it is not proper to speak their names yet, don't know if it will ever be."

"So you were a Ranger, wow," I said.

"Yes. And I am proud of that."

"You know, the first Ranger was Benjamin Church, the Indian Fighter."

This found Noke's 'funny bone' once again, and he slapped me on the back, while laughing and shaking his head, "Oh yes, I know all about Benjamin Church and King Philip's War. Benjamin Church was a big man, a true athlete in his time, and a great warrior. But just remember who taught him those techniques that he adopted so well."

"*Touché*, I said. Then I mentioned that he seemed rather well-spoken for a rangy Indian on a motorcycle hanging out in desert bars in Nevada. This seemed to amuse him greatly. "So I don't fit the profile of Tonto, eh?" Oh my. Quanah Parker, perhaps? You know, my mother was Irish and Comanche. I'll tell you, that's a mixture. Talk about a quick and deadly temper!"

He had gone to college, actually, and then had joined the Army and had been promoted to Lieutenant. He had ended up in a very elite unit of Rangers fighting first with the Contras in Nicaragua, then in Desert Storm in Iraq; after he returned, he had married, put on a suit, and made a fortune on Wall Street. "And then I finally blew out my front tire," he said, "I lost my track, went off the trail. The war had poisoned my spirit and it had taken a long time for it to finally catch up with me. But it was like a rot deep within a tree, a rot that you cannot see from the outside, but all the time it is eating away at the core and weakening the tree."

"What happened?" I asked.

He chuckled. "Well, the fucking tree fell!" he exclaimed. "I lost the fortune that I had made; I gambled most of it away in the casinos of Las Vegas. At the same time I lost my wife; she left; good for her. It was the best thing that she could have done for herself. So I got rid of my suit, got rid of my shirt, even, and began working in construction, framing houses throughout the Southwest, working outdoors all the time within sight of the snow-capped peaks of the Sierras. Even when it was ninety-nine degrees in the valley, I could look up at the snow on the mountains where it was cold and pure and it was a comfort just to know that it was there, I'm not sure why. The sun burned my skin so brown that people who did not know native peoples thought that I was of African descent. And yet always there was the fresh scent of raw spruce, fir and pine around me as I put up framing, and that was a comfort, the smell of clean-cut wood. But then I lost my way again and I was beginning to become a terrible drunk. So I had to stop that before it killed me, and bring myself under control again. It's like sailing your boat, yes? When you drift off course, you have to make a correction so that you don't end up on the rocks."

"That's the idea," I said. "So what do you do now?"

"Just what you see," he answered. "This country is a very big place, and I have much to see before I die. I know that I will not see it all. But I am a wanderer, and will see as much as I can. The more I see, the more, hopefully, I will understand about the world, and people, and then by extension, myself."

"Do you work?" I asked.

"Here and there, from time to time, as I feel the inclination. When a tree falls to the ground, it is not always dead. New shoots will come up out of the stump, or from the trunk itself, and begin life anew. I didn't gamble away everything that I had made; I put some aside, like a small slow-growing sapling. You know, like one of your New England maple trees? You draw away some sap every year to make sugar, but never so much as to kill the tree. You want it to keep growing, even if it grows slowly. My needs are few; I learned a long time ago that a man can survive tolerably on very little. What do I need? Gas for my bike, grease and oil and some occasional parts. I camp in the desert and once in a while sleep in a real bed. My spirit is free; my mind and my eyes are the things that advance my life right now. My wheels have seen many, many miles of road, both straight and winding. And I am at peace with myself."

"Are you satisfied?" I asked.

"Never," he replied instantly. "That would be a kind of death for me."

"I'm glad that you have found peace," I said. "I cannot. I don't think I will ever find it. I have been searching for it, like the 'Pearl of Great Price', all my life. I set out on a voyage alone to find it. Perhaps only death will bring it."

"Does peace seem to be far away?" he asked, studying me intently now.

"Like the distant stars," I replied.

"And yet for all of us, it is so close as to be within our grasp, if only we knew how to grasp it."

"I wish I could believe that," I said.

"Well then gas up your Scout and come with me. I will show you how to find it. But first I must see your bike."

We traveled many days and many miles across the Southwest, camping at night out in the middle of nowhere, eating and drinking at dingy saloons, biker-friendly eateries, and truck stops along the way. In the evening we would talk about many different things, drinking whisky by the firelight while Noke told stories about his childhood, and of his people, and especially stories and legends that had been handed down, orally, by his people.

One evening, after we had crossed into Colorado, he crouched down and scratched patterns, slowly and deliberately, in the dirt with a small stick. It was very dark now in the desert and the shadows cast by the firelight made the figures he drew seem deeper than they probably were, like small canyons.

"The human spirit is like a very deep well, full of dark, unquiet waters," he began. "But every well, no matter how deep, finally has a bottom. And if you were to drain all the water out of one, the well would not be dry, to your surprise, because you see, there are small cold springs at the very bottom, sometimes they are no more than a trickle, but they are clean and pure and crystal-clear and they will slowly refresh the well and refill it if you give them time. They come from the great goodness that ultimately inhabits all things, all creation and all life, that nurtures and sustains everything good in the world. But you cannot seek them, or find their source; you simply have to wait for them to slowly refill the well and refresh your soul, like gradually awakening after a long sleep."

He continued, "People think, every day, that they are successfully escaping something, or getting themselves out of a bad or unpleasant situation. But that is an illusion. A man does not get out of something, truly, as much as he actually gets into something else, which might be better, but also could in fact be even worse. As I said before, a man looking backwards cannot see what lies ahead. By the time that he realizes that he is getting into something else, well, he is already there, and may or may not have to repeat the cycle of extricating himself from a situation once more. Do you understand this?"

I think so," I replied.

Outside of Denver, we rode our bikes up to the top of Mount Evans. Even though it was late summer, and warm in the valleys, we knew that it would quite possibly be cold nevertheless at the summit. We passed a very ancient grove of bristlecone pines, and saw white, long-haired mountain goats on the slopes as we climbed, our bikes laboring in the thin air and steep incline of the winding mountain road.

When we reached the top, it was very cold and windy, and there was what appeared to be a pile of rubble and an abandoned stone ruin of a building a few yards from the summit. Noke parked his bike and with the cold wind in his face started out ahead of me up the short, winding path to the summit, and he seemed to lope along easily, without much effort, while I gasped for breath in the thin air of fourteen thousand feet of altitude, and walked slowly like a Centenarian. The brisk, chill wind blowing against me made me shiver and made my progress even slower.

"Come on!" he called back to me, laughing, "You walk like an old woman!"

"That was once the Summit Lodge," he said, pointing to the stone ruins. "Now look," and he pointed to the sun setting across the Continental Divide, and all I could see in between were the lesser peaks of other mountains off to the west.

"Here you are, at the end of day, at the roof of the country," he said to me. "You have been to the peaks, now, as well as the valleys, and everything in between. Are you not now satisfied?"

We walked back down from the summit and sat behind a natural stone windbreak near our bikes. "Why should I be satisfied?" I asked.

"You have been over the sea, seen many places, much happiness, much sadness and sorrow. You have known love and friendship. You have as I have said been to the top and to the bottom, the bottom was when we rode through the deep valleys of Nevada. You have met every kind of person that there is in the race of mankind, just about. Now there is one place left to go, and the path is straight and clear."

"To die?" I asked.

"No!" he replied, slapping the back of my head, affectionately but hard, chiding, slightly disapppointed at my reply. "It is not your time to die! Did you not learn that in the Pacific? You are young yet; even your soul is still young though you probably don't realize it right now. Every tree with green leaves that loses its leaves in the fall and throughout the winter seems to be dead. But it isn't dead, and there is a spring-time for all things, including you, and of course your spirit."

"What about those who have gone before us?" I asked.

He stared ahead, wistfully, at the clouds. "I believe in a great spirit being above all, and in the continuation of life. We are born to cycles. Why should all things, planets, seasons, abide in cycles, but our own existence be linear, with a defined beginning and a definite end? That does not follow. No, I believe that life goes on, somewhere, and in some way that we do not understand. We all have a purpose, and answers to our questions do not come easily or quickly. Sometimes they are terribly obscure for a very long time. But by living, and struggling, eventually they become clear."

"I thought I was dead in many ways when I left on this voyage in the beginning," I said. "My life seemed to have come to an end in the place where I was at. I sought a new life. A new beginning, leaving all else behind, memories, responsibilities, and I wanted to be needed nowhere, as one sailor once told me. But in the end, that wasn't what I wanted at all. That is the dark bottom of the well, I came to realize. There is no life down there."

"You remember perhaps the quote from the fictional Lame Beaver in the writer Michener's book. He observes that 'only the rocks live forever'. But of course rocks do not live at all, and even they change; the highest mountains, over time, are worn down to foot-hills. So there is always change. And you? You must go home. You must head east, back to the place where you started, for in his end, a man finds his beginning, and in his beginning, the image of where his trail finally ends. Now let's motor down the mountain a ways and make camp. I'm feeling cold up here."

We pulled our bikes well off the road down near the base of the mountain. Noke knew a spot, he said, that would make a good camp. How he found it in the growing darkness, I will never know, but after we parked our bikes in the woods, a hundred feet or so in from the road, we walked on further to a place where the woods opened up into an open area next to a copse of redwoods and pines, a place where the cool, crisp air was aromatic with balsam and the forest floor soft with a thick mat of brown pine needles. Noke pushed away the needles, made a small circle with stones and lit a campfire. We had brought our blankets and rucksacks with us and I helped Noke build a shelter of pine boughs big enough for us both. "I don't think it will rain at all tonight," he said, gazing up at the bright pinpoints of stars visible through the opening above. We were well enough into the woods that we could no longer hear the sounds of occasional cars driving by out on the mountain road.

Noke brought his little teapot out of his pack, and I watched him putting what looked like tea into it. Then he filled it from his water skin and put it on the coals to heat up. In a little while he handed me something that looked like the dried up bud of a cactus. "Here, chew this," he said. "It will help you relax, and understand things better."

"God, this tastes awful," I said, "It's bitter and it's drying out my mouth." He handed me a tin cup of the tea that he had brewed.

"Moisten your mouth with this," he suggested.

"This tastes a lot like it," I replied, "What is this stuff? You aren't poisoning me?"

He laughed. "No, no. Never. This is a very old Native peoples' medicine that we have used for many centuries to cure a variety of ills."

"Is this peyote?" I asked, between chews.

"Yes. Don't swallow it, just take your time and get all the goodness out of it."

I chewed, and as I did so, after a while, my head began to feel strange and light. I began to forget that I was with Noke or even where I was, or that I should care, and I became strongly focused, riveted if you will, on the fire. It grew to consume my entire attention and vision, and as it did so, I became awestruck and fascinated by the constant permutations of the flames, such that they became not terrifying but rather a constantly changing source of wonder, and I began to believe that the fire was actually a living thing, the flames becoming individual captivating dancers in some great Sultan's seraglio, twisting, undulating, and spinning in a dance of veils, shedding and tossing aside glowing, flowing robes, scarfs, and silks as they danced in incredibly enticing ways, Siren-like, pulling me in.

But then the flames seemed to darken, and I must have fallen asleep, because I dreamt then that I was back in that dark cavern on Bermuda, and to my horror, I stood once again in front of the writhing, impenetrable black cloud of an apparition at the far end of the passageway. Once again it filled my entire vision, terrifying and undefinable, moving and undulating like a bucket of liquid pitch being stirred. And then it spoke to me for the first time. It called out my name.

"Who are you?" I spoke up in reply, no longer terrified, but growing angry at this apparition that I had never wanted to see again apparently drawing me back. I did not think that I was dreaming but thought that I was actually there, and could feel the fresh air from outside the doorway blowing in and on my back.

"You know me," the deep voice growled, resonating through the stone cavern.

"You are Death," I replied. "And you have taken away people dear to me. I should have recognized you when I first met you here in this cave."

"Did you not?" it replied, mockingly. "You should have, for you have sought me all your life. You were seeking me when you first sailed out of Bristol."

"I was not seeking you. I sought life. A new life."

"And have you found it yet? No. Nor have many other sailors like you. Dream-chasers and fools."

"You took my child. And then you took Amélie. You took my father. When will you be satisfied?"

"*I take them all,*" the darkness said, slowly and with great emphasis on each word. "And I am never satisfied. And I will take you, too."

"That may be. But I will not come to you willingly, or easily, or quickly. I am not ready to die, and I no longer fear you."

"Many have said that," the thing replied, laughing derisively, mocking me.

"You are the Father of Lies," I replied in disgust. "I will waste no more time listening to you." And with that, I walked toward the mass in the darkness, waving my fists, and as I did, moving into the black cloud, I came upon a wall, a hard, stone wall, and banged on it with my fists in my rage and rejection. And then I remembered nothing more.

When I awoke in the morning, the pine needles were flat where I had lain on my stomach and pounded the earth with my fists. The sun was high in the sky and the ashes within the circle of stones were cold. My mouth was dry and tasted horrible, my head felt dizzy, and Noke was gone. I stumbled over to where the bikes had been parked, and his bike was gone too; only mine remained. But on the seat of my bike was a small round silver amulet on a rawhide string, jewelry of Native American make, very old, crafted with a sliced section of a walnut shell that had been filled with turquoise chips and lacquered. The side-by-side openings in the thin sliver of nut shell created the image of two feet, side by side, filled with turquoise chips. "The Bear's Paw," I remarked aloud, remembering what Noke had told me, "Inner strength and healing. Strength of spirit. Turquoise for good fortune. This is very powerful." I put it around my neck, and felt my eyes moisten as emotion welled up within me. I had to sit down on a stump for a little while, until at last I felt ready and strong again. I packed my gear, started up my bike, and headed down the mountain.

The wind dried my eyes and blew through my hair and quite suddenly I felt an immense freedom, more immense than I had ever known in my life. It was then that I recalled the solo sailor Jason's words in the breakfast shop that early, cold, windy Block Island morning so long ago; and I knew then that I, too, had been allowed to pass.

Chapter 26

Endings

Your journey never ends. Life has a way of changing things in incredible ways.
—*Alexander Volkov*

I realized that everything comes to an end, ultimately, in one way or another. Life does; it has a beginning, and it has an end, at least on earth. If you want to believe that it's cyclical, like many other processes in the universe, that's a matter of faith, but not of practical reality as far as I know. The constant in all things, people, voyages, or lives, is change, change that you can see, and change that you cannot. A voyage has a beginning, a port of departure, and a final destination, or a final harbor, beach, reef, or resting place in the mud of the abyssal plain. What we remember about the voyage are the waypoints along the way, places on land or on the sea that are marked only by our memories of a place in time on the eternal sea, or footprints in the sand of an island, footprints that, in turn, are eventually effaced, and the people who have become part of our lives. Life is a passage between waypoints, connecting all in succession, connecting all as one, and once we are gone, there is nothing to tell the story that we were ever there. The voyage lives on within each and every one of us, like a home movie, intensely personal and individual, the light reflected by a single facet of a precious gem with millions of facets.

The sea seeks to claim all boats. Its claim on *Rugosa* had been delayed and denied for many years, but finally in her old age, it claimed her, not through her own faults or weaknesses, but through the destructive hand of Man, the same creature that had brought her timbers together from out of the Maine forests and had given her birth. Shot full of holes, she lay in permanent blackness on the ice-cold floor of the Pacific. That was a nobler end ultimately, I reasoned, than broken and scattered across a reef, or rotting away against an eroded bank of eelgrass somewhere in a forgotten tidal estuary. And moreover, she held protectively still within her battered and beloved hull, at the cold bottom of the Pacific in everlasting darkness, what for me was a treasure, one that I could not for a moment think about. I could not go there yet in my mind; would I ever be able to, without busting open my seams and becoming totally sprung? I did not know. All I knew now is that I had to focus on survival, and only because I wanted it, because she would want it. She would want me to make every possible effort to endure, and so I was committed to that end, '*Il faut (d'abord) durer*'. But what was the purpose of hanging in there, ultimately? To struggle relentlessly to survive, yet for no other purpose, is in itself pointless, absurd. But then, I thought, that would mean that our very existence is utterly pointless and absurd; put here for no other reason than to procreate, and then die; to perpetuate the species? Is survival without purpose ultimately a purpose in itself? And if so, how utterly dumb, dull, and unimpressive; all that pain for nothing.

Dieter was gone. I never heard from him again before he died, but was contacted by one of his sons that he had lost his boat on a reef, and had subsequently flown back to the United States where the authorities were waiting for him. He had run away from jail time, fled the country after multiple drunk-driving arrests had led to a conviction and a prison sentence, and upon his return he served three months in jail for running away from what is termed 'justice' in America. He would never be granted a license to drive a motor vehicle again, at least not in the U.S. He drifted down to Florida, where he met a widowed crank of a desiccated older woman who drank almost as much as he did, who croaked like a frog when she spoke, or rather barked, and moved into a small bungalow near the Everglades with her because she agreed to take him in. She lived on what money she had been left when her own husband drank himself to death a decade earlier. So now they drove around in her battered old station wagon (she drove) and collected cast-off shipping pallets on Sundays. Dieter cut these up and they burned them for heat in her brick fireplace on colder nights in the winter months. Eventually he drank himself to death as well, collapsing one morning in the bathroom. He died without dignity, lying motionless on the dirty linoleum floor curled up into a fetal position around the base of the toilet, and she shipped his cremated ashes back to Massachusetts to his second wife.

I never learned what happened to Poppa Jon, but Poppa was a survivor, first and foremost, and I heard later on that after the loss of Dieter's boat, he found passage on a ship back to Trinidad, where he may still be today if he has not passed on. His soul was a truly Caribbean soul and could not exist long outside of that environment, much like a quirky tropical fish that cannot live long in the cold waters of the North Atlantic. His very being was like a bottle of blended dark rums, a mixture of so many exotic flavors, rum and vanilla and cacao and coconut, absinthe and guavaberry. His soul was at one with the mystic tropical nights and colorful dancing Jumbies on wooden stilts singing and lurching about in the blazing golden firelight, gangly figures moving in flashes of vibrant color and billowing cloth, with roots as old as the African continent and the deep and dark superstitions of men. That was Poppa Jon, practical and wise with folklore, and always alive within the world of the spiritual. He was timeless, and he faded back into the envelope of island culture and island time, where there is no real beginning, and no foreseeable end, living from one full moon to the next.

Captain John Carver, with his crewman Billy, and Jack aboard as his engineer, sailed away in old *Gleam* toward the South China Sea, or so I heard told, with the intention of landing on the white-sand tropic shores of some empty, palm-forested island off the coast of Thailand where he could hopefully find wild women, free and powerful ganja or other exotic mind-altering drugs, and magnificent tall rock-structures, stacks and pinnacles of a million different shapes sculpted by the sea. He hoped to eventually explore the fabled temple ruins of Angkor Wat, or to uncover the yet undiscovered, whatever it might be, or dig up ancient treasure somewhere and retire in a tropical paradise under the gentle pulsating feather-fans on long poles tended by beautiful and nubile nearly naked young women. Carver was quite literally, if even poetically, born to sail the seas; he had done it for so many years since childhood that it had become his natural habitat, and he could not feel at ease in any other environment. And yet I wished that I could have gone with them, with that jolly, aging, wastrel crew on the old wooden *Gleam*, off on a new adventure; to fling defiance into the face of advancing age and infirmity, or growing poorer, or at any stiff and scowly-faced rule or convention that dictates that a man must have a Puritanical work ethic or productive occupation. I yearned to offer a middle-fingered gesture of refusal, rebuttal, and Devil-may-care rejection of any hint of implied or imposed responsibility, fiscal or otherwise, patriotic, religious, or whatever the source, that might say, "No! You cannot, or must not, go!" Not to be a pirate, but to be in some ways like the pirates of old, outside the law, outside the strictures, rules, and silly regulations and mores of society, ultimately independent and incredibly free to wander the briny roadsteads of the earth wherever I chose to go, wherever I pointed my bowsprit, or wherever I allowed the wind to blow me. I would be one beating heart like millions of other beating hearts in the world, yet unlike the rest of them, at one with these few on this vessel beating in freedom, and in the spirit of those pirates of yesteryear, with ample guns, powder, and shot to defend that freedom or, not succeeding in that, to at least die free, unencumbered, and never enslaved.

But I was not free to go with them now. I had been wounded, damaged in a way that I had once promised myself that I would never allow to happen again. I had lost two friends, one made of flesh, one made of wood, both dear to my heart, and yet not equally so, for the depth of loss in losing another beating heart close to one's own is utterly bottomless. The heart, in free-fall, waits for the hard, sudden stop, the point when descent into sadness and depression ceases, but that hard stop never comes, and if there is at last a bottom to that black well, it is beyond the scope of my vision or experience.

The boat embodies the soul's and heart's wanderlust dreams, and it is the tangible embodiment of freedom, the vessel and cocoon within which all those aspirations are contained and held secure. But the love, the flesh partner, the like-minded soul and object of one's affections, is in herself the fulfillment of dreams. Thinking, as I did, that I could never again suffer such wounds of loss was, I now realized in retrospect, ultimate folly. As long as we live, we will seek out the companionship of others for sharing, because life and love is to be shared. Perhaps that is the point of it all, of life, of continuation, of existence, in refutation of my earlier and darker musings. The reason for being here is first and foremost to share one's heart with another. It is an intangible thing, like a phrase of Mozart played vibrantly and floating on the still night air; here for a moment, to be sensed, heard, enjoyed, and shared, but which cannot be captured, contained, or preserved, only replicated or imperfectly reproduced. Such is life; when the candle flame is extinguished, all is darkness and cold. All else that we create is ultimately a dust-gatherer of limited value, a by-product of the true energy of mind and heart. Creations do not live; they only remind us of what life can be, seen, as Milton said, as through a glass, darkly. So we must strive to make the music; for in that harmonious sound we find purpose and the true satisfaction and fulfillment in being alive.

I needed to heal. My wounds were all inside, and I did not think that I could ever heal completely, nor if in fact I truly wanted to. But I had no choice but to continue on, to keep walking down the trail, following it to the end, wherever that end might be. Having been allowed to pass, I now had a mandate to continue onward; this is part of what Noke had been trying to impress upon me. And so I continued eastward along the straight, flat roads that crossed the Great Plains, geometrically like a giant chess board when seen from the sky. Truck stops and road houses came and went in seemingly endless succession through the nights and across the days of my wandering until the weather grew noticeably colder. My travels were taking me northeastward, and I was soon a long way from the deserts of the southwest.

One morning, after a couple of days of increasingly hillier country, I crossed through the western mountains of Pennsylvania, then New York State, and found myself in the Green Mountains of Vermont and then the White Mountains of New Hampshire. I had arrived back in sweet New England, albeit in winter.

I stepped inside the boat shed, and pulled the big wooden door shut behind me. Outside the Maine winter sky was leaden gray, and dry snow flurries were blowing almost sideways in the sharp wind from the northwest. Because it was a dry snow, and the wind was strong, it did not build up on the boughs of the tall spruces around the building, but rather dusted down periodically as they dumped their snow loads, sending miniature blizzards of blinding white clouds of snow powder descending to the ground from the boughs above. Snow coated the marine railway that led the short distance from the double barn doors of the shed down a moderate slope to the waters of the bay, where they disappeared beneath the edge. The sharply pointed, angular pines that stood densely all along the rock-ribbed shore were etched dark green against the gray sky, leaning in the wind, while the sound of the low surf wash sang its endless song of the Maine coast.

Once I found myself inside the shed, I noted with pleasure that it was much warmer, a pleasant contrast to the bitter dry cold outdoors. The bluish haze of aromatic wood smoke tinted the air. I could smell the slight aroma of burning pipe tobacco. It took a few moments for my eyes to become accustomed to the darkness after the whiteness everywhere outside, and then I saw the black wood stove in the corner, hissing and crackling and occasionally belching a puff of smoke out of the damper whenever a wind gust outside buffeted the metal chimney.

Several naked bulbs, hundred-watt size, hung at the end of cords from the ridge pole at the roof peak. A wiry, tall man dressed in buffalo plaid wool hat and jacket, with olive-drab canvas work pants and high laced boots, was carefully planing the gunwale of a new lap-strake dinghy on a braced frame in the middle of the shed.

"You the feller that Josh sent over?"

"Yes, I'm Nate."

"Yep. Told me about you. Said you want to build boats."

"I do. I have plenty of experience. With wooden boats, that is."

"Well, that's all we build in this boat-shop," he replied.

"That's just what I want," I said.

"How are you with fixtures? Plumbing? Engines? Finishes?"

"I can do all of that, and do it well."

"Well, it doesn't pay much, so if you're planning to become a millionaire, or if you have great expectations, this isn't your place," he added.

"I just want a chisel in my hand, and the chance to focus on my work," I said. "I need very much to focus. To think only about what I need to do."

He looked up at me, and studied me for a moment. His eyes were steel-blue and steady, but not unkindly. His features were weathered, gaunt and drawn, but his was the face of a craftsman of very many seasons.

"Yes, Josh told me a bit about you and your story. So all I ask is that you work hard and be honest. No liquor in here or any of that funny stuff. You'll get a decent day's pay for a solid day's work."

I nodded in agreement, and that seemed to suit him. "Well you can start any time you like. I'll show you around the tool crib and such. Maybe sweep up some of these shavings first."

I paused a moment to study the boat that he had just been working on. I ran my hand along the gunwale. The dinghy was freshly built; he saw me smile.

"Fair, isn't it?" he asked me.

"Very smooth," I answered. "Fresh and clean. I love the smell of fresh-cut wood. It seems like it still has the life of the tree in it. Don't you think?"

"Yes, it does. Like medicine, some say. At least to a boat-builder."

He looked up, and around at the overhead beams, the roof, the walls. "Maybe in time you'll build your own boat in this shed," he offered.

"I just might," I said, running my hand slowly along the planking, savoring its gently curving shape. "Yes indeed, I just might."

The End